Praise for *A Shot in the Dark*

Winner of the CrimeFes

'A farce that gathers hilarious pac[...]
Marx Brothers than Agatha Ch[...]
turned on its head – a giddy spell of sheer delight' Barry
Turner, *Daily Mail*

'It takes a writer of Lynne Truss's wit and intelligence to take
on both the cosy and comic fields, shaking them up to forge
something fresh and beguiling ... Not only is the whole thing
delightfully witty – more early Evelyn Waugh than Agatha
Christie – it also functions very successfully as a novel in the vein
of the genre it is satirising: the police procedural ... [Twitten]
is a delightful creation' Barry Forshaw, *i*

'The ingenious plot involves such period attractions as the
Ghost Train, theatrical landladies, Pathé News and cherry
Genoa cake. Hilarious' *Sunday Times Crime Club*

'This book is as much a comedy as a crime novel ... Lynne
Truss is a national treasure, and this is a gentle, complicated,
humorous tale' *Literary Review*

'We all know that Truss can work miracles ... but I doubt even
Constable Twitten could work out how she has produced a
whodunit that exudes heartwarming cosiness while boasting
Game of Thrones levels of violent death, or given her cast of
amusi[...] [char]acters I've
encou[...] [Tele]*graph*

uples suspense with dark hilarity in the
black comedy film *The Ladykillers*,
in time) the funniest crime novel of 2018'
Wall Street Journal

'Set in 1950s Brighton, *A Shot in the Dark* is an intricately plotted murder mystery that's darkly humorous and beautifully written' *Herald*

'Lynne Truss's first crime novel, based on her radio script, is a success ... It is funny, clever, charming, imaginative, nostalgic and gently satirical' Marcel Berlins, *The Times*

'A witty delight' *Country Life*

'Truss's affection for a rollicking, twisty caper has transferred to the page with ease. Perhaps too comfortably – never has a book that starts with a massacre seemed so gentle – but there's some fine storytelling on display here' *Observer*

A Note on the Author

LYNNE TRUSS is a columnist, writer and broadcaster whose book on punctuation *Eats, Shoots & Leaves* was an international bestseller. She has written extensively for radio, and is the author of five previous novels, as well as a non-fiction account (*Get Her Off the Pitch!*) of her four years as a novice sportswriter for *The Times*. On radio, she is currently engaged in writing a continuing sequence of short stories for Radio 4 entitled *Life at Absolute Zero*. Her columns have appeared in the *Listener, The Times*, the *Sunday Telegraph* and *Saga*. She lives in Sussex and London with two dogs.

A SHOT IN
THE DARK

LYNNE TRUSS

RAVEN BOOKS
LONDON · OXFORD · NEW YORK · NEW DELHI · SYDNEY

RAVEN BOOKS
Bloomsbury Publishing Plc
50 Bedford Square, London, WC1B 3DP, UK

BLOOMSBURY, RAVEN BOOKS and the Raven Books logo are trademarks of
Bloomsbury Publishing Plc

First published in Great Britain 2018
This edition published 2019

A catalogue record for this book is available from the British Library

ISBN: HB: 978-1-4088-9051-6; TPB: 978-1-4088-9052-3;
PB: 978-1-4088-9048-6; EBOOK: 978-1-4088-9049-3

2 4 6 8 10 9 7 5 3 1

Typeset by Newgen KnowledgeWorks Pvt. Ltd., Chennai, India
Printed and bound in Great Britain by CPI Group (UK) Ltd, Croydon CR0 4YY

To find out more about our authors and books visit www.bloomsbury.com
and sign up for our newsletters.

For Gavin
Let's hope you were right

'Twas on a Monday morning,
  The gas man came to call.
                    – FLANDERS AND SWANN,
                        'The Gas Man Cometh', 1953

The Middle Street Massacre of 1951

The day of the notorious Middle Street Massacre dawned like many another in those happy, far-off days. In fact, any Brighton visitor hypothetically strolling seawards down Middle Street early on that June Saturday would have thought, 'How normal for the seaside!': the sparkling sea beyond, herring gulls wheeling and calling overhead, the comforting sound of a horse-drawn milk cart trundling along the seafront, the heady whiff of seaweed mixing intriguingly with warm sugar and peppermint from the humbug shop on the corner.

And then, having tripped over the freshly butchered corpse of an Italian gang member murdered outside the Hippodrome overnight, this hypothetical person would have chuckled, 'Ah, Brighton!', and continued his perambulations. Because it was all of a piece somehow, in those heady mid-century years; all part of the sheer breezy romance of the place: chips and vinegar wrapped in newspaper, larger-than-life Knickerbocker Glories, bloody torsos left in suitcases at the railway station.

Ask people in 1951 what they knew of Brighton and they would confidently list: crime, gangs; cockles and mussels in vinegar, shiny shingle, sunburned shoulders; more crime, more gangs; reprehensible Max Miller jokes, saucy postcards; then more crime, and more gangs. Clearly, the popular appeal of Graham Greene's *Brighton Rock* (and the film featuring the young Richard Attenborough as Pinkie Brown) had a very great deal to answer for.

Where were the police in all this? Well, if those same respondents had been required to think of a policeman in the context of Brighton in those benighted times, 85 per cent would have pointed either to the ineffectual constable in the Punch & Judy show (beaten violently to the ground with a big stick), or to that excellent fairground attraction, the Laughing Policeman, a paunchy animated doll in a glass-sided box that stood less for maintaining law and order, more for shrieking, 'AAAHHH-ha-ha-ha, Ha-ha-ha-hah-haah!'

All this was about to change, however. That famous Saturday in June saw a new star appear in the Constellation of the Helmet. His name was Inspector Steine.

From now on, anyone asked about the Brighton Constabulary would picture something new: not a puppet begging for its life while receiving blows to the side of its head; nor a sinister dummy roaring dementedly at a private joke; but a real man – a tall, slender, dignified grey-haired man, in fact, with blue eyes and a strikingly thoughtful far-away expression. A man about whom a middling British black-and-white film would be released in 1953, and several slapdash biographies would later be written.

In the years following, this man would come to represent the Brighton Police in a new way – in a way that said, 'Come to this town by all means, have fun, enjoy yourselves; get drunk, throw up; copulate under our stately piers like beasts of the field, if you must; but don't commit crime, matey, not on my patch.'

He was no Laughing Policeman, this paragon. In fact, it was a foolish person who dared even to mention the Laughing Policeman in his stern, unsmiling presence. All of the biographies of Inspector Steine (pronounced *Steen*, incidentally) detailed how one of his first acts on arrival in Brighton in April 1951 was to have all the Laughing Policemen in the penny arcades confiscated in early-morning raids, surgically dismantled and destroyed in bonfires behind the police station.

This act of authorised vandalism naturally caused ructions with the arcade owners, but Steine was above such concerns. If there was one thing about post-war Britain he abominated, it was the systematic inculcation of disrespect for the appointed guardians of the public.

Yes, Inspector Steine, formerly of the City of London constabulary, had arrived in Brighton with a mission. Of police corruption there would be no more. Of violent gangs with flick-knives there would be no more. Of mispronouncing his name there would be no more. And of Laughing Policemen – well, within days there was nothing remaining of that ghoulish Marionette Division beyond piles of ash and melted plastic with blackened springs and levers sticking out.

A little film was made by Pathé News: 'The Bonfire of the Effigies'. This rare and disturbing newsreel is honestly worth watching. It substantiates the legend that when the last (and greatest) Brighton Laughing Policeman was put to the flame, its body thrashed, it stopped laughing, and when it fell forward, the flames literally wiped the smile from off its face.

Now, to return to the events of Middle Street: while it truly was commonplace for people to trip over lifeless villains in Brighton at this time, the corpse discovered on 9 June 1951 was special for two reasons. First, the dead man had not been sliced, stabbed, skewered, mutilated or otherwise dispatched with a blade. He had been shot, twice, from behind. Second, he was no expendable journeyman gangster; he was 'Frankie G', a junior member of the Giovedi family, and therefore ranked as underworld aristocracy.

The Giovedis owned various legitimate restaurants in the town while also running very lucrative extortion and gambling rackets, and the teenaged 'Frankie G' was the apple of their collective eye. An ambitious, illiterate and cocky boy, he performed his hoodlum work with a passion – especially when it came to threatening people or roughing them up. Frankie's doting parents regarded him as a trainee criminal psychopath of pleasing potential, and his death at such a tender age (sixteen) was devastating. For his next birthday, they had planned to give him Worthing.

'Oh, Frankie G! My Frankie G!' each of them wailed, when they were brought the news in their modest flat upstairs from their Old Neapolitan restaurant in Preston Street. They were so upset that they briefly stopped counting the heaps of notes, coins and IOUs that had been delivered by henchmen to their drop-box overnight.

'Mama!' wailed Papa.

'Papa!' wailed Mama.

Young Frankie had been a model son. He had loved his mama's cooking! He had loved his hokey-pokey ice cream! He had loved cutting people's thumbs off! He had seen *Brighton Rock* five times at an impressionable age!

Naturally, the Giovedi family's thoughts turned swiftly to revenge – but who had murdered Frankie G? The fact of his being shot contained no clue. Whereas six months before, guns had been a rarity in the town (casino owner Fat Victor being the only hood to flash one around), now they were everywhere; everyone was 'packing'. When Frankie G's body was discovered in Middle Street, his own gun was clamped in his cold, dead hand – apparently unfired.

The suspect pool was limited, however, because only three gangs operated in town: the Giovedi Family (based on the seafront); Fat Victor's crew (based at the Casino); and the more nebulous satellite gang of a London outfit supposedly led by the legendarily unstable and sadistic Terence Chambers (not so easy to pinpoint a base for this particular gang, on account of the nebulousness).

Mama and Papa Giovedi wasted no time jumping to the obvious conclusion.

'Those Casino Boys done this to my Frankie!' wailed Mama Giovedi.

'They pay for this, Mama,' said Papa, grimly.

But was it the case that Fat Victor had thrown down this suicidal gauntlet to the Giovedis? In the few short hours it took for the bloody Middle Street Massacre to be organised and take place on that fateful Saturday, it now appears (with hindsight) that none of the participants stood back from events sufficiently to ask the right questions. No one asked, for example, just who would benefit from the Italians and the Casino Boys eliminating each other in a hail of bullets. Was some nebulous third party possibly behind it? Had some nebulous third party also been behind the sudden proliferation of firearms in the first place?

When the film of *The Middle Street Massacre* came to be made, the lovely John Gregson was cast in the lead role. The inspector was portrayed as a plain-clothes man, which in fact he never was – but there was no way you could dress Gregson in police uniform and peaked cap, he'd look ridiculous; so he wore the usual loose suit, trilby and mackintosh-over-the-arm ensemble, which added to his air of cool capability. *The Middle Street Massacre* struck lucky being released just after the hugely successful *Genevieve*; Gregson was red-hot box office at the time.

'What's all this about the gangs, Sergeant?' he asked in an early scene, handsomely entering his office, hanging his hat on a peg and tossing a folded newspaper onto a desk.

His sergeant was played by a very young (and unknown) Stratford Johns. 'It's Middle Street, sir. Bit of trouble brewing, so they say.'

Steine/Gregson perched on the corner of the desk, looking debonair. 'Middle Street where the Hippodrome is?' he enquired.

'That's right, sir. Where young Marty S was found murdered early this morning.' (The names had been changed slightly.)

'Marty S has been murdered?' Steine/Gregson jumped up and reached for his hat. 'The Sabatos won't take *that* lying down.'

'They've already retaliated, sir. Gunned down one of Fat Trevor's boys as he came out of the barber's. In my opinion, it looks set for all-out gang warfare, sir.'

'Get all the men together, Brunswood.'

'Yes, sir.'

Brunswood's face showed a mixture of emotions, in close-up. Steine/Gregson put a hand on his shoulder.

'I'm sorry, Sergeant. You were going to see that girl of yours today, weren't you?'

'She can wait, sir.'

'Good man. That's the spirit. Keep them keen, eh?'

Brunswood coughed, politely. 'The villains will all be armed, sir.'

'Will they, indeed?' said Gregson/Steine. He narrowed his eyes, as if hatching a plan, then put on his hat and opened the door. 'I want you to clear the area, Brunswood. Then I'll meet you at Garibaldi's on the seafront at half-past two.'

Criminal historians have had a difficult time accounting for the sheer stupidity of everyone involved in the Middle Street Massacre. Why did two entire gangs turn up that afternoon? Who started the shooting? Why didn't it stop? And out of forty-five participants, why did *no one whatsoever* survive?

Again, hindsight allows us to guess at a nebulous third-party influence, but the 100 per cent mortality rate meant there could be no eyewitness accounts of (say) guns fired from upstairs windows into the crowded narrow roadway below, blocked at both ends by police cordons. Many men, it seems, were shot in the back. All accounts agree that by the time Steine and his officers arrived, the street contained two heaps of bodies (in the telltale shape of cresting waves), a number of loose hats (lost in the rush) and an overpowering smell of cordite.

Conspicuously absent from the dead was Fat Victor; his serious fatness prevented him from taking part in face-to-face confrontations; he disappeared from Brighton that very afternoon, to be apprehended in a Littlehampton love nest in 1954. But every senior member of the Giovedi family ignominiously bit the dust – and Inspector Steine's clear-sighted decision to delay his men by buying them ice creams at Luigi's on the seafront (again, the name was changed for the film) was seen as a stroke of tactical brilliance. The Middle Street Massacre made his reputation, in every way.

Inspector Steine was given his own celluloid copy of *The Middle Street Massacre*, and over the next few years he often rigged up a projector at home and watched it. Having at first quibbled over the swap from uniform to plain clothes, the swap from grey-haired, middle-aged inspector to young, dark-haired inspector (not to mention the outlandish idea

8

that his maudlin sergeant would ever have a 'girl' to go out with on a Saturday afternoon), he gradually came to believe its version of events. The film cuts back and forth between the villains in Middle Street squaring up to each other and the scene at Luigi's/Garibaldi's where Stratford Johns looks serious and tense, holding his truncheon in a deathly grip.

'The villains, sir,' he pleads. 'We must arrest those villains!' After which he memorably explodes, 'Eating flaming ice cream at a time like this!'

But Steine/Gregson is firm, and buys everyone an Ovaltine by way of a *digestif*. He adopts a striking faraway expression, quite similar to Inspector Steine's own. The camera looks down vertically on Ovaltine, swirling round in the inspector's cup, and expressionistically cuts back to the bloodbath taking place just a couple of streets away. Since then, Inspector Steine has never had a cup of Ovaltine that didn't make him beam with pleasure at this associated memory.

What worries Sergeant Brunswick (real name) sometimes these days is that when Steine reminisces about the Middle Street Massacre, he refers to the 'Sabato family' when he means the Giovedis – to 'Marty S' when he means Frankie G. That's how far the fiction has supplanted, in Inspector Steine's mind, the actual events. Steine even thinks he remembers saying the words (written for the film), 'I have no blood on my hands this day, just a smidgen of raspberry sauce.'

Because there is something about Inspector Steine that needs to be disclosed, which has probably not been quite apparent up to now. Despite his great success as a policeman, despite his fame, despite his popularity as a regular broadcaster on the BBC's Home Service and despite the look of profound seriousness that sometimes settles on his face, Inspector Steine is not as clever as he thinks he is.

Six Years Later

Twitten's First Day

One

As his Brighton train drew out of Victoria Station five minutes behind schedule on the last day of his life, the theatre critic A. S. Crystal made a note in tiny handwriting: 'Complain to train company.' He had often travelled on this notorious line, and it had often disappointed, but until today he had let it pass. Today, however, he was in no mood to be charitable; the delay was unacceptable, and a complaint would duly be made.

Crystal was under no particular time constraints, as it happens. He would be spending the whole day in Brighton before attending a new play at the Theatre Royal in the evening. The lost five minutes were arguably immaterial. But he was a tightly wound man at the best of times and today he was especially tense, mentally girding himself for *A Shilling in the Meter*, whose reputation preceded it.

An angry play, by all accounts. A shocking play. A 'new' play, by a northern writer. Crystal hated it already, hence his fury with the train for starting late. Had he not met his end in Brighton within the next twelve hours, a swingeing letter on *Daily Clarion* headed notepaper would have been typed and dispatched as soon as his secretary Miss Sibert arrived the next morning at his serviced flat in Great Russell Street.

A middle-aged man in a smart grey raincoat, with a beaky nose and wire-rimmed spectacles, Crystal did not conform to the popular idea of the theatre critic. He had none of the flamboyance (long hair, opera cloaks, affected speech impediments) usually associated with the trade. His speaking voice was thin and reedy, and he had apparently never heard of deodorant. Arriving for a glamorous first night in the Haymarket or Drury Lane, Crystal looked more like a man sent in by the Revenue than an influential writer with millions of readers, who could decide the fate of a production by the use of one single, devastating adjective.

But he was rightly feared by everyone in the theatre. Today's paper contained a Crystal opinion piece lambasting the principle of knighthoods for actors; last year he had famously exploded the chances of a gritty northern drama called *Clogs on the Batty Stones* by dismissing it in just twelve (now-legendary) words: 'Wooden clogs, wooden dialogue, wooden acting; and thicker than two short planks'. There was something of Robespierre about Crystal. He was Robespierre with BO. It was his plain duty to point out deficiencies in every aspect of life. When something *needed to be said*, it was unthinkable that A. S. Crystal would not step up to the mark and say it.

Years before, in fact, when he had been assistant manager of the Aldersgate Branch of the Albion Bank, he had spoken up even when armed criminals were holding him at gunpoint. Not to beg for his life, or to reason with the robbers. No, he had spoken up purely to press home some unwanted critical points.

'You're doing this very badly,' he had said, addressing a masked woman armed with an exotic Luger pistol.

'Put a sock in it, Stinky,' she had replied, pointing the barrel straight at him.

Those were her exact words. In his statement to the police afterwards, Crystal was able to reproduce precisely many things this masked woman had said; it was his facility with remembering dialogue on a single hearing that was the basis of his later confidence as a critic.

'You've also chosen the wrong day,' he had objected later, from his position tied to a cashier's swivel chair with a canvas bag over his head. 'There would have been far more cash in the safe if you'd come tomorrow afternoon.'

But no one cared what this little bespectacled assistant manager thought. Loud shots were fired at the ceiling, as the two robbers gathered the bags of loot in the middle of the banking hall. This was especially terrifying for Crystal. With his head in the sack, he alone couldn't tell the direction she was firing.

'I'm not kidding!' The woman was concluding the proceedings. 'I promise I'll shoot the next person who speaks. Now, I'm asking: any more for any more?'

At which point, she and her confederate had left the building with untraceable notes to the value of £25,000, never to be caught.

Crystal had at first seemed untroubled by the bank raid. For three months or so after the Aldersgate Stick-up (as the incident came to be known), he waved aside all offers of sympathy, and continued his work at the Albion Bank. And then one day he found himself on a number 8 bus in New Oxford Street, weeping and shaking uncontrollably. For the next six weeks, his mother fed him oxtail soup in bed at home in Hoxton, and when he finally re-emerged, unsteady, into the world, he found strange but wonderful solace in the theatre.

There was something cocoon-like in the darkness and the plush seats of those West End spaces; even if guns were fired in the plays, the bangs were planned for, written, part of the design. He loved drawing-room comedies and well-made plays. He revered the work of Terence Rattigan. Above all, he loved the community of the audience together in the dark – although people sometimes noisily vacated the seat next to him. After a while, he started submitting critical articles and feature pieces to the weekly papers, which he was delighted to see in print.

Not that he was a pushover as a critic; quite the reverse. He simply applied his own rule of thumb. When he saw beauty and wit and order reflected on the stage, he hailed it. Conversely, when he saw ugliness, passion and violence, he bowed to no one in his determination to stamp them out. It was the same feeling he had had during the bank raid: *when something needed saying...*

Tonight's play stood for everything Crystal detested. True, he hadn't seen it yet, but he knew all about its writer Jack Braithwaite's infantile ambitions to shock and outrage the theatre-going public. This being 1957, a revolution was already tearing down the comforting old French doors and drawing-room scenery; in its place were kitchen sinks, man-gles, and actors in string vests. Beautiful diction was out; regional invective was in.

Jack Braithwaite was not a leader in this revolution, but he was an articulate follower, and a forthright spokesman, with the sort of youthful arrogance and broody bespectacled looks that evidently made quite sensible women fall at his feet. An actor-turned-writer, too (they were always the worst). Crystal had already gone head to head with him on a BBC discussion programme, during which Braithwaite said, memorably, that if he ever wrote anything *well-made*, he'd have to 'cut off his own two guilty hands'. He had also said that old-school critics like Crystal should be 'put out of their misery'. Miss Sibert, speaking out of turn for once (she usually knew her place), had begged her employer not to go and see the new play. 'It vill only upset you!' she had said (she had a German accent).

But he could not shirk a challenge, so here he was on the train. Also, there was someone he desired to speak with in Brighton, so he could kill two birds with one stone. *A Shilling in the Meter* was bound to be sordid, hectoring, formless, northern in origin, and long – Crystal's top five dislikes. As the train picked up speed on the outskirts of the capital, and the bombsites became fewer and farther between, he picked up his notebook. He had an observation for the review.

'Rather than putting his shilling in the meter, perhaps Jack Braithwaite should have given a bob to a Boy Scout, to write the play for him,' he wrote. (It had been Bob-a-Job Week quite recently; Crystal always enjoyed a topical reference.) 'The Boy Scout would undoubtedly have done a better job than our long-haired northern friend in his absurd black turtleneck sweater and winkle-picker shoes.'

If this excellent sentiment turned out not to work in the context of the review, he could save it for another day. It was all grist to the mill. If it worked nowhere else, he would squeeze it into the memoir he was currently writing with Miss Sibert's help – a memoir linking a) the restorative world of the theatre with b) the life-changing trauma of the Aldersgate Stick-up, and c) the role of chance in a person's life. The book was thus far tentatively titled *A Shot in the Dark*.

* * *

The same morning, in the Lanes in Brighton, a prematurely bald antiques dealer named Henry ('The Head') Hogarth paid

£50 for a set of antique coins that he knew for a fact to be stolen. The anonymous seller of these dodgy goods – who sported an improbably large nose and a jet-black moustache – hinted that, all things being equal, there might be more business they could do. Henry the Head said he welcomed such news. He was 'always in the market', he declared, cheerfully – and tilted his head forward to show the words 'Always in the Market' tattooed in cursive script on the top of his shining, shapely pate.

Before he left, Henry's customer paused at the door and asked a bizarre question.

'You don't need to answer this,' he said, 'but would you say you are a fond father, Mr Hogarth? Would you say you love your children beyond the usual bounds?'

Henry the Head hesitated. Was this a threat? A threat to his kids? He tensed up. Under the counter – out of sight – was a cricket bat, and instinctively he grasped its handle.

'I'd never grass, mate,' he said.

The man held up his hands in a reassuring gesture.

'No, you misunderstand, Mr Hogarth. It's just an intuition I have about you. I wondered if I was right?'

Not letting go of the bat, Henry the Head decided to answer. 'I'd die for my kids,' he said. 'Now, what do you want to make of that?'

'Nothing,' said the man, opening the door. 'I'm very pleased to hear it, that's all.'

* * *

In the preceding two weeks, the police in Brighton had become aware of a spate of house burglaries. In all cases, there was little to go on, and the officers could only take note of the valuables stolen and 'circularise' (official word for circulate) the details to pawnbrokers within the town.

Appearing on the most recent list was the same collection of priceless antique coins that had just come into the possession of Henry the Head. When the file of witness statements was perused by Inspector Steine of the Brighton Constabulary, nothing in particular stood out as offering a helpful clue, beside the fact that all the break-ins had taken place between 7.30 and 9.30 on weekday evenings when the houses in question were empty.

On the day of A. S. Crystal's visit to Brighton, Inspector Steine spent the first half hour of the morning in his office examining this file, which had been prepared for him by his 'bagman' Sergeant Brunswick. It didn't make him happy. Being a sensitive soul, it pained Steine to think of innocent citizens arriving home in the evening to discover they'd been robbed; it was very depressing, and he was rather inclined to be angry with Brunswick for bringing it to his attention.

But he took some small comfort from this file nevertheless. Two or three of the victims, he noticed, mentioned that on the day of the burglary a smartly dressed woman with bright auburn hair had called at the house in the afternoon and interviewed them on behalf of the national Public Opinion Poll. She had stayed around forty-five minutes and taken a particular interest in whether the householders kept a dog, whether they had any plans for the evening, and whether any window catches at the back of the property were especially in need of repair. This was all great news as far as Inspector Steine was concerned. He had always hoped one day to be interviewed by the Public Opinion Poll. How pleasing to discover that attractive female pollsters were operating in the Brighton area!

'Circularise details to pawnbrokers,' he wrote on the cover of the file, and handed it to Sergeant Brunswick, who was standing patiently beside the desk.

'Yes, sir,' said Brunswick, reading the instruction. 'You don't think the red-head is important?'

'Not really,' said Steine. 'She was only mentioned by one or two people. But I certainly hope she calls at my house, don't you?'

And there the investigation might have ended. But as Brunswick turned to go, the station charlady, Mrs Groynes, entered Steine's office with his ten o'clock cup of tea and plate of custard creams, accompanied by a tall young police constable in a helmet, who politely helped her with the door.

Inspector Steine acknowledged him, with a questioning raise of an eyebrow.

'Constable Twitten, sir,' said the unknown young man. He sounded well educated and unusually keen. He also sounded as if he thought his arrival was expected. 'Reporting for duty, sir,' he added, in a rush. And then, unable to suppress his excitement: 'Reporting for duty to the great Inspector Steine!'

Steine nodded. 'Thank you, yes, that's me,' he said, quite kindly. 'You may remove the helmet.'

'Thank you, sir,' said Twitten.

Steine hoped this would mark the end of the interview. 'Good, good,' he said, and shuffled some papers on his desk. The day ahead looked unusually demanding: first, he had to finish writing a talk for his weekly BBC Home Service series entitled *Law and the Little Man*. Later, the theatre critic of the *Daily Clarion* was intending to visit him at the police station. Evidently this man remembered Steine from a long-ago case called the Aldersgate Stick-up.

Crystal had been a witness, apparently; Steine the investigating officer. In his letter to Steine, typed on *Daily Clarion* headed notepaper and postmarked WC1, Crystal claimed that the trauma had altered the course of his life. Steine's total lack of success in breaking the case at the time (by finding no leads) had robbed Crystal of both his chance to obtain justice, and also to shine in court. Steine sincerely hoped he wasn't about to receive some sort of ticking off.

'He's seen that film of yours any number of times, isn't that right, dear?' said Mrs Groynes, nodding towards young Twitten, who was still standing awkwardly to attention in front of Steine's desk, helmet under his arm. She flicked a feather duster over Inspector Steine's Outstanding Policing Award certificate in its ornate silver frame. Mrs Groynes wore a floral overall and brown lace-ups. Her hair was tied up in a paisley scarf. Steine had spoken to her before about her habit of wittering on, but it turned out that the wittering was non-negotiable if you wanted the tea and biscuits.

'It was *The Middle Street Massacre* that made me decide to become a policeman, sir,' gushed Twitten. 'Father wanted me to study kinship systems in the Fens! But I saw *The Middle Street Massacre*, and then I read all the books about it, and I'm afraid I defied Father and enrolled for Hendon, and – I'm sorry, sir, you'll know all this already from my file, of course. The awards and commendations and so on. So I'll pipe down, shall I, sir? Yes, I think I should probably pipe down.'

Steine smiled again. He had no idea who Twitten was. He had seen no file. He looked optimistically at Brunswick, but from the sergeant's dazed expression, it seemed that he didn't know anything about Constable Twitten either.

'Just so,' Steine said.

And then Mrs Groynes said something that brought Inspector Steine a strange discomfort, and had such a powerful effect on Sergeant Brunswick that it seemed to raise the temperature in the room.

'This young man won a prize at Hendon for forensic observation,' she said.

'Did you, son?' said Brunswick, powerfully interested. 'Forensic observation?'

'Yes, sir,' said Twitten, blushing.

'Top of his year,' added Mrs Groynes.

Steine said nothing. Was this young know-it-all coming to work *here*? He hoped not. It was bad enough keeping Sergeant Brunswick in check.

'How do you feel about criminals, son?' Brunswick demanded.

Twitten looked surprised by the question, but answered it. 'I wholeheartedly oppose them, sir,' he said. 'Don't you?'

At this, a mixture of unfamiliar emotions appeared on Sergeant Brunswick's face – his usual pained expression giving way to amazement, disbelief, a little bit of triumph and (most unfamiliar of all) hope.

* * *

At the Theatre Royal, the five cast members of *A Shilling in the Meter* were assembling onstage for a meeting with the author. Prior to its opening night in London the week after next, the play was being 'tried out' in Brighton – a place famous for the regular tipping up of seats during performances, as outraged retired colonels struggled to their feet and hobbled out in noisy protest. The actors were right to be worried about tonight's first public performance. *A Shilling in the Meter* was overlong, quite hectoring, utterly sordid, unapologetically northern in origin and completely formless – the five top dislikes of retired south-coast colonels (although they wouldn't have been able to compile the list themselves: they relied on A. S. Crystal to do it for them in their favourite establishment newspaper).

The play's protagonist was a disaffected youth who made speeches about the evils of conformity; water dripped irritatingly from a fractured pipe in the ceiling into an old tin bath below; a dirty lavatory was on show throughout; and to top it all, in one of his rages, the unappealing central character Nick murdered his hapless girlfriend by first assaulting her with a hot iron and then smothering her under an old, stained mattress.

But it wasn't any of these unpleasant particulars that had precipitated the cast rebellion. Playwright (and director) Jack Braithwaite had instructed the management that, at the end of the play, the National Anthem should not be played. It was possible there would be a riot tonight – which in terms of publicity, of course, would do the play no harm. But for the actors, it was worrying; the three older members of the cast had pressed for this meeting with Braithwaite, to ask him to reverse his decision. Having Braithwaite's luminously beautiful current girlfriend amongst them in the cast – young Penny Cavendish, in her first leading role – was an advantage here. She could act as a bridge to the author, who otherwise scarcely gave his small troupe of players the time of day.

But they would have to wait for Braithwaite. He was in the circle bar, about to give a quick interview to a youth from the local press – a youth who had, literally, drawn the short straw. Braithwaite was a famously difficult interviewee (it contributed to his sex appeal), so the call for volunteers at the *Brighton Evening Argus* had been fruitless, hence the drawing of lots, using matchsticks.

'Did you say you *don't want a drink?*' Braithwaite now called to the young man from where he was standing at the bar.

Ben considered his response carefully. Was this a trick question?

'Yes, thank you,' he called back, politely.

'Now, what the bloody hell does that mean? "*Yes, thank you*"?'

'Well, it means –'

'Yes, please, you DO want a drink? No, thank you, you DON'T want a drink?' Braithwaite had evidently never heard anything more stupid than 'Yes, thank you'.

Ben Oliver chewed the inside of his cheek and then said, with care, 'I meant, yes, thank you for asking, I did say that I didn't want a drink.'

'Huh!' said Braithwaite, as he returned to the table and sat down heavily. 'God's *boots*,' he muttered, in an unnecessarily northern kind of way.

'Um,' said Ben, and cleared his throat. 'Um, I wondered if you could tell me about your play's title, Mr Braithwaite.'

'What about the title?'

'I just wondered if you could explain for our readers why it's called *A Shilling in the Meter*.'

'Bloody *hell*!' exploded the easily offended playwright. 'Where do these papers get such slobbering cretins? Why do you *think* it's called *A Shilling in the Meter*?'

Ben looked at his notes while he decided what to do. No one had ever described him as 'slobbering' before. He had never slobbered in his life. It seemed a trifle unfair, in this professional context, to direct such slurs at people who were in no position to retaliate.

'Well,' he said, 'I'm wondering, not having seen the play yet, if it's to do with the last gasp of England – the last shilling running out on empire, and that kind of thing. Maybe the play concerns the frustrated energy of youth in post-war Britain, symbolised by a gas fire that keeps going out on an endless dark February Sunday afternoon.'

He looked up from his notes. Braithwaite, with a stunned expression, wordlessly waved him on.

'If so,' Ben continued, 'I think that the great well-crafted plays by playwrights such as Rattigan and Priestley are about to be blown to matchwood by this hurricane-force new spirit of sexy naturalism emanating from the North.'

Braithwaite sat back. He was actually impressed. He particularly appreciated the word 'sexy'.

'But that's just my guess,' added Ben. 'Speaking with the disadvantage of not having seen the play yet, and also as a slobbering cretin. By the way, I noticed from the cuttings that you were actually born in Portsmouth. Is that true?'

* * *

Back at the station, Inspector Steine was hoping that the others would leave his office so that he could press on with the talk he was writing. For this week's *Law and the Little Man* he wanted to draw attention to the legal aspects of a notorious London football match in 1945, known as the Battle of Fulham Road, which had been such a hot ticket that fans had run amok. They had scaled buildings using stolen ladders; residents answering a knock on their front door had been rudely pushed aside by fans who took to the upper floors or stormed through gardens to get a view of the pitch; fences were torn down to be used as battering rams against locked gates.

So, on the one hand, this match had been a morale-boosting affair between Chelsea FC and a famous Moscow team (which Steine had a feeling was called the Dominoes, but some female dogsbody at the BBC would be able to check); on the other hand, there had been an enormous number of chargeable offences committed by a large group of individuals acting, as it were, with a single criminal purpose.

Inspector Steine was masterly when it came to explaining law to people who hadn't studied it; in the years since the Middle Street Massacre, such entertaining explication had become his main career. For example, did you know it was illegal to take a billiard cue on a bus? Do you know about the origins of 'legal tender'? If the young Queen's playboy husband hypothetically requested you to pay his gambling debts, would it be treason to refuse?

Well, you would be well informed in such fascinating areas if you had listened to *Law and the Little Man*, which over the past five years had confirmed Inspector Geoffrey Steine as a household name, and had familiarised the public with such arcane legal statutes as the Public Service Vehicles (Conduct of Drivers, Conductors and Passengers) Regulations, 1936. Honestly, if it weren't for Sergeant Brunswick constantly trying to expose criminality in Brighton, Steine would be more than happy with his lot.

Because the point was this: Steine loved the law, but he found the entire concept of criminals morally repugnant. When he adopted the famous faraway expression, he was not (as all supposed) thinking deeply: he was strenuously attempting to place himself in a calm green place beside a tinkling stream, with kingfishers flashing overhead and a snatch of Elgar on the breeze. It suited him perfectly to believe that, in a single afternoon, all the serious criminals in Brighton had killed each other, leaving the town crime-free for ever. Policing for him was about upholding the law and protecting the public, not dealing with unprincipled louts who would shoot you as soon as look at you.

'All the Brighton criminals are dead, Brunswick,' Steine had said to him a thousand times. 'You saw them dead with your own eyes. And may I remind you, they even made a film about it!'

'Yes, but that's not quite correct, sir,' Brunswick would reply. 'Two gangs were wiped out, sir, I grant you. But there are still dozens of villains, sir. Dozens!' And then he would start tiresomely reeling off names like Stanley-knife Stanley and Diamond Tony, Fiveways Potter and Ronnie the Nerk. 'It's my belief they're all controlled by Terence Chambers in London, sir. Working through a trusted deputy, as yet unidentified.'

It had been hard work suppressing Sergeant Brunswick's policing zeal for all these years. Of late, Steine had resorted to a regular, meaningful reply to all of Brunswick's reports of robberies and assaults: 'I fear this case will baffle all our efforts to solve it.' It had become a kind of mantra. No wonder Steine looked at this young Twitten now with a certain dread – especially when Brunswick handed Twitten the file concerning the break-ins.

Steine tried to object. 'Brunswick! We don't even know who he is!'

But Brunswick defied him. To Steine's annoyance, he asked the young man, 'Would you study this for me, son, and tell me what you make of it?'

To which Twitten, anxious to impress, replied, 'I already have, sir. And it's surely obvious that the flame-haired female is the key.'

* * *

A. S. Crystal of the *Daily Clarion* alighted neatly from the train at 11 a.m., and adjusted his spectacles. He was happy because he had already composed a large part of his review. Technically, any critical assessment of the play need not be written until the week after next, when it had officially opened in London. It was also unfair (and deeply frowned on) to review a production before it was ready. But Crystal had decided to dispense with the usual protocol. His intention was to kill off *A Shilling in the Meter* before it was even born.

As he left the station amid a herd of shrieking holiday-makers, he felt the cool punch of sea air in his face and stomach, and recoiled. There was nothing about Brighton that wasn't tawdry and second-rate, he thought. Stuck badly on an old wall opposite the station entrance were garish, tattered posters advertising the delights on offer in the town beyond: the Palace Pier, the Hippodrome. At the Hippodrome the current star act was evidently 'Professor Mesmer, the Last Living Phrenologist' – which just about said it all. A fake, outmoded science exercised in a fake, outmoded place. 'Come and have your bumps felt by the Great Professor Mesmer!'

'Ugh!' said Crystal, closing his eyes in disgust. Thank goodness the *Clarion* never required him to cover acts like that. He would rather (in that memorable image) cut both his hands off – except that, unlike Braithwaite, he appreciated what logistical difficulties that bloody job would present, if you actually tried to do it.

* * *

At the Theatre Royal, Braithwaite had finished with the reporter, and reluctantly met with his cast onstage in the darkened auditorium, on a set built to represent a grimy basement room lit by an upper, barred window and two naked light bulbs. On behalf of the others, who perched on the tea crates that comprised the major furnishings, Penny begged him to reconsider about the National Anthem.

What he wanted this morning was to run a dress rehearsal of Act One. After that, he intended to take Penny to a boozy lunch in the Queen Adelaide with a chum of his from drama-school days, who happened to be in town. He was in no mood for protests and naysayers; in no mood for these irksome actors. He had embarked on his theatrical journey believing that he liked everything about it, but now he realised there was one small part that didn't suit him at all: this disagreeable requirement of working with other people.

He surveyed his cast now with genuine dislike. The young leading man Todd Blair was a vain little insect, of course – but since he played the part of Nick (and therefore delivered three-quarters of the dialogue), Braithwaite had been obliged not to express this opinion too openly. Sporting a fashionable quiff, Blair had recently appeared as a hopped-up juvenile delinquent in a Dirk Bogarde film, and was, truthfully, the main reason people were buying tickets, so if he wanted to address Braithwaite as 'Daddy-o' occasionally in rehearsals, that was clearly his prerogative.

Where Braithwaite's patience had not stood the test was when Blair challenged any single detail of Nick's behaviour ('I'm just wondering if *even Nick* would say something so mean, you know?'). Such impertinent questions were off-limits, and had resulted in a few nasty scenes, with Jack telling Todd that until he was Marlon Brando he could keep his ruddy trap shut.

Penny, of course, playing the girlfriend Ruby had been a delight to work with, mostly because she loved him and thought (rightly) that he was not only masterly in bed, but a genius in an active relationship with the *zeitgeist*. Being a classy girl, she also knew when to keep quiet.

But the others! The couple playing Nick's stick-in-the-mud parents were obstinate time-server types who never expended a pound of effort if half an ounce would do; as for old Alec Forrester, who played the unnamed Man from the Gas Board, he'd been a thorn in Jack's side from the start. Casting a former matinée idol in such a demeaning role had appealed to his iconoclastic nature, but any malicious pleasure had soon evaporated once rehearsals had begun. The man with the smallest part was the biggest irritant – forever campaigning to change his lines; making suggestions for improvements to the script; reminiscing at length about playing one of the Lost Boys in the original production of *Peter Pan*; making odious comparisons between this play and great works by Priestley, Rattigan and Maugham.

It was true that this was Jack Braithwaite's first mainstream production, and that a bit of humility might not have gone amiss. It was true that Jack Braithwaite knew pitifully little about the history of the British stage. But he was a rising star whose picture had appeared in magazines, and he wasn't going to be humiliated by the actor playing Man from the Bloody Gas Board, however many anecdotes the tedious old stager could tell about what 'Larry' said to 'Vivien', and what 'Johnnie' had said to them both.

Things came to a head between Alec and Jack at this meeting. It was hardly good for cast morale that a violent spat should break out between writer and Gas Board Man with a first performance looming later in the day. It was unfortunate for Braithwaite, too, that young *Argus* reporter Ben Oliver was sitting quietly at the back of the stalls in the dark, and witnessed the whole thing.

But resentments had been building between the two of them ever since Alec had first tactlessly pointed out that Man from the Gas Board was a 'colourless cipher' and needed (at the very least) a Scottish accent. Today, under the spotlights, as tempers flared between them, and Penny tried to intervene, Jack accused Alec of being a 'pathetic toupéed has-been', while Alec called Jack 'jumped-up' 'talentless', 'derivative' and (worst of all) 'totally cloth-eared'.

The two men behaved very differently during their argument. Jack became restive and loud, and started pacing the stage – from tin bath to ironing board, and back to tin bath – while Alec sat upright on his tea chest, hands on his knees. Todd Blair and the others started to quite enjoy it. The exchange might be acrimonious, but it was packed with home truths. For example, Alec Forrester actually *was* a has-been, and he *did* wear a toupée, and he *was* pathetic.

And then Alec dropped his bombshell. 'Well, we'll see what Algernon makes of it, shall we?'

For a moment confusion reigned. Algernon who?

'You know him as A. S. Crystal, I suppose. Of the *Clarion*. I've invited him to see the play tonight, and asked him to pay particular attention to the under-written part of Man from the Gas Board. If I know Algernon – and I *do* know Algernon – his review will appear tomorrow.'

Braithwaite was so shocked that he stopped pacing the stage, coming to rest near the ironing board. The others held their breath. 'He can't do that,' he said. 'It's the first bloody performance!'

'He shouldn't, but he can,' laughed Alec, nastily. 'As you would know if you knew *anything about the theatre*.'

And then Braithwaite did something that shocked everyone. He grabbed the iron from the ironing board and threw it full force at Alec Forrester. Penny screamed; Todd Blair shouted 'My face!'; and all took cover, including Alec, whose ginger hairpiece fell off in the mêlée.

Fortunately, the iron didn't travel far, being heavier than it looked. It dropped like a stone without hitting anybody, just as the house manager yelled from the wings, 'What's happening here?' and switched on the house lights to reveal a tableau of disarray on the stage, and at the back of the stalls a cub reporter from the *Brighton Evening Argus* nestled into his seat, making notes in an excited manner.

'You!' shouted the house manager. 'Out!'

'Just going,' Ben Oliver called back, preparing to leave. 'But bravo, everyone. Bravo!'

* * *

Back at the police station, Twitten explained how he had come to read the file on the break-ins.

'It was while I was waiting for everyone to arrive in the office this morning,' he said. 'I'm sorry, sir. Perhaps I should have waited?'

'You most certainly should,' said Steine.

'But I found the statements so interesting I couldn't put them down, sir. The fact that several of the victims received a visit from the same red-headed Opinion Poll lady – well, what a lead! She was obviously casing the joint for the burglar who came along later in the evening.'

Steine harrumphed. 'There's no "obviously" about it.'

'The inspector's right,' said Brunswick, loyally. 'This is the real world, son. You're not in Hendon now. It was only a couple of the victims who reported this woman, isn't that right, sir?'

'Just one or two, as I recall,' said Steine.

'It was four, sir! And I hope you won't be cross, but I decided to telephone all the other victims to see if they'd had a visit from the Opinion Poll lady themselves –'

'You did what?' said Steine.

'It seemed like the obvious next step, to establish the pattern. Witnesses are notoriously unreliable when it comes to mentioning details they think the police won't consider relevant. At Hendon we were taught about it as "FOWPT", or Fear of Wasting Police Time, sir. I can show you the relevant section in the latest training handbook if you like.'

'No, thank you,' said Steine.

'Anyway, my hunch paid off, sir. *All* of them had received an identical visit!'

'What?' said Brunswick, a half-smile of astonishment on his face. This surely couldn't be happening. Who *was* this boy?

'I know, sir. All of them including the woman who lost the antique coins. She lives quite nearby in Upper North Street, so I've made an appointment to go and interview her this afternoon at half-past two.'

Twitten paused. From the way everyone was looking at him, he sensed something was wrong, but he had no idea what it was. So he pressed on.

'There's just one more thing?' He looked to his superior officers for a signal to continue, but they were too stunned to give it. There was an awkward pause. Spotting the problem, the charlady spoke up.

'Go on, dear,' she said, kindly.

'Thank you, Mrs Groynes. The thing is, the Opinion Poll lady always gave her respondents tickets to the Hippodrome for that evening, as a way of thanking them for their time, and no one had mentioned that in their statements, had they? To my mind, this omission was a classic example of witness "FOSTMAOS", Fear of Saying Too Much About One's Self, which is a recognised sub-division of FOWPT, Fear of

Wasting Police Time. So if she's handing out tickets to the Hippodrome, she might have some connection to that establishment, which I believe is in Middle Street, sir.'

'I know where the Hippodrome is, thank you, Twitten,' said Steine, feeling himself on firm ground at last.

'There's an old phrenologist topping the bill at the moment, sir,' added Twitten. 'But that might not be relevant.'

He stopped and looked round expectantly. Oddly, there was no round of applause.

Brunswick put his hands to his face.

Mrs Groynes turned away, saying, 'I'll put the kettle on, shall I, dears?'

Steine looked out of the window. His expression was suggestive of deep thought. (He saw *two* kingfishers, and heard the sound of distant panpipes.)

'You can come with me this afternoon to Upper North Street if you'd like to, Sergeant Brunswick,' Twitten added, excitedly. 'After all, it is your case.'

Two

Sergeant James Brunswick – known to his family as Jim – was thirty-eight years old, a tall man with regular features and a slight limp from being shot in the leg by the villain Fat Victor on the one occasion the police managed to arrest him.

He lived in a second-floor flat above a bicycle shop on the London Road with his auntie Violet, not far from where he'd been educated at the London Road Academy for Orphans, Waifs and Foundlings. His parents, who were now dead, had (interestingly) still been alive when little Jim was accepted as a pupil, aged five, by the foundling school, but they had managed to use some influence. In the years between the wars, you see, the London Road Academy had been one of the best of its kind in the country, financed by a generous bequest, and known as 'the Eton of the Poor'. Alumni were now in parliament and in many branches of entertainment.

'I was at school with him!' was Brunswick's regular cry, when listening to variety shows on the wireless with his auntie Vi on Saturday nights. He would often surprise people with the unlikely fact that the popular band leader Edmundo Ros was originally from Brighton, not Trinidad. No one believed him. (He was, in fact, mistaken.)

Having joined the so-called 'Boys' Army' straight from school in the 1930s, Jim Brunswick was twenty when hostilities broke out, and in the war had been a paratrooper dropped into various theatres of action, most notably Italy. While Inspector Steine had spent the period 1939–45 on the Home Front in the City of London, successfully guarding the Bank of England, and Constable Twitten had spent the war years as a precocious child begging to be allowed to solve enemy codes and thereby put paid to the protracted Battle of the Atlantic, Sergeant Brunswick had been jumping out of aeroplanes shouting 'Geronimo!', landing – alive, against the odds – behind enemy lines and engaging in mortal hand-to-hand combat.

He never talked about the war. In Italy, there had been a woman – but Brunswick never spoke about her, either. He carried her picture in his wallet, though, as he carried her memory in his heart. Brunswick was still handsome in a certain light; he had a delicate mouth and good cheekbones; he had a full head of neatly cut brown hair; but he looked older than his age, and had an aura of despair that was, sadly, very off-putting to women.

Much of his anguished state could be traced back to the Middle Street Massacre. From his point of view, that apocalyptic shoot-out had been a mixed blessing. Of all the lines in the film that people remembered, the outburst, 'Eating flaming ice cream at a time like this!' (which tended to raise a laugh), was the only one that had not been invented by the writer of the screenplay. Brunswick had in fact exclaimed, 'Eating flaming ice cream at a time like this' four times in Luigi's that day, and if the circumstances ever repeated themselves, he would say it again. Forty-five criminals could have been charged with arms offences! What a policing bonanza! So, on the one hand, yes, it was like a miracle to Brunswick that the town's worst and most notorious villains were wiped out at a single stroke, as if by an atomic bomb. The Giovedi family in particular had been a blight on the reputation of Brighton, operating so blatantly that police corruption was not so much suspected as assumed.

But when the Giovedis and the Casino Gang were wiped out, Brunswick was painfully aware – as Inspector Steine was not – that it created no power vacuum in Brighton's criminal underworld. 'It's just more nebulous now,' he would sometimes complain to Mrs Groynes, the charlady, with a sigh. And she would say, 'Nebulous, you say? That's a bit vague, dear, how do you mean?', while making him a nice cup of tea to take his mind off it.

Oh, that nebulousness! It was so indistinct and hazy, so vague and unclear! Villainy still abounded in this town, but its source was obscure. The great Terence Chambers, safe all those miles away in the East End of London, was obviously the man in charge, but how? Who acted as his deputy in Brighton? Who were his men, even? In the old days, Brunswick at least knew the chain of command in each of the gangs. He also had informers in both camps – Dodgy Pierre (not actually French but affecting a French accent) worked as a waiter in the saloon bar at the Queen Adelaide and helped him with the Casino Boys; Barrow-boy Cecil (who sold wind-up toys from a tray outside the Regent Kinema) was his inside man with the Giovedis. But since the Massacre, Dodgy Pierre seemed to know *rien* and Cecil had slowly unwound, like one of his plastic toys. They were both still worth a few bob a month for keeping their eyes open, but that was it. The

Massacre had been a massive setback to Brighton crime, but it had been a massive setback to detecting it, too.

And so Brunswick had grown demoralised. As far as the world was concerned, he belonged to the most successful police constabulary in the country. But from the inside, if you told Inspector Steine that you had suspicions about a thug called Stanley-knife Stanley, he would merely joke, 'I'd look out for him, if I were you, Brunswick. I hear he's quite sharp!' Ask, 'Permission to go undercover, sir!', and permission would be denied. Come up with a promising case, and Steine would say, 'I fear this case will baffle all our efforts to solve it.' Sometimes Brunswick seriously considered joining the Foreign Legion.

'It's his pride, Auntie!' he would say sometimes at Sunday breakfast-time, when she served him his fried rashers and special black pudding. 'If he's forced to accept there's still crime in Brighton, it will hurt his flaming pride!'

His one consolation over these years had been the silver screen. Brunswick adored the pictures – and Brighton had a plethora of picture-houses. Police films were his favourite: *The Blue Lamp*, *The Long Arm*. He also loved the B-features with Edgar Lustgarten outlining successful investigations from the files in Scotland Yard. He attended the theatre quite frequently too, but he was less comfortable there because of the sheer envy that overwhelmed him in his seat in the royal circle: he yearned to join the actors on the stage; he felt (deludedly) that, at heart, he was one of them.

Brunswick had actually stopped reading his favourite newspaper, the *Daily Clarion* – which covered crime stories especially well – just because its theatre critic A. S. Crystal was sometimes so vile and destructive where defenceless thespians were concerned. It was morally wrong to bully actors, in Brunswick's view; like punching kittens.

But more than the legitimate stage, Brunswick was drawn to variety, and that was why he relished Brighton. He visited the Hippodrome at every opportunity – ostensibly to pump old Stage Door Albert (another of his useless informants) for titbits, but mainly to slip inside and experience the buzz, the glitter, the cymbals, the 'Ooh!'s and 'Ah!'s. To adopt the words of Sir Arthur Conan Doyle, it seemed to Brunswick that there was no smell in the world like that of the hot oil in the footlights and the oranges in the pit.

This past month, with Professor Mesmer at the top of the bill, Brunswick had been in the audience three times already. It was unusual for a novelty act to be the star turn: you'd expect a big-name comedian, or a pop star in blue jeans for the kiddies. But Mesmer was hugely popular. A terrific and genial showman with a bushy beard and Victorian top hat, he was a hypnotist who practised not only on the volunteers from the audience, but on the audience as a whole. Brunswick adored him. He could read a person's character by touch alone! He could stimulate areas of the skull and induce laughter, tears, grandiosity.

Of course, the audience expected the usual hypnotist-act items, such as making people squawk like chickens, bawl like babies and turn cartwheels, flashing their underwear. But what Professor Mesmer did was more impressive than that. Somehow, he entertained you whether you wanted him to or not. At the end of Professor Mesmer's forty-five-minute spot, you felt that you sort of woke up, snapped out of it and, with a pleasant shudder, thought, 'Where am I?' And then, of course, you started applauding him to the rafters.

* * *

38

After the upsetting altercation with the Man from the Gas Board, Jack Braithwaite had preferred not to take his dress rehearsal after all, and had gone straight to the pub with Penny. He did not apologise about the iron. He did not explain to the house manager. But on the plus side, he didn't stride over to Alec Forrester and kick his head in, either. He just said, angrily, 'Penny, come with me,' and exited, stage left.

She caught up with him in the street, outside the stage door in Bond Street, where the brightness of the day, and the colour and noise of the milling holiday crowd, added to the unreality of what had happened inside. Jack was moving at speed through the throng on the pavement, but she ran and caught his arm.

'Jack!' she said. 'Come back. You have to apologise.'

She was scared at this moment; scared he would turn his anger on her. But when she saw the expression on his face – a look of shame and panic; a look of boyish mute appeal – she thought, 'This is why I love you,' and took him in her arms. He didn't hug her back, but nor did he wriggle or push her away. It was about as tender as Jack Braithwaite knew how to be.

'I don't know why I did that,' he said, quietly.

'He provoked you,' she said, supportively.

'That kid from the paper saw it all!'

'I know.'

She gave him a steady look. 'I need a drink,' she said, with a laugh.

'You're on.'

And she felt, as they walked wordlessly to the Queen Adelaide together, that maybe a deeper intimacy had been created between them by this unpleasant affair – which is the sort of thing that nice women like Penny sometimes sweetly delude themselves with, when involved with irredeemable egomaniacs like Jack.

What preoccupied Penny as they walked along was that the trigger point for Jack's violence had been the idea of a (slightly) premature review of *A Shilling in the Meter*. That's what made it so hard to understand. She could appreciate why he was angered by Alec's taunts, and by Alec's entire pompous personality, and indeed by everything that Alec stood for. Where she lost sympathy was over this reviewing business.

Jack's hatred for critics in general, and Crystal in particular, was ridiculously exaggerated. Plays had to exist in the real world. They had to be seen, and judged. What was the point of performing them in a void? Personally, she was keen to land a part in a film quite soon, possibly alongside the dangerous-looking Todd Blair (they looked dreamy together on the poster for the play). There was no chance of a film part if the critics weren't allowed to come and see her as the lovely, battered Ruby, whose Act One curtain-line ('Nicky, please don't! I was only stitching some nets!'), was guaranteed to break even the stoniest heart.

Bobby Melba happened to look up just as Penny and Jack arrived in the saloon bar. He would never forget that first glorious sight of Penny at the side of his old drama-school acquaintance. He always remembered Jack's demeanour with Penny – regarding her on his arm as if she were the lucky one: the little actress girlfriend of the charismatic theatrical genius. Whereas what Bobby saw immediately was the truth: Penny was a star.

As it happens, Penny would never forget her first sight of Bobby, either: a slender young man in his twenties, wearing a fashionable suit and Italian leather shoes. In later life, when she was indeed a colossal star of stage and screen (and had been married five times), she often thought back to this first encounter with the man she so quickly loved and lost.

He was so *right* for her. It was like meeting her other half, and she never got over him. She measured all the subsequent husbands against the feeling of intense attraction that she had on first seeing Bobby, and none of them came close. When she and Bobby locked eyes in that saloon bar, he stood up and simply smiled at her with his arms wide as if to say, in astonishment, 'Now I am complete!'

'Jack!' said Bobby. 'You're early.'

'Bobby Melba,' chuckled Braithwaite. 'Well, look at you. Like a peach!'

While an oddly French-accented waiter was dispatched to get drinks, and Jack went to buy cigarettes, Penny and Bobby sat down. Bobby smiled at her conspiratorially, and she smiled back.

'I'm Penny,' she said, quickly shaking his hand – glad that Jack, occupied with feeding coins into the cigarette machine, couldn't see. She knew from past experience that Jack could react badly when his bad manners were drawn attention to. Interestingly, however, this never taught him to have better manners in the first place.

Bobby was soft-spoken without being quiet. 'I wish I could come and see the play, Penny,' he was saying, as Jack returned with his pack of Woodbines. 'I'm sure you're sensational.'

As Jack sat down, and the drinks arrived, Bobby repeated what he had said to Penny – or part of it, anyway.

'I was just saying, Jack, I wish I could come and see your play.'

'Oh, yes?'

'But I go on myself at half-past nine.' He turned to Penny to explain. 'I'm the so-called Last of the Phrenologists,' he said, with an air of self-deprecation. He lifted his glass. 'Professor Mesmer, at your service! At the Hippodrome for a month – a whole month, Jack! It's unheard of.'

Penny's eyes lit up. 'Is that feeling people's heads for bumps?' she asked.

Jack gave her a mocking push. 'Don't pretend to be interested, you phoney cow!' he barked, laughing, and lit a cigarette. Bobby winced, but Penny didn't seem to mind.

'You're very young to be a professor,' she said. Her eyes were green, he noticed.

'It's more of an honorary title.' Bobby smiled. 'Self-conferred.'

'Do you wear a self-conferred beard?'

'Yes, I do. And a hat. I am a master of disguise.'

He turned to Jack. 'So are your cast behaving themselves?' he asked. At which point Penny felt she should dive in and change the subject, and ask how they had met at drama school.

It turned out that Bobby had been a very promising actor, getting good parts in student productions, but then something had happened ('beyond my control, I'm afraid'), and he'd decided not to go into the profession, after all. He had dropped out in the final year, swapping Hamlet for head bumps, apparently without a qualm. 'A thousand people a year play the Dane; no one else can do what I do,' he had told the affronted school principal on the day he officially hung up his tights.

The last time Bobby and Jack had met, they were both in shows in Leeds – Bobby as Professor Mesmer at the famous City Varieties, Jack upstairs in a pub playing an activist Geordie miner in an outstanding little play called *Clogs on the Batty Stones* – a play that had received such a crushing and vindictive twelve-word review from A. S. Crystal when it reached London that the mortified writer had left the business altogether and gone to live in Nova Scotia.

'I thought I saw him the other day,' Bobby said, conversationally. 'He must have come back.'

'Who?' said Jack, confused. 'Not *Crystal*?'

Penny reached out a restraining hand.

'No, no. I meant your friend Harry Perks. The man who wrote *Clogs on the Batty Stones*.'

'You've seen him?'

'Yes. Here in Brighton.'

'But he went to Canada.'

'Well, he must have come back. He's working in an ice cream place on the seafront. I suppose he felt he couldn't face going back up north.'

'Oh, poor Harry!' said Jack.

'He hasn't forgotten or forgiven, either. He says if he ever sees A. S. Crystal, he'll kill him.'

'Not if I do it first!' said Jack.

Bobby laughed, but he noticed that no one else did.

So Penny explained how Crystal was possibly planning to review Jack's play ahead of the opening. 'We're all quite cross about it,' she said, brightly. And then, heroically changing the subject, 'But tell me about the time when you were both in Leeds. What was it like?'

Jack gratefully went along with Penny.

'Leeds, well, yes.' He racked his brain for an anecdote – sensibly avoiding anything that involved mentioning previous beautiful girlfriends (all actresses). Amazingly, one came up. 'Well, here's a thing, Bobby,' he said. 'You remember that stuck-up landlady I was staying with?'

'The one who fancied you?'

Jack ignored this. For a start, all his landladies fancied him. 'I told you she had those nice bits of Lalique glass, do you remember that?'

Bobby pulled a funny face. 'Not really,' he said.

Penny laughed. Why *would* he remember?

'Well,' Jack continued, 'silly mare. A day or two after you and I met, she got this posh bint calling round in the afternoon pretending to be doing an opinion poll of some sort, and she fell for it. And that same bloody evening she was robbed!'

* * *

Brunswick and Twitten were on their way to interview the lady in Upper North Street, whose antique coins had been taken in a break-in. It was a beautiful summer day, warm but with a brisk sea breeze, and Brunswick was lighter of step than he had been for years.

He raised his hat to say 'Good day' to holidaymakers; gallantly offered help to a woman with a little dog; gave directions to the Pavilion; he even held up the traffic to let a party of French children cross the road. He was out on proper detective business and it felt good, even if he had to suffer this precocious young Twitten at his side, explaining the latest thinking (at Hendon) on using cross-checking of criminal records to detect crimes. ('I could draw you the basic diagram, sir.')

Normally Brunswick spent his days begging the inspector to let him go undercover, with the inspector refusing to let him on the grounds that a) he never learned anything of importance by doing it, and b) the one time he'd gone undercover before, he'd been shot in the leg by Fat Victor. Being out and about in the sea air, on a legitimate police investigation, accompanied by a fresh-faced young copper, made for a very agreeable change.

'I hope you won't mind my asking this, sir,' said Twitten, hesitantly, as they walked uphill on North Street. 'But is it true that the inspector won't even countenance the idea that crime takes place in Brighton?'

Brunswick didn't know how to answer. 'Where on earth did you hear that, son?' he asked.

'Mrs Groynes the charlady, sir. She seems to have taken me under her wing. Is it true, sir?'

This was awkward. 'Well, yes and no,' said Brunswick, tactfully. 'But mainly yes. I suppose it's better that you know about it straight away. It's a flaming nuisance, son, but it's true.'

'But if that's true, it would be a scandalous dereliction of duty, sir. I have to say, I can't quite believe it.'

Brunswick shrugged. He didn't really care whether Twitten believed it or not. As they passed the Regent Kinema on the hill, he gave a secret wink to Barrow-boy Cecil, who was attempting to flog small wind-up rabbits from the top of a box covered in a green velour tablecloth, calling out, 'See the bunny run! See the bunny jump! Only half a crown!'

'Who was that, sir?' said Twitten, eagerly, when they were safely past.

Brunswick looked shifty. 'Who was who?'

'The man you signalled to, sir. With the bunnies. Is he a *grass*, sir?'

'I didn't signal to anyone.'

'You did, sir, I saw you.'

But Brunswick refused to answer, and as they crossed by the Clock Tower, there was a brief, welcome lull in the conversation. He never seemed to stop talking, this boy.

Sadly, the lull was soon over.

'Well, I must say, I think we're jolly lucky we caught on to the Opinion Poll scam before some innocent householder was murdered,' Twitten said, brightly.

'Murdered? Why should anyone get murdered?'

'I fear it's inevitable, sir.'

'Is it?'

'Oh, yes. This sort of crime, involving disguise, is commonly associated with narcissism, you see. And a cornered narcissist is highly dangerous. It's pure bally luck that so far none of his victims has come home at an inconvenient moment and been struck down. Yes, it doesn't do to underrate the latent turbulence of the narcissist personality, sir.'

Brunswick didn't like the sound of any of this, especially as it seemed to be mostly in a foreign language. He decided to say nothing.

'Psychology is a bit of an interest of mine, sir,' Twitten explained. 'But to be honest, I was brought up with it. My father is the pre-eminent criminal psychologist in Britain. He's the author of *Inside the Head of the Law Breaker*, which was a best-selling book about ten years ago. He followed it up with *Behind the Eyes of a Killer* and *Under the Lid of a Psycho*. It was a very lucrative line of work for a while. I think that's why he hoped I'd turn to anthropology instead. He knows too bally much about the dark side of human nature, sir.'

They had reached the Clock Tower, and Brunswick stopped walking. Together they looked down West Street to the sea.

'Look,' said Brunswick. 'About the inspector. About what you said just now. The hard part is, he thinks I see villainy just to spite him.'

'But why would you do that? I don't understand.'

'He says I want to *disprove* the success of the Middle Street Massacre out of some sort of envy, or revenge, just because I was portrayed as an idiot in the film.'

They moved on again, uphill.

'Well, I hate to speak out of turn, sir,' said Twitten, at last, 'but I do think that's a very unfair analysis on his part. You are clearly a very dedicated, if unimaginative, policeman. Although he does have a point: they did make you seem quite stupid in the film.'

Brunswick groaned. 'I know, son.'

'It was terribly funny, sir!'

'I know. But the result is, every cocky kid in Brighton knows he can get a rise out of me, doesn't he, just by talking about eating flaming ice cream. *Eating flaming ice cream at a time like this, Sergeant Brunswick?* I hear it every day of my life, son. It's even more annoying when I'm actually eating flaming ice cream.'

They had arrived at Upper North Street.

'This is the house, sir!' exclaimed Twitten, unlatching the painted garden gate. 'Would you like me to take the lead in the questioning?'

Brunswick pondered this outrageous suggestion.

'No, thank you, son,' he said. 'But I'll tell you what. I'll do the questioning and you can draw a diagram of it afterwards, how's that?'

* * *

Inspector Steine left a message for Crystal at the station, telling him to rendezvous at Luigi's on the seafront. It was far too nice a day to spend entirely indoors: along the promenade the bunting strung between the lamp posts was dancing and rattling in the breeze, and from the modest bandstand between the piers came distant comforting oom-pah-pahs.

But it wasn't just that Steine wanted to be out and about for its own sake. He preferred to meet Crystal in a public place. The tone of that letter had not been friendly; it seemed to imply that Steine should have 'solved' the Aldersgate Stick-up – as if such a thing had been possible in the absence of information! Demanding for crimes to be 'solved' was an ignorant and unreasonable position to take, in Steine's view. It was simplistic. Many crimes went unsolved in this world; it was *very common* for a crime to go unsolved. In many ways, Steine felt that an unsolved crime was more satisfying – in philosophical terms – than a solved one. Complete in itself, it had more integrity as a concept. Once you started trying to solve it, it came apart in unattractive ways.

But you couldn't expect a mere layman to grasp such a high-minded abstract argument. Not many people knew this, but Steine had at one time hoped to become a professional philosopher. The nearest he'd got, however, was years ago in Bloomsbury, helping Bertrand Russell onto a number 14 bus, while at the same time informing him that he couldn't carry his billiard cue.

So Steine had chosen Luigi's partly because it was a public place, but also out of instinct. He was uncomfortable about seeing Crystal, and it was his usual practice, when he felt uncomfortable, to eat ice cream. Later, when the day's events had unfolded in their unexpectedly grisly way, Steine was glad that at least Crystal had experienced a superlative chocolate sundae at Luigi's before meeting his spectacular end.

'Speaking personally, I think if *I* were going to be assassinated later in the day, I'd certainly want one of Luigi's ice creams to be *my* last meal,' he announced to the gentlemen of the press – and for many years afterwards Luigi's adopted this dubious endorsement in their advertising.

Old Luigi himself served Inspector Steine, as he always endeavoured to do. It was a busy and bright ice cream parlour, with high swivelling stools at a chrome-edged counter, and eight booths, each with red leatherette upholstery, and shiny-topped tables the colour of HP sauce. In the next booth, sitting alone facing Steine, was a delinquent-type youth with rolled-up sleeves, flicking through the pages of an *ABC Film Review* with a picture of James Dean on the cover. On the walls were black-and-white photographs of Luigi's on the day of the Middle Street Massacre: the place packed with members of the Brighton Constabulary all intently eating Knickerbocker Glories with special long-handled spoons.

In reality, no one had brought a camera to Luigi's on that famous day; the shots had been staged afterwards, which explained why Sergeant Brunswick was absent. He had refused to take part in the reconstruction. Partly, he thought it undignified; partly he disapproved of fabricated evidence of any sort. But mainly he could never square it with his conscience that while he had indeed fumed about eating flaming ice cream, he had, in the end, been persuaded by Inspector Steine to consume a delicious rum-baba.

The man who brought Inspector Steine's *tutti-frutti* and Ovaltine to his table was a rugged-looking individual Steine had never seen before, but the inspector took little notice of him as he approached, having brought along an ancient file concerning the Aldersgate Stick-up, to refresh his memory. Consulting the contents, he was reminded that Crystal had been the assistant manager of the bank, and had been an out-standingly helpful witness. He had also recklessly antagonised the armed robbers while they were about their nefarious business, virtually asking to be shot.

A police photo of Crystal was attached to the file, and Steine was studying it in his booth when the man carrying the *tutti-frutti* arrived and let out a cry of surprise. Luigi was there in a moment. 'Harry!' he beseeched. 'Wassa wrong with you?'

Luigi took the bowl of ice cream and mug of Ovaltine from Harry's shaking hands, and placed them on the table. 'Isspector, I so sorry,' he said. 'I get you wafer, yes?'

And Steine – somewhat baffled, but latching on to the word 'wafer' – instantly cheered up and put the whole incident behind him.

Crystal arrived at Luigi's soon after. He was evidently cross about finding Steine absent from the police station; he had been redirected by a wittering charwoman.

'Steine,' he said, as he reached the table.

'Crystal,' Steine responded, standing up – not noticing how the boy with the movie magazine in the next booth reacted as if electrocuted at the name (it was Todd Blair, of course). The two men shook hands. Steine sniffed the air, bothered by something. A tiny whiff of Crystal's body odour had reached his nose. He sniffed again, and shrugged. 'So what brings you to Brighton?'

'Some ghastly play,' said Crystal, unbuckling the belt of his raincoat, and removing it. As he did so, a pungent gale was released, which made the inspector gape in shock and sit down involuntarily. Crystal sat down opposite.

'A play, you say?' said Steine in a strangled voice, coughing.

Crystal opened his briefcase and withdrew a sheet with the bare details typed on it. He handed it to Steine and then studied the menu with his glasses off.

'*A Shilling in the Meter* – thrilling new play by *enfant terrible* Jack Braithwaite' the announcement said. Below was a plot outline and a list of cast members. It might have been in Sanskrit for all the sense it made to Steine. He hardly ever went to the theatre; he was more of a Home Service and Slippers man himself.

'Alec Forrester's name rings a bell,' he said, at last. 'If it's the same man, I'm surprised he's still alive. My mother saw him in Ivor Novello musicals in the 1920s.'

The youth in the next booth was now taking such an obvious interest in the conversation that he had quite forgotten his magazine and was narrowing his eyes, while running a practised hand through his quiff. He was quite handsome, Steine noted. A bit like an actor.

'Terrible ham nowadays,' said Crystal, referring to Alec Forrester. His thin voice somehow made every utterance sound mean. 'Deluded, too. Thinks he's a theatrical Olympian, when in fact he's just a has-been.'

'Poor chap,' said Steine.

'Oh, don't waste your sympathy there, Steine. Oh, no, no, no. But the things he's been telling me about this play! He loathes it! He's hoping I'll say he's the best thing in it, but there's no chance of that.'

Crystal lowered his voice. 'He's playing the part of Man from the Gas Board! And he wears a toupée!'

* * *

After saying goodbye to Jack and Penny, Bobby took himself down to the Palace Pier. He often went to noisy places when he needed to think. So he positioned himself between the ghost train and the helter skelter, where the train rattled loudly on its narrow track and bells jangled, and ghoulish 'Whoooo!' noises resulted in demented female screams, and hooters hooted, and bodies thundered down the spiralling slide on thick prickly mats – and there he stood and lit a Senior Service and thought about Penny.

He thought she was the most beautiful person he had ever met. He thought that Jack was a vain brute who didn't deserve her. He also thought, regretfully, that she was a moral sort of girl to whom he could never confess the sorts of things he did under cover of being Professor Mesmer. Even Jack would be shocked if he knew about those.

Was Jack's behaviour getting out of hand, though? When he had briefly popped to the Gents, Penny had told Bobby about the incident with the iron that morning; she had defended Jack's actions on the grounds that emotions were running high, and that Alec had committed a very disloyal act by inviting that critic down from London. She also said Jack had been wonderfully contrite. But she was obviously worried.

Bobby thought she was right to be so. He didn't tell her the story, but once, at drama school, Jack had deliberately wounded another student during a fencing class. At the time everyone believed it to be an accident, but Bobby knew better: it had been coldly premeditated. Jack had harboured a grudge for eighteen months, just biding his time for a shot at revenge. And when the chance came, he took it.

'I think he's quite *vengeful*,' he had said to Penny, leaving it at that. And it was true. He was. Although Jack had indeed been born in Portsmouth, he had absorbed much from his Yorkshire-born mother. 'Keep a stone in thy pocket for seven year,' she had told him, in his cot, like something out of a Brontë novel. 'Turn it and keep it seven year longer, that it might be ever ready to thine hand when thine enemy draws near.'

'Bobby! Is that you?' He turned and saw with pleasure his favourite person in Brighton ('Brighton Auntie' he used to call her), waving from the crowd, conspicuous by her neat, wasp-waisted figure and her striking auburn hair.

* * *

From that convenient booth in the ice cream parlour (luckily upwind from Crystal), Todd Blair heard quite a lot to amuse him over the next half hour. What Crystal had said about Alec Forrester was hilarious; he could hardly wait to get back to the Theatre Royal and tell stuck-up Alec what his old chum Algernon really thought of him. 'You're toast in tomorrow's paper, granddad,' he would inform the proud old-timer. 'He's clocked the rug, and all.'

But there was even more to listen to. Blair sipped his second frothy coffee and eavesdropped with delight. After giving Steine his spare ticket to *A Shilling in the Meter*, and finishing his complimentary sundae without once commenting on its outstanding quality, Crystal had become quite heated over some long-ago robbery in London. The page in Blair's magazine concerning Marlon Brando in *Tea House of the August Moon* started to swim before his eyes.

'On the contrary, you had a LOT to go on!' Crystal was saying, his high voice almost shrieky.

'I keep telling you, I appealed for information.'

'Your appeal said, and I quote, *Does anyone know who did this?*'

'Of course it did! What's wrong with that?'

'Don't you have underworld connections?'

'I most certainly don't!' The inspector sounded shocked. 'Do *you*?'

Crystal stood up and gathered his things.

'You're an idiot, Steine. And I think it's time people knew.'

'I beg your pardon?'

Crystal put on his raincoat and buckled the belt.

'*Law and the Little Man*? You're the little man, Steine. Pretending to be the policing genius. Living on the legend of the Middle Street Massacre. Lecturing the public on the Rights of Way Act 1935!'

'I think you'll find that's 1932,' corrected Steine, hotly.

Crystal turned to go. He saw the smirking Todd Blair for the first time, and a look of vague recognition flickered on his face. But he hadn't finished with Steine. At the door he called back, 'I could have been shot that day at the Albion Bank, and you did nothing!'

'Well, I wish you *had* been shot, you odious man!' Steine called after him, for all to hear. 'Right now I wouldn't mind shooting you myself!' And as the door slammed, he added, 'And get yourself a bar of Lifebuoy, for pity's sake.'

Three

What Constable Twitten had failed to establish before arranging the interview with Mrs Eden in Upper North Street was whether or not she was blind. Somehow the question hadn't occurred to him. When she opened the front door that afternoon, wearing bottle-green glasses and holding a white stick, Brunswick let slip a groan of annoyance – but Twitten shot him such a look of disapproval that he corrected himself.

Of course, in the next half hour this blind woman helped them establish far more about the phoney Public Opinion Poll lady than they might have got from a dozen witnesses with perfect vision. As Twitten eagerly explained to the inspector when they were back at the station, all the sighted witnesses had been so struck (or misdirected) by her improbably bright red hair that they couldn't remember very much else about her.

Steine wasn't interested. He was fed up with this woman. He was fed up with this Constable Twitten. His enjoyment of Luigi's had been ruined (how could *anyone* not comment on how good the ice creams were?), and he now had a ticket to see a play that sounded awful, in the company of a man he'd like to throttle. What he needed this afternoon was the usual peace and silence of his office, interrupted only by the occasional rattle of bone china cup on saucer brought in by a tiptoeing charlady. But instead he was faced with two excited policemen with an annoying story to tell.

'She was definitely casing the joint, sir,' said Brunswick. 'That Opinion Poll lady. Tell him, Twitten. About Mrs Eden. She was *blind*, sir.'

'Then I'm sure she was a lot of help.'

'Oh, but she was, sir,' said Twitten. 'It is often the case in blind people that their other senses are heightened, sir. Smell, touch, hearing, and so on.'

'I know what the five senses are, thank you, Twitten,' said Steine. 'And I'd like to point out that since no one alerted me to this posting of yours, technically you might not actually work here. You might just be a clever imposter with a uniform from a theatrical costumiers.'

Twitten wondered whether he was supposed to respond to this bizarre accusation. He glanced at Sergeant Brunswick, who reassuringly pursed his lips and shook his head.

'Mrs Eden gave us so much, sir,' Twitten went on, undeterred. 'About the Opinion Poll lady's voice, her accent, her manner of speech. She remembered from shaking the lady's hand that there were protuberances on the top knuckles of the fingers, such as pianists sometimes get. And she brought with her a strange mixture of smells, among which were –' Twitten consulted his notebook '– face powder, Brylcreem, lavender, rubber adhesive and *explosives*.'

'None of which necessarily makes her a *criminal* Opinion Poll lady,' objected Steine, complacently. 'Just a law-abiding Opinion Poll lady with a laudably wide variety of hobbies.'

'But there was something else,' said Brunswick. 'Mrs Eden lent her a blotter to rest her papers on. Young Twitten here asked if he could rub a soft pencil over the indentations to reveal what might have been written there. And it worked, sir! They had been discussing public transport facilities in Brighton, and what do you think the Opinion Poll lady had written down, sir?'

'I have no idea.'

'Oh, go on, sir,' said Twitten. 'Guess.'

'Something about trams?'

'No. Guess again?'

'This isn't a game, Twitten,' snapped Steine.

But both his men were looking at him expectantly, so he had another go. 'The regular late running of trains to the capital?'

Twitten read triumphantly from his notebook. 'She had written *back window – broken latch*; *NO DOG* in capitals; and *cash in bureau top drawer*!'

Brunswick patted Twitten on the back. 'Well done, son,' he said.

'Thank you very much, sir.'

Steine, however, was still not satisfied.

'However,' he said, 'I fail to see how all this advances matters. We already knew she had *red hair*, didn't we? It's surely easier to spot someone with red hair than go around sniffing people for a mixture of lavender and gunpowder.'

'But the hair is obviously a wig, sir!' blurted Twitten. 'Any fool would guess that!'

Peregrine Twitten, aged twenty-two, had been a super-brain all his life. And like many a super-brain, he found it difficult to interact diplomatically with people slower-witted than himself, especially when they were in positions of authority. There was one particular error he made again and again: expecting people to thank him for explaining things to them. It was astonishing to him how often they just took offence instead.

'Would you care to repeat that, Constable?' said Steine, stiffly. 'Did you actually say, *any fool would guess that*?'

'Gosh, sir. I'm very sorry. I didn't mean to imply –'

Twitten turned in confusion to Sergeant Brunswick, who chipped in, 'But it probably is a wig, sir. When you think about it.'

Steine looked out of the window for a moment, adopting the faraway thoughtful look that had become his trademark. The others waited for him to speak. When he did so, it was with an air of finality.

'Constable Twitten,' he said. 'I've made a decision. I expect you mean well, but I've come to the reluctant conclusion that you will never fit in at this station, so I'd like you to make your goodbyes and gather your personal things.'

'But sir, I only started this morning!'

'I feel obliged to tell you that your whole approach is simply annoying, Twitten. You're like a dog with a bone. You are an impetuous, arrogant pipsqueak. What were you going to do *next* in this case, I'd like to know!'

Steine had meant this as a hypothetical question, but Twitten was more than happy to answer it.

'I was going to follow up the Hippodrome angle, sir, which I think is strong. It occurred to me that the explosives smell might be associated with a theatrical effect of some sort. And the sergeant, who's seen the current show a couple of times, confirmed to me that one of the highlights is indeed, as I suspected, a midget being shot out of a cannon.'

'It's amazing, sir,' said Brunswick. 'Not a mark on him. There's also a woman who tears up telephone directories with her bare hands.'

'Apart from that,' Twitten continued in a rush, anxious to prove himself, 'I thought I would contact all the major wig emporiums in London and check sales of red wigs in the past year. I've already put in a request to the criminal records department at Scotland Yard to establish whether similar crimes have been committed in other towns and cities. Also, having realised that those tickets to the Hippodrome were complimentary ones, I was going to ask the box office for a list of the people entitled to have them.'

He lowered his voice and stood more to attention. 'Please don't move me on for being too clever, sir. It's not my fault. I've already been transferred six times in my first three months.'

This emotional appeal, coming out of the blue, was very affecting. Brunswick looked heartbroken for him. 'Six times?' he repeated. 'That's awful, son.'

'I know,' sniffed Twitten.

'Keep out of this, would you, Brunswick?' said Steine. 'Look, Constable. For one thing, I didn't say you were *too clever*. I said you were annoying.'

'I'm afraid other people have used the words "too clever", sir. The words "too clever" are all over my personal file. Even Deputy Chief Inspector Peplow at Scotland Yard said I was too clever! That's probably why you didn't get any notification of my arrival. Until last Friday, I was working there. I had cracked the case of the Kennington Butcher, sir, which had frustrated him and his division for several years. They had unaccountably overlooked a human tooth embedded in a floorboard in the prime suspect's scullery! When I pointed this out, my transfer was ordered almost immediately.'

This startling news put a new complexion on things for Steine. DCI Peplow was someone he loathed with a passion. Peplow had a suspiciously high clear-up rate that had three times secured for him the title 'Policeman of the Year', twice pipping the more high-profile Steine to the title. Twitten's news changed things considerably. 'The great Peplow couldn't cope with you, you say? Because you were *too clever*?'

'That's right, sir.'

'The famous Deputy Chief Inspector gave up on you? He washed his hands? He threw in the towel?'

'He said I brought him out in hives, sir.'

'Hives, you say?'

'It's a sort of aggravated rash, sir.'

'I know what hives are, good grief.' Steine shook his head. It was very hard to be patient with this boy. But he wouldn't mind outdoing the great Peplow for once. He imagined shaking hands with Peplow at some all-male Top Ranks gathering (possibly in a smart bar at the Festival Hall, for some reason) and saying, smugly, 'You found him too hot to handle, I believe? What an error! Young Twitten is a positive asset if you know how to manage him.'

'Look, just leave this with me, Constable,' he said.

Twitten looked relieved. 'Thank you, sir. You're my last hope, sir.'

'But I'd rather you didn't go to the Hippodrome tonight.'

Steine had made a decision that he considered would kill two birds with one stone: it would slow Twitten down a bit, and also remove the loathsome and vile-smelling Crystal from his own life.

'I want you to take this ticket for a play called something like *A Bob in the Slot* at the Theatre Royal. And I want you to stay there, and not do any detecting, and watch the whole thing. Give those little grey brain cells of yours a rest.'

If this was meant to ruin Twitten's day or put a spoke in his wheel, it failed. An excited grin appeared on his face.

'You don't mean *A Shilling in the Meter*? Oh my goodness. Thank you very much, sir.'

'You've heard of it?'

'Who hasn't, sir?'

Steine sighed. 'Well, don't get too excited. You'll be sitting next to A. S. Crystal of the *Daily Clarion*. Your biggest challenge will be not to murder him. Meanwhile Sergeant Brunswick can make enquiries at the Hippodrome about red-haired women with hammer-fingers, and with you two Sherlock Holmeses safely out of my hair, I can finally – *finally* – write my talk for the wireless on the rather thorny subject of the law on joint enterprise when applied to marauding mobs.'

Twitten had a bright idea. 'If you ever need help with subjects for your talks, sir –' he began, but Brunswick hustled him out of the room before he could say anything more.

'Well done on the Kennington Butcher, son,' Brunswick was saying, as they shut the door behind them, and Steine could hear Twitten reply, 'There was a rug over it, sir. Can you believe that no one at Scotland Yard had ever thought to look underneath the rug?'

* * *

In advance of the first performance of *A Shilling in the Meter*, the cast were on edge. The technical rehearsal went well enough, though: the water dripped perfectly as directed into the tin bath (*plip!* – *long pause* – *plop!*); the expressionistic lighting effect for the arrival of the Man from the Gas Board at the end of Act Two looked excellent. For this grand moment, the door needed to swing open (and not swing back again), and a strong backlight cast a lengthy shadow of Alec across the raked floor of the stage, pointing to the exact spot where the hapless Ruby (Penny) lay dead. 'I've come to read the meter,' was the sonorous curtain line, as Alec shuffled in.

Braithwaite was very proud of this moment. It made him shiver. He insisted that Alec's leather shoulder bag be filled, authentically, with heavy coin, even though the spindly Alec had nearly buckled under its weight several times in rehearsals. From the auditorium the heavy bag had clear significance: this bent old man collecting the dues was Death. And it helped the effect considerably (so Braithwaite always said to the others) that Alec looked a lot like death already.

* * *

On the shingly beach, by the bandstand, with the small murky waves dragging loose pebbles down the shore, and herring gulls dive-bombing grubby cockney tots unwisely holding unprotected ice cream cones, a diminutive, aggressive-looking Punch & Judy man was setting up his booth, muttering to himself in a Greek accent.

'This ruddy pole go ruddy *here*?' he was saying, as if he'd like to garrotte the person who designed this thing. 'But *that* ruddy pole go ruddy *there*?' He picked up a rock to start knocking the posts into the shingle, but was interrupted by the telltale crunch of footsteps on the shining stones.

'Help you with the tent, Vince?' offered Sergeant Brunswick, approaching. The sergeant walked taller than usual this afternoon, Vince thought. Vince was one of those people who don't miss a thing.

Tent? *Tent*? Vince, in his old brown waistcoat worn over a slightly ragged collarless shirt – still holding the rock – gave Brunswick a withering, murderous look and spat on the ground. 'Assa *booth*, mate,' he said. 'Not a ruddy *tent*!'

'Sorry, I forgot. Help with the booth, then?'

'Not on your ruddy life, Sergeant ratface ruddy Brunswick policeman rozzer ponce.'

It had often been noted that Ventriloquist Vince was not possessed of ideal qualities for the world of innocent seaside entertainment. Along with anger issues, it was possible he suffered from undiagnosed Tourette's. If children gaily heckled the Punch & Judy (and they soon learned not to do this), Vince would step out from the booth, a puppet on each hand, and shout in their faces to shut the fucky-fuck up.

The police received complaints about Vince every single day of the summer, but he evidently had friends in high places. His public entertainment licence was often reviewed, and occasionally suspended, but inexplicably it had never been revoked.

He had been nicknamed 'Ventriloquist Vince' in the dim and distant past by underworld associates, and to be honest it had never made sense. Vince used no ventriloquism in his act; he didn't even do much to inhabit the various characters in his show. Mr Punch, Judy, the baby, the hangman, the policeman – they all sounded the same in Vince's rendition of the traditional story, apart from the heart-stopping screams for mercy, which he had definitely made his own.

'Take that, you ratbag Judy bitch-face – *Help! Help! You beating me a death, you ruddy psycho* – I hit you on a head, you slag, I hit you smack, smack, smack on the head – *Help, help! You want me to ruddy die? You go prison, mate, you hang by ruddy neck* – What I fucking care, you brass, take that, smack, smack – *I dying! Punch, you killing me! Stop! You killing your Judy! Stop! Stop! STOP!*'

And so on, and so on, for as long as he could reasonably string it out. Sometimes he would emerge from the booth and find people holding their heads back with trauma-induced nosebleeds; sometimes he found that his audience had scattered in horror. It didn't bother him. Punch & Judy was a great British seaside tradition, and it had never had a more dedicated or passionate practitioner than Vince.

Brunswick had not come here about the Punch & Judy, though.

'Maisie about?' he asked, laconically.

'What for you want my Maisie?'

'Got tickets to the Hippodrome later. Thought she might like to come. And she's not your Maisie, is she, now, Vince? There's no call to say she's yours.'

'You lay one ruddy ratbag finger on that girl –'

'Yeah, yeah,' said Brunswick. 'You'll beat my ruddy ponce policeman ratface head in?'

Brunswick was, in fact, terrified of Ventriloquist Vince, but he did a very good job of disguising it.

At that moment a girl appeared from the beach-ball stall in the arches behind the bandstand. She was sucking on a gob-stopper in a somewhat provocative manner. This was Maisie. She was nineteen years old, well developed, bottle-blonde, with buck teeth, a pink hairband, blue dress and white bobby socks worn with red kitten heels. In short, in common with most teenagers of this period, she transmitted a blizzard of teasing mixed signals, and both Vince and Brunswick would gladly admit she drove them wild with confusion and desire.

And she was more than happy about that. She also enjoyed the way that every time she uttered the name of another man ('Jim', for example), it made Ventriloquist Vince twitch with barely controlled homicidal jealousy. It pleased her to have such power over him. The place where she sold beach balls, buckets and spades, and little windmills on sticks, was just yards from the Punch & Judy, but for some reason hearing Vince once an hour shrieking, '*Stop! Don't kill me! I never do sex with that policeman bastard ratbag! I woulda do that, Punch! I good girl, Punch, I good girl!*' didn't alert her to the obvious peril of flirting with him day after day, while reserving the right to say 'Jim' to other men.

'What colour's my tongue, Jim?' Maisie asked Brunswick now, with hand on hip. She poked it out. It was disgusting.

'Mauve,' said Brunswick. They were not alone. Vince stood just inches behind. He was still holding the rock.

'Mauve? You sure?' She poked it out again.

'Pretty sure. Look… fancy going to the Hippodrome with me tonight?'

'Don't you go with 'im, Maisie!' said Vince, in a threatening manner.

She made a screwed-up face at him, teasingly, as if to say, 'You can't stop me.'

'What time, Jim?' she said to Brunswick. Her buck teeth dazzled in the afternoon sun. Brunswick swallowed. He didn't dare look down at those seductive ankle-socks.

'I could pick you up at seven.'

'All right, then, Jim.'

'My treat.'

'I should think so. I like port with Tizer. Remember? Vintage port if they got it.'

'How could I forget?' said Brunswick, smiling. As he walked away he noticed Vince take his heavy rock to the tent pole and, using both hands, pound it violently into the stones.

* * *

At Luigi's on the seafront, a busy afternoon was not helped by the unexplained absence from work of Geordie Harry from Nova Scotia. Luigi felt sad and exploited. You train up a friendless drifter to make Knickerbocker Glories and then he just quits? Making Knickerbocker Glories was a good job! Squirting the raspberry sauce was an art in itself! But Harry had seemed unsettled ever since he'd seen the file on the table in front of Inspector Steine. Whatever was in that file had given Geordie Harry a nasty turn.

Employing him had been a charitable act of Luigi's, because the man was so emotionally damaged that he was virtually a basket case. What with his tics and trances, it was as if he'd just returned from the trenches of the First World War. When pressed to explain his unusual nervous condition, all he would say was that he had been 'a miner and a playwright', and that it was being a playwright that had done for him.

This had made no sense to Luigi. Surely writing plays was the softest of soft jobs, while being a miner was the hardest of the hard. But Harry had stuck to his guns. The threat of imminent pit collapse, shared with your mates, was as nothing compared with the lonely anxiety of dramatic composition; and at least when you emerged from the pithead cage at the end of the day, blackened and exhausted, you got the rewards of light and air, ale and birdsong; you weren't immediately beaten to the ground in a ritual of public humiliation.

It was nearly closing time when Luigi noticed a small sealed envelope in the till with the words 'To Luigi, I'm sorry' written on the outside. Reading its contents, he called in panic to his sons Alfredo and Giuseppe. They hastily shut the doors, dropped the blinds and searched the building, and soon found Geordie Harry's stiff, icy, lifeless body on the floor of the big freezer. He had taken an overdose. In the note he thanked

Luigi for giving him this last chance. He explained that Crystal was the man who had destroyed his life. 'They say a bad review never killed anyone,' he wrote. 'Allow me to disagree.'

* * *

While Twitten waited at the Theatre Royal for Mr Crystal to turn up on that summery evening, he reflected on his first day with the Brighton Constabulary.

Most first days of this kind were presumably less busy or momentous – you found your way to the canteen, obtained a locker key, had an introductory chat with your divisional chief, and went home early to the station house – which was where Twitten would be boarding for the time being, a couple of streets away from the police station, until he could afford independent lodgings. First days probably didn't usually include being ordered to gather your things and leave, on account of half-solving a case that would otherwise have languished unexamined.

On the other hand, they also didn't usually include receiving a ticket to one of the most talked-about play openings of the decade, or meeting one of the most influential broadsheet newspaper critics. So it sort of evened out, he thought. Threatened with the sack; treated to a glittering landmark theatrical experience. If Twitten still didn't know where the police station canteen was, and hadn't got a locker, he didn't feel too hard done by.

Twitten knew who to look out for in the pre-theatre throng; he had a good mental picture of A. S. Crystal. He also knew Crystal's reputation. There were stories of glamorous leading ladies in their most stylish Parisian slingbacks kicking Crystal in the kidneys in Soho doorways. Flora Robson always denied it, but during a nasty fracas in Long Acre in

1954 after a royal command performance, she did bite a lump out of Crystal's right ear. The writer of this play tonight, the attractively spiky Jack Braithwaite, had said on the wireless that critics like Crystal ought to be physically exterminated!

Looking at the people now gathering for this famously gritty and modern play, Twitten had to admit that his sympathies were more with Braithwaite: something was very out of kilter here, sociologically speaking. The foyer was sweatily packed with people dressed up for the evening in smart suits and satin gowns and evening gloves, as if they were going to a reception at Buckingham Palace. The women's hair was set, stiff and lacquered; the air was dense with *L'Air du Temps*. It was hard to marry the promised slice-of-life drama with the type of people who were gathered to see it – all self-importantly crushed together, shouting to make themselves heard, while clutching shiny theatre programmes along with their expensive drinks and dainty boxes of soft-centred chocolates.

When Crystal arrived, Twitten introduced himself and apologised on behalf of Inspector Steine. He then suffered a short, inexplicable asthma attack, but waved away all offers of help, and soon recovered his breath to carry on. As for the oblivious Crystal, he was initially outraged at Steine's rudeness in sending a deputy, but quickly placated. The young constable was polite and knowledgeable, and seemed very keen to learn about the theatre from an expert. But what pleased Crystal most – as they pushed their way past the fragranced buffoons who had, unaccountably, paid money to witness the upcoming abomination – was Twitten's genuine interest in the Aldersgate Stick-up. The young constable had spotted the file on the inspector's desk, and put two and two together. It was an unsolved crime, he explained, that had fascinated him when he first studied it as a schoolboy, and he would love to hear anything that Crystal, as a highly reliable eyewitness, could add to his understanding.

Which was why, before the play started, Twitten and Crystal spoke only about a long-ago armed bank robbery in the City of London, and not about the theatre. As the seats filled up around them – and a woman in a seat behind asked Twitten (not unreasonably) to remove his helmet – Crystal took a piece of paper from his coat pocket, and produced a small fountain pen. On the paper, in tiny handwriting, was evidently a short list of points he had hoped to raise during his meeting with Steine; well, it was too late now. Having scanned it, though, he adopted a thoughtful expression and unscrewed the top of the pen, as if intending to add a new item.

'May I ask what that is, sir?' asked Twitten, standing up to let a fellow playgoer shimmy past. It didn't help the flow of their conversation that Crystal's seat was on the end of a row – position of choice of all newspaper critics from time immemorial, so that they can dash for the exits at the end of the play, under cover of the applause.

'Well, Constable, since you ask, a few new angles on the Aldersgate Stick-up have occurred to me recently, since I've been working on my autobiography, *A Shot in the Dark*. My secretary Miss Sibert teased out some details and I was very grateful to her. You see, although I gave a splendidly thorough witness statement at the time, it should be remembered that I was suffering from shock; unsurprisingly, there were further memories that needed to be unlocked.

'Fortunately Miss Sibert is a remarkable woman, who came to London from Vienna with Sigmund Freud back in 1938. She has helped me to remember all manner of things about my mother that are frankly staggering. Have you ever realised, for example, that for a mother to serve *oxtail soup* to her grown-up son is tantamount to castration? But I digress. I made these notes for Steine, but he was so pig-headed that he wouldn't look at them.'

Naturally, Twitten was wildly excited to see the list, but merely said, politely, 'May I see, sir?'

Crystal ignored the request. 'But something new occurred to me today, Constable,' he said, still gripping his list and gazing into the middle distance. He was evidently searching his memory. 'I just can't quite put my finger on it.'

Afterwards, Twitten wished their ensuing exchange had not been quite so explicit (or so loud), considering there were strangers around them in a position to overhear. At the time, however, there seemed no reason to be more discreet; in any case, raised voices were necessary in all the hubbub.

'Something of importance in the case of the Aldersgate Stick-up, sir?'

'That's right.'

'You're saying it came to you today, sir?'

'Yes.'

'Might it provide a breakthrough, sir?'

'Well, it might if I could remember it.'

'Oh, sir. Do try.'

'Well, I will attempt to visualise. Miss Sibert taught me to do that. Perhaps I should take off my coat.'

'Oh, please don't do that, sir,' said Twitten in alarm. 'I mean, I expect you were wearing the coat at the time, weren't you?'

'Good point. I'll keep it on. It was after I got off the train. Between getting off the train and meeting Steine at the ice cream parlour. But what? Something took me right back to that scene in the bank! It was just a flash, but I was in the dark again, shaking with terror, with a canvas bag over my head!'

'Gosh, sir. I wish you could remember what it was.'

'So do I. It was momentary, but vivid.' Crystal dropped his voice to a whisper as the lights went down. 'Let me think. I came out of the station and I saw the posters on the wall, and then – was it a name? A voice?'

'A smell perhaps,' said Twitten. 'Smells are very evocative.'

'Shhhhh,' someone said behind them.

'Don't shush me, madam,' Crystal said, half turning. But then he realised that, sure enough, all the rows were full, and curtains had been swished across the exit doors by the ushers.

'Tell me later, sir,' whispered Twitten. 'In the interval.'

And so the play began. The stage curtains opened on a dark and crazily angled set representing a dingy basement room on a Sunday afternoon in Halifax, with a tin bath in front of a glowing gas fire. It was such an ugly sight that the well-heeled audience let out a shudder of revulsion – a communal expression of 'Ugh!' At its centre, however, was the beautiful, luminous Penny, smoking, one arm in a knotted sling, holding an open letter in her hand. A door slammed, offstage, and she looked about, as if deciding what to do.

'Nicky?' she called out, hastily tucking the letter under the mattress of the unmade bed. 'Is that you, dear?'

A door opened and a scowling youth in a donkey jacket stepped into the room. It was Todd Blair, of course. This cheered the audience up somewhat – most of them recognising him from his recent breakthrough part as the murderous juvenile delinquent in a film; even Twitten thrilled when he came on.

'You still here?' he said, menacingly, to the lovely Penny – and then, yelling, 'You make me SICK!', picked up a chair and hurled it across the stage. The audience gasped. Crystal groaned with displeasure.

'Oh, Nicky,' breathed Penny, with emotion. 'I thought you'd gone and left me!'

Twitten didn't know quite what to make of the play, and after the first five minutes or so, it was hard to concentrate anyway with so many people getting up and leaving. It was definitely something new, he thought. But was it art? He noticed that his critic companion made no notes – as was well known about Crystal, he trusted to his excellent memory, and had never been known to misquote. He groaned repeatedly, though. He made pained noises while squirming in his seat. It was pretty clear he was not revising his original prejudices about the play.

But about twenty minutes in, Crystal went rigid in his seat. 'That's it!' he said out loud, and was shushed again from behind. Placing the piece of paper on the upholstered armrest, he excitedly scrawled something on it in the dark. Twitten, watching, was desperate to ask what had happened. Was it something in the play? Onstage the passionate Nick was lengthily berating his beautiful girlfriend Ruby for being the breadwinner (which seemed a bit rich to Twitten). The burden of Nick's complaint was that it was emasculating for a man to see his woman working as a clippie on the bus. It seemed to Twitten that this speech was no more annoying and unconvincing than anything else in the play, and yet the effect on Crystal was extraordinary.

'Sir, are you all right?' whispered the constable, putting his head close to Crystal's.

What happened next would always be unclear. Again, it wasn't the sort of thing that happens to most police constables on their first day – to be showered with blood and brains in seat D2 of the stalls, an ear-bursting bang making your own head ring so painfully that you can scarcely think. Afterwards he recalled that Crystal whispered urgently to him, 'I knew it! Tell Inspector Steine from me he's even more of a fool –' And then, just as a shower of 'shushes' was sent in his direction, and Twitten was turning to apologise, there was a shot in the dark, and Crystal fell forward, dead.

Twitten temporarily lost sight, hearing, everything, but instinct made him stand and turn to face the auditorium. The audience was still. On the stage behind him, the actors froze.

'Fucking hell,' said Blair Todd. 'I didn't mean –'

Then the curtain came down, and as the audience rose like a flock of pigeons, Twitten – acting still on pure instinct – put his whistle to his lips, and blew.

* * *

By the time help arrived, Twitten was seriously regretting he had not had the usual first day of a police constable.

Although he had appealed for calm, and had especially insisted that no one leave the auditorium, a hysterical stampede had ensued, and the theatre had emptied in half a minute, leaving just two still figures: a bloodied and stunned Constable Twitten, his police whistle still upraised, and beside him in the aisle seat, a slumped corpse with a crumpled piece of paper in its hand.

The house lights were up, and Twitten could see all the litter on the floor between the seats: the programmes dropped in the frantic exodus; the abandoned boxes of Orchard Creams; the odd high-heeled shoe; a diamond earring; a slender pistol glinting against the red-patterned carpet in the aisle. It was only as he climbed over his seat to retrieve the murder weapon, taking a hankie from his pocket, that he realised he was in tears. He took a seat at the end of Row H and sat in silence until help arrived.

The management had called for the police. In particular they had asked for Inspector Steine, who arrived quite promptly with other uniformed officers; the theatre staff who had gathered in the foyer stood aside respectfully to let the great man through. Ben Oliver of the *Evening Argus* flashed his press credentials and followed behind. For someone who had drawn the short straw in the office that morning, he was having an excellent, possibly career-changing day.

'Constable Twitten!' exclaimed Steine, entering the auditorium, and taking everything in. 'So it's true. Someone's shot him. I knew you'd be trouble, Constable. I just knew it.'

Twitten, one side of his face coated with blood, stood up from his seat, wobbling, and carefully held up the pistol, using the hankie. His voice, when it came out, was small.

'I think this is the weapon, sir.'

'Well, it's unlikely someone did this with a popgun, Constable. Of course it's the weapon.'

'May I sit down again, sir?'

'Certainly not. There's a lot to do. And put your helmet on.'

'Yes, sir.'

Steine turned to the three constables who'd come with him from the station. 'Carry on,' he said – but they just stood there awkwardly. It wasn't clear what they should carry on with exactly, until someone with the right qualifications had come to inspect the corpse and take it away.

'What's happened? Who is that?' said a frightened voice behind them. All turned towards the stage. It was the actress from the play, Penelope Cavendish, peering through the curtains, and then stepping onto the apron. Her arm was out of its sling, but she looked no less fragile. Despite the circumstances, Twitten couldn't help thinking what a beautiful girl she was. He also had another thought and

74

acted on it while Steine's attention was captured elsewhere. He swiftly removed the bloodstained Aldersgate Stick-up list from Crystal's stiffening hand and slid it inside his tunic.

'This man has been shot in the head, madam,' said Steine.

'Oh, no!'

'The sight is not for the faint-hearted, I'm afraid. Gore and brains everywhere. Good grief, is that an eyeball down there? Don't tread on it, Twitten.'

Penny sensibly stayed where she was. 'Oh my God,' she said.

'Can you account for your movements when this incident took place?' Steine demanded.

'She was on the stage, sir,' said Twitten, faintly. He felt increasingly disorientated. The auditorium appeared to be spinning. Perhaps the adrenalin was wearing off. The bang still rang in his ears; he had witnessed his first murder; flesh and chips of bone from another man's head were in his hair under the helmet; worst of all, he had knowingly removed evidence from a crime scene, an offence so serious it was punishable by imprisonment.

But true to his nature, he carried on talking. 'When the shot rang out, sir, she was being told off for being a bus conductress, for reasons I didn't quite understand.'

Then he piped up for Penny's benefit, 'It needn't concern you, I'm sure, madam. He was an aggravating man, admittedly, but at the same time one of the great theatre critics of our time.'

The effect of this news on the beautiful Penny was curious. 'An aggravating theatre critic?' she said.

'An extremely aggravating theatre critic,' said Steine. 'And quite smelly, too.'

'Not… *Crystal*?' she whispered.

'Yes, that's the man,' said Steine, surprised. 'Did you know him?'

She recoiled as if she'd walked into a plate-glass door. 'Jack! You didn't!' she gasped. And then she fainted onstage – just as Twitten said, 'So sorry, sir', and fell to the floor as well.

Four

At just about the time Twitten and Crystal met at the Theatre Royal, Brunswick and Maisie were outside the Hippodrome, halfway back in a loud, excited queue of holidaymakers, most of them swaying unsteadily, already the worse for wear. Brunswick himself had consumed three halves of Watney's in twenty minutes at the Queen Adelaide; Maisie might be only nineteen years old, but she had easily kept pace with her disgusting port-and-Tizers.

It's an aspect of old-school Variety that is often overlooked in respectful academic accounts of the genre's sad and lonely death-by-television in the 1950s – that what made the weak comedy routines sound so funny in the halls (and the tawdry 'glamour' even passable), was the audience's prior consumption of alcohol in quantities that would nowadays be considered catastrophically injurious to health.

So Brunswick wasn't at his sharpest, perhaps, when he saw an elegantly dressed woman with striking red hair cross the road to the Hippodrome and enter through the stage door. What caught his attention was how fast she was moving: trotting in her high heels, head forwards – and holding a gloved hand to her face, as if in some distress. She was also wearing an extra-large raincoat, which was odd given the balminess of the evening. Brunswick looked back down the street. Was someone chasing her? For a while he did nothing, knowing that Maisie would strongly object if he abandoned her; but in the end, he just had to make a move. Instructing Maisie to keep his place in the queue, and promising to be quick, he raced to the stage door, cursing himself for not following the suspect instantly.

Curiously, the thought flashed through his mind, 'Wait till I tell Twitten!' – which he realised ought to be grounds for concern. He wanted *Constable Twitten* to be pleased with *him*? And yet, there was no doubt about it. If this woman turned out to be the Opinion Poll lady, he glowed with pride at the thought of young Twitten patting him on the back and saying, 'Jolly well done, sir. I think you've solved the case!'

Stage Door Albert greeted him. Albert was seventy-five years old, chesty and as deaf as a post. He was also one of Brunswick's hopeless 'irregulars' who happily received ten bob from time to time, and in return never came up with the goods.

'Albert, did you see a woman come through here? Five minutes ago? Red hair?'

Albert coughed. 'Pardon?' he said.

'A woman! Red hair!'

'Went down there,' said Albert, pointing to the dressing rooms. 'Been here a few times. Someone's bit on the side, most likely,' he said.

'Whose?'

Albert shrugged. He'd seen it all, of course. The animal acts were the worst. Through force of habit, Brunswick slipped him a florin, and made his way down the foul-smelling distempered corridor lined with closed dressing-room doors. Every name was thrilling to him: Buster Brown the human cannon-ball! Tommy Tricks the magician (probably not his real name)! Joanne Carver the strong woman!

Was Carver possibly the Opinion Poll lady? Having seen her perform, Brunswick had noticed how feminine she could make herself look, despite the amazing power in her hands. Onstage, to emphasise her feminine assets (and to draw attention away from her manly wrists), she dressed in fishnet stockings, high heels and a strapless bodice; she spoke beautifully to the audience, like Lady Isobel Barnett on *What's My Line?*; and then to general amazement she would pick up a table by just one leg and hold it high above her head.

Brunswick knocked on Miss Carver's door, but there was no answer. He tried the handle. It was locked. He was sure he was on to something. Hadn't one of the break-in victims reported that a heavy bookcase had been moved by the robber? Previously this had seemed to indicate the Opinion Poll lady wasn't working alone. Well, maybe not. Maybe the lady and the intruder were one and the same. In the corridor, Brunswick could smell lavender, make-up and explosives. He was sure he was on the right lines.

But besides knocking and trying the handle, he could do nothing more at present. Breaking in would require a warrant. It was frustrating, but there it was. In the meantime, he couldn't help noticing, at the end of the corridor – with the biggest star on the door – was Professor Mesmer's room. Brunswick, gripped by a desire to meet his hero (and emboldened by the Watney's), knocked on it impulsively.

'Not now, Albert!' came a pleasant call from within, but Brunswick's beer continued to work its magic: he grasped the handle and entered. And there he found the great Mesmer sitting at his mirror with his back to the door, applying a fake beard. The room was a mess of costumes and paraphernalia, and overflowing linen baskets, and on the wall were large coloured charts of the human head. There was a full tumbler of whisky near Bobby's hand, with the half-drunk bottle beside it.

'Sorry to interrupt you, sir.'

'Who the hell are you?' said Bobby, with an easy smile. 'I'm sorry but members of the public aren't allowed in here, you know.'

'Police, sir.' Hat in hand, Brunswick produced his identity card. Bobby raised his eyebrows to acknowledge it, but still didn't look round from the mirror. The beard now secured, he started work on his eyeliner.

'I still don't know why you're here,' he said.

'Sorry, sir. I'm looking for a woman,' said Brunswick. 'Would you happen to know a woman with red hair? She came down here a few minutes ago, you see, sir. And as far as I'm aware, she hasn't left.'

'Well, she's not in here,' said Bobby. 'You're welcome to search. Try Tommy Tricks. He has females coming and going all day, lucky devil. He makes them laugh, apparently.'

'That's very helpful, sir. But can I ask – Miss Carver, sir. Have you ever seen her in a red wig?'

Bobby frowned and took a sip of his whisky. 'Miss Carver? You mean Jo? Not that I can remember. But she's not here all the time.'

'No?'

'Not many people know this, but she holds down a very lucrative day job as a brickie. Doing shifts on building sites. Hod carrier *extraordinaire*.'

'Well, thank you, sir.' Brunswick turned to go and then couldn't help himself. When would he ever get the chance again to tell Professor Mesmer how brilliant he was?

'I'm a great fan of your abilities, sir,' he gushed. 'I hope you don't mind my saying. What you do is astonishing, absolutely flaming well astonishing.'

Bobby smiled, and at last swung round to look at Brunswick. He waggled the beard, which made Brunswick laugh.

'I've seen you three times, sir.'

'No!'

'You're a genius, sir. I wouldn't ever want you feeling *my* head bumps, that's for sure. By the way, you're much, much younger than I imagined.'

Brunswick realised he was quite nervous now that he and Professor Mesmer were face to face.

'What was your name, officer?'

Brunswick was overcome. 'Sergeant Brunswick, sir. Jim.' He swallowed. 'Jim Brunswick,' he clarified. 'Jim. Or Jimmy, if you like. Well, thank you, sir. Sorry to bother you. I'd better go, there's someone waiting.'

'And you're looking for a red-haired woman, for some reason?'

'Yes, sir.'

'May I ask why?'

'It's in connection with some break-ins. Police business, that's all. Someone answering her description came in here.'

'You saw her yourself?'

'I did, sir.'

'Well, I wish you luck in finding her, Sergeant.' Bobby stood up and pointed at Brunswick's forehead. 'But before you go, I feel I ought to tell you that you show a very well-developed organ of Causality. Though I expect you know that. It's what you use as a detective, tracing things back to their causes.'

Brunswick felt embarrassed. 'Causality, you say?'

'If I may –? Look, could you sit on that chair for a moment and face away from me?'

Brunswick hesitated. What an amazing thing to happen! 'Well, I shouldn't really –'

'It won't hurt a bit.'

So Brunswick did as he was told, and the next thing he knew, Professor Mesmer's fingers were massaging his cranium in precise little circles. It made him feel warm and light-headed, but in a good way. He closed his eyes. He was aware of the coloured patterns on the insides of his eyelids. Whatever Mesmer was saying to him (was he saying anything?), it was soothing, and lovely. He felt a bit like one of those blown-up plastic lilos the kiddies floated on sometimes, lying stretched out, rocking gently on a sea that buoyed him up.

'Yes, it's as I thought,' said Bobby, suddenly removing his hands from Brunswick's head, and jerking him back to reality.

Brunswick opened his eyes.

'A large organ of Hope, Sergeant. That's the real thing that drives you. You should rejoice in it. No one ever came to much who didn't have a pretty big organ of Hope.'

Brunswick was happy to hear it. 'Thank you, sir,' he said, standing up. He felt dizzy. 'And good luck with the show tonight.'

'You're very kind. And I've just remembered. I think I *have* seen Jo in a red wig once or twice. Is it important?'

* * *

When Constable Twitten woke up, he was horizontal on a trolley, travelling in a speeding ambulance with its alarm bell ringing. What was he doing here? His vision was bleary; there was a buzzing in his ears; his mouth was dry. Opening his eyes, he was puzzled to see Mrs Groynes, the station charlady, sitting beside him. She appeared to be dressed in quite smart black clothes and a fashionable turban-style hat. Was he delirious?

'Mrs… *Groynes*?' he said.

'That's right, dear. Only me.' She turned and called out, 'He's woken up!'

'Good!' was the reply from the driver. 'Nearly there!'

'Where am I?' Twitten croaked.

'You're going to the hospital, dear. The inspector packed you off, see, on account of you fainting and then babbling like an infant. In your defence, the inspector said it was a regular bloodbath in there. Imagine, in some directions the gore flew twenty feet.'

Twitten struggled to sit up.

'I shouldn't be here, Mrs Groynes,' he said. 'Could you ask them to stop the ambulance, or turn it round?'

'I'll do no such thing.'

'I should be there, at the theatre. I could be jolly useful. I'm good at working things out! I won a medal for forensic observation!'

He found he couldn't hold himself upright, and fell back with a groan.

'Would you like some water, dear?'

'Yes, please.'

But when Mrs Groynes asked for water, the ambulance man said Twitten ought to wait till he arrived at the hospital. It would only be a couple of minutes. So instead, she took a miniature bottle of 4711 *eau de cologne* from her handbag, and dabbed a drop behind each of Twitten's ears. Bizarrely, it did make him feel a bit better.

'But why are *you* here, Mrs Groynes? I don't understand.'

'Search me, dear. Think of me as your personal bodyguard.'

Twitten shut his eyes.

'I really ought to be helping! The boy on the stage said something important after the shot was fired. Inspector Steine needs to know that.'

'It's all right. He does know that, as it happens. I told him already, dear.'

'But how –?'

'Because I thought it was strange myself. He said, "Effing hell, I didn't mean –" And then he stopped.'

'That's right. That's exactly what he said.'

'And then of course the girl on the stage, she said, "Jack! You didn't!" Inspector Steine knows all about that, dear, too. They're looking for Jack Braithwaite as we speak. And also Alec Forrester, one of the cast. Both of them have made themselves scarce, apparently. No one saw either of them this evening before the curtain went up. He had a *lot* of enemies, that Crystal. You'd never guess, to look at him.'

Twitten moaned. It still didn't make sense that the charlady was with him in this ambulance. 'Were you *there*, Mrs Groynes? At the theatre?'

'I was, dear. Row S. I led the charge out the door, dear! And I was outside with everyone else when the inspector arrived.' She seemed mildly offended. 'Blimey, dear, I do have a life, you know, besides making tea and dusting the inspector's desk!'

'Of course. I'm so sorry.' Emotions welled up in Twitten: contrition, helplessness, shame. She patted his hand.

'When you were babbling back there, dear,' she said, kindly, 'you asked quite loudly for a "huggie from mummy". I thought I should tell you because everyone heard it, and quite a lot of people laughed, and it's the sort of thing you'll probably never live down in this town, dear, no matter how hard you try, no matter how long you live.'

* * *

Sergeant Brunswick had just stepped out of the Hippodrome stage door and put his hat back on when two breathless constables caught up with him. Being informed that he had a specially large organ of Hope had really cheered him up, but he had no time to enjoy it. He was wanted at the Theatre Royal at once. The critic Crystal had been shot dead, they said; Constable Twitten was unharmed but on his way to hospital with symptoms of shock (including some very entertaining babbling); the inspector was now interviewing the cast and management. Two suspects were at large.

Pausing only to apologise to Maisie – who was still waiting outside while the rest of the queue had gone in, and duly outraged to be abandoned mid-date (and whose tongue was lemon yellow, for the record) – Brunswick raced through the Lanes to the Theatre Royal, his heart thumping loudly in his chest.

'Ah, here you are,' said Steine. He was up on the stage, with four-fifths of the cast in front of him – Penny, Todd Blair and the two older generic character actors whose particulars are happily immaterial. Old Alec Forrester was missing.

Brunswick recognised Todd at once as the menacing presence from the Dirk Bogarde film, and was astonished by how small he was. Todd had just confessed to spilling the beans to Alec about what he'd overheard at the ice cream parlour.

'I told him. I said, you'll be toast once that review comes out, mate.'

'You didn't!' gasped Penny.

'Well, he made me sick. Always playing the big I Am. Always talking about his flaming rounded vowels. All he did was carry a satchel and stagger into the room! Him and his rounded vowels.'

'I *thought* I caught you listening to our private conversation,' said Steine sternly to Todd, having finally put two and two together. 'And let me say, I very much disapprove of such underhandedness.' Steine spoke to Todd as if he were a hooligan, not a film star.

'He must have been very hurt when you told him,' said Penny. 'He thought Crystal was his friend.'

'He wasn't hurt, he was livid,' said Todd. 'I'll tell you what he said. And there were no rounded vowels in it. He said, "That's it. That bastard. I'll fucking kill him." Sorry, Penny.'

'No, don't mind me.'

'Oh, all right, good. Because then I said, "Well, you'd better do it tonight before he writes that review, mate." And he said, and I quote, "That's a good fucking point, Todd. I fucking will."'

'Oh, God,' said Penny. 'Why didn't you tell someone?'

'I didn't think he'd actually do it!'

Steine had a thought. 'Has any of you ever seen Mr Forrester with a gun?'

They all shook their heads. 'No,' said everyone.

'Well, it can't be him, then, can it?' said Steine, exasperated. He tore up the piece of paper he'd been writing on. Honestly, had these people never heard of FOWPT?

Brunswick used this moment to join the inspector on the stage and produce his own notebook. He tipped his hat to them all and stood to one side, respectfully.

'So what can you tell me about this missing writer?' said Steine. 'What's his name, Jack something?'

The others all deferred to Penny in a rather obvious manner.

'I'm Jack Braithwaite's girlfriend,' she explained. 'All I know is that he wasn't here for curtain-up. I've been very worried. He does have a temper, and he was furious about the review Crystal was planning to write! I keep telling myself Jack couldn't have done this –'

'Oh, I think he could,' said Todd Blair.

'– but he was quite violent earlier today when he first learned about it! And he did say, "I'll kill him"!'

Steine nodded and made a note. 'So he was murderously angry about a review that hadn't been written yet. In ordinary circumstances, that wouldn't make much sense, but I happen to know personally that Crystal was planning a stinker.'

'He certainly was,' agreed Blair.

Brunswick took over, and addressed Penny. 'What time did you last see Mr Braithwaite, miss?'

'Around seven, I think,' she said. 'He said he needed to pop back to his digs. He said he was worried about something there, but he didn't say what.'

'Was he fetching a gun, perhaps?' said Steine. 'That would fit in nicely, if it was a gun. Did he mention a gun?'

'No, of course not.'

Steine made a note. 'Shame,' he said. 'I thought we had him, then.'

'My point is, he never came back.'

'Do you have the address of these digs, miss?' said Brunswick. 'I can go there immediately, sir.'

'I think we should both go, Brunswick.' Steine looked at his watch and sighed. 'I've missed half the concert on the

Light Service already. Picking it up at the interval is rarely satisfactory. So, in for a penny, in for a pound, I suppose.'

Ten minutes later, accompanied by uniformed officers, Steine and Brunswick arrived at Jack Braithwaite's digs, in the Clifton Hill area of the town. Braithwaite had been staying with a Mrs Thorpe, a rich widow who kept a spare room for visiting theatricals in a nice Regency house painted white, with views across trees, gardens and rooftops to the glittering sea beyond. It was nearly sunset and the sky in the west was flaring with pinks and oranges. Starlings in their thousands were massing and swooping aerobatically above the West Pier.

As Steine and Brunswick approached the house, the inspector tried to remember the exact form of words used when making an arrest, but for some reason they wouldn't come easily to mind. So he gave up.

'You take over from here, Brunswick,' he said, magnanimously.

'Really, sir? Thank you, sir.'

'You remember the exact form of words used when making an arrest, I hope?'

'Of course.'

'Then carry on.'

Brunswick knocked at the door, and they waited for a response. He knocked again, without success. Steine felt that by now someone should have answered. Brunswick evidently felt it too.

'I feel a bit deflated, Sergeant,' said Steine. 'You have my permission to find a side window and break in.'

But before Brunswick could act on this instruction, a middle-aged, blue-rinsed woman in an expensive fur stole arrived at the gate and asked them what they were doing. It was Mrs Thorpe. She had been in the audience for *A*

Shilling in the Meter, using a ticket provided by her lodger, Jack Braithwaite. Like everyone else, she'd arrived home a lot earlier than expected (although she had stopped for a stiffening drink or two en route). Unfortunately, she hadn't been able to help the police taking statements outside the theatre; she'd been so fixated on the play, she said – which she had found raw and original and full of promise – that she really hadn't noticed anything untoward until the shot. She and the inspector discussed all this on the doorstep, and then she asked him again why he was there.

'To arrest Mr Braithwaite for the cold-blooded murder of A. S. Crystal, of course,' said Steine.

'What?' she exclaimed. 'But Mr Braithwaite would never –!'

Brunswick chipped in, reassuringly, 'Or possibly to eliminate him from our enquiries, sir. We don't actually know he's guilty yet. If he has an alibi, he could be in the clear.'

Steine shrugged. That wasn't how he saw matters at all.

'But why would he be *here*?' asked the landlady. 'Surely he was at the theatre?'

Brunswick explained that Jack had told his girlfriend earlier in the evening that he needed to pop home to his digs. 'She said he seemed worried about something here. He wouldn't tell her what.'

'Oh, no,' said Mrs Thorpe, crossly, producing a key from her handbag. 'And I begged him not to! Not on his special night!'

She opened the door. 'Mr Braithwaite?' she called, as she stepped inside. 'Mr Braithwaite, the police want to talk to you! It's very important! Are you here?'

In the hallway, she turned back. 'I don't think he's in. But if it's helpful, I think I can clear up why he might have come back here this evening. This afternoon I had a visitor from the national Public Opinion Poll – an absolutely charming young woman.'

'You did?' exclaimed Steine. He sounded slightly aggrieved. 'Was it fascinating?'

'Well, yes. I suppose it was. But –'

'Wide range of topics?'

'Yes, very.'

'Did you feel you were doing something of civic importance?'

'Well, yes.'

'I knew it!'

'But the point is –'

'What colour hair did she have?' interrupted Brunswick.

'Oh.' Mrs Thorpe didn't have to think about it. 'Red,' she said, 'bright red.'

'Bingo!' said Brunswick. 'Sorry, do go on.'

'Thank you. The point is, I happened to tell Mr Braithwaite about this visit, and the effect on him was extraordinary. He was outraged on my behalf! He said he was sure she wasn't genuine; that she was really some criminal or other doing research for a crime! He said he was worried someone would break in this evening to burgle the house and take my pearls! I said he was being ridiculous and not to give it another thought, but he said, no, he had come across this exact scam before.

'Mr Braithwaite has quite a temper, it's true – well, it's the wonderful magnetic passion one saw in his play tonight. But he does mean well. I'm sure you'll find he's perfectly inno-cent. May I offer you a sherry before you go?'

And then she opened the door to her front living room, and let out a scream of horror. Furniture was in disarray; ornaments shattered, curtains torn; blood dripped from the fireplace and was sprayed in arcs across the walls. There was no doubt that a life-and-death struggle had taken place inside this room – the biggest giveaway being the lifeless remains, on the best Persian rug, of the magnetic young playwright Jack Braithwaite, whose own personal Gas Man had arrived unexpectedly to read his meter and collect his dues.

* * *

That evening, while Constable Twitten begged to be released from hospital, and the sympathetic Mrs Groynes insisted on soothing his brow with refreshing dabs of *eau de cologne*, two arrests for murder were promptly made in Brighton.

Steine was in no mood to hang about; the concert on the wireless was by now a completely lost cause; why string things out longer than was necessary? Thus, at 9.38 p.m., the veteran actor Alec Forrester was arrested in the saloon bar of a discreet, all-gentlemen pub in Hove. He was virtually unconscious by the time he was tracked down, having been drinking there for several hours – some witnesses said he had been there since mid-afternoon, long before the shooting at the Theatre Royal had occurred. But since these witnesses were legless themselves, Steine saw no reason to take account of their testimony.

On standing up to hear the charge, the swaying, blinking Alec adopted a profoundly confused expression, and then visibly brightened.

'He's *dead*?' he said, as the information sank in. His face was a picture of pure relief. 'Thank *fuck*!' he cried (an ejaculation that was recorded by Brunswick in his notebook with a certain amount of awkwardness).

On motive alone, Alec Forrester might have faced two charges of murder had it not been so obvious he was physically incapable of overpowering Jack Braithwaite in hand-to-hand combat, and finally slitting his throat with a regimental sword (once the property of General Thorpe, and displayed above the fireplace in Mrs Thorpe's front room). Even Inspector Steine was forced to conclude that the murder of Jack Braithwaite had clearly been committed by an interrupted intruder.

The absence of all Mrs Thorpe's pearls was a pretty big clue here, not to mention the way a back window had been forced from the outside. The most likely explanation was that the regular accomplice of the Opinion Poll lady must have arrived at the house expecting it to be empty, and found Jack Braithwaite waiting for him. They had fought, and Braithwaite had copped it.

Just one detail didn't fit this theory: two sherry glasses in the room had been used. Mrs Thorpe was adamant that when she left the house, all the glasses had been clean, and that there had been a good two inches more of sherry in the decanter. Had the two men shared a couple of genteel glasses of fortified wine and *then* tried to kill each other? Steine allowed Brunswick to make a note of this inconvenient piece of evidence, but remained firmly married to the surprised-intruder hypothesis. It pained him to do it, but he now felt obliged to concede that perhaps the Opinion Poll lady was not the real McCoy, after all.

'But who was the intruder, Brunswick? Have you got any closer to identifying even the bogus Opinion Poll lady? I mean, what have you and Clever Clogs Twitten been *doing* all day?'

'I have reason to believe that the Opinion Poll lady and the intruder are one and the same, sir.'

'It would have to be a very strong lady, Sergeant!'

Brunswick beamed. 'It is, sir.'

Which is why, at 10.20 p.m., at the Hippodrome Theatre, policemen led by Inspector Steine of the Brighton Constabulary raided the dressing room of professional strong lady Joanne Carver. They found her in a silk dressing-gown with her wrists in little baths of iced water and her feet up, a women's magazine in her lap; she screamed as they burst in. While two men restrained her, Brunswick conducted a superficial search, which proved fruitful. In among her costumes, he found not only a carefully hidden red wig in an old canvas money-bag but also a briefcase full of pearls. She looked shocked.

'I've never seen those before!' she cried. Brunswick noticed that she didn't sound quite as posh now as she did onstage. Less the Lady Isobel Barnett, more the Diana Dors.

'A likely story,' said Inspector Steine. 'Well, you've gone too far this time, young lady. We were willing to turn a blind eye to those robberies of yours –'

'No, we weren't!' objected Brunswick.

'– but now you've killed a man, it's the hangman's noose for you, miss, I'm afraid.'

She struggled. 'I don't believe this. Someone's fitted me up. I've been here all evening. Listen, I was at Gatwick all day working on the new terminal building… just ask them! Then I got here and had my usual early-evening kip with the door locked. Then I did my act – and that's it. Where's Professor Mesmer? He can tell you.'

'He's due offstage shortly,' said Brunswick, with authority.

'I'm here!' said Bobby, entering in full Professor Mesmer costume. A blast of music, hubbub and applause accompanied him. Fresh from his curtain call, he gleamed with sweat; his hands reeked of hair products. He recoiled when he took in the scene. 'Joanne, love, what's going on? Unhand that woman at once. There's obviously a mistake.'

'We are arresting Miss Carver on a charge of murder, sir,' said Brunswick.

'That's ridiculous!' said Bobby. 'I'm sure you've got the wrong person.'

'Help me, Bob!' she said, her eyes huge with fear. 'They're saying they found evidence in here. Pearls!'

'And we also found this, of course,' said Brunswick, indicating the red wig. 'So thank you for the tip-off, sir. It's very much appreciated.'

* * *

Young Ben Oliver of the *Evening Argus* took a calculated risk that evening. He reported Crystal's sensational murder directly to the *Daily Clarion*. Any reporter in his place would probably have done the same: sitting on such a juicy story until the *Argus* came out tomorrow afternoon would be absurd. On the other hand, it was the *Argus* that employed him, and it's pretty much the first rule in journalism: don't give stories to rival newspapers. So Oliver knew he was gambling with his career when he stepped into the telephone box on the corner of New Road and called the *Clarion* news desk with this story of national importance concerning their own controversial theatre critic.

Oliver's reward was to hear the news editor bark, 'Hold the front page!' and 'Get Jupiter here right now!' (Harry Jupiter being the *Clarion*'s legendary crime reporter.) But then, to be honest, the excitement wore off quite quickly as he was obliged to feed the story down the line to a more experienced reporter who kept – with evident exasperation – demanding facts and details he didn't have.

By the time Oliver hung up, he was deflated. Had he really imagined the *Clarion* would be so grateful they would offer him a job in Fleet Street? And now he would have to face the music in the morning with his own news editor, while the big boys from London, doubtless led by the great Harry Jupiter, swept into Brighton and took over.

* * *

Twitten was released from the hospital at midnight with some tranquillisers to take home. He was still unsteady on his legs, but said he would prefer to walk back the mile or so to the station house, as he needed time to think. It was only after he set off that he realised he didn't know the address.

When he reached the indigo, moonlit seafront, he stood for a moment listening to the waves, watching the lights from cross-Channel ferry-boats in the distance, and trying not to remember the *Bang!* that had, just a few hours ago, exploded the head of a human being in the seat beside him.

What was it that Crystal had remembered? At the hospital, when he was briefly alone, Twitten had retrieved the critic's precious list from his tunic and studied it. There was no doubt in Twitten's mind: Crystal had been killed, not because he was a loathsome individual or an outstandingly unkind critic, but because he'd remembered something incriminating about the Aldersgate Stick-up.

Had Twitten known at this point that poor Alec Forrester was under arrest for shooting Crystal, he would have despaired. Only a fearless professional criminal would have shot Crystal in the theatre like that. First thing in the morning, Twitten would call Crystal's secretary Miss Sibert in London and demand to see the notes for his chapter on the bank robbery.

If London gangland boss Terence Chambers could be linked to the shooting of A. S. Crystal, it would blow the lid off all the crime committed in Brighton since 1951!

'Whatever's that, dear?' Mrs Groynes had said, when she returned to his cubicle and saw the list in his hand. Guiltily, he'd stuffed it into his pocket.

'I'm afraid it's *evidence*, Mrs Groynes,' he whispered.

'Evidence of what, dear?'

'I took it from the scene. It's a list. Please don't tell anyone. I just felt it might not be safe there. It might be overlooked. I think it points to the killer.'

Twitten wasn't sure how he could explain his thinking to someone with Mrs Groynes' limited experience of crime. True, she worked in a police station, but only to make the tea and swab the lino. So he said, 'I think it's to do with a London bank robbery from years ago. But it's nothing to worry about. I mean, from your point of view, it's better if you remain in blissful ignorance.'

Mrs Groynes laughed. 'Right you are, dear.'

After that, she had left him – to get her beauty sleep, she said. But he felt he had found an ally in Mrs Groynes tonight. She hadn't exactly offered him a 'huggie' (and how his blood ran cold when he remembered about the babbling), but she had offered friendship, and had shown she was much cleverer and more observant than she made out. He and she seemed to see things the same way. For example, at one point, he had said, 'The inspector will jump to the wrong conclusions!' And she'd replied, 'Oh, let him, dear. That's what he's good at.' And they had both laughed, which had felt good.

Then she had said, thoughtfully, 'The inspector threatened Crystal himself, you know. Luigi told me. He shouted after him, "I wouldn't mind shooting you myself!" In front of witnesses. I don't suppose he'd be very happy if anyone brought that up and used it against him, would he?'

And now, on the seafront, alone in the moonlight, Twitten sat on a bench on the upper promenade and looked at the paper again. The original, neatly written list contained just four items:

own bags?
'Palmeira'?
run-over policeman?
a sneeze?

What Crystal had added was just the start of a word:

Dai

Twitten wished he could call Miss Sibert right now to ask what it all meant. Nothing here obviously linked the robbery to either Terence Chambers or Brighton – unless the 'Palmeira' referred to Palmeira Square, perhaps – a fashionable address in Hove, with landscaped gardens, close to the sea. But perhaps it was a misspelling of Palmyra, the ancient city in Syria Twitten had visited as a schoolboy with his father. They had gone to see the Roman ruins, and afterwards Twitten had made an impressive papier-mâché reconstruction of the Baths of Diocletian that had won him a prize at school. Thinking back to the glory days of schoolboy projects isn't hard when you're only twenty-two. Twitten's last papier-mâché model had been made only two or three years in the past.

Twitten felt his mind wandering. He needed to concentrate. If he had removed evidence from a crime scene, there had better be a good reason. What Crystal had written – still neatly – in the dark at the bottom of this list was the key thing, but it was incomplete (unless it was a Welsh name). He remembered how Crystal had urgently whispered, 'Tell Inspector Steine he's even more of a fool –' and then, *Bang!* He'd been dead.

And now, as Twitten peered closer at the paper, *whoosh!* It was snatched from his hand by a juvenile delinquent cyclist, who, screaming with laughter, whizzed off along the promenade and disappeared from view.

The Day After Twitten's First Day

Five

In all the thrill of that momentous evening of law enforcement – consisting in the swift but slightly under-considered arrests, for violent murder, of an old, feeble actor and a female novelty artiste – Sergeant Brunswick forgot about one quite significant thing: the potential wrath of the buxom, toothy nineteen-year-old girl he had publicly abandoned in the rowdy queue for the Hippodrome.

True, Brunswick had paused to apologise to Maisie as he sped off to the crime scene at the Theatre Royal. Even in the thick of events, he had gamely reported the vibrant colour of her tongue, which was clearly her principal interest in life. But essentially he had ditched her and then forgotten her. Earlier in the day, he had glowed with pleasure at the thought of Maisie spending the evening on his arm, calling him 'Jim' all the time in that thrilling way she did; once he had heard the clarion call of duty, however, the delectable Maisie might never have existed.

In his defence, it had been an exceptional night. No wonder he barely slept, and was up the following morning by half-past six. As he dressed and shaved quietly (so as not to disturb his doting auntie Violet), Brunswick realised he was especially happy at one incidental aspect of the affair: that he and the inspector had conducted the entire evening's transactions without the help of PC Clever-clogs Twitten. Wouldn't that kid be impressed when he found out what they'd achieved? Such prompt arrests in two gruesome killings would surely cast Twitten's own successes – in the age-old 'Kennington Butcher' case, for example – completely in the shade, tooth-in-that-flaming-floorboard or no tooth-in-that-flaming-floorboard.

So, at seven-fifteen, Brunswick was surprised, as he gently pulled shut the downstairs front door to his auntie's flat on the London Road, to find an avenging Ventriloquist Vince on the dusty pavement, awaiting him with a baseball bat.

Alarmed, Brunswick played it cool. 'What's all this, Vince?' he said, adjusting his hat. 'A bit early, aren't you?'

Vince toyed menacingly with his blunt instrument. He was pretty pumped up (not that this was unusual). Brunswick swallowed nervously.

'You hurt my Maisie, you ratface ruddy policeman ponce,' snarled Vince, weighing the bat in his hand. 'You make her feel like ruddy *lemon*, mate!'

Brunswick thought quickly. Was there any justice at all in this accusation? He'd only left her for ten minutes, after all. He raised a finger. 'But the point is, Vince –'

'You make her ruddy cry, mate!'

'Mm,' said Brunswick, turning, as if making an important decision. 'Right, well, in that case, there's not a minute to lose.'

And then he started to stride briskly along (proceeding in a southerly direction), so that Vince was forced to trot at an uncomfortable speed beside him. For a while, Brunswick said nothing, then he stopped and looked quizzically at Vince, as if surprised to see him still there. Vince (thankfully) looked slightly uncertain now; slightly bewildered. The bat was looser in his grip. Brunswick might not have won a medal for forensic observation at Hendon, but he knew a thing or two about defusing violent intent, especially when it was directed against himself.

'Well, I'd just like to thank you for telling me all this, Vince,' he said, with an air of authority. 'Where can I find her? I'll apologise.'

Vince scowled. He wasn't sure how – or when – he had lost the advantage here. Daringly, Brunswick placed a hand on Vince's shoulder and applied a little weight.

'Where can I find her?' he repeated.

Vince shrugged. He looked fed up. 'She's in Luigi's.'

Brunswick held out his hand, which Vince reluctantly shook. 'That's excellent. Now, you're free to go. Thank you for your help. I'll take it from here.'

At which Brunswick strode off down the London Road, then made a quick right turn up one of the lesser streets (as if to proceed in a westerly direction) and – remembering first to remove his hat – was vastly sick in an alley.

* * *

It was a day for starting early. Even before Sergeant Brunswick had left his auntie's place, Constable Twitten was having a cup of tea with Mrs Groynes at the police station, and sharing with her his shock and disbelief at how events had unfolded the previous night. He had not slept at all. Not knowing the address of the station house, and not having money for a hotel, he had spent the pre-dawn hours walking the empty streets, making notes, familiarising himself with the town.

In his short career to date, he had found that it was useful to know how quickly one could get from A to B, or from C to F, via E – even if, after a few days, you generally found yourself transferred elsewhere and had to start all over again.

At around 2.30 a.m., outside a house in the pleasant, leafy Clifton Hill area, he had found a young constable on duty, guarding a crime scene (but actually asleep). It was from him – firmly shaken awake – that Twitten learned all the astonishing news of the night: that Brunswick and the inspector had come here to arrest Braithwaite and had found him murdered; that from here they had arrested old Alec Forrester in a Hove pub (for the shooting of Crystal); and from there they had arrested a strong lady at the Hippodrome (for the Opinion Poll lady burglaries and unpremeditated murder of Braithwaite).

Twitten's initial reaction to all this was despair. A disgruntled *actor* was supposed to have shot Crystal? What about the Aldersgate Stick-up?

For a while the two young officers stood together in the moonlight. Then Twitten thought of something.

'Where are the suspects detained?' he asked.

'In the cells at the station, sir. I mean, in the cells at the station.'

Calling Twitten 'sir' had been an embarrassing slip, but an understandable one.

'What do the cells look like?'

'How do you mean?'

'Walls or bars?'

'Bars.'

'*Bars*?' repeated Twitten, significantly.

'Yes. Like cages.' The other constable didn't see where this was going. He thought Twitten must be slow, or something. 'You know. Cages made of iron bars. It's quite normal.'

'Doesn't that woman famously *bend* iron bars as part of her act?'

'Ah,' said the PC, finally understanding. 'Blimey, that's a point.'

Twitten had sprinted back to the police station and demanded to be let in by the night desk sergeant, who laughed merrily at his suggestion of a prisoner escape until he went downstairs to check and found that, yes, unfortunately, while the old man was still safely asleep and groaning on his hard wooden bunk, the young woman's cell next door was empty, with a significant bendy gap in the bars big enough for a body to squeeze through.

'Oh, *bugger*,' said the desk sergeant, with feeling.

'Yes indeed,' sympathised Twitten. Exhausted from the night's events, it was all he could do not to climb through the gap, fall onto the strong lady's vacated bunk bed and shut his eyes at last. But he dared not give in to tiredness, so instead he headed for Inspector Steine's department and spent the rest of the night furiously typing.

'So she'd scarpered, had she?' asked Mrs Groynes, delightedly, pouring Twitten his second reviving cup of tea. Next to him was a pile of typed notes half an inch thick. 'Well, you've got to laugh.'

'I know. We searched the whole building. After a while, the desk sergeant said he remembered seeing an unidentified person in a big overcoat and trilby hat waving goodnight at about 1 a.m. When I pressed him to recall if there was anything odd about this unidentified person, he thought about it for a minute or so and then said yes, he'd heard the incongruous click of high heels on the tile flooring, but unfortunately hadn't put two and two together.'

Twitten swallowed, and then lowered his voice to a whisper. 'Mrs Groynes,' he said, 'I feel awful saying this, and

I know it can't be literally true, but it's as if this station is run by idiots.'

Mrs Groynes sat down beside him, smiled, and patted his hand. 'I know, dear. Sometimes it seems that way to me, too.'

Twitten took a deep breath. 'Thank you so much for coming with me to the hospital last night.'

'That's all right; it was the least I could do. You was in such a two-and-eight, babbling about lists and such removed from the scene of the crime!' She smiled at him, conspiratorially. 'Ooh, now, that reminds me. I've had a little think about that precious list of yours, and my advice is this. Give it to Inspector Steine at the very first opportunity, dear, without delay, and say you did it when you wasn't in your right mind. He'll be cross, all right; but he'll forgive you, for sure.'

Twitten bit his lip. 'Give it to the inspector?'

'That's right, dear. It's the right thing to do.'

'But I can't, Mrs Groynes. I lost it!'

She looked puzzled.

'How do you mean, you lost it?'

'A boy on a bike snatched it out of my hand. He must have thought it was a five-pound note! It wasn't my fault!'

Mrs Groynes gasped. 'You're saying you *lost* a piece of vital evidence that you'd *removed from the scene of the crime*?'

'Yes.'

Mrs Groynes put her hand to her mouth in horror.

'Please don't tell anyone, Mrs G,' said Twitten. 'The thing is, I do remember everything that was on the list, so in a way it doesn't matter.'

'*Doesn't matter?*'

'No, I mean it. In the night, you see, I traced Mr Crystal's movements precisely from the railway terminus to the ice cream parlour by way of the police station, so I'm already forming ideas about what might have jogged his memory, and I'm sure I'm on the right track! Did you know, for example, that there are all sorts of posters on the wall opposite the station – for the Hippodrome, for the Punch & Judy, for sand-castle competitions, all sorts! On his way from the station, he would also have passed a man selling wind-up toys on a tray outside a cinema, calling out: "See the bunny run! See the bunny jump!"'

'I'm not with you, dear.'

'I'm just saying, it was some small thing that triggered his memory. Perhaps it was the bunnies, it's too early to tell. But once it's eight o'clock, I'll telephone Mr Crystal's secretary in London and get her to come down on the train with the manuscript of his memoirs. I've got her home telephone number. She worked with him extremely closely on memory-retrieval and she'll be familiar with his very thought patterns. I've got it all worked out! I'll also request a copy of the play so that I can check precisely what was being said onstage when Mr Crystal got excited. So you see the list was only the starting point.'

'But if you haven't *got* that list, dear,' said Mrs Groynes, gravely, 'who's going to believe it even existed?'

'I'm not a liar, Mrs G! You saw the list yourself!'

'I saw a piece of paper, dear.'

'But –'

Mrs Groynes stood up and moved away. She picked up her mop and bucket. Twitten felt bereft. Wasn't she on his side, after all? After a few seconds, she turned to face him, and her expression was serious.

'Look, dear. You probably don't want me sticking my oar in. But I'm afraid after what you've told me, my advice is let the whole thing lie.'

'What? No.'

'Listen. They've got to catch that escaped strong lady first, haven't they? And they've already got that actor bloke for the shooting –'

'But he can't have –'

'I'm just thinking of you, dear. Thinking of your reputation; your career. They already know you're someone who wants a huggie from his mummy. They already think you're an annoying brainbox. You're *this close* to being moved on again, am I right? If they thought you'd made up phantom evidence –'

'I can prove it all without the list, Mrs G,' said Twitten, firmly.

Mrs Groynes put down the mop and bucket. 'Can you, though, dear?'

'Yes, I think I can. But I do appreciate your trying to help me. You've been so awfully kind.'

Mrs Groynes threw up her hands in mock defeat. 'Well, it's up to you, love,' she said. 'It's no skin off my nose. How about a nice fig roll?'

* * *

Bobby Melba woke at 9 a.m. in his Ship Street B & B, and was initially puzzled by three things. Why was he on the dusty sofa with a heavy overcoat on top of him? Why were the curtains open? Why could he hear the unmistakable sound of female emotion?

A few seconds' reflection brought everything to mind: after the sensational arrest of poor Jo Carver at the end of last evening's performance, he had rushed into the night to find Penny. So great was his urge to protect and comfort that wonderful young woman that he hardly paused to take off the beard.

As he raced across town, he felt slightly ashamed that he had so little compassion for the slaughtered Jack; that all his thoughts were for Penny – but that's just the way it was. Although he had technically been friends with Jack since drama school, he'd had good reason never to like him particularly; whereas Penny! The very idea of a stricken Penny filled him with passion. So beautiful, so vulnerable, and now in such a fix! Not only had she lost her budding-playwright boyfriend, but she was probably out of a job as well, since it's quite a well-known rule of the theatre that plays don't usually survive a first performance cut short by two brutal murders and the arrest of one of the cast.

He had found Penny in the pub next door to the theatre, drinking brandy, with hollow eyes and tear-stained cheeks. Initially she'd gone there with Todd Blair to get over the shock of the shooting in the stalls, and to await news of Jack; when they later learned of his death, she had wailed piteously. Todd hadn't been of enormous comfort. His main concern being whether he might be the next target himself, he kept wondering aloud whether he should reach out to the Brighton Teddy Boy community for protection. But then Bobby appeared at the door and Penny rushed to him. Bobby had never felt so strong a natural (or instant) connection with anyone in his life.

'I heard what happened,' said Bobby, his voice breaking. She was pressed tightly against him; instinctively, he cupped the back of her head.

'We argued!' she said. 'The last time I saw him, I begged him not to go back to his digs. I was angry, Bobby! I called him a bastard! I called him selfish!'

'Oh, Penny. I know. But to be fair, he *was* a bastard, wasn't he? And he was selfish.'

'And then someone took his life!'

'I know. I know. I mean, I bet he was asking for it, but I know.'

'I can't take it in! I just can't take it in!'

'It's impossible, Penny.'

'I keep expecting him to walk in.'

'Yes?'

Penny's eyes filled with love. 'He'd say, "There you are, you posh tart!"'

Bobby flinched, but agreed with her. 'Yes, he probably would.'

He ordered more drinks from the waiter, and they sat together for another hour in the pub, talking quietly (Todd Blair soon gratefully made his excuses and left). With difficulty, Bobby explained to her how he knew what had happened: it was one of his own co-stars at the Hippodrome who'd been arrested for killing Jack; evidently she was a cunning thief who had turned to violence on this occasion for reasons as yet unknown. She used to tell everyone she was a brickie by day, but in fact she must have been out posing as an Opinion Poll lady and 'casing joints' before returning in the early evening to steal the valuables! Jack must have challenged her, not realising that she was a hundred times stronger than she looked.

'So there was a struggle?' said Penny.

Bobby said he imagined so. What with all the blood up the fireplace, the torn curtains, disturbed furniture, and so on.

After the landlord had rung the bell at closing time, Penny had asked if she could sleep at his digs – she couldn't face her own lonely hotel room – and he had led her back there in a complicated state of happiness.

And now it was morning, and Bobby was blearily aware of his surroundings, and Penny Cavendish was dressed and standing by the door, which she had noiselessly opened.

'Bobby, you're awake,' she said. 'I'm sorry. I thought I should go. I left you a note. It's not goodbye. It was so sweet of you to let me spend the night here. Let's meet again later.'

'Penny, please don't go.'

'I needed to pin my hair so I used this comb-thing, is that all right?'

Bobby didn't look. Of course it was all right.

Taking a deep breath, he pushed aside the oppressive over-coat he'd been sleeping under, and rocked himself into a sitting position on the settee. 'Please stay and talk,' he said, gently.

'Bobby, I'm very confused,' she said. He longed to rush to her and put his arms around her.

'I love Jack, you see. I mean, I loved Jack. I do love Jack!'

'I know, Penny.'

'I need some time to think.'

'Of course you do. I'm not trying to take advantage of you, Penny, it's just that –'

'Oh, why do you have to be such a lovely man?' she wailed.

And then they both laughed, weakly, and she let herself out.

It was his cue to go back to sleep. But the last thing he saw as she left the room made him jump to his feet in alarm, run to the mantelpiece and punch it with his fist. On the back of Penny's head, holding her hair in an improvised knot, something had sparkled like a diamond – in fact, just like the exact large diamond decorating a stolen Victorian hair-comb illegally in Bobby's possession, with an estimated value of a thousand pounds.

* * *

By the time Brunswick had located Maisie – not at Luigi's in fact, but opening up her little shop under the arches – he was angry.

'Guess who called at my house this morning, Maisie!' he demanded.

He hadn't reckoned on the girl being quite so angry herself. After all, he hadn't left her last night out of choice, had he? There had been a flaming murder to attend to! But not a bit of it. She was seriously furious with him. When she saw him approaching, she pointedly turned her back – shoving colourful windmills-on-sticks into a blue bucket and setting her little pink mouth into a pout. When she finally turned to face him, holding a scarlet windmill-on-a-stick in her hand, her eyes were blazing and he noticed a tiny pucker in her otherwise unlined brow, which ought to have scared him, but in fact had an immediate electrifying effect on his loins.

What *was* it about this girl? Maisie looked magnificent in her fury, and also (he couldn't help noting) the neat white socks were transcendently white and virginal today.

'You left me, Jim. You left me like a lemon.'

'Look,' he said. 'Two people were murdered last night, Maisie. What was I to do? I'll make it up to you. Name the day, name the place, I'll take you.'

'You left me before that.'

'What do you mean?'

'You went in by that stage door and left me outside on my own.'

'But only for ten minutes!'

'Ten minutes? It was more than half an hour, Jim!'

Brunswick couldn't let this go unchallenged. She was being completely unreasonable. 'It was ten flaming minutes, Maisie.'

She stamped her foot. The little plastic windmill caught a bit of breeze and started to whizz in her hand. 'No, it flaming wasn't! And then, when you finally do come out, you run off and leave me altogether. If Vince hadn't been there, I'd have had to go home on the *bus*.'

'Hang on, Maisie. Vince was there?'

'Blimey, didn't you see him?' she laughed, nastily. 'Call yourself a policeman, he was right behind us in the pub, Jim!'

'Was he?'

'Then when we were in the queue, he was watching from opposite and pointing us out to that bloke Stanley. Are you blind or something?'

'What, Stanley-knife Stanley was there, too?'

'If you say so.'

'Flaming heck, Maisie, why didn't you say?'

Maisie shrugged. She liked it that Vince showed such an insanely passionate interest in her. It made her feel special.

'Vince is very keen on me, if you hadn't noticed.' She leaned her face close to Brunswick's, but not in an affectionate way. She had chewing gum in her mouth; it was identifiable as spearmint. Perhaps the shop had run out of multicoloured gobstoppers (which would be a blessing). She chewed in a meaningful manner. 'So you'd better watch out, *daddy-o*,' she said.

Sensing that she was softening towards him, Brunswick decided not to challenge the 'daddy-o' thing. She'd only started saying it in the past ten days; he hoped it was a passing teenage fad.

'Yeah, yeah,' he said. 'Look, Maisie, all I can do is apologise and offer to take you out again. And I've done that, so I'll get off to the station. There's a lot to do today.'

As far as he was concerned, their tiff was over. He leaned towards her to kiss the top of her head.

But Maisie hadn't finished. 'But you didn't apologise, Jim,' she said, firmly, backing away with her hands on her hips.

Brunswick was confused. 'Yes, I did. That's why I flaming came here!'

'No, what you said was, *Two people were murdered last night, Maisie.*'

He considered this. What point was she making?

'You didn't say: I'm so sorry, I apologise, I did a thoughtless thing to a defenceless teenager.'

'Defenceless?' he scoffed. 'I wouldn't say you're defenceless, would you? Vince was at my place this morning with a baseball bat!'

'Was he?' Her eyes lit up. She smiled, to reveal the devastating buck teeth.

'Yes, he was.'

'Oh.' She laughed rather unpleasantly and gave Brunswick a little push on the chest. 'Well, then. That settles it. Run along then, Mister Policeman. Go on. Shove in your clutch.'

'What?' (He had never heard the expression 'shove in your clutch' before.)

'You can practise your apologies on some other girl from now on. Don't bother asking me out again.'

Just then, Vince appeared a few yards behind her, and stopped to watch while his rival received his marching orders.

'What?' begged Brunswick. 'Oh, Maisie, come on. Why are you being like this? It was only ten minutes.'

'It was *half an hour!*'

He backed away. She seemed to be truly enraged. Her eyes were bulging.

'No, I've made my mind up. I've had enough.' She stamped a foot again. The windmill whizzed. 'Yes, mate, that's it, you've had your chips.' She didn't care at all that she was mixing her metaphors. 'I said, on your bike, piss off, and sling your ruddy hook!'

* * *

Falling into step with Brunswick in Prince Albert Street, Inspector Steine hailed his sergeant companionably. He didn't notice that Brunswick looked more miserable than usual. It was such a beautiful day that Steine had left his car at home and walked into town. He felt full of optimism.

'Splendid day, Brunswick.'

'Is it, sir?'

'I slept like a log. Did you?'

Brunswick thought back. 'No, sir. To be honest, I had a lot to think about.'

'Really? About what?'

'About the murder suspects, sir.'

'Oh, yes, of course. Those.'

'We have to interview so many people.'

'Ah, yes.'

'We have to organise an identity parade, search dwellings, check that Alec Forrester's fingerprints match any on the weapon, take statements, check alibis. For a start, that strong lady insists she's been working as a brickie at that new airport every day, which would mean –'

'Yes, yes,' interrupted Steine. 'Well, I don't envy you any of that, Brunswick. But I must say, I did enjoy the arresting part. It was surprisingly bracing.'

Brunswick stopped walking, and Steine gave him a look.

'I'm sorry to say this, sir.'

Steine sighed. It was one of the burdens of leadership that occasionally one had to listen to the trifling concerns of one's underlings.

'What is it, Sergeant?'

'I'm sorry to say this,' Brunswick repeated, 'but I think on reflection we might have been too quick to dismiss Alec Forrester's watertight alibi, sir.'

'Was he the elderly man in the pub?'

'Yes, sir. When a whole bar full of people say they saw a man come in at half-past three in the afternoon and drink gin-and-it solidly from then on, it does seem a stretch to place him at a scene three-quarters of a mile away firing a gun at seven-forty-five and making an escape. Also, his reaction when he heard that Crystal was dead – well, what did you think, sir?'

'Remind me, Brunswick.'

Brunswick opened his notebook. 'He said, "Thank fuck", sir. It was heartfelt and convincing.'

'But he used to be an actor, don't forget.'

'I know, sir. He still is. But I've seen him in many productions, and I have to say that a performance like that would be well beyond him. He is the worst kind of terrible old ham, sir.'

'I see.' Steine pursed his lips, irritated. 'You realise this will mean rethinking the whole thing?'

'Yes, sir. But in the interests of justice –'

'But you still think the strong lady did the other one, I hope?'

'Oh, yes, sir. Definitely. Apart from the possible alibi placing her twenty-five miles away in the afternoons, which might mean we have a problem identifying her as the Opinion Poll lady. But at least we've got the wig and the stolen goods, though, sir. She's got to be in on it, at least.'

'All right, then.'

They stood awkwardly on the pavement. Steine felt that all his splendid–day–Brunswick bonhomie was leaching out of him. But he sensed there was even more of this to come.

'I have another request, sir.'

'Oh, *what*?' Steine was getting testy now. He had been looking forward to his first cup of tea.

'I think Constable Twitten might confuse the investigations, sir.'

'Ah. Now. Yes.' Steine didn't mind talking about Twitten. He already had quite a lot to say on the subject himself.

'He's very clever, I know, sir –'

'*Too* clever, so people say.'

'My very point, sir. I think he might be too clever.'

'Go on.'

'It worries me that he will over-complicate my investigations by being too clever, so my request is that I can ignore his findings or suggestions if they are unhelpful. I don't like to tell tales, but he talked to me yesterday about –' (and here Brunswick lowered his voice) '– about *criminal psychology*, sir! In the *street*! As if it was a normal topic of conversation!'

'Criminal psychology? Good grief. I mean, what does that even mean?'

'He actually said that, given the nature of the Opinion Poll lady's criminal personality, you could predict she might turn to violence and that it was only a matter of time!'

'Dear me. What sort of hocus-pocus was that? Detecting crimes before they even occur?'

'I know, sir. Anyway, I just think a capacity for forensic observation can make a person quite annoying on its own, but when it's combined with looking for flaming *inner causes*...'

'I agree, Brunswick. I mean, good heavens, we're not living in Vienna. We fought a war to protect ourselves from that sort of decadent nonsense. You yourself jumped out of aeroplanes, if memory serves.'

'I did, sir.'

'While I protected the Old Lady of Threadneedle Street.'

'Pardon, sir?'

'The Bank of England.'

'Yes, sir.'

'Leave Twitten to me.'

'Thank you very much, sir.'

Brunswick looked up. 'He's coming, sir!' he reported.

And so Twitten arrived to intercept them on their way to the police station and inform them, breathlessly, and in one long sentence, that the strong lady had escaped, that the contractors building the passenger terminal at Gatwick Airport could confirm that Miss Carver had worked an afternoon shift there every day for the last fortnight, that Alec Forrester was obviously innocent, that a famous journalist from London called Harry Jupiter was already waiting for Steine inside, and that he (Twitten) was actively pursuing leads on all fronts to link the murder of Crystal to the long-ago Aldersgate Stick-up, which was why he was hotfooting it to the railway station to meet Miss Sibert from the next London train, and collecting a copy of the script of *A Shilling in the Meter* from the green room of the Theatre Royal en route, with twenty-five shillings taken from petty cash to cover any unexpected expenses, hoping that that was all right.

Getting no reaction to any of this important news, Twitten then added, to Steine's evident relief, that Mrs Groynes had just made a fresh pot of tea and was waiting for him with a nice half-pound of coconut ice.

'Well, carry on,' said Steine, which was apparently the right thing to say, because Twitten raced off in the direction of the Theatre Royal.

Steine noticed Brunswick's disappointed expression.

'Well, I'm sorry, but he took me by surprise,' he said, helplessly. 'It's a bit like having a dog. All that energy. Twenty-five shillings sounds like a lot, to me. And what's all this nonsense about Crystal's death being linked to the Aldersgate Stick-up?'

'I did warn you, sir. Not to listen.'

'Quite right, Brunswick. By the way, did you hear him say that the strong lady has *escaped*?'

* * *

The hilarious news that Joanne Carver had effortlessly absconded from the police cells was all over town in no time. At the Queen Adelaide, where Bobby had arranged to meet his Brighton auntie, jolly toasts were raised at opening time at 11 a.m. to the stupid woodentop in Brighton nick who'd put a famous strong lady in custody behind a bunch of bendable bars.

Bobby laughed along with everyone else, but in truth he had mixed feelings about Jo's being on the loose. On the one hand, he liked Jo and admired her; but on the other, he had very good reason to be scared of what she might do. After all, it was his fault the police had arrested her! If he hadn't mentioned seeing her in a red wig, she wouldn't even have been a suspect. He kept remembering, with a groan, Sergeant Brunswick holding up the wig in Jo's dressing room and saying, 'Thank you for the tip-off, sir. It's very much appreciated.'

Thank goodness there were only a few more nights at the Hippodrome. Next week Professor Mesmer was on the bill at the London Palladium! This stint in Brighton had been memorable in many respects – for meeting Penny, principally. But he would be more than happy now to pack up his trunks and boxes and move on. He just needed to retrieve that comb from Penny, ask her to be with him in London, and also to marry him (the order still required a bit of thought).

Bobby took a sip of his drink and continued to watch the door for the arrival of his Aunt Palmeira. He was confident that she'd understand why he was glad to go. She hadn't always lived here herself. True, she'd been his Brighton auntie for a few years now, but he had fond memories of former times in London. It was this Aunt Palmeira who had come up with the idea of the phrenology act. He had always been so good with his hands – he'd been brilliant at the piano as a child. But there were thousands of other pianists in the world, Aunt Palmeira said; thousands of card sharps; thousands of illusionists and magicians. And then she remembered how, as a child herself, she'd been taken to have a reading from the great Jessie Fowler (a legend amongst phrenologists), and it had changed her life.

'It was uncanny,' she told the young Bobby. 'She'd been feeling heads for decades. She'd read the heads of Queen Victoria and Teddy Roosevelt, and Oscar Wilde and Rasputin, and she still said I had the largest organ of Deceit she'd ever come across!'

Aunt Palmeira had bought Bobby some books and charts, and he had never looked back. He discovered that phrenology was not just an act, it was an art. Once he had placed his hands on a person's head, he felt he was playing them, like a great sonata, but one that had never been heard before. There was something mystical about it: at the same time as he drew out his sitter's essential character, he kneaded it back in, wise to its strengths and weaknesses. He could even open their minds and close them again without his sitters' conscious knowledge.

And when, aged twenty, he tested his new-found skills on his Aunt Palmeira, he found that the great Jessie Fowler had not been exaggerating. The organ of Deceit on his auntie's head was, truly, staggeringly enlarged.

* * *

While Sergeant Brunswick checked up on poor Alec Forrester in his cell, Inspector Steine returned to his office with a nice cup of tea (and a slice of lovely shiny pink-and-white coconut ice) to polish the talk he'd be recording later in the day at Broadcasting House in London. It was his regular compositional habit to set his manuscript aside for a day or two and then return to it on the day of the recording, embellishing it with a few fresh turns of phrase. Mainly, however, he would read it aloud, timing it for length with a stopwatch, as the talk needed to be nineteen and a half minutes precisely.

This week's subject – the case of the Battle of Fulham Road – was perhaps not the strongest theme he'd ever chosen, but he looked forward to explaining to the clueless populace the legal principle of a mob (consisting of many people all capable of exercising individual free will and moral responsibility) together committing a single criminal act.

Had he been feeling remotely charitable towards young Constable Twitten before he sat down, he certainly wasn't afterwards. On top of his script was a note from Twitten, evidently written (typed!) during the early hours of the morning, offering the insight that while joint enterprise was a fascinating area for legal scrutiny, surely the most interesting aspect of the Battle of Fulham Road was whether the stampede came within the words of the Riot (Damage) Act of 1886?

'This is intolerable,' said Steine, turning to the second page of Twitten's missive.

If memory serves, sir, [Twitten continued] *there was much debate after this famously well-attended football match about whether the police should compensate the people whose properties were invaded – and also whether the Riot Act of 1714 had been publicly read or not. But it's a brilliant piece anyway, sir! Well done! I just feel it would be incomplete without some mention of the 1886 legislation, which I'm sure you are familiar with. Also, the Russian team was called the Moscow Dynamos, sir, not Dominoes, a classic schoolboy error that would leave you open to derision!*

* * *

At the railway station, Twitten watched Miss Sibert's train arrive. She wasn't on it. While energetic groups of day-trippers streamed across the concourse dressed in their most colourful, scanty and sexually alluring attire, there was no one who looked remotely like she had arrived from Vienna with Sigmund Freud in 1938.

This was worrying. He had spoken to her once this morning at her own home, and she had promised to take the 8.32 from Victoria, bringing the manuscript of Crystal's memoirs. Their conversation had been very clear, especially when she had voiced her reaction to the news of Crystal's death.

'I'm so frightfully sorry about what happened last night to Mr Crystal,' Twitten had said.

And she had replied, in a Mittel-European accent, 'Don't vorry, it was bound to happen sooner or later. He voz a horrible man. *Ein schweinhund*. I often haff fantasy of shooting him myself.'

Once he was sure Miss Sibert had not been on the train, Twitten raced to the public telephone outside the station, beside the taxi rank – narrowly beating an elderly working-class woman in an unseasonal fur coat, who exclaimed, 'Ruddy nerve!' as he slipped into the telephone box ahead of her, removing his helmet and resting it on the floor.

Realising he had no penny coins, he dialled the operator. 'I am a police constable,' he announced, 'and I need to be connected at once to a flat in London's Great Russell Street, telephone number Museum 0488.'

After several demoralising rings, during which Twitten became guiltily aware that a short queue was now waiting for the telephone behind the original outraged fur-coat lady, the call was finally answered.

'Miss Sibert, it's me. Constable Twitten.'

'Ach, I am glad it iss you, Mr Twitten,' said Miss Sibert, evidently relieved. She sounded flustered, a little breathless. 'It will sound ridiculous, but I was unsure vether to pick up.'

'Has something happened, Miss Sibert? I was worried when you weren't on the train.'

'I'm afraid it has, yes.' There was a catch in her voice. 'I'm afraid the manuscript of Mr Crystal's memoir is no more!'

Someone knocked on the glass and Twitten spun round. It was the fur-coat lady. He opened the door. ''Ow much longer you gonna be?' she demanded.

Twitten, in agitation, ignored her and shut the door again. He had a lot to take in. If Crystal's memoir had been stolen, it was jolly bad luck, but at the same time proved his investigation was on precisely the right lines.

'Did you hear vot I said, Mr Twitten?' Miss Sibert asked, shrilly, down the line. 'It is gone. Even the carbon copy! When I arrive this morning, the door is open; Herr Crystal's book is *gone*!'

'Crikey,' said Twitten, with feeling.

'Months of *verk*, Mr Twitten!' She sounded very upset. 'It was all in there! We verk for months on the trauma –' (she pronounced it *trow-ma*) '– of the Aldersgate Stick-up. We veep together; we howl like wolves; we place bags over our heads and fire loaded pistols in the air. Loaded pistols! In this very flat in Great Russell *Strasse*!'

'Goodness,' said Twitten. 'Was that *regression*?'

'Of course it was regression!'

Twitten made a decision. 'Perhaps we don't need the manuscript. You can just tell me what you discovered. Would you wait there at the flat for me? I can catch the next train, I've got twenty-five shillings. I took it from petty cash this morning, which was jolly prescient of me, I now realise.'

She took a deep breath. She was evidently pulling herself together. Outside the telephone box in Brighton, a man in a flat cap (third in the queue) was alternately indicating the station clock and shaking his fist at Twitten.

'Ach so,' Miss Sibert said, 'I suppose I could stay here. It is true there vill be much secretarial work for me for a little vile.'

'People writing with condolences, I suppose.'

'*Jah*, and also people writing to say how much they hated and detested Mr Crystal and are so glad that he is dead. But for now, *auf Wiedersehen*.'

'Before you go! Just one thing!' Twitten said. To a groan of annoyance from the small crowd now watching him, he pulled the script of *A Shilling in the Meter* from his pocket, opened it and quickly found the relevant passage.

'At the play last night, you see, just before he was shot, Mr Crystal got very excited when Nick, the passionate young protagonist, berates his girlfriend for working as a clippie on a bus.'

'*Jah*? What is *clippie*?'

'Ooh, sorry. Bus conductress.'

'OK.'

'Now. Nick particularly hates hearing her say, as a bus conductress, "*Any more for any more?*" And I'm pretty sure it was at exactly this juncture that Mr Crystal got very excited. Can you explain that?'

Miss Sibert gasped. 'The breakthrough!' she said. '*Mein Gott.*'

Twitten waited for more, but evidently 'The breakthrough! *Mein Gott*' was all she was going to say.

'I don't understand,' he said, at last. 'Why are those words important?'

'Because they must have been the exact verds of the woman in the bank robbery! We verked for veeks to retrieve zem and they would not come!' she said, and in her excitement hung up the phone.

Twitten stared at the receiver briefly, then out at the eight or nine people now waiting restively in the queue. He put his helmet back on his head, composed himself, then opened the door, and strode past his disgruntled audience in a purposeful manner, taking no notice of the jeering and swearing as he headed for the Brighton Station ticket office.

Six

Harry Jupiter, author of such bestselling publications as *The Art and Craft of Murder* and *Heroes of the Yard*, had never set foot in Brighton before. His work for the *Daily Clarion* generally kept him in London, and his special relationship with the elite of the Metropolitan Police – in particular, his well-established and mutually beneficial alliance with that famous London policeman Deputy Chief Inspector Philip Peplow – meant that he was perfectly well occupied from day to day without the bother of taking steam trains from the capital.

He would have denied living in Peplow's pocket exactly, but when the call had gone out last night from the news desk, 'Get Jupiter here right now!', the *Clarion*'s minions had wasted no time scouring the local taverns of Fleet Street, or checking with the long-suffering Mrs Jupiter at home in High Barnet; they had known to take a cab straight to Peplow's private gentlemen's club in Pall Mall, where Jupiter was reliably to be found proudly hobnobbing with senior Yard detectives, and ostentatiously addressing them by their first names.

It was certainly a cosy arrangement. DCI Peplow ensured that Jupiter got first dibs on anything juicy the Yard was investigating, while Jupiter ensured that the Metropolitan Police's CID came out of all investigations brilliantly, even when its officers failed to nail the culprit, or mishandled the evidence, or were otherwise lazy, stupid, incompetent or corrupt. As a result of this simple reciprocation, public trust in both Jupiter and Peplow was sky high; meanwhile both were equally revered by their peers. When Jupiter attended a crime scene with other reporters, he literally led the pack (they trotted in his wake in an elongated arrow formation), wearing an expensive camel coat draped over his broad shoulders, in the style of Edward G. Robinson – with whose unimpressive physique the small, rotund Jupiter had quite a lot in common.

Jupiter was, therefore, the universally acknowledged sun in the sky of crime reporting, and there was no doubt that he enjoyed his power. It would be an exaggeration to say that men had been hanged on his say-so, although he sometimes made this claim privately. But he was a great supporter of the rope, and the readers of the *Clarion* adored him for it, even when, awkwardly, the hanged men were discovered afterwards to be innocent.

Detail was Jupiter's great interest when it came to all crime stories. His way of introducing himself had, over the years, perfected itself to, 'Jupiter of the *Clarion*, now just tell me what's going on here and don't spare the particulars!' In the case that first brought him to prominence – concerning the sparse, gruesome remains of a murdered woman found in a sludgy acid bath – he had made brilliant use of the ghastly details: the half-set of dentures that had not dissolved; the bit of handbag; the pair of National Health specs with the broken lenses.

This famous half-set of dentures was a particular that Jupiter had audaciously made up, having asked a forensic scientist to suggest the sort of materials that would not have melted in the acid. But Peplow was so pleased with the impact of Jupiter's lurid story on the general public ('Those dentures!' they thrilled) that he not only never contradicted the detail but decided to go along with it. Indeed, he borrowed an upper set from his own old mother to show as Court Exhibit G (luckily his mother was happy to live on custard, soup and macaroni pudding for the duration of the trial).

But the acid-bath murder was in the past, and now the great crime correspondent was in Brighton Police Station, and the place was naturally abuzz. Passing through the ground floor, Sergeant Brunswick spotted Jupiter in an outer office and recognised him at once from his famous byline picture. Jupiter was a short but feisty-looking man, snazzily dressed, with a full head of hair, who looked like he could take care of himself in a fight – all of which fitted with his punchy, Hemingway-esque style of writing.

> Night. Light glinting on policemen's helmets. Good men. Great men. Heroic men. Men without fear. A half-set of dentures. Whose? Not theirs.

(At the *Clarion* offices, incidentally, it was understood that if anyone dared to insert a verb in a Harry Jupiter story, they were automatically dismissed. Likewise anyone who attempted to soften his emphatic punctuation. In a cupboard on the home-news floor was proudly preserved a heap of old, unusable Jupiter ex-typewriters whose full-stop keys were missing, having snapped off from persistent overuse.)

Brunswick was a huge fan of Jupiter's, full stops and all. The idea of being written about made him feel faint with excitement.

'Does he need anything?' he asked the desk sergeant, jerking his head towards Jupiter's door.

The sergeant replied that he shouldn't think so. Jupiter had arrived half an hour ago with the words, 'I'll need a Remington in good repair, some foolscap paper with new carbons, a large ashtray, an up-to-date street map of Brighton, a half bottle of Bell's, a green visor, some functional sleeve garters, and a place to hang my mac *where I can see it*.'

Right now he was finishing a piece for tomorrow's paper about an astonishing new discovery in the old 'Kennington Butcher' case (the name had been his own idea; Peplow had long ago made him Case-Namer-in-Chief at Scotland Yard). The public needed to know that just last week, the great and tireless Peplow had found an incriminating human eye-tooth embedded in a scullery floorboard! After all these years! What a great example of sheer, honourable diligence and application. What a great example of how a tiny detail makes all the difference.

When he had finished this piece, he must of course turn his attention to the death of Crystal, in which the *Clarion* naturally took an interest, since he was one of their own. But so far he had only come up with the name for the case: 'The Blood on the Plush'. He had telephoned Peplow and asked him what he thought of it, and Peplow had wholeheartedly given him the double-thumbs-up.

* * *

It was one of the lovelier things about Inspector Steine that he not only didn't care about the great 'Policeman's Friend' Harry Jupiter, he hadn't even heard of him.

Others would have advised him to invite Jupiter into the investigation as soon as possible, in his own best interests.

However, there was no chance of that. Steine loathed journalists, for the simple reason that they were always asking questions he couldn't answer. He also blamed journalism in general for the way the public so quickly forgot landmark events such as the Middle Street Massacre. Other news stories relentlessly captured their attention; 'news' created a kind of collective amnesia.

This was why he liked to talk on the wireless about long-ago riots at London football matches: to restore a sense of perspective; to give people a break from the never-ending 'news'. The Middle Street Massacre had been a massive policing triumph that people would still be celebrating, if only a constant accrual of 'news' hadn't made it slip their minds.

Because, six years after the event, people were indeed beginning to forget the Middle Street Massacre. Instead, to Inspector Steine's considerable annoyance, the image of Brighton that still prevailed was the purely fictional (and irresponsibly depressing) version contained in Graham Greene's book *Brighton Rock* and the subsequent film of the same name. This was bizarre, inexplicable and very upsetting. Quite often, when walking along the seafront, Steine overheard visitors saying excitedly, 'Look, there's the tea shop from *Brighton Rock*, Janet!' or 'Perhaps we'll spot Kolley Kibber from *Brighton Rock* and claim the ten guineas!'

On all such occasions, Inspector Steine stopped the misguided visitors in their tracks, introduced himself, and gave them a talking-to. Didn't they realise that the events of *Brighton Rock* had actually never taken place? If they were genuinely interested in crime, why not take a tour to Middle Street, where they could see the site where forty-five authentic bad people – real armed villains – had been deliberately left to shoot each other to death, thus rendering Brighton the charming and safe holiday place that it was today?

This kindly intervention usually did the job of rescuing people from any morbid delusions about Brighton. It also took the wind out of their sails, and ruined their day. (Many of them just went home.)

'We ought to question Mr Forrester now, sir,' said Brunswick, entering Steine's office. 'He's got a terrible hangover, but I think we should get it over with.'

'Any news of the strong lady?'

'I sent someone to check her lodgings, sir, but she was evidently long gone. Unfortunately her alibi of the brickie job at Gatwick does check out; it precludes her from being the Opinion Poll imposter, but what with the pearls found in her possession, she could still have been the interrupted burglar.'

'But why wear a red wig for that?'

'I know, sir. Good point. Doesn't add up, does it? I suppose it means we're still looking for a woman and a man working together, and the woman must be someone else.'

'Regrettably, I suppose it does mean that, yes. I'm sorry, Brunswick.'

Brunswick tried to look brave, as if his whole case had not just collapsed around him.

'Oh, and by the way,' said Steine, 'there's a strange little fat man in one of the offices downstairs just smoking and typing and looking pleased with himself. Wearing a double-breasted suit. I don't know how he got in, but it's highly irregular. Could you go and tell him to leave?'

Brunswick was shocked. 'That's Harry Jupiter of the *Clarion*, sir.'

'Well, whoever he is, tell him he can't write here. This is a police station.'

'But it's Harry Jupiter, sir.'

'Yes, yes. So you said.'

'He's on our side, sir.'

'I beg your pardon?'

'Mr Jupiter is "the Policeman's Friend", sir. At Scotland Yard, I expect he types wherever he likes.'

Steine furrowed his brow. 'That doesn't mean he can do it here.'

Mrs Groynes appeared at his office door. 'Cups of tea, dears?' she asked.

'Yes, please,' said Steine. A thought occurred to him. 'I hope this Jupiter man doesn't know that the strong lady escaped during the night?'

'I might have just told him that, yes, dear, sorry,' said Mrs Groynes, pulling an apologetic face. 'He found it ever so amusing.'

* * *

Alec Forrester was demanding to be released, and he was in full voice, as if projecting to the Upper Circle.

'I won't pret*end* I'm not *glad* the fucker's *dead*,' he said, grandly. 'But *I* had *nothing* to *do* with it.'

They were sitting in a room bare but for a table and chairs: Brunswick, Steine, Forrester. They all had cups of tea, and Forrester was smoking. Steine was finding it hard to care about what the suspect was saying. He was a little preoccupied. He kept thinking, was Twitten *right* about him missing the bigger picture in his Home Service talk? If this Forrester man could be dispatched quickly enough, there would be time to revise it, and include mention of the 1886

Riot (Damage) Act. (He had already grudgingly corrected the Russian team name from Dominoes to Dynamos, and he had to admit it looked better.)

Brunswick opened his notebook. 'Mr Forrester, as you know, you are charged with the murder of Mr Algernon Crystal.'

'Yes, and I *demand* to know *why*.'

'Well, I'm afraid we have a witness to your saying earlier in the day yesterday, and, er, pardon the language, sir –' Brunswick checked with Steine whether to continue. Steine nodded at him to get on, but only because he had forgotten the exact words Brunswick was about to quote; otherwise he would have asked him to tone it down.

'Thank you, sir. The witness says that you said, "That's it! That bastard! I'll fucking kill him!"'

Steine made a disapproving noise.

'You were talking about Mr Crystal, sir,' said Brunswick. 'With Todd Blair, another member of the cast. And you were angry because you had invited Crystal to Brighton to review the play, and Mr Blair informed you he was intending to say in print that you were a ham; moreover, a ham with a toupée.'

Forrester couldn't hide the pain of the recollection. His face contorted and he twisted his body (ham-like) while putting the back of his hand to his brow.

Brunswick referred back to his notebook and continued. 'Mr Blair says that he remarked, "You'd better do it tonight before he writes the review," and you said –'

Steine closed his eyes. This time he did remember what was coming.

'– "That's a good fucking point, Todd. I fucking will."'

'Is there much more of this, Brunswick?' asked Steine.

'That's everything, sir. Except that when we arrived at the King Henry last night and revealed to Mr Forrester that Crystal was dead, he said, "Thank fuck", sir.' He closed his notebook. 'During the arrest itself, Mr Forrester said nothing at all, being virtually unconscious. However, the night desk sergeant informed me this morning that he heard a cry of "Good fucking luck to you, strong lady!" in the early hours, which he now thinks was Mr Forrester encouraging Miss Carver in her escape. At the time, however, it seemed to be the mere ravings of a drunken man.'

Forrester raised his eyebrows and took a swig of tea. He had no recollection of a strong lady.

'So we have threats, Forrester,' said Steine. 'We have a strong motive. We also have opportunity. All your fellow cast members concur – even the mousy middle-aged pair who don't say much – that you did not arrive for the performance and that the house manager had been hastily recruited to play your part. Thankfully, he was never required to go on, but such sheer unprofessionalism speaks volumes against you, to say the least. A man who can be guilty of such irresponsible conduct – what else might he do, if he had a grudge and an opportunity… and a gun?'

This being Steine's most hopeful line of questioning, he delivered it with an impressive *je ne sais quoi*. For a moment there was a thrilling silence. Then Forrester ruined it.

'What, me? But I don't have a gun.'

'No, I'm saying, *if you had a gun.*'

'But I don't have a gun. I've never had a gun.'

Steine threw up his hands and turned to Brunswick. 'Do you think he's got a gun?'

Brunswick was startled by the question. It was hardly standard interrogation procedure for the police to talk amongst themselves during an interview.

'Perhaps we should step outside, sir. Mr Forrester doesn't need to hear this.'

'Oh, don't mind me,' said Forrester.

'Look,' said Steine, again addressing Brunswick. 'What's the point of carrying on with this? I believe him. I don't think he ever had a gun. I distinctly remember the cast said they'd never seen him with one.'

'Did they? Oh, bless their *hearts*,' chipped in Forrester.

'Didn't you make a note of them saying that, Brunswick? It was very important.'

'Well, no, sir.' Brunswick flipped through his notebook. He felt awkward to be talking about this with the accused man listening. 'It was just as I arrived at the theatre. But I did hear it. I think *you* made a note but –'

'Look, I think we should let him go.'

'What?' said Brunswick. 'But, sir –'

Forrester started to put on his jacket.

'Cool it, Mr Hambone,' said Brunswick, sternly. 'Not so fast.'

Forrester settled back into his seat. Brunswick wasn't happy. For one thing, he couldn't believe he had just said 'Mr Hambone' (or indeed 'cool it') in the heat of the moment.

'Sir, shouldn't we keep him another day or two? We haven't searched his lodgings yet.'

Steine hesitated. But only for a second. He'd made up his mind.

'No. You can go,' he told Forrester. 'But if I ever find out you *did* have a gun, and that you *did* kill Mr Crystal, I'll be absolutely furious, is that clear?'

* * *

Steine was back at his desk, substantially rewriting his radio talk with just a few hours to go, when the door burst open and a man appeared in the doorway. It was the same strange, spherical man in a pepper-and-salt double-breasted suit he had seen typing and smoking in an office downstairs without so much as a by-your-leave.

'Jupiter,' said the man, extending his hand and walking in. 'Awkward time, I imagine?'

Steine was confused, but answered honestly. 'Not really,' he said, indicating his well-ordered desk. 'Why?'

'Two murders on your hands?'

'Well, I wouldn't say they were on *my* hands, exactly. I had nothing to do with either of them.'

Jupiter pulled a face and then laughed loudly, as if getting a tremendous joke. Steine shrugged. Accustomed to deference, he was finding it difficult to adapt to such a pally approach from a complete stranger.

'So what suspects have you got, Geoffrey?' asked Jupiter, taking a seat and opening a notebook.

Steine was exasperated. 'Sorry. And you are –?'

Jupiter laughed again, assuming this was a wind-up. Every policeman in the country knew who he was, unless they were idiots.

'Look, man,' he began – the word 'man' making Steine gasp in outrage – 'it's not my policy to step on anyone's toes! I know my place. But Crystal was a colleague, and the *Clarion* wants two thousand of my very best by sixteen hundred hours. I've already visited the murder scene and interviewed the cast. That Penny Cavendish is a corker; they've sent a local snapper to get some come-on-big-boy shots for the picture desk. But if you can tell me anything about what it was like at the scene last night, I want details, man. Details.'

'Look,' said Steine, 'if you would stop calling me "man" –'

'The public laps them up. How about shoes lost in the scramble? They love a lone lost shoe. Two they aren't so bothered by, for some reason. An abandoned prosthetic limb would be even better. In fact, I'll make a note of that, in case there was one.'

'You can't just walk in here.'

Jupiter opened his arms. 'Yet here I am.'

'You're a journalist!'

'Yes, I am, and a bloody good one. Oh, come on, man. You want to catch who did this, don't you? It's a fantastic story and I'm the boy to tell it. Imagine you're Mrs Bloggs of Blogg Street. You want to know, can you and the little Bloggses walk safe in Brighton; can you and Mr Bloggs go to see faddish kitchen-sink dramas at the Theatre Royal without fear of having your heads blown off?'

Steine closed his eyes.

'Come on!' Jupiter went on, undeterred. 'What lines are the police pursuing? How does the murder of Braithwaite fit in? Crystal was a witness to the Aldersgate Stick-up – you do know that? Well, they never caught the culprits, did they? It's common knowledge that Terence Chambers was behind it, but no one's ever been able to make the link. This murder could be that link! It could be a professional hit to silence the only useful witness! DCI Peplow sends his regards, by the way.'

'Does he?' Steine reluctantly opened his eyes. This was all moving too quickly for him. What did Scotland Yard's DCI Peplow have to do with this awful man? Who was Mrs Bloggs? Why wouldn't people stop talking about the blessed Aldersgate Stick-up? Where was Blogg Street, and did Mrs Bloggs live there by coincidence or by design?

'Look, whoever you are,' said Steine, firmly, 'I am first of all shocked that you've seen the crime scene. You should never have been admitted, and besides, it's disgusting. When I was there I nearly stepped on an eyeball. Second, please remember to address me as either "Inspector Steine" or "sir". Anything else is highly irregular.'

Jupiter laughed. Nothing could shake his idea that Steine was being deliberately funny. But he was pleased to make his second note (after 'prosthetic limb'): 'eyeball'.

'But you haven't answered my question, man. I know you charged some old actor for it, but the rumour downstairs is that you're letting him go.'

'Again,' said Steine, firmly, 'you should not know that. It's inappropriate for you to know that. How do you know that?'

Jupiter smiled. He found that, in police stations, people just told him things. He also knew the strong lady had hilariously escaped through the bars, but for the time being, he was tactful enough not to mention it.

'So, you must be pursuing the Aldersgate Stick-up angle?'

This was too much for Steine. Until yesterday, he'd completely forgotten the Aldersgate Stick-up, and now everyone seemed to be determined to rake it all up. 'Look, Mr Jupiter –'

'Old Peplow saw it straight away, of course. "Jupiter," he said to me last night at his club; and I said, "Yes, Philip?" because I call him Philip when we're on our own; that's the kind of man he is. And he said, "The Aldersgate Stick-up will be in the background to this somewhere. That case was appallingly badly handled."'

Jupiter smiled at Steine in a pointed way, assuming that a small-time Brighton inspector would admire the great Scotland Yard man just as much as he did. 'Really,' he added, 'it's no wonder Peplow always wins Policeman of the Year.'

Steine was very torn about how to respond to such provocative stuff, especially from a man who looked like a bookie. Part of him wanted to say that actually, one of his officers was strenuously pursuing the Aldersgate Stick-up angle *at this very moment*; meanwhile a further small part of him knew that whatever he admitted to Jupiter would end up in print, which was the last thing he wanted. And finally, the last part of him (by far the biggest) just wanted the whole damned thing to go away.

Steine therefore took a deep breath, stood up, and said, 'Well, good luck, Mr Jupiter. Our enquiries are at a delicate early stage, and we can't discuss them. I personally disagree about the handling of the historic Aldersgate Stick-up case, which DCI Peplow is in no position to criticise. I am quite persuaded that Mr Crystal was shot because he was simply odious and made enemies in unusually high quantities in the world of greasepaint. But more importantly, I'm afraid I need to finish this talk for the Home Service, so I'll say good day.'

Jupiter realised he needed to adapt his approach. He searched his memory for anything connected to Inspector Steine (it was a shame that he never listened to the wireless) – and, distantly, something stirred. 'What about the Middle Street Massacre?' he said, inspired. 'Wasn't that you?'

'Of course it was me,' said Steine, still bristling. He sat down. 'But what about it? It has nothing to do with the cases at hand.'

Jupiter started making notes in his notebook, as if feverishly interested in the Middle Street Massacre. Trying to impress Steine had got him nowhere. It was time to turn things round.

'The link is *you*, man. Don't you see?'

'Me?'

'Yes, you. The great Inspector Steine! The link is that you will not stand for violent crime on your patch.'

'Well, that's true.' Steine sat back in his chair. 'That's very true, actually. I won't, and I never have.'

'And that's the story.'

'Is it?'

'1953, wasn't it, the Middle Street Massacre?'

'1951.'

'That's it. 1951, of course.' Jupiter made a note. 'What a triumph over crime that was. You were admired by every policeman in the country. And by the public too, of course.'

'Thank you.'

'A very unconventional kind of triumph.'

'If you say so.'

'I do, I do. That's what makes it special. How many villains dead?'

'Forty-five.'

'Forty-*five*?' Jupiter clapped his hands in *faux*-admiration. For all his huge self-regard, he was a talented toady, who knew from experience that even the most intelligent people were blind to preposterous flattery, if you told them what they wanted to hear. Sometimes he had only to exclaim, 'But you don't look old enough!' for people to melt like snow on a bonfire. In the present situation, it helped that more and more of the Middle Street Massacre stuff was coming back to him as they talked.

'People should be reminded of this,' he declared. 'People deserve to be reminded. What was that line in the film, "I have no blood on my hands this day –"'

Steine helped him out: '"Just a smidgen of raspberry sauce."'

'Great stuff.'

'Thank you.'

'Did you actually say it?'

Steine had been hoping for years that someone would ask him this question.

'Yes,' he said. 'I did. Or something very much to that effect.'

* * *

All this explains why Steine allowed himself to be persuaded to go out and about with Jupiter in search of particulars (or 'colour') for the *Clarion* piece. Ten minutes later, they were on the seafront, near the bandstand, and Jupiter was back to being quite demanding.

'Don't forget,' he said, his voice raised to be heard over the wind and the seagulls and the open-topped buses roaring past, 'I want detail, man – detail.'

'I did ask you not to call me "man",' said Steine, but he didn't say it with his usual force. He was slightly distracted by a scene he had fleetingly witnessed when they had left the station together – it was Alec Forrester, being hugged and kissed on the front steps by the two mousy cast members of *A Shilling in the Meter* whom no one ever took an interest in. The man was saying, 'They just let you go, Alec? After what you said? I don't think *I* would have done!'

What Steine could not have known about Jupiter up to this point, of course, was that – like everyone else in the world, apparently – he was obsessed with *Brighton Rock*. But as they walked along, it was becoming horribly, depressingly obvious that, whatever Jupiter's ostensible interest in the Middle Street Massacre, he was planning to bring up all the old *Brighton Rock* stuff again in his front-page report on Crystal's murder.

It would be no good telling him that last night's two killings had been the first murders in Brighton since 1951, or that the town had been free from gangs for six whole years. This famous crime reporter was going to take the obvious route, and invoke the same old *Brighton Rock* hoodlums, in spite of the fact they had never existed.

'I can't believe you didn't know which tea shop was the one in *Brighton Rock*, man,' said Jupiter now, as they walked along the breezy seafront. 'That tea shop is one of the most famous landmarks in Brighton!'

'Well, I'm sorry you see it that way,' said Steine. 'And may I repeat, Mr Jupiter, that there is something much too familiar in your tone.'

'If that woman in that souvenir shop hadn't been able to help –'

'Look, she did help, Jupiter. She helped. You saw your blessed tea shop! Much good may it do you. It's just a tea shop like any other.'

'But I can't get over the fact that you didn't know which one –'

'It's a book, Jupiter! It's not real! I don't have to know about it!'

'It's a very famous book.'

'It's still a book!'

They walked on, until they came to the end of Middle Street. Steine paused significantly.

'Why are we stopping here?' asked Jupiter.

'This is Middle Street.'

'Ah.' Jupiter glanced up it. He tried to exhibit interest. 'So this is where it happened, then?'

'Obviously, yes.'

'Mm,' said Jupiter. 'Forty-five?'

'I think we've established that, yes.'

Jupiter had a thought. 'Why is it called Middle Street? What's it in the middle of? I bet a lot of people have asked you that question over the years.'

Steine couldn't believe what he'd just heard. *What's it in the middle of?* 'No, you're the first,' he said. 'But anyway –'

'So what's it in the middle of?'

'I have no idea.'

'Oh, come on, man. Haven't you ever wondered?'

This was precisely why Steine disliked journalists. 'No, I've never wondered. Middle Street is just its name.'

'Haven't you even tried to work it out?'

'Look –'

'It's called Middle Street, you say?'

'Yes.'

'So what's it in the middle of?'

'I don't know. Look –'

'Is it in the middle of Brighton, for example?'

'No. I don't think so.'

'So why is it called Middle Street?'

'I told you, I just don't know!'

By the time they reached the Palace Pier, Steine was ready to abandon the whole expedition. Jupiter would be setting the death of Crystal against the murky world of *Brighton Rock* – it would be all Pinkie Brown, or Brownie Orange, or whatever his name was; razor gangs at the racetrack; busty women drinking strong liquor in the middle of the day – whereas if Jupiter would only look about him he would see flocks of happy holidaymakers on a sunny day, paying their pennies at the turnstile and flooding onto the pier, to ride the cars of the roller coaster, or shoot rifle pellets at rows of tin rabbits to win a fluffy toy. Many of these visitors carried candyfloss and freshly made humbugs, or long sticks of rock wrapped in white tissue paper. It made Inspector Steine so angry that his town had been cursed by that dismal, nasty book.

Jupiter paid for them to go through the turnstiles. 'Say thank you to Lord Otterdale,' he grinned – which made no sense to Steine, who had no knowledge of newspaper proprietors, and who was hardly familiar with the concept of the expense account, either. Afterwards, when questioned about it, the turnstile man clearly remembered the little man in the smart suit paying for himself and the tall, distinguished-looking police inspector. It was a transaction that had stood out from the norm.

'Can't you do the rest without me?' Steine said. 'I think you've grasped the fact by now that I haven't read that blasted book, which is all you seem to be interested in.'

But Jupiter led him up the Palace Pier, homing in on a sound that he evidently found significant.

'Here it is!' he said, stopping at the ghost train. He checked his watch. 'Perfect timing. It will only take ten minutes. Come on, man. Lord Otterdale can treat us to this as well, I think.'

'You don't expect me to go on that thing?' The ghost train? Why on earth?'

'Two, please,' said Jupiter at the little window where they sold the tickets. 'And can I have a receipt? Could you make it for four tickets, actually? Good man, good man.'

Steine couldn't believe this was happening. 'A lot of people come to Brighton for the sunshine and sea air, you know, Jupiter. They come for the Knickerbocker Glories and the saucy seaside postcards and the general sense of well-being.'

But Jupiter merely said, 'Get on, get on,' and so they took their seats in the ghost train, their little open carriage shunting forward unsteadily, causing Steine to yelp in alarm.

'I don't like this,' he said, gripping the side of the car. 'I don't like this at all.'

But it was too late to get off. They lurched forward on the tracks and then swerved abruptly through a rough, thick curtain, into suffocating darkness.

What happened next was simply horrible. In the gloom, Steine heard a clanking noise and felt his stomach lurch back to knock his spine. Jupiter seemed to be laughing a lot, as green luminous faces appeared in front of them, and hands and cobwebs touched their hair and faces, and the carriage picked up speed as it dodged and snaked in the rattling dark.

'I don't like this!' Steine said, loudly.

'I reckon the spot is round the next bend or two!' shouted Jupiter back.

'What spot?'

Something rubbery hit Steine in the face. 'Get off!' he cried, batting it away.

'Relax, man!' yelled Jupiter.

'What?'

'I said relax!'

Steine was frowning in confusion when, terrifyingly, he felt two hands tighten on his windpipe.

'Get off!' he shouted, trying to stand up. 'Help! Help!'

'Don't wriggle, Steine!'

'Help! Help!'

Ahead of the carriage, they could see to a point where bright daylight came up through the tracks, and the wavy reflections of the water below hit the walls and ceiling around them. The little carriages were hurtling towards it. Steine struggled against Jupiter's grip. What on earth was happening?

'What are you doing? Get off me!'

'Look, man –' Jupiter stood up, and was trying to push Steine back down when the train reached the place where the sea lay beneath.

'Help! Help! Get OFF!' yelled Steine, pushing Jupiter so hard that he lost his balance and let go with a cry.

Steine was so relieved to be free from Jupiter's grip that he didn't notice his assailant fall out of the carriage and plummet seawards, banging his head on an iron cross-beam on the way down. He also failed to hear the splash.

All he knew, when the little carriage rattled back into daylight and stopped with a jolt, was that no one was trying to throttle him any more, and there was an empty seat beside him, which the small Policeman's Friend had formerly occupied.

Seven

Fortunately, Sergeant Brunswick was unaware that Inspector Steine was in the process of endangering the life of the world's most police-friendly newspaperman by knocking him into the sea. The knowledge might have dampened his sense of excitement, which was perversely high this morning, given that he had already lost not only the girl he fancied but also both his principal suspects in the murders.

But sometimes the mind works like this when things are at their bleakest: darting so quickly between intractable subjects that it lights on none of them long enough to register the true dismal hopelessness of the situation. The activity itself keeps one's spirits up.

Who killed Crystal? Well, good question, don't know, I'll come back to that. So who killed Braithwaite? Again, not sure, but at least we know it's to do with the break-ins, or do we? OK, where is the Strong Lady? Well, there's nothing to go on there, really. If the Strong Lady isn't the Opinion Poll lady, who is? Actually, no idea, but moving on… Will Maisie change her mind and take me back? Don't go there, she's insane with all that 'half an hour' nonsense, and it's less important than solving who killed Crystal – but who did kill Crystal?

And so on, round again.

But being a methodical man, Brunswick had a mental list of what to do, and the first task of the day was to re-interview Mrs Thorpe – Braithwaite's Brighton landlady – and also to search Braithwaite's room and talk to the neighbours. Looking back on the proceedings of the night before, Brunswick was conscious of having rather rushed to a conclusion about Jo Carver's guilt, and of having therefore neglected proper procedures. While he disliked admitting it, he had rarely seen anything so upsetting as the body of the slain Braithwaite: the attack on him had been ferocious. Twitten had warned that a cornered narcissist could be dangerous – but he couldn't have meant anything on this scale. Flaming heck, how many cornered people, narcissists or not, would reach for a sword above a mantelpiece and frenziedly hack a person to death?

So Brunswick had been overexcited last night; he saw that now. He had been so intent on leading the inspector to Miss Carver's dressing room that he had very nearly overlooked important evidence at the scene of the crime. Luckily, the forensics men had done their job properly and taken the sherry glasses for fingerprint examination. Otherwise, they would have been left behind for Mrs Thorpe – or for her daily cleaning woman, more likely – to give them a soapy wash in the morning and put them back on the tray.

He had high hopes of Mrs Thorpe as a witness. She was the most recent person to meet the Opinion Poll lady, and she had evidently become quite friendly with Braithwaite during his stay. She had been adamant about the sherry glasses. And she was evidently kind to actors, which always counted for a lot with Brunswick.

There was a wide range of theatrical digs available in Brighton, and Braithwaite had hit the flaming jackpot with this one, which was more like living with a rich relative in her gracious home. Brunswick had been particularly impressed by the framed signed photographs in the hallway of legendary theatrical guests – the identities of most of whom had been lost on Braithwaite. What he had apparently most appreciated about Mrs Thorpe's house were the excellent breakfasts (served at the considerably late hour of half-past nine) and the pleasant ten-minute stroll downhill to the theatre.

Understandably, Mrs Thorpe looked less impressive this morning. Her demeanour the previous night had been that of a rather stately householder, offering sherry to the police, but that was before she knew that a bloody murder had occurred in her own front living-room, and that the nice lady from the Opinion Poll – with whom she'd had such an enjoyable conversation – was a wicked fraud in league with a desperado house-breaker.

Today she looked smaller, faded, with untidy hair. Her fluffy slippers aged her. This morning the role of theatrical landlady appealed so much less to her that she was thinking of selling up and moving to France. One of her posh neighbours had earlier informed her – with unpleasant relish – that during the attack he had heard through the wall raised voices, a violent scuffle, and then blood-curdling screams.

'My house, it happened in *my* house, in *this road*,' she said now, to Brunswick, with misery in her eyes. 'Poor Mr Braithwaite. Poor Mr Braithwaite! Such a terrible thing.'

The front living room still being closed off as a crime scene, Mrs Thorpe offered Brunswick coffee in her drawing room on the first floor, with its view across the gardens and rooftops to the glittering sea and wide horizon. It was very beautiful. The inevitable 'daily' brought the refreshments on a silver tray, and Mrs Thorpe attempted to pull herself together. Brunswick expressed his sympathy, and told her to take her time, but was secretly impatient to get on with his questions.

'Mrs Thorpe, I wonder if you would tell me about the conversation you had with Mr Braithwaite yesterday concerning the Opinion Poll lady who had visited in the afternoon?'

She took some deep breaths, wiped her eyes with an embroidered handkerchief and gave him a brave smile.

'Well. I was at home in the afternoon yesterday, at around four o'clock, when the doorbell rang and I answered it. A woman was on the doorstep. She gave me her card and –'

'Do you still have the card?'

'I think so. But it will be downstairs.'

'Thank you. Do carry on.'

'So, she gave me her card and came in. We sat in the front living-room. I've been thinking about her a lot since last night, as you can imagine, Sergeant. And it occurred to me: once she was in the house, all the while she was asking me questions and writing down the answers on her forms, she kept her head down. It meant that I didn't see her face very much. Do you see?'

'I do. That's very helpful, Mrs Thorpe. It occurs to me that you're what we call an observant witness. But you must have seen her when she arrived and when she left?'

'Oh, yes.'

'Can you describe your first impressions of her for me?'

'Quite tall. Slim hips. Strange fingers, when she took her gloves off. A lot of make-up.'

'What was wrong with the fingers?'

'They were a funny shape. It's hard to describe.'

'Accent?'

'Well educated. A soothing voice. Like you hear on the wireless.'

'Did she ask questions about your possessions?'

'No, no.'

'Really?'

'No, nothing like that. There was nothing suspicious. She seemed to have a list, and she stuck to it. She asked how often I went on a bus, how many different ways I cooked potatoes, what I thought of Independent Television, did I know who Hughie Green was, and was I scared of the atomic bomb. Or perhaps it was, did I know what the atomic bomb was, and was I scared of ITV. Anyway, I really enjoyed it. She stayed about forty-five minutes and at the end of it offered me a ticket to the Hippodrome for last night, but I said I already had a ticket to see Mr Braithwaite's play, so she smiled and left and that was it.'

'Was she on her own in the room at any point?'

'I did go to ask Mrs Browning to make us some tea.'

'She's your daily?'

'Daily woman, yes.'

'And did the Opinion Poll lady possibly ask to visit the WC before she left?'

'Yes, she did. Is that how the murderer got in later? Through the window in the WC?'

'It's possible, yes.'

Mrs Thorpe reached for a handkerchief in her cardigan pocket and dabbed at her face. 'So if I hadn't let her –?'

'None of this is your fault, Mrs Thorpe.'

'I feel so stupid,' she said.

'You shouldn't. She's fooled countless people, this woman. But anyway, after she'd gone –'

'I've just remembered something,' she interrupted. 'I beg your pardon. But it was on the doorstep, as she was leaving. She said something odd.'

'Yes?'

'Well, as I said, she had a beautiful accent, but as we shook hands she said, with a smile, "Well, all this standing around jawing won't buy the baby a new bonnet, will it?" And I thought that was very strange, for a well-educated person.'

Brunswick didn't see why, but pretended to make a note. The important thing was how Braithwaite had reacted. 'So later you told Mr Braithwaite about it?'

'I did. I thought he'd be pleased for me, but he got all serious and said I should call the police! I told him he was being silly, but he said he'd been talking to his friend Bobby about this just a few hours before – about how when they were both in Leeds once, a landlady of his had been robbed on the very day an Opinion Poll lady had visited!'

'Who's Bobby?'

'Oh, I don't know. I think they went to drama school together. Bobby Melbourne, I think he said. No, Melba. Bobby Melba. Mr Braithwaite was looking forward to seeing him.'

'And you're sure it was Leeds?'

'Yes, I'm sure, because I said, "That's where the big City Varieties theatre is?" And he said yes. Anyway, I told him not to be silly, and not to vex himself about something that wasn't going to happen – which is why I was so cross when you told me he had left the theatre before the curtain just to check that my house was safe. If only he hadn't! If only I hadn't told him about that woman!'

'Now, I've told you already, you mustn't go blaming yourself, Mrs Thorpe,' said Brunswick, closing his notebook.

'I'm sorry,' she said, on the verge of tears. 'Mr Stephenson next door said he heard shouts and screams from in here! But if he did, why didn't he do something? Why didn't he try to intervene? I mean to say, someone could have been murdering *me*!'

'People generally think it's not their place to do anything, I'm afraid. But I must have a word with Mr Stephenson, thank you. Now, I won't be much longer, but do you think you're up to showing me Mr Braithwaite's room?'

Mrs Thorpe led him upstairs to the top floor, and stood in the narrow doorway as he opened the curtains (to views of seagulls adjusting their wings on a jumble of rooftops) and then poked about, searching through drawers and picking up framed pictures.

'Penny Cavendish?' He held up a studio portrait of Braithwaite's girlfriend.

'That's right. She's a lovely girl. She came here once to see him. They've been going out about six months, I think. She must be devastated.'

Flicking through Jack's diary, he discovered the entry for the day before, 'Bobby and Penny, Queen Adelaide, noon', and made a note.

'This Bobby Melba you mentioned downstairs,' he said. 'Any idea what he does for a living now? Presumably he's an actor, too? Or is he a writer now, like Mr Braithwaite?'

'I've no idea. I don't think Jack mentioned it.'

Brunswick noticed something else. Next to the diary was an old, faded programme for a drama school production of

Noel Coward's *The Vortex*, with a line of ten thin young student actors smiling at the camera in 1920s period costume, the caption including Jack's name, and also that of 'Robert Melba'.

Brunswick was puzzled. He held it out for Mrs Thorpe to see. 'Which one is Bobby here?' he asked. 'I can't work this out.'

'I'm afraid I haven't met him,' she said.

'Of course. I forgot.'

Brunswick took the picture to the window and laboriously counted along the figures in the photograph, assigning a name to each. Halfway along he was finally sure he had got to 'Robert Melba'. What had confused him initially was that, despite the presence of real females in the cast, the woman in the middle with the shiny bobbed hair and cupid's-bow lips and flapper-length dress was evidently played by a man.

Brunswick felt a thrill of excitement. 'Bobby Melba's dressed as a woman here!' he said. 'Look at this!'

'Well, a lot of actors do that, of course,' said Mrs Thorpe, regretfully. (She knew a thing or two about actors.) 'You wouldn't believe the number of times I've come home unexpectedly and found them wearing my frocks and jewellery.'

'Yes, but –'

'Big, hairy men, some of them. Decent shoes have been completely ruined!'

'Mrs Thorpe?' Brunswick said, beckoning her to the window. Excitedly, he pointed to the picture. 'Is there any way that the person in this photograph was the woman who called on you yesterday afternoon?'

She took the programme from him and held it up for more light.

'Yes, that's her,' she said, with surprise. 'You clever man. That's definitely her.'

Penny Cavendish had just received some startling news. She had been packing her things at her seafront hotel that morning when she'd learned from the Theatre Royal that, if she was willing, *A Shilling in the Meter* would resume its run tonight, in a show-must-go-on sort of spirit. Evidently the theatre itself was ready to reopen its doors.

True, the carpet and seats in the stalls would smell a bit of disinfectant, and there were some unsightly stains on the flock wallpaper that had proved resistant to repeated applications of Handy Andy, but if they took the dim bulbs out of the wall-lights along there, it would look all right. Basically, there was no reason – now that the events of last night had been dealt with by the authorities – not to get back down to business. Or there was no reason other than the potentially tender emotional state of the cast – all of whom had lost their director and writer, one of whom had spent the night in a cell, and one of whom was a beautiful young woman who was grieving for her boyfriend, victim of an unusually violent homicide.

It was the Theatre Royal's manager himself who had come to see her, which was an interesting concession on his part as he had always been very offhand with her up to now, being someone who openly hated Jack's work, and couldn't stand Jack, either. *A Shilling in the Meter* was the sort of dramatic offering he personally loathed. Once, while the play was in rehearsal, Penny happened to pass the box office, and overheard him advising a would-be ticket-buyer to save her money. 'Come back next week, Mrs Plumley,' he told her. 'We've got *The Desert Song.*'

But today the manager was singing a different tune. Last night's sensational events had led to an unprecedented rush for tickets – especially for Row D in the stalls, where Crystal had been sitting – and although he still couldn't bring himself to say anything nice about the play, he said that the rest of the cast were up for it, even Alec Forrester, and that *A Shilling in the Meter* might now be a huge theatrical success (instead of the failure it so obviously deserved to be). But it all depended on Penny. Would she agree to appear?

Penny wasn't sure. She had already been interviewed by Harry Jupiter that morning, and photographed for the press, which had been horrible. She felt raw and numb, and she felt angry with Jack, whom she irrationally held responsible for the whole thing. She wished he were alive just so that she could tell him how furious she was with him for being dead.

But mostly she felt that she had let him down by allowing herself to have feelings, so quickly, for his old friend Bobby. It was irrational to think this way, but she couldn't help it. If she had never met Bobby, Jack's death would somehow be easier to bear.

What she wanted right now was to run home to her parents in Wiltshire and sleep for a month. But what would Jack think of her if she ran away?

'Can I think about it?' she'd asked, but the manager said no, sorry, box-office staff were standing by, with cash drawers open in readiness.

All that mattered was whether Jack would have wanted it. *Would Jack have wanted the show to go on and be a success, even if it was a success for the wrong reasons?* Penny knew that the answer to this question was yes.

And so she had consented, and the manager had sped back to the Theatre Royal, literally rubbing his hands. There would be a rehearsal at 2.30, he called back over his shoulder as he left the room. And she could change anything she liked in the script, by the way: now that the cat was away, the mice could play. Alec Forrester was already working on making his Man from the Gas Board hail from Finland.

* * *

To Twitten's disappointment, there was no reply when he buzzed the communicating doorbell of Crystal's service-flat in Great Russell Street later that morning.

'Miss Sibert!' he called up from the street. 'It's Constable Twitten from the Brighton Constabulary!'

So he buzzed for the caretaker instead and was soon admitted to the rather wonderful (but curiously empty) flat, with its inspiring view of the blackened pillars of the British Museum's portico. He was pretty pleased with himself for taking the initiative of coming up by train in this way. However, if truth be told, it was a rare day when Twitten didn't feel pleased with himself.

But where was Miss Sibert? He looked round quickly. It wasn't a large flat: just one big room with floor-to-ceiling bookcases and two old desks, and a bedroom/dressing room to the side, with tiny bathroom beyond. No kitchen, of course, because with this sort of flat the meals were brought in. Briefly, he pictured Crystal and Miss Sibert seated at their respective desks, working on the great memoir. He also tried to picture them making their dangerous experiments with regression, down on the carpet on all fours, 'howling like wolves'. And now Crystal was dead, and Miss Sibert wasn't here (she'd left with two men, the caretaker said – which sounded ominous), and there was nothing here to help him with this Aldersgate Stick-up theory, after all. Just one thing was clear: someone really didn't want to be exposed for their part in that robbery of the Albion Bank all those years ago.

But why? As Twitten closed the door firmly against the rather nosy caretaker (who had tried to come in), he realised he was asking himself this question for the first time. What could the significance of the Aldersgate Stick-up possibly be? True, it had been a successful bank raid, but despite shots being fired, no one had been injured or killed. The public had not clamoured for justice. Inspector Steine had not been vilified – or even much criticised – for failing to solve it. In police circles, the job was always assumed to be the work of Terence Chambers. The present cover-up was so ruthless and well organised that it implied a large criminal network – which again pointed to Chambers himself.

But why would such a big cheese work so hard to keep secret the details of this relatively peaceful historic bank rob-bery? Chambers had allegedly done far worse things in his life than the Aldersgate Stick-up: he'd got away with torturing his rivals by electrocution and dismemberment; he'd once done something unspeakable to a pet proboscis monkey; and he was known to carve up the faces of his own gang members if they forgot his mother's birthday. A routine successful bank raid from seven years ago was hardly the thing to stop Terence Chambers from getting to sleep at night.

Twitten decided he would ponder this matter properly later – assuming he made it alive out of Bloomsbury. But he wasn't leaving his survival entirely to chance. On the way to the flat, he had cleverly purchased two brown canvas hold-alls from a shop on Shaftesbury Avenue. Into one of these bags he now stuffed every scrap of paper from Crystal's desk, including telephone pads, typed theatre reviews and bulging notebooks. Then he tackled what was clearly Miss Sibert's desk (it had a silk scarf tragically draped over the back of the button-backed swivel chair).

Sadly, there was no trace of the autobiographical manuscript in any of the drawers; no trace of the carbon copy this secretary had so efficiently made. But Twitten refused to be downhearted: he just took everything remaining, including her battered volumes of Sigmund Freud's works in German, and (an inspiration) all the used carbon paper in her desk.

It was while he was doing this that he glanced out of the window and saw that amid the throng of excited antiquity enthusiasts heading towards the gates of the British Museum, two men in raincoats and hats across the street were standing worryingly still, smoking cigarettes and taking turns to glance up at the building.

He darted back out of sight and then carefully looked again. They might be police, in which case he was probably safe (although who knew how far the conspiracy reached?); on the other hand, they might be villains planning to come in; or villains waiting for him to come out.

Again, he was not unprepared for this eventuality. Opening the other bag, he quickly put his helmet in it, and began to undress. The main thing was not to be wearing the boots, of course – any criminal could spot a policeman's footwear a mile off. Heavy as they were, he placed his boots in the second bag along with his uniform. In the tiny dressing room, Crystal's closets contained more than enough outfits for him to choose from, but for obvious reasons, putting them on was not going to be easy. Just opening the closet had brought on another attack of breathlessness. But after some diligent searching, accompanied by deep breathing, Twitten found items that appeared to have just come back from the laundry, on which the taint was less vile. He also found some shoes that were only a tad too small, and finally a hat and coat.

The whole outfit, when complete, made him look like an unkempt travelling salesman – which was perfect, since he would be carrying the two bags. Dressing with speed, he tried not to admit he was frightened (and a bit nauseated), but he noticed, when he finally closed up the bags, that his hands were shaking.

Looking again out of the window, he was at first alarmed: the men had gone! Were they already on their way up the stairs? But then he saw they had moved to a telephone box on the corner of Montague Place. This was his chance. He took one last glance round Crystal's study, and opened the door.

'Who are you?' said the caretaker, who'd been waiting outside. Twitten jumped in the air.

'Here, what are you wearing? What's going on?'

Twitten grasped the man's arm. 'Don't let anyone else in,' he instructed. 'Once I'm out of the building, you must call the police and ask for protection.'

'I thought you were the police.'

'I am,' said Twitten firmly. 'But I'm just one man and I can't do everything.'

* * *

Back at the Palace Pier, Inspector Steine was feeling a bit dazed. Holidaymakers pushed past him to board the ghost train; someone dropped an ice cream cone on his foot; a child stumbled into him and wiped candyfloss on the knee of his trousers. All this he failed to notice. A piercing hoot meant the train was trundling off again. At this baleful sound, he actually placed his hands over his ears.

'You all right, dear?' said a friendly voice (muffled). 'You look like you've seen a ghost!'

He took his hands away again, and focused on the person speaking; he was surprised to see it was Mrs Groynes. Or was it? She looked different without the usual comforting ensemble of overall, turban, thick stockings, tin of Vim and plate of fancy biscuits. Regrettably, she looked less motherly.

'Mrs Groynes? Oh my God. Am I… dead?'

'I don't think so, dear,' she laughed. But then she saw how stricken he looked. 'Sorry, Inspector. Ghost train too much for you, was it?'

He smiled weakly. 'You could say that.'

'Well,' she said, giving him an encouraging pat on the elbow, 'all this standing around jawing won't call a halt to the unfortunate myxomatosis epidemic, now, will it? Forget that silly old ghost train. I was looking for Mr Jupiter. Is he here?'

'I'm sorry?'

'That Mr Jupiter from the newspaper, dear. Little bloke shaped like a ball. Is he here? They sent me out to look for him. He's wanted by his office in London and there wasn't anyone else to come: the sergeant's out getting statements and that new young constable of yours seems to have disappeared off the face of the Earth!'

Steine chewed his lip. 'I think there's been an accident,' he said.

'What do you mean? What sort of accident? To the young constable? Oh, I do hope not.'

'No. To Mr Jupiter. Quite a serious sort of accident.'

Mrs Groynes laughed and looked round. 'I'm sure there hasn't, dear. You're imagining things. Now, where is he?'

But then, from the beach came shrieks – not the general happy shrieks that one tends to hear every day at a popular British seaside resort; the sort that come when freezing cold water slaps suddenly against sun-warmed human flesh in the sensitive top-of-the-inside-leg area; no, these were more the incredulous and horrified shrieks of people on a pebbly beach noticing a fully dressed, unconscious male body with a head injury bobbing on the waves in the shadow of a famous south-coast recreational pier.

Mrs Groynes ran to the railings and looked down. Steine followed.

'There's someone down there,' she reported. 'Oh, my good gawd, is it Mr Jupiter?' She looked at Steine, confused. 'Did he fall in?'

Steine said nothing. He still wasn't entirely sure what had occurred on the ghost train. He remembered horrible laughter, and the suffocating pressure of hands round his throat. All he knew was that he had acted in self-defence.

'People are swimming out to reach him, dear,' said Mrs Groynes. 'Look, dear. Wading, then swimming. There's a lot of splashing, anyway. But *is* it Mr Jupiter, dear? I hardly met him. Look, dear. Is it him? He does float well, I'll give him that.'

But Steine did not look. While public-spirited members of the public struck out to reach the poor man in the water below, and then started to pull his body back to shore – and while St John's Ambulance men scuttled down the shingle with a stretcher – Steine determinedly looked the other way. What if Harry Jupiter turned out to be dead? This was an intolerable situation. None of this was his fault! He had done nothing. But should he give himself up? Should he at least come clean to Mrs Groynes?

'What happened?' she said.

Steine shrugged. 'I'm not sure. I don't know.'

'Did he jump?'

'No. No, he didn't jump.'

'Did he fall?'

Steine hesitated. Technically speaking, Jupiter had definitely fallen. Otherwise he wouldn't be in the water.

'Did you push him, dear?'

'I don't know.'

'You pushed him!'

'I said, I don't know. We were on that ghost train thing, and it was dark and noisy, and he suddenly attacked me. And then – he was gone.'

By now the body had reached the shore and was being lifted onto the stretcher on the beach.

'Look, there's an ambulance coming,' Mrs Groynes reported. 'It's nearly over, dear. What you need is a nice cup of tea.'

She wasn't wrong there. Inspector Steine had never wanted a nice cup of tea more in his life. What if the man was dead?

'They've got him safe,' she said. 'Someone's giving him mouth-to-mouth resuscitation!'

And then she let out a little scream – which was echoed in a collective cry of alarm from the people on the beach.

'What happened?' said Steine, finally forcing himself to look landward towards the centre of the commotion, where, on the stretcher, the distant figure of Harry Jupiter was suddenly sitting up, pale as a ghost, and pointing an accusing finger in the direction of the pier.

* * *

Penny Cavendish had just finished her unpacking when there was a knock on the door (which was still open) and Sergeant Brunswick entered with his notebook, asking if she could answer some questions. He had come via interviewing Mr Stephenson – the nosy neighbour up in Clifton Hill – who had been able to provide not only the time of the fracas in

Mrs Thorpe's house, but a description of a figure who had fled the scene.

Brunswick felt that the identity of Jack Braithwaite's murderer was inexorably emerging. This was honestly one of the most exciting and fulfilling days he had experienced since the unfortunate cessation of global hostilities in 1945 had brought an end to his jumping out of planes.

'Going somewhere, Miss Cavendish?' he said, not unpleasantly, indicating the open suitcase. Penny explained what had happened; how she had hoped to go home, but that the play would go on, in response to the ghoulish demand for tickets. She looked broken, Brunswick thought. It was terrible that something like this should happen to a woman so young and lovely.

She invited him to sit on the only armchair in the room, while taking her own place at the dressing-table. She swallowed, and briefly closed her eyes. 'Is this about Jack?' she said, bravely.

'Yes. Well, it's more about a friend of Mr Braithwaite's, actually. A man named –' (and here he consulted his notebook) '– Bobby Melba?'

Penny was alarmed; her immediate thought was that she didn't want Bobby to be dragged into this. He had been so kind to her last night. She also didn't want to admit she had spent the night in his digs. She knew how it would look.

The sergeant smiled at her reassuringly. 'It's probably nothing. Just doing my job.'

'Of course,' she said, as if reassured (she wasn't). 'Look, do you mind if I do my hair while we're talking? I've suddenly got quite a lot to do. I have to make my way to the theatre as soon as possible.'

Brunswick said he didn't mind at all, so she turned to her mirror, and for a moment he was slightly overwhelmed. It turned out that Penny was as beautiful from the back as she was from the front.

'So. This friend of Jack's?' she prompted.

'Ah, yes. I'm interested in someone called Bobby Melba, and I believe you met him yesterday morning.'

Penny took a steadying breath and then answered, as offhandedly as she could, 'Bobby? Yes, I did meet someone called Bobby yesterday.'

'That's excellent.'

'He's an old friend of Jack's. They were at drama school together.'

'That's right. They were. Did he happen to mention what he does for a living nowadays? Is he still an actor, for example?'

Penny hesitated for a moment. 'Is he under suspicion for something? I do hope not.'

'Well, I'd like to ask him some questions, let's put it like that. He was definitely one of the last people to see Jack Braithwaite alive. So, *did* he say what he does for a living, miss?'

She turned to face him, adopting what she hoped was a guileless expression, and pretended to search her memory. 'No, I don't think so,' she said, carefully. 'I think the subject just didn't come up. We talked mainly about Jack, you see. Jack was like that. He tended to dominate proceedings and he had a lot on his mind. But Bobby seemed awfully nice.'

Brunswick smiled. 'I see,' he said, making a note. It was obvious she was lying. She was terrible at it.

'Is this Bobby staying down here in Brighton, do you know? In a hotel or some such? Does he live here, perhaps? Or was he down for the day?'

'Oh. Down for the day, I think,' she said, quickly – glad of being handed a convenient lie to use. 'Yes. 'Yes, he definitely mentioned he was down for the day.'

'Well, that's very helpful, miss. Thank you. Just one last thing: did he and Mr Braithwaite talk about being together in Leeds at some point?'

Penny could see no harm in admitting to that. She brightened. 'Yes, they did. How did you know that?'

'Can you remember what in particular they talked about?'

'Yes. It was quite strange. Jack mentioned a landlady there who'd experienced a robbery at the same time Bobby was in Leeds too – although what Bobby was doing there, er, I don't remember, but it was something else, somewhere else, not in the play with Jack.'

She realised she wasn't lying very convincingly, but didn't know how to set it right. 'What I'm saying, you see, is that Jack was acting in a play there, but Bobby wasn't. It was a play called *Clogs on the Batty Stones*. It never came to anything because Mr Crystal destroyed it in the paper. That was why Jack first hated him – for attacking that play. Apparently the man who wrote it is working in an ice cream parlour on the seafront here. Bobby told Jack that yesterday. His name's Harry Something.'

Penny stopped. She realised she was trying too hard. 'Sorry, I'm prattling on, aren't I? Jack would have said, "You never know when to belt up, you silly bitch!"'

'Really?' Brunswick was surprised. 'And you'd have let him?'

'Oh, he didn't mean it. It was just his way.'

Brunswick stood up. He was aware she was on the brink of tears.

'Miss Cavendish, I know this must be very hard for you. I was there last night at the scene, and I promise I'll do all I can to bring the person who did this to justice.'

'Thank you,' said Penny, her eyes brimming with tears. 'I keep thinking of it myself, the furniture all overturned, the curtains torn... Blood on the fireplace!'

'Exactly,' said Brunswick, then paused. 'Hang on, how do you know about the blood on the fireplace?'

'Oh.' She pretended to think about it. Bobby had mentioned the state of Mrs Thorpe's living-room when they'd met last night. 'The manager of the Theatre Royal must have told me, just now.'

'Must he?' Brunswick said. But the answer seemed to satisfy him. He merely added, in a bemused tone, 'Well, I wonder how he came to know about it.'

Brunswick pocketed his notebook and extended his hand.

'Miss Cavendish, that's all very helpful, and it's been a pleasure to meet you, and I wish it could have been in more pleasant circumstances. I also wish you a great success with the play tonight.'

'That's very kind. Thank you.'

He hesitated, then said, in a rush, 'I expect this isn't the right time to mention it, but I saw you a couple of years ago in a production of Lillian Hellman's *The Children's Hour*.'

'Really?'

'And you were wonderful – flaming wonderful.'

'You remember me in that? It wasn't a big part.'

'No, but you really caught my eye. I think you'll be a great star one day. In fact, I'm sure you will.'

'Oh.' Penny didn't know what to say. Brunswick felt awkward, too.

'And if you happen to see Mr Melba –'

'Oh, but I won't. I'm sure. He was just down for the day, as I said.'

She felt bad about lying to the nice policeman, especially now that she knew he was a fan. But it was too late to change her story. She turned her head away.

'Well, as I say, if you do see him –' repeated Brunswick, but then he stopped dead. He seemed to have noticed something about her appearance, but what?

'Is there something wrong, Sergeant Brunswick?'

'That's a very lovely hair-thing you've got there,' he said. 'Can I take a look?'

She was relieved. 'Of course,' she said, carelessly. She took it out of her hair. 'Here it is. I picked it up this morning.'

But she instantly regretted saying this, when she saw how Brunswick was studying it.

'Picked it up?' he queried, still smiling, with the Victorian emerald-and-diamond-studded hair-comb in his hands – a piece whose photograph had been circulated to all the pawn-brokers in Brighton two weeks ago after its theft from a wealthy colonial widow in Hove.

Penny looked scared. 'Yes. Why do you ask?'

'No reason, miss,' he said, handing it back to her. 'But that's a real find, if you ask me. Don't wear it out in daylight, whatever you do. There are some desperate people about.'

Brunswick left Penny's hotel sensationally happy with his progress. He still didn't know how to find Bobby Melba, but two hours ago he had never heard of him, and now he knew three significant things about him: that he had been posing, cross-dressed, as an Opinion Poll lady; that he was definitely resident in Brighton; and that he had stupidly given priceless stolen jewellery to the grieving girlfriend of Jack Braithwaite. On top of which, it was possible that Bobby Melba had actually described the murder scene to her as well, because someone had.

Back at the station, Brunswick would see whether foren-sics had come up with anything, then he would telephone the constabulary in Leeds and find out what else had been happening there (specifically, in the world of entertainment) in the precise week last summer when *Clogs on the Batty Stones* was playing. Meanwhile, he would need to find someone to tail Penny Cavendish, who was clearly protecting Bobby Melba, for reasons unknown. Brunswick felt he was walking on air. He was solving a murder! It was his first proper case in years! He had told Penny Cavendish that she was good in *The Children's Hour*! And to top it all, the great Harry Jupiter was on hand to write in the *Clarion* about how brilliant a detective he was!

Eight

Constable Twitten alighted from a taxi in Aldersgate, carrying his two canvas holdalls, and entered the Albion Bank at a brisk pace. If there was one place he could hide safely until the coast was clear, surely it was here. He felt scared, but confident. Crystal's hat might be too large for his head; Crystal's shoes might be too small for his feet; but what fitted him perfectly right now was the task ahead: of mentally unpicking the events of yesterday and identifying Crystal's murderer. (We won't mention the clothes, because of the latent smell, which was beginning to revive in response to Twitten's body warmth.)

Within his bag of evidence – which included not only the scraps from Crystal's flat but also the play-text of *A Shilling in the Meter*, the original file on the Aldersgate Stick-up (commandeered from the inspector's desk) and his own personal typed-up notes – was surely contained the answer to who had shot Crystal and why. Was it a stroke of absolute genius to return to the very place where the stick-up had occurred? Twitten rather thought it was. What unfortunately hadn't occurred to him was that the Albion Bank in Aldersgate might still employ people who'd been in some way complicit in the Stick-up. This was an error he would later have cause to regret.

On his arrival, Twitten asked for the manager, and there was a brief period of confusion because he wasn't in uniform; then he was ushered through to the office of Mr Arnott, who was expecting him. Coming here had not been a spur-of-the-moment decision. Twitten had conceived his plan while at Crystal's flat, and had telephoned ahead, explaining to Mr Arnott that he was from the Brighton Constabulary, pursuing new leads in the Aldersgate Stick-up case, consequent to last night's shocking cold-blooded murder of Mr Crystal in Brighton.

Arnott had absorbed this information and offered whatever help he could give. And now they sat opposite each other in Arnott's office – a dark room reeking of pipe tobacco and brass polish, with a loudly ticking clock. Beyond the solid oak door could be heard muffled voices and the odd tinkle of female laughter; also distant footsteps on the tiled floor of the echoing banking hall. Twitten was quite excited. So this was where it had all happened! Where persons unknown had produced firearms seven years ago and got away with £25,000!

Taking his seat, he dispensed with preamble and flipped open his notebook. 'Can I ask you what you remember about the Stick-up, Mr Arnott? Were you the manager then?'

Arnott sucked his pipe, which was unlit. He seemed nervous. 'No, I was the deputy undermanager. Mr Crystal was my superior. It will all be in your files. I was sorry to hear what happened to poor Mr Crystal last night. You surely don't think it was connected with the bank robbery? That was so long ago.'

'It's just one line of enquiry,' admitted Twitten, truthfully. 'Mr Crystal had quite a large number of enemies. He was a terribly unpopular figure. Was he always so hateful, I wonder?'

'Oh, yes. Well, we all loathed him here, I must say. The chief cashier, old Mr Lyons, didn't mind him so much, but of course he'd lost his sense of smell at Passchendaele.'

Arnott's nose twitched. 'You'll find this odd, Constable,' he said, 'but ever since you came in today, I've been oddly aware of Mr Crystal again. A kind of presence. It's like he's *in the room.*'

Twitten fidgeted on his chair. 'Very warm today,' he said.

'Perhaps you'd like to remove your hat and coat?'

'Oh, thank you,' said Twitten, jumping up. He felt foolish. But having hung the hat on a convenient hat-stand, he thought better of taking the coat off, and stopped. 'Perhaps later,' he said, sitting down again. And then, quickly, 'But you were telling me about the robbery.'

'I'm afraid I can only tell you what I told the police on the day, Constable. There were two of them, dressed in everyday clothes; it was a quarter to twelve. No one took much notice of them, as they appeared to be just ordinary customers, huddled together with their heads down in the corner. Suddenly they turned, and they had masks over their faces, and had produced guns.'

'And one was a woman.'

'Yes. I can't remember whether I knew that at the time, or found out afterwards…'

His dot-dot-dot was audible, as his expression and voice became oddly wistful. It was as if he were narrating a flashback in a film.

'It had been a fine morning, constable. I do remember that, for some reason. We had all the top windows open.

The banking hall was full of dappled light on account of the ancient plane trees outside. I wouldn't say we were less than vigilant that day; I would never say such a thing. But I must confess there was no reason to expect criminal interest. On the seventeenth of the month, you see, we generally handled a large sum of cash from a particular diamond merchant in Hatton Garden; this made us a target, we knew. But the Stick-up occurred on the sixteenth, as you know.'

'That's right. And it's very interesting. That the robbery took place on the *wrong day*.'

Arnott laughed. 'Mr Crystal actually informed them they were robbing the bank on the wrong day, did you know that?'

'Yes, it's in the file.'

'*You should have come tomorrow*, he told them. That's the kind of person he was, I'm afraid. Very critical. Quite obnoxious. Even when tied to a chair with a bag over his head. But he paid for it later, of course. He had a breakdown a few months after, you know, poor man, and then he had to give up banking altogether.'

Arnott made it sound as if having to give up banking altogether was the most devastating thing that could happen to anyone.

'Can you give me any description of the robbers?'

Mr Arnott shrugged. 'I really didn't see them. I was on the floor from the minute they told us to get down. Crystal was the one who bandied words with them.'

'Would anyone else here remember anything new?'

'I don't think so. But if anyone *had* remembered any detail after all this time, they would have told Mr Crystal himself – the other day, you know – and they didn't.'

Twitten was puzzled. 'I don't understand,' he said. 'What do you mean, *the other day*? Did Mr Crystal visit the bank?'

'Oh, yes. He was here quite recently. I assumed you knew.'

'When did he come?'

'About two weeks ago. It was very upsetting for all of us – raking it up again. He interviewed both myself and Miss Hutchinson – she's my secretary – wanting us to recall details about the day of the robbery. And I'm afraid he was very disappointed, almost angry, that we couldn't help him.'

'Angry?'

'He seemed a bit desperate.'

'Gosh, I wonder why.' Twitten made a note. 'Was he alone?'

'No, he came with a bossy German woman. She said she was his "assistant" – "helping him" to write a book – but between you and me, I could clearly see that she was the person driving things, not him.'

'Really?' said Twitten, looking up. 'What an interesting remark, Mr Arnott. What makes you say that? Are you sure you're not just being anti-German? Or even anti-lady?' (Twitten knew that Miss Sibert was actually Austrian, but decided to let it pass.)

Mr Arnott bristled. He didn't appreciate being called anti-anything. 'What makes me say that she was driving things is that she kept shouting at him.'

'Shouting?'

'Yes.'

'Why?'

'Oh, it was horrible. They were engaged in some sort of psycho-nonsense exercise, and Miss Hutchinson and I were very uncomfortable, being forced to witness it. "*Bring it beck!* [He pronounced 'back' with the German accent.] *Bring it beck, Algernon! It iss vital that you bring it beck!*" At one point the poor man was rolling on the floor of the banking hall with tears streaming down his cheeks. Thank goodness we did all this after closing time.'

'And what did he *bring back*?'

'Ah, that's the thing. He didn't. Nothing came. And you'd think she would be sympathetic, but she wasn't. She seemed furious.'

Twitten felt inspired. It was time to get thinking. 'Mr Arnott, that's all very helpful. Is there somewhere private I can sit for an hour or two?' The clock on the wall said 1 p.m.

Arnott stood up. 'You can use this office if you like. I have an appointment at the Holborn branch. I'll tell everyone not to disturb you. We close at three.'

'That's marvellous, thank you. I'll take off these shoes, if you don't mind. They're killing me.'

'As you please,' said Arnott. At the door he paused and looked round. 'I just can't get over the sense that he's *here*, Constable,' he said, shaking his head. 'But I can't quite put my finger on it.'

* * *

Penny needed to be at rehearsals, but she also needed to talk to Bobby. As soon as the sergeant was out of sight, she slipped out of the hotel by the back entrance and made her way to the Hippodrome. It was her only chance of seeing him before the evening.

'Bobby!' she said, bursting into his dressing room – and was embarrassed to find he wasn't alone. He had evidently been in the middle of a serious conversation with a woman – a woman who was quite a bit older than he was, and very smartly dressed with just the slightest scent of *eau de cologne* to her. They both reacted guiltily to Penny's arrival.

'I'm so sorry,' said Penny, backing out of the room. 'I'll go.'

'No,' said the other woman, smiling. 'I have to run.' She gave Bobby a significant look, and said, 'Tomorrow night then?'

'Tomorrow night,' he agreed. 'All fixed.'

And then the woman quickly tiptoed out of the room, closing the door behind her, and Penny stood alone in the room with Bobby. She was very confused. Should she run into his arms, or should she slap his face? She stayed where she was.

'Bobby, the police came,' she said. 'They weren't asking about Jack, they were asking about you!'

She had hoped he would be innocently surprised. But he wasn't. Bobby put his hands to his face and sank down on a chair. 'Oh, no,' he groaned. Then, carefully: 'What did you tell them?'

'Bobby, did you kill Jack?'

'No!'

'Oh, but you did! You did!'

'No! Penny, no. I swear.'

'What about this comb?' She tore it out of her hair. 'I could tell when he saw it. It's stolen, isn't it?'

Bobby took a deep breath. 'Yes,' he said.

She looked like she might cry. 'I hate this. I can't believe it's happening! I panicked and lied, Bobby. I lied to the police. When he asked me about the comb I said I'd "picked it up" in Brighton and he shot me such a look of disbelief, it made me feel like a thief myself. Bobby, what have you done?'

He gave her a steady look. 'I've never met anyone like you before, Penny. I want to tell you everything, I *ought* to tell you everything, but I can't.'

'Just tell me. Please. Are you a *thief*, Bobby?'

Her eyes filled with tears.

'Yes, I am. I'm a thief. I'm sorry.'

'*Did you kill Jack?*'

'No!' He grabbed her hand. 'No. No, I didn't. I wouldn't. I've never hurt anyone.'

Penny broke down in sobs. 'I don't believe you. You told me about the furniture and the curtains in the room where he was killed! How do you know about that if you weren't there?'

Bobby took a deep breath. 'Because I *was* there, Penny.'

'No!'

'I'd gone there to rob the place and Jack confronted me, and then –'

'And then what?'

'Oh, Penny. You've got to believe me. All I did with Jack was have a glass of sherry!'

* * *

At three o'clock that afternoon, the persons of interest in this story were all individually occupied in such interesting ways that an overview of what they were all doing simply cries out for description, preferably in the dramatic present tense.

For example, by 3 p.m. Penny Cavendish is rehearsing Act One of *A Shilling in the Meter* at the Theatre Royal, and bringing a previously unseen gravity to the part of Ruby. Her acting seems to have acquired a new dimension. The weight of her arm in its sling is perceptibly heavier; her innocent love for the loathsome Nick is profoundly touching.

The rest of the cast naturally put this development down to her shock and grief over the death of Jack, but they don't know the half of it. She is also wrestling with the knowledge that Bobby – to whom she's been drawn like a magnet from the moment she met him – is a professional transvestite burglar who hints that he perhaps might have prevented the violent death of her boyfriend, but adamantly refuses to explain why or how he didn't.

Meanwhile Alec's strange Finnish accent as Man from the Gas Board has brought real interest (and mystery) to the part, and the two mousy actors playing Nick's parents are thoroughly energised in their roles (it turns out they just couldn't stand working with Jack Braithwaite).

At the Hippodrome in Middle Street, in preparation for a matinée, Bobby Melba is applying his make-up with a shaking hand – praying that he has not done the wrong thing by confessing his crimes to Penny. He has just taken every item of stolen loot – including the precious comb – to Harry the Head, the pawnbroker in the Lanes whose prominent organ of Philoprogenitiveness (love of children) can't help but draw Bobby's professional interest every time he meets him. Bulging out of the back of his head, it's the size and shape of a small coconut (but obviously less hairy).

Disappointingly, Harry has given Bobby less than half the money he had expected, but in the circumstances he's just glad to be shot of everything. Bobby's mind runs to Penny constantly, to the look of fear and revulsion on her face when she asked, '*Did you kill Jack?*' – and the scene of the killing runs through his mind over and over again. That sword slicing into the flesh of a human being. The blood everywhere. His own screams of horror. But he also thinks deeply about tomorrow night, because tomorrow night needs an enormous amount of thinking about.

In the Royal Sussex County hospital, Harry Jupiter of the *Clarion* is loudly demanding to be discharged, but the doctors are refusing to let him go until he can at least remember his own name. He keeps reciting short, verbless declamatory sentences, such as: 'Night! Moonlight on dentures! A half-set of helmets! Great men, great men!' Rather shockingly, Inspector Steine has not come forward with information about how Harry Jupiter happened to fall in the sea.

Instead, he is in London, in a musty studio at Broadcasting House, delivering his hastily rewritten weekly talk. He is in his element. Having telephoned the hospital anonymously and enquired after the man recovered from the waves, he has been immensely encouraged to learn of the poor chap's amnesia, which surely (for the time being, anyway) puts him in the clear.

The talk goes down well with his dandruffy producer, who afterwards particularly remarks on all the bits put in on Twitten's recommendation. 'More rigorous this week, Geoffrey,' says the producer, pointing a pencil at him. 'I like this new-found rigour.'

On the breezy seafront in Brighton, Maisie sells a red-and-green beach ball to a small child. She is sucking a multi-coloured gobstopper, and finds herself wishing she had a handsome, tall, slavish admirer to monitor the ever-changing unearthly hues of her tongue.

On the shingle, a few yards away, the Punch & Judy show is in full horrific flow, with children running screaming to their parents. There is so much violent energy to Vince's puppet performance today that the booth itself jumps about and threatens to topple over.

'*I bash your head in, Judy ratface brass!*' The breeze blasts Maisie's downy cheek; plastic bunting rattles above her head like distant machine-gunfire; she bares her buck teeth to the bold afternoon sun; she ponders what she has lost.

At the police station in Brighton, Sergeant Brunswick waits for a call from the Leeds City Police and wonders where everyone else has got to. He's been looking forward to sharing his discoveries about new prime suspect Bobby Melba, but has found the place unusually empty. The inspector is, of course, in London, which is customary on recording day. But where is Twitten? Where is Mrs Groynes? Where is Harry Jupiter? And most important, what has happened to all the coconut ice?

In the Queen Adelaide public house in Ship Street, newly unemployed young reporter Ben Oliver is scanning the Situations Vacant in the newspaper, while in another corner a woman with abnormally thick wrists nurses a port and lemon. A waiter with a dodgy French accent asks her if she'd like another. He also asks if she would (*'sea-view play'*) please stop breaking the glasses by gripping them so tightly. Ben Oliver, trying not to appear interested, secretly makes a note.

In the forensics lab at the police station, fingerprint analysis on Mrs Thorpe's sherry glasses finds a set of prints from the deceased, and a set from a person unknown. The unknown prints do not match those on the murder weapon, which suggests a third individual at the scene.

And finally, in the manager's office at the Albion Bank in Aldersgate, Constable Twitten yawns and stretches, emerging from one of the most satisfactory but exhausting mental workouts he has ever attempted. Some of it has required real physical activity – impatiently riffling through papers and shouting, 'Yes, yes! It all fits!' And some of it has required him to lie back in his chair, staring at the ceiling in strenuous contemplation.

It has been an exemplary performance of muscular mental endeavour. He has cast aside lazy assumptions; interrogated evidence; skewered unhelpful prejudices; and dared to think the unthinkable. He can now proudly say he has worked out who killed A. S. Crystal at the Theatre Royal last night, and why. It is time to go back to Brighton, change into his uniform, create a small ceremonial bonfire out of Crystal's rancid clothes and make his astonishing report.

It is only as he tries to put the shoes back on that he realises the bank is now very quiet and that he hasn't seen anyone for more than two hours. Well, he must summon Mr Arnott and thank him for his wonderful co-operation! But when he tries the door, it doesn't open.

'Hello?' he calls. 'Mr Arnott? Hello!'

He rattles the handle again, and looks round the room. There are no other exits.

He puts his ear to the door, and hears a muffled conversation which fills him with alarm. Can he also smell *eau de cologne*?

Oh, no. The door is unlocked and he braces himself. A waft of 4711 assails him.

'Now, there you are, dear,' says Mrs Groynes, entering with a rattling tray covered with cups and saucers, a little plate of biscuits, and a gun. 'I thought I'd find you in here. How about a nice cup of tea?'

* * *

It was Mr Arnott who had called her. Just as he had called her when A. S. Crystal had turned up at the bank two weeks before with his so-called assistant.

'I know it was you, Mrs Groynes,' said Twitten now, brazenly. 'I know it was you who killed Crystal. I worked it out.'

She didn't seem to mind. 'Good for you, dear,' she said, taking the gun from the tray and placing it on the desk. 'I rather guessed you would.' She smiled. 'You look a lot less impressive out of uniform, dear.'

They sat across the desk from each other. She rested her chin on her hands, expectantly. Had female bank managers been a remote possibility in 1957, the scene might have been Twitten asking nervously for a loan to start a bookshop. Instead of which he was a newish policeman in a dead man's clothes, who had deduced from scrappy evidence that the woman opposite, who had masqueraded brilliantly as a charlady in a police station for several years, was a hardened criminal who didn't stop short of murder.

'But to be honest,' Twitten admitted, 'I hadn't yet worked out what I was going to do after telling you that I had worked out it was you.'

'I appreciate your honesty, dear,' she said, and sipped her cup of tea.

Twitten drew a steadying breath. 'Look, it would help if I knew,' he said. 'Are you planning to kill me?'

'I don't know yet. I'm deciding.'

'Oh, good,' he squeaked, and then coughed to get his voice back to normal. 'Oh, good. So, when you've decided, will you let me know?'

'Oh, you'll know, dear. Don't worry.'

Twitten bit his lip. He felt he was blushing; he couldn't control it. 'May I tell you how I worked it out, Mrs Groynes?'

'If you like.'

'There might be a few holes.'

Holding the gun, Mrs Groynes leaned back in her seat, gesturing for him to go ahead regardless of the few holes.

'Thank you.' Twitten took a deep breath, as if to start a recital. 'Now, I'm sure you won't believe this, but I think I suspected you from the very start.'

She shook her head. 'No, you bleeding didn't!'

'I mean, not consciously, of course. But there were some little things that did catch my attention. For example, you were so keen to tell the others about my qualifications from Hendon – which personally I would never have mentioned. You had somehow wheedled them out of me. *He won a prize for forensic observation*, you said. *He came top of his year*. These were matters that would of course mean nothing to Inspector Steine; you mentioned them, you see, only because they meant something to *you*. It's a classic psychological "tell", Mrs Groynes. A real charlady wouldn't have taken any interest in my academic achievements, do you see?'

Mrs Groynes narrowed her eyes. 'Go on, dear.'

'Well, then of course it was bizarre that you were present at the Theatre Royal for the first performance of a controversial modern play, wasn't it? And that you then volunteered to look after me in the ambulance – but that was because you wanted to know what I had found out from Mr Crystal.'

'I was very nice to you, as I recall. Very kind and motherly.'

'Yes, you were. That's true. Perhaps I didn't suspect you then, actually. I started to think of you as a friend. But the main thing was that you tried to talk me out of exploring the Aldersgate Stick-up angle once I'd lost the list – and of course it was no coincidence that once you knew I had Mr Crystal's list, it was snatched from my hand by a boy on a bike at midnight. And once you knew I wanted to read Mr Crystal's memoir, it was stolen from his flat, and now poor Miss Sibert has disappeared too!'

Mrs Groynes tried to interrupt, but he pressed on.

'Also, when we spoke of Mr Crystal, you made the telling remark, "He had a lot of enemies, that Crystal. You'd never guess, to look at him" – a remark to which I will return. But if I may say so, it's all part of a much more interesting broader picture, you see; a broader picture which is even more –' He stopped. Unfortunately, he couldn't think of a better word. 'Which is even more *interesting*.'

'Is it, dear? Do tell.'

'Oh, yes. You see, ever since the Middle Street Massacre, there have been so-called "nebulous" forces running crime in Brighton. Sergeant Brunswick speculated that since the original Italian and Casino Gangs had so stupidly wiped each other out, the famous Terence Chambers must somehow be doing it from London – "through an unknown deputy", the sergeant said. Of course, Inspector Steine denies that *anyone* is running crime in Brighton, but that's because he holds a sadly irresponsible attitude, so his perspective can be set aside for the purposes of this argument as largely immaterial.'

Twitten took a breath. That last sentence had been rather beautifully put together, given the immense pressure he was under, so he wanted to leave it hanging there. He also wanted to pause before his big finish.

'It's my belief,' he announced, proudly, 'that the person who's been in charge of all things criminal in Brighton since 1951 is in fact you, Mrs Groynes.'

Mrs Groynes put her head on one side. 'Me?'

'Yes! Bally well, yes! And you have been operating from the very heart of the police station, where bally well no one takes any notice of you!'

'I thought Terence Chambers was supposed to be behind everything, dear. Am I working for him, then?'

'No. Not at all!'

'No?'

'That's all part of how clever you've been. Letting people think Terence Chambers is behind everything. I put it to you that you are *not* working for Terence Chambers; but that you used to be in cahoots with him. My suspicion is that you were at one time very close. But then – and here I haven't got a lot of hard evidence to go on, but I think this makes sense – in 1950, when Chambers was planning to rob the Albion Bank in Aldersgate – this very bank – on the *seventeenth of the month*, when large sums of cash would have been in the safe, it is my belief that for reasons unknown you led your own small gang here the day before, thus scuppering his plans and earning his everlasting enmity!'

'You've got nothing to back this up, have you, dear?'

'Not really, no. But please don't interrupt, Mrs Groynes, because I've only just worked this out, and if I lose the flow I'll have to go back to the bally beginning. Now, I was talking about earning Terence Chambers' everlasting enmity. So, the thing is, earning Terence Chambers' ever lasting enmity is such a terrible thing, Mrs Groynes, that no sane person would do it without a very good reason, and for the moment I have to admit that I don't know what your very good reason might have been. However, all this does explain why you have gone to such lengths to cover up your role in the Stick-up, and to prevent Mr Crystal remembering any incriminating details. It's not that you fear police arrest; it's that you fear what Terence Chambers will do!'

Mrs Groynes picked up the gun and weighed it in her palm. She was impressed, but she had to correct him on a couple of things.

'May I speak now?'

Twitten reflected on whether there was anything more for him to say. 'All right.'

'Have a biscuit, dear.'

'Ooh, thank you.' He took a garibaldi.

'Now, for one thing, Sibert wasn't snatched,' she said. 'Don't worry about her. *Poor Miss Sibert*? She was working for Terry all along. If anyone took that manuscript, it was her.'

'Good heavens.' Twitten held his head at an angle while re-processing a few things. 'She was a plant?'

'She was. If she's who I think she is, she's not even from Vienna. But you're right about a lot of the other things, so well done.'

It occurred to Twitten that his father would have loved to meet Mrs Groynes. In all his extensive investigations of the deviant mind, he had never studied a female master-criminal, not once. To look at her now – a small, respectable middle-aged woman with a nice leather handbag, smelling of *eau de cologne* with an undertone of ammonia – you would simply never guess what she was capable of.

'So it was you who deliberately called the existing Brighton gangs together on the day of the Middle Street Massacre? Why?'

'Well, mainly because it was so easy, dear! They were spoiling for a shoot-out. All I had to do was make sure none of them got out alive, and that Inspector Steine came out a hero. Then I could have the place to myself.'

'But how did you know the police wouldn't arrive and stop it? Wasn't it a spur-of-the-moment decision by the inspector to take all the men for an ice cream?'

'No, dear. It wasn't. But I'll always be perfectly happy for him to claim that it was.'

Now, it is one thing to work out logically – lying on the floor of a bank manager's office with your eyes closed – that a harmless-looking charlady of your acquaintance is actually a callous master-criminal; it is quite another to have her admit to everything face-to-face in a dark-panelled room with a loudly ticking clock and a loaded gun in the equation. Especially when it occurs to you that you are unarmed, your feet are agony, you stink to high heaven of someone else's body odour, and that no one – aside from the person who might murder you – has the faintest clue where you are.

'But you're wrong about me and Chambers. I mean, you're right that we used to be close. You're right he was planning a robbery on the seventeenth. But I'm not worried he'll connect me to the Stick-up, dear. Chambers already knows perfectly well it was me.'

'He *does*?' Twitten exclaimed in disappointment. 'Oh, *flip*.'

'Yes, sorry, dear. He's always known. I left him in 1950 after eight years together as a team; he knew I was leaving; he knew I did the Stick-up; he knows I set up the Middle Street Massacre and made those idiots shoot one another. And if he ever wants to find me, he knows exactly where I am.'

Twitten was naturally upset that his excellent theory contained such flaws, but it was impossible to deny that his main emotion here was excitement. What Mrs Groynes was confessing was amazing.

'Well, I have to say, Mrs Groynes, you are an absolutely enormous villain.'

'Thank you, dear.'

'I can't believe how enormous you are.'

'You'll get used to it.'

'And no one has ever suspected?'

'That's right. I'm invisible, dear.'

'How many people work for you?'

'That's a good question. I'd say two hundred, give or take.'

'Well, you're a bally genius!'

This wasn't quite the way the conversation ought to be going, Twitten realised. He ought to be attempting to arrest Mrs Groynes, or at least denouncing her.

'The clinching thing for me,' he went on (because he couldn't stop himself), 'was the way Crystal reacted to the words in the play, when they talk about Ruby being a bus conductress, saying *Any more for any more?*'

'He clocked it then, didn't he, dear?'

'Yes! That's when he got really agitated and started writing something down. He'd been desperately trying to remember an incident that had jogged his memory earlier in the day, you see, and he knew it had happened between getting off the train and meeting Inspector Steine at the ice cream parlour. At first I thought it might have been a thought triggered by the posters outside the station. I wasted a lot of time on that.'

'You wondered if it might have been the bunnies on Barrow-boy Cecil's tray.'

'Yes. I did.' He stopped. 'Barrow-boy Cecil? Is that his name?'

'It is, dear. He's a good boy, Cecil.'

'Oh. But anyway, then I thought again about where else he'd been, and I remembered that, of course, he came to the police station first, and was "redirected by a charlady". And then you let slip to me that you'd seen him, when you said the words, *You'd never guess, to look at him.* He recognised your voice, Mrs Groynes, didn't he?'

'Yes, dear. And I saw it in his face. A flicker. I'd heard that Chambers had been working on him to remember the day of the Stick-up. Arnott here had telephoned me about the woman with the accent turning up with Crystal at the bank and yelling at him to "bring it back". But I wasn't too worried. I reckoned if all that failed, Chambers would have to give up on it.

'And then there he was, A. S. Crystal, in my very own police station, asking me where Inspector Steine was! I'd never expected to see that man again in my life. I said as little as I could, of course, but I saw that something clicked. So that's why I bought the ticket for the seat behind you in the Theatre Royal – the bloke made me give him fifteen quid, cheeky sod – and I listened to everything you said, the pair of you. And then, when that line came up – well, it was the very words I'd said on the day of the Stick-up, dear, and that's when he almost jumped to his feet, wasn't it?'

'It was.'

'So I had no choice. Luckily for me, people were leaving at such a rate, I could just get in among them and fire. Then I dropped the gun and joined the stampede for the exit. I had quite a bit of blood on me, but I'd made sure to wear black – and then I gave you a cuddle as soon as I could, dear, to explain away any marks on my face and whatnot.'

She produced a note from her pocket. It was Crystal's bloodstained list. Twitten gasped at her boldness in showing it to him. 'What do you think he was trying to write? The last word, there?'

Twitten swallowed. The last shred of doubt was now gone. If she was holding this list, she had engineered everything. If she was showing him the list, she didn't care what he knew.

He looked at the three letters. 'I think,' he said, 'he was going to write "daily", as in charwoman.'

'Of course,' she said. '*Daily*. You're very good at this, you know.'

'Oh. Thank you.'

They both drank their tea, and Twitten took another biscuit. He looked at the clock: it was nearly 4 p.m. 'I am so glad we've had this conversation,' he said, carefully.

'Me too, dear. Clears the air.'

'I've just realised that the word "massacre" in the name Middle Street Massacre wasn't quite the misnomer I always thought it was. I'd been unhappy with it before.'

'No, it was perfectly well named, in fact. It was literally a massacre, really, you see.'

Twitten felt he had a million questions to ask, but at the same time had run out of things to say. Perhaps it was because of the gun, and the fact that he had uncovered the identity of an absolutely enormous female villain with two hundred people working for her, one of whom poor deluded Sergeant Brunswick actually paid for information.

'Have you decided yet, by the way? About killing me?'

She made a 'tsk' noise. 'Not yet.'

'The thing is, you see, I am a policeman. And you are a cunning criminal. And while I am incredibly proud to have worked everything out, obviously that's not enough for me. It's now my duty to take you back to Brighton and turn you in.'

He opened the bag with this uniform in. 'I've got some handcuffs in here, I think.'

'Ha!' she said. 'I'd like to see you try.'

'Look, you did kill a man in cold blood, Mrs Groynes! I can't let you get away with that, can I?'

'And I say, *ha*. I thought you understood, dear.'

'Understood what?'

'Well, for one thing, that I can tell you all this because no one will believe you.'

'But it's the truth, Mrs G. I'll make them believe me.'

Mrs Groynes shook her head. 'Look, dear, all this talk of the charlady involved in stick-ups and massacres? They'll just think you've gone stark staring mad. Where's your evidence for any of it?'

'Well –'

'The inspector already dislikes you for being too clever; even the sergeant's in two minds. You've got nothing on me, dear. And you cannot underestimate how much those two love me and trust me and think nothing of the simple cockney woman who makes the tea and remembers to make them pink blancmange on a Friday.'

'Yes, but you can't –'

'They think that anything said by a woman can be classed as *wittering*.'

'Yes, but you just can't –'

'Now, listen, dear. I want to prevent you saying "But you can't get away with this", because it will make you sound very silly.'

'But you *can't* get away with this!'

'I've been getting away with it for seven years!' Her voice was raised. 'You said it yourself. They're idiots! I've removed evidence from their very hands! I talked them into having an ice cream instead of stopping a shoot-out. It's incredibly easy. All I have to do is give them a plate of biscuits and they will discuss anything right in front of me. How do you think Fat Victor got caught in Littlehampton? *I told them where he was.* They will never suspect me because I'm a *woman*, dear. And because, on top of that, I'm *working class*. The inspector once said to someone on the phone, "Yes, I am completely alone", and I was standing right next to his desk with my feather duster. You can't beat me, dear. You just can't.'

Twitten attempted an expression of defiance. It failed.

'Now, as it happens, dear, I like you.'

'Do you?'

'I do. And I've got an idea that might save you. In fact it might give us all a solution. Listen to this. It's clever. This is what I think happened to Mr Crystal. I think he was killed by that playwright, Jack Braithwaite.'

'What? But he wasn't. *You* killed him, Mrs Groynes!'

This annoyed her. She picked up the gun and stood up. 'I said, *Listen*, Mister Smelly, I'm doing you a bleeding favour! And the timing works out, just. Braithwaite could have done it, you see.'

'But he didn't!' Twitten squeaked, unable to stop himself.

'For crying out loud, dear! Look, Braithwaite had a motive, didn't he? You remember that actress saying: *Jack, you didn't?*'

'Yes, but it wasn't a very strong motive – just something about a play he'd been in getting a bad review.'

'Fair enough, but something else has come to light. Something that might help you change your mind. Did you know that an old friend of Braithwaite's killed himself yesterday in a fridge at Luigi's?'

Twitten recoiled. 'No. What? In a fridge? Oh, please put the gun down, Mrs Groynes. Please. I'm finding it very hard to concentrate, and it's also making the smell much, much worse!'

But Mrs Groynes was enjoying waving the gun around.

'This man in the fridge was the man who *wrote* the play that Jack Braithwaite appeared in, and that your Mr Crystal destroyed with one of his nasty reviews. Seeing Crystal again tipped this bloke over the edge of despair and he took his own life. Now, what I think happened is this: Braithwaite hears about his friend's sad, cold death, and is furious. He also has a history of violence, did you know that?'

'No.'

'Well, he does.'

'How do you know that?'

'I just do. So he turns up at the theatre and shoots Crystal –'

'Oh, this is preposterous.'

'Then, having killed Crystal, he rushes home to his digs,' said Mrs Groynes, raising her voice in triumph, 'and in a frenzy of remorse, cuts his own throat with that regimental sword!'

Twitten stared at her. 'What?'

'It can be done, dear, I checked.'

'*It can be done?*'

'I mean, in the time. I'm not saying it's psychologically feasible, dear, I'm just saying it can be done in the time. He could have done it. Technically.'

'But no one would ever believe that!'

'That's what happened, though. Trust me. And think how neat it is. If Braithwaite did it all – well, sadly, he's dead, he's killed himself; so there's no need for further enquiries. And I have to say, given the choice between *your* explanation of what happened to Mr Crystal – involving London gangs, long-ago bank robberies and Freudian memory retrieval, not to mention the police having to admit to being outwitted for years by a mere woman – and *my* explanation – putting everything down to Braithwaite who won't even need to go to trial – I think we know which solution the inspector would prefer, don't we?'

'But your explanation is beyond preposterous, Mrs Groynes.'

'I admit it. But it's no more preposterous than that the station charlady is a master criminal, dear. And much less paperwork, do you see?'

Twitten understood what she was doing by proposing this bizarre alternative solution. She was saving herself but also offering to save him as well. If he was prepared to go along with it, it was a lifeline.

She looked at him expectantly. 'What do you say, dear?'

By way of helping him decide, she performed a quick comic mime of a person leaning over backwards, sawing at their own throat with a sword, while rolling their eyes with their tongue hanging out. It wasn't funny in the slightest.

'Oh, come on, dear,' she said. 'Do yourself a favour.'

He closed his eyes. It was no use. 'No, I'm sorry. I can't go along with that. Not in a million years.'

She sat down, disappointed. 'Well, I'm sorry too. I don't mind admitting it was really nice to meet someone clever for a change.'

Twitten acknowledged the compliment. Perhaps it could be engraved on his headstone. There was just one last question he felt compelled to ask.

'Since I might be dead soon, Mrs G, are you going to tell me your real reason for covering up the Stick-up?'

She froze. 'No, I'm not.'

'I'm guessing you're protecting someone else from the wrath of Terence Chambers. But who?'

'That's *enough*!'

Mrs Groynes' manner had changed significantly. The little window of opportunity she had offered him was closing very swiftly.

'Lads!' she shouted. Three large men entered the room. One of them was Barrow-boy Cecil. 'See the bunny run?' he said, with a wink.

Twitten quailed.

She gave him a last, steady look. 'The Braithwaite Version, dear?'

Regretfully, Twitten shook his head, and sniffed. 'Never,' he said.

'All right, boys,' she said, turning away. 'You know what you have to do.'

The Day After That

Nine

James Brunswick had not joined the police force for the fame it might bring him. Personal celebrity was something he neither sought nor valued. Quite the reverse, in fact: as a policeman he aspired to walk in the shadows and also – one day, if Inspector Steine would ever let him – infiltrate the underworld unsuspected.

The arrival of Harry Jupiter in Brighton, however, had knocked all Brunswick's usual good sense aside. To be immortalised by the greatest ever crime reporter! Who cared if every villain in the town recognised him after that? (To be fair, they did already.) It would all be worth it to cast off – at last – the image of himself in the film of *The Middle Street Massacre* fuming in Luigi's.

Brunswick had long been a fan of Harry Jupiter. His principled stand against the *Clarion* – when he stopped buying it out of a sincere (but misplaced) solidarity with the acting profession – had hurt him a lot more than it had hurt the *Clarion*, and it had been agony to maintain. How could he live without reading those juicy crime reports? Well, it turned out that he couldn't. Among his colleagues, he had become famous for feverishly snatching up discarded copies of the paper in the police station canteen, or from deckchairs on the beach. He had been known to fish the *Clarion* out of bins. On one occasion, he had confiscated a copy from a blameless holidaymaker, saying, '*I'll* take that, sir, thank you very much', when the chap had merely been asking him the quickest route to the railway station.

Jupiter's stories were always so *detailed*. They were also very *reassuring*. Over the years, Brunswick had consumed all of Jupiter's best-selling books as well, including *The Art and Craft of Murder*, *Just an Ordinary Saturday (in Scotland Yard!)* and *Don't Just Give Them Your Money*. Having exhausted Jupiter's police-based oeuvre, Brunswick had even gone on to read the less commercial – and quite surprising – autobiographical works (*Fishy on a Dishy* being the first and best) concerning Jupiter's highly impoverished infancy in Stockton-on-Tees.

Finding out this morning – two days after Twitten's first day – that such a great apologist for all upright servants of law and order was now lying in a Brighton hospital with total memory loss was therefore a profound sadness for Brunswick. It drained away all the excitement of the previous day.

'Yes, he's lost his memory, apparently,' said funny old Mrs Groynes that morning, when Brunswick accepted his ritual wake-up cup of tea and sat down at his desk.

She was as cheerful as ever, of course. Thank goodness for the stability of Mrs Groynes. The day had dawned grey and overcast, with heavy rain pattering on the shop awnings, and little rivulets running down the gutters. Visitors in their guest houses would be looking out at the brooding clouds, feeling glum and cheated: the seafront shelters were comfortless places on a day like this. Most landladies insisted that their guests vacated the premises between eleven and four. Inside the police station, Mrs Groynes had switched on the garish overhead lights.

'Shame, though,' she carried on. 'They're saying it's all gone, his memory, every bit. Seems when he fell off the pier he banged his head on the way down and now he doesn't know his own name, bless him, let alone remember who might have stupidly pushed him off that ghost train, or whatever it was that happened, not that I know anything at all, dear, not having been there at the time, only afterwards, and then not really, only a bit. Now, that's quite enough about Mr Jupiter, dear. Hark at me wittering. How's your tea?'

Throughout this speech, she had been mopping the floor with sudsy water. But now she paused and laughed. 'Yes, it's a funny thing, life. A funny thing.' She looked at him. 'Oh, cheer up, love. You look like you've lost a half-crown and found a sixpence.'

Brunswick stirred his tea. He couldn't smile. This news about Jupiter was appalling. What bad luck! Also, something in all Mrs Groynes' wittering had registered in his mind, even though it had been said by her. 'Did you say someone *pushed him*?'

'Did I, dear? Well, you can't go listening to the likes of *me*, now, can you? Handsome young detective like yourself. What on earth do I know?' She laughed again. 'But I'll tell you this for nothing. If someone *did* push him, dear, I'm sure it was no one you know! No policeman would do it, would they? They'd have to be mad! Or stupid, of course. Especially a senior policeman. Oh, by the way, the inspector's coming in a bit late this morning. Something about a haircut.'

Brunswick sat back in his chair. 'I can't believe it,' he said, at last.

'Really? Oh, he definitely needs a haircut, I told him so myself. You don't want to get taken for a dirty beatnik, I said.'

'No, not about the haircut. About Jupiter. I can't believe what's happened to him. I feel a bit sick. If someone did push him –! I mean, he's written so much about villains, Mrs G. What if one of them got their own back on him? In Brighton, as well! The first time he ever came here. This is going to reflect badly on us. We should have been protecting him… why weren't we protecting him?'

'I'm sure the inspector did the best he could, dear.'

'What? Was Inspector Steine there?'

'Of course, dear. Oh, yes. Didn't I say that? But don't you go blaming him, just because he can be a bit slow on the uptake, that's hardly his fault, is it?'

On the windowsill a bedraggled seagull chick was sheltering. It tapped its beak feebly against the glass. Brunswick stared at it. He was just saying, slowly, 'So if Inspector Steine was *there* –?' when Mrs Groynes banged the window and the bird flew off, and Brunswick's half-formed thought went with it.

'And in any case,' she continued, sitting beside him and patting his hand, 'you take too much on yourself, that's your trouble. All this detecting you've been doing, and on top of that you've got your lovely auntie Violet to think of, and your little Maisie as well, doubtless still driving you doolally with unrequited lust. I suppose you realise she's a minx, dear? The way she strings you along, it's criminal.'

'Maisie's finished with me, Mrs G. As of yesterday.'

'Finished with *you*?' Mrs Groynes pursed her lips in sympathetic outrage. 'Little madam!'

'It's all right. I was too old for her, anyway.'

'Of course you were, but who cares about that? But I will say this. I've held my tongue till now, but just picture those teeth of hers in the face of a forty-five-year-old! They're all very well when you're a kid, but –'

'Please, please, let's not talk about Maisie. It's not about her, Mrs G. I was just so excited about telling Mr Jupiter about the case.'

'Going well, then, is it?'

Brunswick smiled. 'It's going *very* well. Do you want to hear?'

She took a seat.

'Oh, go on, then. I don't mind. Tell old Mrs Groynes. My life can't be all Vim and Squeezy, can it, now? I'd have to top myself.'

He laughed. This had been their early-morning routine for several years now. The nice sergeant kindly spicing up the day of the funny cockney charlady with stories of exactly how his enquiries were going, vis-à-vis fur-shop robberies or the tracing of stolen goods. And to her credit, the charlady always took such a respectful interest – even when the enquiries eventually (and oddly) came to nothing, after all.

What he appreciated about Mrs Groynes was her selfless enthusiasm. Where Inspector Steine refused to see the point of most detective work, Mrs Groynes was sometimes genuinely agog. On one or two occasions, when he'd told her specifics about banks or post offices with faulty security arrangements, she had even asked him to stop for a minute, produced a pencil from behind her ear and made a little note.

And so Brunswick told her all about Bobby Melba being his prime suspect in the Jack Braithwaite murder. He described how he first discovered Bobby Melba's existence; he showed her the picture of Bobby in female attire (at which she marvelled); he told her about Penny Cavendish awkwardly covering for him, and about the clinching evidence of the stolen jewelled comb, and Penny's second-hand knowledge of the crime scene. He said he was sure Bobby was in show business.

'My belief is that he's never killed before,' Brunswick concluded, 'but he was cornered, do you see?'

'I suppose so.'

'And a cornered narcissist can be very dangerous.'

'A cornered what, dear?'

'Narcissist.' Brunswick looked grave and lowered his voice. 'To be honest, I'm not completely sure what a narcissist is, but I think it's someone who *does drugs*.'

Mrs Groynes pulled a face of horror, while Brunswick nodded, as if to say, 'I know.'

'So who *is* this Bobby Melba, dear?' she asked, helpfully steering the conversation back to a safer channel. 'I mean, how do you go about finding him, that's what I'd like to know?'

Brunswick grinned. 'I'm very close, Mrs G.'

'Well, that's marvellous!' She was all admiration. 'But specifically, dear. I'm curious. What I meant just then was, how *do* you go about finding him, *that's what I'd like to know*.'

'Oh, I see. You mean, you'd like to know actually how I'm going about it?'

'Yes, dear. If it's no trouble.'

'It's quite simple, really. Miss Cavendish said that Melba was in Leeds last year at the same time as Braithwaite was in a play there. I've asked the Leeds City police to look through the papers for that week and tell me about any other entertainers advertised. They were supposed to call yesterday but they didn't. So today I'm not leaving this desk until I *get that call*.'

He thumped the desk three times, to show how much he meant it. 'I'm not moving an inch! Which reminds me, where were you yesterday afternoon, Mrs G? I was here all by myself for hours.'

Mrs Groynes ignored the question. 'Well, I think you're a bleeding genius, dear.'

'Oh, not really, Mrs Groynes.'

'Yes, you are. Putting all that together, while the rest of us are only good for cleaning windowpanes with vinegar and newspaper!'

She gave him an affectionate push.

'But what's his motive?' she said. 'That's what I don't understand.'

'Motive, Mrs G?'

'Well, say he's at the house, and stealing the jewels, and his friend Jack jumps out and says, "Bobby! It's you!" I don't understand why he then goes berserk and all but slices the man's head off.'

'Perhaps Braithwaite threatened to turn him in, Mrs G. Braithwaite says, "I'm shocked at what you're doing and I've got to turn you in," and Bobby turns nasty. Criminals will stop at nothing when they think they'll be exposed.'

Mrs Groynes tutted. 'Well, I'm shocked. What, you mean they'd *kill* someone rather than risk facing the music?'

'It happens all the time, I'm afraid. You're lucky you don't know about this kind of thing. People being *silenced*. There are supposed to be at least half a dozen bodies built into the new runway up at Gatwick already, did you know that? And as for the people given concrete boots every Friday night by the likes of Terence Chambers and dropped in the Thames…'

He looked round, remembering something. 'Where's Twitten?'

Mrs Groynes frowned. 'Who, dear?'

'The new constable. I haven't seen him since – well, since his first day, the night of the murders. Last I saw, he was being lifted into an ambulance. Where's he flaming got to? I know he must have had a shock, but he should still be here, helping.'

'Do you know what I think?' she said, getting up. 'I don't know where he is, and I don't care. I think he wasn't cut out for police work at all.'

'Really? Too clever, you mean?'

'My point exactly, dear! Too clever. No, I wouldn't be surprised if we never saw him again. Now, another cup of tea?'

'I wouldn't mind, thank you.'

Brunswick was happy. Listening to his own case against the mysterious Bobby Melba, he found it very satisfactory. The gruesome murder of a promising playwright would soon be avenged. And now he could have a pleasant morning at his desk, having cups of tea with Mrs Groynes while the rest of the world got soaked to the skin outside.

He opened a copy of the *Police Gazette* at the 'Your Star Sign' page and found that today's lucky colour for Scorpios was dark blue, and today's lucky word was 'handcuffs'. Lucky direction to be proceeding in was 'westerly'. Outside, on the windowsill, the sodden baby seagull had come back.

He was just sighing contentedly while Mrs Groynes put down a small saucer of biscuits beside him, when she suddenly stopped dead and slapped her hand to her mouth.

'Oh, my good gawd, I've just remembered something.'

'What's that?'

'The telephone call.'

'What telephone call?'

'Vince! Vince whatever-his-name-is, that Punch & Judy man who's always threatening people. He called just before you arrived.'

'What?'

Mrs Groynes banged the window and the poor wet bird flew off again.

'He sounded very upset, dear! Oh, how could I have forgotten, I'm so sorry, dear! And we were just talking about her! I said awful things about her teeth!'

Brunswick froze. 'Maisie?'

'I called her a minx.'

'Maisie?' repeated Brunswick, this time more like a squeak.

'Yes, dear! It was about Maisie. I made a note… oh, where did I put it?'

She started searching the room, going through her pockets, while Brunswick followed her about, very agitated. 'Has he hurt her? Oh, please no, has he hurt Maisie? Mrs G, just tell me!'

'I can't find it, dear.'

'It doesn't matter about the note. Just tell me.'

'He said she's disappeared.'

'What?'

'She didn't go home last night, apparently.'

'Oh, *no*!'

'Her mum's in a right two and eight. He said, could you meet him by the bandstand as soon as possible? I'm so sorry I forgot!'

Brunswick already had his hat and coat on, and his hand on the door handle. So much for his lovely morning in a warm, dry office.

'But what about your very important message from them Leeds City people, dear?'

Brunswick groaned. 'Can you take it for me, Mrs G? I've got to go.'

She smiled. 'Of course I can.'

He wanted to give her a kiss, but there was no time to lose. *If something had happened to Maisie…*

'Here, hold on,' she said. 'I've just had a thought about this case of yours.'

'Can't it wait, Mrs G?'

'If this Bobby is the guilty party, then that strong lady you arrested – was she *framed*, then?'

Brunswick frowned, confused. Now that he came to think of it, he supposed she was.

'So won't she be out to get the person who did it? All I'm saying is, I hope you find this Bobby bloke before she does. He might need protecting.'

After Brunswick had left, Mrs Groynes locked the door to the office and looked around. The bird had come back, but she didn't care. She quite liked seeing it there, dripping on the sill. She propped her mop against the wall, sat down at Brunswick's desk and lit a cigarette, narrowing her eyes in thought. Then she picked up the phone and asked to be put through to a Brighton number. While she waited for an answer, she tipped ash from the cigarette into the pocket of her floral overall.

'Ronnie? We're on,' she said. Having hung up, she crossed to a large, double-doored built-in cupboard, producing a key from a string round her neck. This cupboard was a favourite topic of conversation for Inspector Steine, who had often been heard to complain, 'What's the *point* of this cupboard? It's locked all the time and no one can find the key!'

Opening it now, she checked its contents: a shelf containing some gold bullion, another shelf with a neat pile of stolen postal orders to the value of £1,500, two coshes, a jemmy, three balaclavas and half a dozen sets of skeleton keys; hanging from hangers, a variety of female outfits and three full-length sable coats with exorbitant price tags still attached; and on the floor, an unconscious young constable in uniform, tied and gagged, along with two recently purchased canvas holdalls.

She regarded all these items with equal satisfaction, then relocked the cupboard, picked up the phone again and asked for another number.

'Bobby?' she said. 'Thanks for picking up, dear. It's me.'

* * *

'Who was that on the telephone?' asked Penny, as Bobby took off his silky dressing gown and got back into bed. The digs had a phone in the dingy hallway, and he had sprinted downstairs to answer it barefoot. This was known to be a good time to ring. It was common knowledge that the landlady at Bobby's theatrical digs took herself shopping between nine and eleven every weekday morning. If her lodgers missed the short, allotted breakfast time (8.15–8.30 a.m.), that was their lookout. (No actor was ever up before 8.30. It saved her a fortune in eggs.)

'Just an aunt of mine,' he said. 'She's my sort-of god-mother, too, as a matter of fact. She's going to help me with something.'

He made a face, indicating that this was all he was going to say. Penny put her arms around him. Rain lashed against the windows.

'I'm scared, Bobby.'

'Well, you're not the only one.'

She stroked his hair. 'I've just found you and you're going to leave me.'

There was no answer to this. They both knew it was true. If Bobby didn't flee the town in the next day or two, he would be arrested for the burglaries at least. His fingerprints were on that sherry glass: on such evidence alone, unless someone else was arrested for Jack's murder, Bobby might even hang.

'Tell me what happened,' she had asked him, again and again. She had asked it gently; she had asked it firmly; she had asked it, finally (and weirdly), while performing a marital act. Penny was highly confused; sleeping with Bobby had hardly made things better. In the night, he had twice woken them both up by screaming in terror. The first time, he'd shouted, 'Jack, look out!' The second time, it was, 'So much blood!'

There was no getting away from it. The fact of Jack's death was so present in both their minds that they might as well have been making love in the same room as the corpse. But they say that every cloud has a silver lining, and in later years, when Penny was cast as a highly sexed Gertrude in an acclaimed *Hamlet* at the Haymarket, she was able to draw, quite consciously, on this fleeting time with Bobby back in 1957 – when intense shock, grief, guilt and overpowering physical attraction had combined and mutated into fire.

When Bobby now kissed her with passion, she responded in kind.

'I still can't believe that you came to me last night,' he said, when they finally broke apart again.

'I know. I know.'

'This isn't disloyal to Jack, Penny.'

She looked miserably unconvinced. 'Isn't it?'

'This is all about him, Penny! You're in his play. You loved him. You got four… five curtain calls, all for him.'

'I know.'

207

'The success of that play is *all for him*.'

'I know. But all the time last night, as I was taking my bows, I wasn't thinking about Jack at all.'

'No?'

'I kept thinking: *Bobby was there, he might be a murderer, yet I want Bobby*. Oh, what am I going to do?'

'I'm not a murderer, Penny.'

'I want you so much. Can't we just run away?'

'It's too late,' he said, sitting up with his back to her. 'Seriously, too late. Wheels are in motion.'

'Let's come clean, then. Tell them what happened.'

'I can't, though.'

'Tell *me* what happened! Please!'

'I can't. I really can't.'

Bobby reached for his cigarettes on the dressing table, then lit one and got back under the covers. He plumped up a pillow and leaned back.

'Let me tell you about phrenology,' he said.

'What, now?' She let out a little shriek of frustration.

'It's relevant, I promise.'

'But Bobby –'

'The thing is, everyone thinks it's Victorian mumbo-jumbo, don't they? I suppose when I started learning how to do it, I thought of it as a kind of trick myself – a reliable trick, but still basically a trick. Up to then, I'd learned all sort of card tricks and stuff – did you notice my fingers, Penny? You've never said.'

'Of course I have. You don't hide them.'

'They started out quite normal; we think it was playing the piano so much as a child that changed them.'

He held them up – the top knuckle of each finger permanently bent, giving his digits the shape of little hammers.

'Anyway, I was sure I wanted to practise some sort of sleight of hand as a profession, and I was brilliant at card magic, but it was frustrating: these strange fingers of mine drew too much attention to what I was doing. And then someone told me about the "defunct" art of phrenology and I suppose I just saw the attraction.

'For one thing, it's a profession that requires dexterity, which I already had; for another, I'd be able to dress as a bearded Victorian, so people would think I was much older than I am, and not recognise me out of costume – and I always saw the value of that; and last, whenever there was a lull in the audience's interest, I could remark on the size of a person's "organs", because it always – and I mean *always* – gets a laugh.

'What I didn't anticipate was the genuine insight it would give me into people. It's like having X-ray eyes, Penny; like being the one-eyed man in the land of the blind. Because when most people look at each other, they just don't *see*. Whereas when I look at a new person – even without laying my hands on their head – I instantly know something of their flaws, their strengths, and even their destiny. Jack, for example, had bulges behind his ears – did you notice?'

'Well, yes. His glasses kept falling off.'

'That was his organ of Destructiveness, Penny. It was very pronounced. But I didn't mean to talk about Jack. The thing is, at first, I just latched on to the broader truths: a high forehead goes with a perceptive mind; a low brow literally indicates less intelligence; the instinctive stuff is at the base of the skull and the more spiritual and perceptive stuff is on the top.

'But the more I continued to study, the more I learned not just about the system of phrenology, but about the richness of human nature. It's an incredible thing, Penny. To see how powerful instincts are either kept in check, or given free rein. When I lay my hands on a person's head and feel for the bumps, it's like the entire personality travels directly into my mind. It's not a trick at all.'

'And then you hypnotise people?'

'That's the other bit of the act. They used to call it phreno-magnetism. Audiences lap it up. But I have to admit, six or seven curtain calls like yours I've never had.'

'What? Six or seven? Oh, you.'

He was teasing her.

'It was four, Bobby.'

'I'm sure you said nine.'

'It was four!'

Penny wondered whether he was about to practise his phrenology on her. She braced herself to resist. So she was surprised when he said, 'So what I'm saying is, I want you to put your hands on the back of my head. Just here.'

'Me?'

He turned his face away and indicated an area of his skull.

'But I can't. I don't know what I'm doing.'

'Just here,' he said, gently. 'I'll talk you through it. I want you to understand.'

Blushing, she placed her fingertips tentatively on the back of his head.

'I'm not sure, Bobby.'

'But that's it. That's good. Now press with –' (he had to work it out) '– the forefingers.'

She followed his instructions, and felt his head grow responsively heavy in her hands.

'That's it. Perfect. Now, that's the area of the head concerned specifically with family relationships, home, loyalty and closeness. In the language of phrenology, it's my organ of Consanguinity. Now, feel about, go on. Gently, that's right. That's very good. What can you tell about it?'

'It's raised.'

'Yes?'

'It's like a bump!'

'Yes.'

She explored some more.

'Yes, there's a definite bump there. Does everyone have it?'

'Not at all. Some people have nothing there; some people actually have a dent.'

He turned his head to face her.

'Penny, you know when people say, "You put your finger on it"?'

'Yes?'

'Well, you just literally had your finger on it. On what drives me. My enlarged organ of Consanguinity. Everything I do starts there.'

* * *

Jo Carver, better known as the Strong Lady, had not left town. But aside from unthinkingly crushing the glassware in pubs in the Lanes, she had done little to draw attention to herself. She was no freakishly massive woman, in any case: part of her stage appeal was that she looked and dressed like a perky, wasp-waisted dancer but at the same time could chop a breeze block in half with one blow from the back of her hand. She easily disappeared into the crowd, just so long as she resisted the impulse to use her superpowers.

Sometimes this wasn't easy, though. Just a few hours ago, sheltering under a tree, she had seen three men – outside the police station, around sunrise – transferring a large, heavy sack from a van and carrying it up the steps, and she had very nearly called out, 'Need a hand with that?'

But, for obvious reasons, she had not been much in the vicinity of the police station. Her main focus had been keeping tabs on Bobby Melba. The scene was still vivid in her memory: police bursting into her dressing room; the sergeant triumphantly holding aloft a red wig and a string of stolen pearls; above all, the sergeant thanking Bobby for his helpful tip-off.

Since her arrest and escape on Wednesday night, she had watched Melba's every move from the shadows. She had seen him with his new actress girlfriend: the girlfriend who was with him right now in his digs in Ship Street, where the terrifying landlady was famously out each day between nine and eleven, leaving the place otherwise empty, and where an anonymous, slender young woman with a grievance – and with the useful ability to break down a side entrance with just her bare hands – could get in, and get out again, without anyone being the wiser.

* * *

Back at the station, Mrs Groynes was sitting at the typewriter. It was evident that typing was nothing new to her. She sandwiched a piece of carbon paper between two sheets, rolled them efficiently into the machine and was just about to start composing when she realised what she'd done.

'Oh, my good gawd,' she laughed. What a mistake! Confident as she was that she could talk her way out of most things, it would be very silly to have a carbon copy of this letter lying around in the police station. So she began again with one sheet, and wrote the following:

TO WHOM IT MAY CONCERN

5 June, 1957

I, Jack Braithwaite, hereby confess
to the murder of the critic A. S.
Crystal, which I intend to commit
later this evening. I do not regret
what I am about to do. My
dear friend Arthur

Mrs Groynes stopped typing. She couldn't remember the name of the playwright who had committed suicide in Luigi's. 'Arthur' didn't sound right. She adjusted the carriage of the typewriter and blocked out the last four words with heavy applications of the capital X.

what I am about to do. XX
XXXX XXXXX XXXXXX A dear friend
of mine was driven to suicide
by Crystal, just ask Luigi, and
I personally feel a deep and abiding
grudge against the vile man which
I can never overcome, coming as I do
from Yorkshire where we can't help
it. I am confessing because I do not
want police time wasted in following
up other fanciful lines of enquiry,
however plausible they might look at
first glance. The killer is me, and
I act alone, using a gun that no one
knows I've got. And damn the man to
hell, I say, because I am known not

to mince my words and to write hard-
hitting northern plays and so on.

After the murder I will take my own
life, as I am a coward and would
prefer not to hang, or go to trial
or anything. I have spotted a sharp-
edged sword at my landlady's digs
that will be just the ticket if
I happen to drop the gun at the
scene of the crime and therefore
can't use that to take my own life.
Again, I am telling you this so
that you don't pursue other angles
pointlessly. Honestly, you police
are busy enough catching people
cycling without their lights on.
I cannot emphasise enough that
although I am planning to commit a
grave offence

Again, Mrs Groynes stopped and backspaced.

although I am planning to commit X
XXXXX XXXXXX two grave offences,
I do respect the police and would
hate to be the cause of unnecessary
detective efforts. I am a big fan
in particular of Inspector Steine
of the Brighton Constabulary, so if
by chance this letter should fall

into his hands, I will just say that
what you do, sir, with your weekly
broadcasts is brilliant, and that you
should by rights be decorated as soon
as convenient by our lovely young
Queen. You seem to me to represent
everything upright and honourable in
our country today. Also, the public
loves you.

But now I must

The phone rang. Mrs Groynes was torn. There were only a couple of minutes before Inspector Steine was due to arrive sporting his new haircut. But she had to answer. It might be the Leeds Police. She must take that message, even if in passing it on she got some of the details askew, being but a harmless, uneducated charlady with limited understanding.

'Brighton Police Station. Miss Fitzherbert speaking,' she said into the receiver, in a bright voice.

A voice on the other end announced, slowly, that it was a Detective Constable Ollerenshaw and could he speak to Sergeant... "oh, what was it, hang on, I've got it here somewhere –" But she interrupted. She didn't have time.

'You'd like to speak to Sergeant Brunswick?'

There was a pause. The pause got longer. 'That's right, love. Who were you again?'

'I'm Inspector Steine's secretary. Miss Fitzherbert. I'm afraid I'm alone in the office right now, but I have been fully briefed. I believe Sergeant Brunswick just wanted to check that in the week of August the eighth last year in Leeds, a certain act was playing at the City Varieties, the act being –' she pretended to be quoting from a note '– a Professor Mesmer, Last of the Phrenologists.'

In the distance, Mrs Groynes heard the telltale noises of Steine's arrival at the police station. She could hear his voice downstairs at the front desk, chatting with the desk sergeant. If only this man on the phone would *hurry up*.

'Hold on,' he said. 'I've got the paper here. I'll have to put the phone down. Only got one pair of hands.'

'Well, do be quick, please,' she said. 'It's of the utmost importance to the case.' For the first time in all this, she was anxious. Steine was not the brightest of men, but if he arrived to find her impersonating a secretary, with a half-written murder confession from Jack Braithwaite sticking out of the office typewriter, even he might be a bit suspicious.

At the other end of the line, she could hear broadsheet pages being slowly turned, while the man hummed nonchalantly. Laughter from the hall below meant that at least the inspector hadn't yet started on the stairs.

'Hello?' she said urgently, into the phone. '*Hello*? Oh, come *on, come on*.'

There was the sound of the receiver being picked up at the other end, then a pause.

'Hello? You still there, lass?' said the voice, at last.

'Of course I'm still here!'

'Well, there's no need to be like that, young lady. Now, was it Mesmer, you said?'

'Yes!'

'Yes, I can confirm Professor Mesmer, Last of the Phrenologists, was performing at the City Varieties, on the bill with Frankie Lane, Arthur Askey, strong woman Jo Carver –'

Mrs Groynes hung up and raced back to the typewriter. Was there time for a final paragraph? But then she saw what she had written.

```
But now I must
```

She looked at the words, baffled. She had no recollection of what she had intended to write next. Now I must what? She couldn't imagine. So again, she backspaced. She could hear Inspector Steine's footsteps on the stairs. She ran quietly to the door and unlocked it. Then she rattled out the last few words.

```
XXX XXX X XXXX That's it. Sorry about
the mess, if I make a mess, that is.
I'll try not to. Bang bang, ta-ta,

Jack Braithwaite
```

She tore the sheet out of the typewriter, folded it and put it in the pocket of her overall. Why on earth had she written 'Bang bang, ta-ta' and all that stuff about the mess? Well, it was too late to change it now. As the inspector reached the door, she grabbed her mop and started to sing 'Getting to Know You' from the recent hit musical *The King and I*.

'Morning, Mrs Groynes,' said Inspector Steine, entering.

'Ooh. Morning, dear. You startled me. That's a lovely haircut, if I may say so.'

He looked around. 'Where is everybody?' he said.

'No idea,' she said. 'They don't tell me anything, and why should they?'

She reached into her pocket and drew out the letter. 'But before I forget, I thought you'd like to know that this came for you.'

Ten

Sergeant Brunswick was not the only fan of Harry Jupiter's in Brighton. Young Ben Oliver – late of the *Brighton Evening Argus* – had grown up reading Jupiter's reports, and had long hoped to emulate the great man's illustrious career as a crime reporter. The decisive moment was when he read the account of the acid-bath murder. From that day forward, to write something half as compelling as the Half-Set-of-Dentures story became his life's ambition.

Oliver's family had expected him to join the thriving family grocery business; instead he started as an office boy at the *Argus* with a view to working his way up. And now he felt awful. It was his fault that Jupiter had come to Brighton and been struck down by some unknown hand! Hadn't he called the *Clarion* and instigated this regrettable train of events?

Oliver had many qualities that would one day make him an excellent newspaperman: he was literate, quick, dogged, shameless, insensitive to atmosphere, a whizz at punctuation, hard to intimidate, and looked good in a hat. During his short and uncomfortable interview with the bullying Jack Braithwaite, he had displayed excellent pugilistic

qualities – parrying well, then getting his opponent helpless against the ropes, before neatly delivering a killer punch.
There was just one fatal flaw in Oliver, from a professional
point of view: he had a conscience.

Arriving at the Royal Sussex County hospital on that rainy
Friday morning, Oliver shook his umbrella, and rescued from
inside his damp raincoat a small bag of grapes. A nurse directed
him to a ward on the second floor, where for five minutes
he was emphatically denied entrance – on account of its not
being visiting hours. But having shown his press credentials
to the right person (at last), he entered the squeaky-floored
male ward where the strong odour of urine was masked only
lightly by carbolic, and found the great journalist awake in
his bed – in borrowed pyjamas, with a thick white bandage
round his head – perusing a newspaper with an expression of
total bewilderment on his face.

'Who are you?' said Jupiter. While the memory had gone,
the personality was gloriously intact. 'What's the big idea?'

'It's all right, sir, you don't know me.'

'I don't know anybody. I've banged my head. Are those
for me?'

Oliver handed over the grapes. Jupiter – characteristically –
failed to thank him, took them and started eating them.

'The thing is,' Oliver pressed on, 'I'm a journalist, like you,
sir. I mean to say, not exactly like you. But I am a journalist,
and the thing is, I want to find out what happened to you.'

Oliver realised he was blushing. He was beginning to wish
he had rehearsed this better. Why did every word out of his
mouth sound so bumbling and stupid?

'I've read everything you've written, you see. When you
were awarded your honorary Silver Truncheon for services to
law and order, I cut the story out of the paper and pinned it

to the back of my bedroom door. I do hope you remember your Silver Truncheon, Mr Jupiter. You're the first civilian ever to receive one.'

Jupiter sighed, and nibbled a grape. It was depressingly clear that no truncheon, of whatever unsuitably weighty element, could impress him much at this moment. 'Look, man, why are you here?'

'Because I think I can help you. And I brought this.'

He produced a slim hardback, dog-eared from multiple readings, published by the *Clarion*'s own book imprint. It was entitled, *You Couldn't Make it Up: Fictional Murders Re-examined by the Greatest Brains of Scotland Yard*.

'Do you recognise this book, Mr Jupiter?'

'No. Not at all. I'm a hopeless case, apparently. But it seems to bother other people more than it bothers me.'

'Well, it's not one of your major works, I suppose, but it's one of my favourites. In here, you see, on page twenty-five –'

Oliver opened it at the page and held it out. Jupiter sighed, and didn't look.

'In here, you see, you challenge Graham Greene and his subsequent film-makers over the murder of the character "Fred Hale" at the beginning of *Brighton Rock*.'

Jupiter was becoming impatient. 'Look, man, whoever you are –'

'It's where Pinkie murders Fred on the ghost train on the Palace Pier and shoves his body into the sea.'

'So what?'

'Well, it all happens *suspiciously quickly*, you see. And it's not exactly clear how it's done. In the film, the train is rattling along, and Pinkie leers in Fred's face, and Fred is terrified, and there are screams from all sides, and then they approach a section where the train goes over water, and then there's a push!'

At the word 'push', there was a tiny flicker of recognition in Jupiter's expression; the merest flinch.

'And when the carriage comes back out, there's only Pinkie in it, and Fred is gone.'

Jupiter put down the grapes. 'I wish you'd go yourself.'

'People are beginning to speculate about what happened to you yesterday, Mr Jupiter. It's my theory that you were on the ghost train trying to test this fictional murder from *Brighton Rock* when you yourself fell through the gap and into the sea!'

Oliver had expected more of a reaction to this excellent detective work. He got nothing.

'So, what I have to find out is, were you alone, or did someone push you?'

'Look I still don't understand why you're doing this.'

'Because I have always admired you, Mr Jupiter. Because it's a Brighton story and I'm a Brighton boy. But also because I have asked witnesses on the pier what they remember, and I think the person responsible for your fall must have been Inspector Steine of the Brighton Constabulary! And if only we could get your memory back, sir, such a sensational story will get me my job back on the *Argus*.'

* * *

At the police station, Steine was celebrating the clearing-up of the two murders with a cup of tea and a slice of cherry Genoa. He had no idea that an interfering turnstile man, with keen observation skills, had just landed him in serious doo-dah.

This written confession from Jack Braithwaite was terrific. It accounted for everything, provided you didn't examine it too closely. To be strictly honest, there were a few details in this excellent document that made even Steine raise his eyebrows: for example, the choice of intended suicide method being to cut one's own throat with a sword, while violently knocking over furniture. But looking on the bright side, Steine was glad he couldn't place himself imaginatively inside the mind of a person as vengeful and murderous as Jack Braithwaite. Not being able to comprehend the warped and disgusting mentality of criminals was, after all, probably what kept him sane.

The cherry Genoa made him think of Brunswick (it was the sergeant's favourite cake). Steine reflected on the many happy mornings he had spent with Brunswick, down the years, both of them eating cherry Genoa, with the sergeant carefully picking out the cherries to eat at the end, and begging, 'Permission to go undercover, sir!', while Steine tried not to stare too longingly at the accumulating pile of sticky loveliness on Brunswick's plate, and said no.

It was a very satisfactory relationship, all in all. Young Twitten, on the other hand – well, what a hopeless young constable he was. He had spent so little time in the station in his first week that even his bakery preferences (one of the first things any policeman learns about another) were as yet completely unknown.

'No, I haven't seen either of them for days,' said Mrs Groynes, dusting, interrupting his reverie. 'I'm sure they're doing their best, dashing about following clues, interviewing innocent suspects, getting trains to Victoria without proper authorisation, visiting banks in the City, bothering their counterparts in the North of England, uncovering conspiracies, and who knows what else – but won't they be in for a bleeding great shock when they get back here with their fancy theories and bits of so-called evidence – and there you'll be, dear, holding the whole solution on one piece of paper! I can't wait to see their crushed little faces, can you?'

Inspector Steine nodded, happily. The sight of a crushed little face was always gratifying, somehow. The idea of Twitten's crushed little face was somehow especially pleasant.

'And all done without leaving my desk, Mrs Groynes. I am like a truth magnet. I sit here patiently, quietly, and the truth just seeks me out.'

'Exactly. Well, that's why you're the famous one, you see. That's why you get Policeman of the Year. Doesn't Mr Braithwaite actually say as much in his letter? I'm sure I saw something about you being brilliant in there somewhere.'

Steine demurred. 'He was a self-confessed murderer and suicide, Mrs Groynes. But yes, he does say some rather kind things about me.' He looked round. 'Where *is* everybody?'

Mrs Groynes dragged a bucket of soapy water into his office, creating a small flood, and started mopping.

'Any news of Mr Jupiter in the hospital, dear?' she said.

Steine winced. He moved his fountain pen from one side of his desk to the other.

'Don't you think you should visit him, dear?'

'Visit him? Oh, no.' Steine didn't like the sound of that. 'As I've explained before, Mrs Groynes, he was *trying to kill me*.'

'But why was he?' She pushed the mop towards his feet, and he had to lift them.

'I tell you, Mrs Groynes, I honestly don't know!'

* * *

It was a horrible day for a Maisie-hunt. Aside from the steady rain, a stiff wind was bowling huge grey-green waves ashore, and smashing them against the shingle, sending up high arcs of cold salt spray – nearly all of it landing directly inside the collar of Brunswick's raincoat while he waited for Ventriloquist Vince beside the seafront bandstand.

Why hadn't they arranged to meet somewhere warm and sheltered? Why not in Luigi's, across the road, where he could be drinking a warming frothy coffee from one of those Pyrex cups and saucers while the wind shook the awnings outside and the rain squalled, comfortingly, against the windows?

Of course, the last time he'd been in Luigi's – a painful memory! – he'd been with Maisie. He had treated her to a banana split, and she'd urged him to put sixpence (his last until payday) in the jukebox, so that she could do a dance to the latest Bill Haley, with her full blue skirt flying out, and her ponytail bobbing. Everyone had looked at her. She'd been wearing a thin red belt to match her red shoes, he remembered. A short, tight sweater and a little spotted scarf.

And now he had a horrible vision of Maisie's body lying broken and wet in a dark alley with the rain falling pitilessly upon it. He had a vision of her being attacked by a gang of men and shouting desperately: 'Jim! Help me!' He saw her following some unknown man with a scar on his cheek up the staircase in the Metropole, giggling and stumbling after one too many port-and-Tizers. He felt sick. All these fates had always been on the cards for poor Maisie – a teenaged temptress who, thanks to shockingly inadequate parental supervision, consorted with members of the criminal fraternity while openly flirting with a policeman.

By the time Vince arrived, Brunswick was weak with anxiety and guilt. It is true to say that, at this moment, any urgent duty to uncover the identity of Jack Braithwaite's wicked murderer had been utterly displaced in Brunswick's mind.

'Vince, at last. Tell me what you know!' he demanded.

Vince looked as wet and worried as he did himself. 'She no go home last night. I go off my ruddy nut, mate.'

'Where was she last seen?'

'She went to Hippodrome! You promised a take her, you ratbag ponce policeman, but you ruddy left her –'

'I know, I know. I said I was sorry!'

'Did you? That's not what she –'

'Look, I said I was sorry!'

'So she go again, thass what! First person who ask! Thass the kind a girl she is!'

The rain fell harder now – so hard that, what with the wind, Brunswick and Vince had to shout to be heard.

'Who with?'

'What you say?'

'Who did she go with?'

Brunswick was praying it was with one of the many girl-friends Maisie never stopped chattering about – Janet with the droopy eye from school, or Hazel next door with the calipers, or Maggie from the fish shop.

'Some slim-slimey bloke,' yelled Vince.

'Oh, no.' Brunswick pictured Maisie in the queue for the Hippodrome once more, giggling and poking her tongue out, while alongside her stood a shadowy, menacing figure in a black hat, playing with a flick-knife in his pocket.

'Name of Twitty,' yelled Vince. 'I never see him afore.'

Brunswick pulled a face. Twitty? What sort of a name was Twitty?

'You know him?'

'No.'

'Thass funny coz he say he know you.'

Brunswick gasped. 'Not *Twitt-EN*?' he said.

'Twit-man, Twit-face, Twit-twat, something. About twenty-two years, she say. Like a toff, mate. And she go off with this ruddy ratbag Twit-features last night and then – thass it! No more Maisie! Oh, MAISIE!'

Brunswick's mind was racing. Twitten? As far as he was concerned, Twitten had been off the radar for at least thirty-six hours, ever since witnessing a shooting at extremely close range. He had discharged himself from hospital without any kind of treatment and had not been seen since. He was almost completely unknown. He might be capable of anything.

'Tell you what, mate!' yelled Vince, as if reading Brunswick's mind. 'I kill whoever done this. If my Maisie hurt, I knock his ruddy brains out!'

'And I'll help you,' said Brunswick, grimly. 'Oh, Maisie,' he groaned.

'Maisie!' yelled Vince, as if hoping she could hear him.

'Maisie!' they yelled together, setting off in the rain. 'MAISIE!'

* * *

There are many people who, after being struck unconscious by a professional hench-person in a London banking establishment and then transported to Brighton by van and left in a cupboard in a police station with a stolen fur coat tickling their face, would simply have given way to self-pity.

'Poor me!' they would have thought. 'I have made a number of classic errors when dealing with an experienced criminal, and now I am going to die because I bally well know too much.'

But Twitten did not think he had made any errors, and he also didn't believe he was going to die. Being in this cupboard was proof enough that Mrs Groynes had different plans for him. True, her burly henchmen had been a bit rough when they bundled him out of the Albion Bank and into the van, but to be fair, they probably didn't know any other method of bundling.

So although it's hard to believe, finding himself now in this pitch-black enclosed space without a lot of air, unable to move his arms or legs, Twitten felt relatively chipper. After all, he was here because he'd been right, and there could be no better consolation than that. He'd been right about the Aldersgate Stick-up being connected to Crystal's assassination; he'd been right about Mrs Groynes being a wicked criminal.

When he was finally in a position to expose her, how foolish the sergeant and Inspector Steine would feel! How they would cringe, and kick themselves! They had doubtless trusted her with all sorts of sensitive information over the years. How diminishing to Inspector Steine that Mrs Groynes had engineered every part of the Middle Street Massacre, from the shooting of young Frankie Giovedi right through to the stopping-for-ice-cream that ensured no one got out alive. And that was another thing: this blanket deception had been going on for *years* at the police station, whereas Twitten had penetrated the truth in just a matter of days!

He wondered if he should try to make a noise, in the hope of rescue, but decided rather to wait and see what happened. If he interfered with Mrs Groynes' master plan, someone might panic and hurt him. No, for the time being, he would just practise shallow nose-breathing, try not to wriggle, or to dwell on the highly disturbing fact that his clothes had been changed while he was unconscious.

Instead, he would use the time to compile a mental list of every single law and subsection under which Mrs Groynes would eventually be charged. So far, including all the conspiracies and frauds and possession-of-weapons (as well as the robberies and murders), he could count seventeen major infringements, with a maximum combined sentence of 245 years (plus, of course, hanging).

* * *

There was no trace of Maisie anywhere. Her droopy-eyed best friend hadn't seen her for a couple of days; the girl in the fish shop became hysterical at the news that she was missing, and in her distress, accidentally burned her hand on a saveloy.

More significantly, however, there was no trace of Twitten either. At the station house, where he was supposed to be lodging, they had seen nothing of him. They had taken delivery of his suitcase, and that was all. In the absence of any other leads, Brunswick asked to see the suitcase, which had been left neatly on Twitten's allocated bed, with its thin white pillow and standard-issue brown blanket.

'Can I open it?' he asked the station-house sergeant, who had accompanied him.

'If I stay here and watch you, I don't see why not. What's he gone and done, then? He's only been in town five minutes.'

Brunswick shrugged and opened the young constable's suitcase. It contained a few clothes, a threadbare teddy and a lot of old, filled-in *I-Spy* books (heavily annotated in pencil by an infant hand), inside one of which was tucked a letter from 'Big Chief I-Spy' to the fifteen-year-old Peregrine Twitten, thanking him for pointing out mistakes in one of the earlier titles.

'Bit of a clever-clogs, is he?' laughed the station-house sergeant, perusing the letter.

'You could say that,' said Brunswick, folding it and returning it to the book.

At the bottom of the suitcase were more books, all about crime. Brunswick was starting to entertain doubts that Twitten could be the man he was after. The teddy, in particular, had given him pause. But then he noticed that among the books were a couple written by Twitten's celebrated father: *Inside the Head of the Law Breaker* and *Behind the Eyes of a Killer*. He remembered his conversation with Twitten about 'criminal psychology'. He also remembered something Steine had said to the young man, which had seemed uncalled for at the time: *You might just be a clever imposter with a uniform from a theatrical costumiers.* What if there was actually some truth to this accusation?

So despite the fact that an agitated Ventriloquist Vince was waiting for him around the corner in the famous *Brighton Rock* tea shop, Brunswick paused to have a look. Interestingly, *Behind the Eyes of a Killer* fell open at the chapter 'The Psychopath Personality'. Ten minutes later, the station-house sergeant said, awkwardly, 'Want to take that with you, then? I can write you a chit.' And Brunswick, not looking up, said yes.

* * *

What few of these people know, at this stage in the day, is that in a few hours they will have a common destination. They seem to be going their separate ways, but they are not. In the evening, they will all convene at the Hippodrome, where a daring and dramatic showdown has been planned in quite some detail for their benefit. Getting them all there is no picnic, however, even for a mind as devious and manipulative as that of Mrs Groynes.

Constable Twitten is the only individual who can be physically shifted (by the van-and-henchmen method again) to the desired location: everyone else will have to be tricked or lured. Luckily, Inspector Steine is an easy task; Mrs Groynes already has a foolproof plan for him. Meanwhile Sergeant Brunswick will be given a last-minute tip-off by Stage Door Albert that Twitten is hiding there; and poor Constable Twitten will wake up to find himself in Jo Carver's old dressing-room, still tied up.

So much for the scope of Mrs Groynes' clever plots. We then get into areas beyond her control, where chance might play a part. For who else might conceivably turn up at the Hippodrome tonight? Will Penny Cavendish rush there from her multiple curtain calls at the Theatre Royal, to tell Bobby she loves him, and beg him once more to turn himself in? Will Ben Oliver and/or Harry Jupiter make the Hippodrome their evening destination for unpredictable reasons of their own? And finally, will the hard-done-by fugitive Jo Carver make an appearance, with bloody vengeance in mind?

For the time being, we are in the dark. But as each of our characters will be drawn, inexorably, towards the Hippodrome, it is important to emphasise that there is nothing slapdash, or airily improvised, or coincidental about all this. Mrs Groynes knows most about what will happen tonight, of course, but – while she would hate to admit this – she does not know quite everything. Meanwhile Twitten knows more than the others, but who will believe him? Sergeant Brunswick knows quite a lot, but will it be relevant? And Inspector Steine knows nothing at all, but will anyone be surprised?

* * *

Back at the station, however, Inspector Steine was aware of something unusual going on. He kept discovering Mrs

Groynes using the telephone, and then breaking off as if caught in secret activity.

'At the Hippodrome?' he heard her saying, the first time, quite loudly. He was sitting at the desk in his own office, but could hear her through the door. 'At seven-thirty, you say? You want me to get the inspector to the Hippodrome for seven-thirty? Yes, but how am I supposed to do that – oh my good gawd, he's coming, I'll call you back again, dear.'

And then, as he entered the outer office, she randomly picked up her own handbag and started polishing it intently with a duster.

Steine didn't know what to make of this, so he asked for a cup of tea, took another slice of cherry Genoa and went back into his own room.

Half an hour later, he heard her pick up the telephone again, so he went straight out, and she quickly put the receiver down, saying, 'Wrong number, dear! Chinese laundry!'

The next time he heard the telltale receiver-lifting, he decided to listen at the door – forgetting that, standing there, his silhouette would be plainly visible to Mrs Groynes through the frosted glass. And what he overheard was thrilling. After asking the station operator for a London number, she kept her voice low and secretive, but everything she said was still clearly audible.

'Of course I've seen the programme, dear!' she exclaimed. 'I know it has to be a surprise! But he could come in at any minute!'

Steine gulped. What was this? What programme? What surprise? He pressed his face to the glass.

'I know, I know. They go in all innocent, thinking they're going to be a guest on the *Sooty Show* or get their ears syringed or something, and then out jumps Eamonn Andrews with the big book, saying, "Geoffrey Beverley Wildebeest Steine, *This Is Your Life!*"'

Mrs Groynes noted with satisfaction that the outline of Steine behind the door had stopped moving. She had especially enjoyed the Wildebeest bit.

'Oh, I wish Sergeant Brunswick was here,' she groaned. 'It was him you discussed all this with in the first place, I suppose? But I don't know where he is, and I'm not sure – look, I've got to be straight with you, dear, I'm not sure I can manage it. I'm just the charlady. And I had plans for the evening, and now you want me to drop everything and get the inspector to the Hippodrome *without him suspecting*? Look, I won't do it, dear. It's beyond me. He is *bound* to be suspicious; he's not an idiot. So that's that, I'm sorry.'

Steine closed his eyes. There was a little pause, as if Mrs Groynes was listening intently to the person on the other end. In fact, she wasn't even bothering to hold the receiver to her ear. Steine strained to catch what was being said.

'What? His *mother*? You've got his mother coming?'

'Mummy?' whispered Steine.

'From Kenya?' she said. 'He hasn't seen her for *how long*?'

There was another agonising pause.

'Oh, all right then,' she said, at last – and, gratifyingly, saw the figure of Steine sink to a crouching position, in relief. 'But I can't be held responsible if he smells a rat, dear. It's just not in my nature to dissemble.'

She then pretended to hang up and marched straight to Steine's office door. He had to dash awkwardly back to his desk and pick up a pen.

'Inspector, dear?' she said, standing by the open door. 'Everything all right?'

'Yes, yes,' he said, flustered.

'I thought I heard a commotion.'

Steine pulled a face. 'No, not in here. I've been sitting here all along.' There was a pause, while he pretended to be wondering what commotion the charlady might have heard. 'Was there something, Mrs Groynes?'

'Look, dear, yes. It's a bit of a long shot, and just say no if you like, but I've got a spare ticket for the Hippodro—'

'Well-I'd-be-delighted,' said Steine, slightly too quickly.

Mrs Groynes held her head on one side.

'Are you sure, dear? You're not suspicious that I should ask you?'

'Suspicious? Why should I be? I would love to come with you, that's all.'

'To the Hippodrome? This evening? Dancing girls and such like?'

'To the Hippodrome this evening, yes, lovely, dancing girls, a marvellous idea. I can't think of anything better.'

Mrs Groynes pulled a face, as if she couldn't quite believe how easy this had been.

'All right then, dear,' she said. 'I thought I'd have to work harder to persuade you.'

'No, no. No need.'

'Right then. If you want to go to the Hippodrome all that much, dear, we'd better go and do it.'

* * *

At the hospital, Oliver was quietly reading to Jupiter from his book about fictional murders, and Jupiter was deliberately not listening, staring out of the high window at the dark and thundery sky, when the doors to the ward banged open, and a Metropolitan policeman of high rank (and even higher demeanour) strode into the room, his shiny boots squeaking on the linoleum, his peaked cap tucked officiously under his arm.

It was the famous Deputy Chief Inspector Peplow of Scotland Yard, responding to the devastating news of Jupiter's plight with a slightly belated mercy dash. To give him his due, he would have arrived sooner, but it had taken a little time to rally his team from Pathé News: cameraman, lighting man and director. While Peplow made his entrance, it was the youthful director (in a donkey jacket, glasses and roll-neck sweater) who had the job of arguing with the ward sister about being allowed in to film.

'My dear Jupiter. Dear fellow! Dear friend!' Peplow boomed. 'I came as soon as I heard. Well, I came, in fact, almost as soon as I heard! I've got an ambulance outside to transport you to London. We'll get you the finest specialists and have you back at the *Clarion* in no time. And if you don't recover, you'll still feature in your very own newsreel, so how about that as a crowning achievement to a brilliant career?'

Peplow waited for a response. Jupiter peered at him.

Peplow introduced himself to Oliver; the reporter (impressed) politely reciprocated. Jupiter looked on without interest. At the door, a man with a tripod tried to push his way in, but it resulted only in an unseemly scuffle with the nursing staff, which made Jupiter roar with laughter.

'He doesn't know who you are, sir,' Oliver explained. 'He doesn't even recognise his own writings. I've talked to him about acid baths, and the Kennington Butcher, and even *Brighton Rock*, but there's not a flicker.'

'So how do you think this happened?' demanded Peplow, brusquely. 'And by the way, we might have to repeat this con-versation for the cameras in a minute, but they don't record sound, so you won't have to worry about what you say. I find that reciting "The Walrus and the Carpenter" gets me through this sort of thing quite well, but of course you can make your own choice. As long as your lips move, it's fine.'

Oliver tried not to be overwhelmed by this whirlwind intrusion.

'My theory, sir, is that he was taking the opportunity of the trip to Brighton to check the details of the ghost train murder at the beginning of the film *Brighton Rock*, as detailed in this book.'

He handed the open volume to Peplow, who scanned the pages quickly.

'Ha! That sounds like Jupiter, all right! *Detail*, that's always been his guiding principle. *Detail*! And if there isn't enough actual detail, make some up! Or perhaps I shouldn't say that.'

'But it went wrong somehow, you see,' Oliver continued. 'I think he got into a tussle with his companion on the ghost train, who unfortunately pushed him into the water – and he struck his head on the way down.'

Peplow sucked his teeth. 'Now, I noticed you were careful to say "*his companion*"?'

'Well, that's the thing, sir. I have reason to believe it was Inspector Steine of the Brighton Constabulary.'

A great smile spread across Peplow's face. He loathed Steine quite as much as Steine loathed him. Steine was known within Peplow's department at Scotland Yard as the 'FBB' or 'Fluky Brighton Bastard' – and Peplow himself had started it. It was unbelievable how pure luck could elevate a person of such meagre talents. 'Ha!' he said. 'Oh, that's perfect. Poor old Fluky. Comeuppance at last. That's wonderful.'

How bewildering this all must have been to Jupiter is hard to imagine: a self-important man in uniform bursting into the quiet ward and then reciting a children's poem about oysters across his bed. The noisy camera whirred for at least an hour, taking shots of Peplow walking in with hat on and hat off; Peplow in earnest poetic conversation with the young reporter; close-ups of all three of them, and of a pretty nurse imported from a nearby baby clinic.

Bewildering for Jupiter, but exciting for Peplow. The dash from London – with the clanging of the ambulance bell, and the flashing light – was going to make a very decent little film, demonstrating the caring nature of the Metropolitan Police. The hold-up on the journey – while they filmed the right shots of the ambulance speeding past a South London milestone saying, 'Brighton 53 miles' – had lost them only two or three hours. But now, a thought occurred.

'Can we take him back to the ghost train before heading to London?' Peplow enquired, looking round for approval. The film crew definitely liked the idea, but Oliver was the only one who could speak for the medical opinion.

'The doctors do think that if Mr Jupiter could return to the scene, the memory might return – but it turns out they won't let anyone remove him who isn't next-of-kin, and for some reason his wife isn't co-operating. In fact, when she heard what had happened, she immediately went on holiday. Also, apparently, the Pier has its own by-laws and –'

'Oh, we can get round all that,' said Peplow. 'Now, what do you say, Jupiter? Fancy that ghost train again?'

'I'm quite happy here,' said the patient, truthfully. 'It's raining. And I wish you'd go away. And I wish you'd stop calling me Jupiter.'

'He shouldn't be moved,' a nurse piped up.

'I'll telephone the office,' said another.

'He's right. It's raining,' said a third.

'Leave me alone,' said Jupiter.

But Peplow got his way, as he always did. Within half an hour, the hospital authorities had conceded, and Jupiter was made to dress in his old suit – wrinkly and misshapen from its dip in the sea – and be taken in a wheelchair across the rainy hospital forecourt to the waiting vehicle with London number plates – making the journey three extra times, for the sake of different camera angles.

'To the Palace Pier!' said Peplow, as he and Oliver clambered into the back alongside Jupiter.

Oliver, for all his qualms about the value of this exercise, appreciated the way the senior policeman was allowing him to stay involved. In the ambulance, he thanked him.

'Not at all, you're doing very well,' Peplow said. 'These film bods make everything a bit complicated, but the resulting newsreels are always top notch, and they're seen by *everybody*. And you can write about this, presumably? Sell a piece to a newspaper?'

'Oh, yes.'

'Well then, good! *The Times* would be nice, for a change. But I'm not going to tell you how to do your job!'

And so they sped to the Palace Pier, on a mission to jolt Harry Jupiter's memory back.

Had Inspector Steine known what was happening, he might have been very anxious. His arch-enemy was poised to uncover what he'd done. An ambitious young reporter was poised to expose him. But he didn't know any of this, so he cheerfully spent the rest of the day with pen and pad listing everyone who might have been rounded up to talk glowingly about him on *This Is Your Life*.

Was it too much to hope for Princess Margaret? He didn't think it was.

Back at the Pier, Peplow brooked no denials from anyone. He and his film crew, and Jupiter and the reporter, took themselves straight to the ghost train, despite by-laws, despite pier regulations, despite protests from angry uniformed men and despite the continuing rain. And while Peplow made suggestions for shots, and pretended to interview the ticket seller in his flat cap (' "*If seven maids with seven mops, Swept it for half a year,*" ' he asked the startled man, ' "*Do you suppose,*" *the Walrus said, "That they could get it clear?*" '), Oliver talked gently to Harry Jupiter, who seemed nervous and unhappy.

'I'm sure you don't have to do this, sir. What are you remembering?'

'*Brighton Rock*?' said Jupiter, with an effort.

'That's right, sir! *Brighton Rock*.'

On account of the pouring rain, there were few legitimate riders on the ghost train, so the operator was happy to keep the carriages still for half an hour while the cameraman set up his lights, and someone held an umbrella over Peplow and Jupiter, and finally a tight shot was taken, with Peplow smiling broadly in anticipation of success.

'Do another one?' said the director. 'You never know.'

So for the next shot, Peplow looked depressed. For the one after that, he put his arm round Jupiter and looked caring. For the final one, he larkily put his hand to his mouth and pulled a face, as if scared of what was to come.

'Right, off you go,' said the director, and the carriage trundled off inside, through the thick curtain and into the dark.

What actually happened once the carriage was out of sight, no one will ever precisely know. It was only Ben Oliver who had any misgivings about the possible outcome. Everyone else believed that Jupiter would come out of the ghost train with his memory restored, and Peplow the big hero of the day. But unfortunately, there were other possibilities.

All that is known for certain is this: when the carriage returned to view, with the camera and lights in place to film it ('Ready, everyone! Now!'), it was empty. The newsreel of that empty carriage rattling into view, in the rain, became one of the great hits with cinema audiences of 1957. People gasped in horror. Women sometimes fainted. That last shot of the two men sitting so awkwardly in the little carriage – the famous newspaperman looking depressed and miserable with his head in a bandage; the star of the Metropolitan Police with his hand to his mouth, pulling a funny face – lived long in people's minds.

Rounding off the newsreel was an interview with Inspector Steine of the Brighton Constabulary. It was filmed a few days after the horrific events, and took place at the entrance to the Pier, on a bright morning, with purposeful holidaymakers in stylish sunglasses queuing for the turnstiles behind him.

Steine's performance was perfectly judged. He was solemn, steadfast, reassuring. He said that a) the whole episode was deeply regrettable, almost unimaginably tragic; and that b) the gap in the Pier was being filled in forthwith, to prevent any more such accidents. What was cut was Steine going on to say that c) DCI Peplow had sadly brought it all on himself by his arrogant behaviour in bypassing proper procedures in a town where he held no jurisdiction, d) there had been a real and irresponsible risk of electrocution and fire with all that filming equipment being used on a wet day on a wooden structure, and e) he personally blamed that damned book *Brighton Rock*, because apparently it encouraged such irresponsible mock-violent behaviour on a moving fairground attraction and led to terrible misunderstandings, sometimes involving blameless people of high rank.

When the filming was finished, the crew thanked him and started to pack up their gear. They were not to know that Steine might also have added f) that he was himself miraculously off the hook, and actually in a better position than he'd ever been. Fluky indeed. With Peplow conveniently out of the way (and having died so needlessly – and so stupidly – in the line of duty), Steine was now not only free of two very serious charges – grievous bodily harm (Offences Against the Person Act, 1861) and absconding from the scene of a crime – but a pretty safe bet for 1957's popular-vote award for Policeman of the Year.

Eleven

Unsurprisingly, Inspector Steine had never been to the Hippodrome before, so he was unsure what to expect, apart from horses (his classical education leading him up the wrong path here, as it so often did). So it was only when he and Mrs Groynes had taken their seats towards the front of the crowded and smoky auditorium that he put two and two together: this must be the place Brunswick was always talking about – with its sweating comedians and high-kicking dancing girls and exotic Portuguese contortionists.

Predictably, the place was hot and noisy and reeked of cheap cigarettes and acrid body odour; it was full of louts and teddy boys and young girls wearing too much make-up. Steine was utterly revolted, but also mystified: why would the makers of *This Is Your Life* choose such an awful place to record their show about him? Why not the Wigmore Hall? At what point in the evening would the true purpose of his presence be revealed?

Again and again, Steine had to repress the urge to ask Mrs Groynes these questions. Again and again he had to remind himself that *he wasn't supposed to know what was going to happen.*

So he pretended to be interested. It seemed the polite thing to do.

'I've never been to the Hippodrome before, Mrs Groynes!' he called, over the noise.

'You haven't lived, dear,' she replied. She was peeling an orange and dropping the peel on the floor. She had brought a pound and a half of oranges from a street stall en route. She offered him the bag.

'No, thank you.' He smiled, weakly. 'Look, I know I shouldn't say this, but I can't help wondering why –'

'Wondering why what, dear?' she snapped, with a worried expression, licking juice from her fingers.

Steine sighed. 'Oh, nothing.'

Every so often he stood up, ostensibly to stretch his legs, but in fact to scan the crowd for Eamonn Andrews. It was so hard to control his feelings: he was excited, but also anxious. The idea of seeing his mother after all this time – after just those curt, functional letters at Christmas for the past twenty years. If she had agreed to come all this way, did it mean that she'd finally forgiven him for what had happened on his last, fateful trip to Kenya in 1937, when he'd accidentally 'bagged' her rich neighbour, the Hon. Hugh Lees-Chetwynde? As Steine had argued at the time, it was an honest mistake: what else could a man expect if he lurked on all fours in the under-growth draped in an animal skin?

'Ooh, it's starting, dear,' said Mrs Groynes, tugging at his tunic. So Steine sat down, but not before noticing the flash of a police uniform from a figure taking a seat in the front row – a figure he couldn't quite make out, as it was surrounded by a group of large men, one of whom was holding a fully extended umbrella, which was preposterous behaviour once indoors, as well as very dangerous.

'Did you see that?' he asked Mrs Groynes.

'See what, dear?'

'Man with an umbrella up. Indoors!'

But the lights had gone down now, and a figure appeared on the stage in a top hat and tails. For a moment, Steine thought he recognised a giveaway Irish accent, and took a deep breath. He turned to Mrs Groynes as if to say, 'Wish me luck', and prepared to stand up – but then he realised the man was in fact from Lancashire, and was the Master of Ceremonies, and was already telling a joke in questionable taste, so he sank back in his seat instead.

For Inspector Steine, much of the show that evening passed in a blur of anguish. One ghastly act followed another: a line of half-naked dancing girls coming onstage sideways, linked at the elbow; a ventriloquist with a huge, unfunny lion for a puppet; a man who caught darts between his teeth (which ought to be illegal); a shiny-skinned body builder in tight swimming trunks, who elicited lewd and depressing wolf-whistles from the women. Steine was so bored and disgusted that he nearly wept.

He kept thinking, *This is the wrong audience*. He pictured his mother, possibly brought here by flying boat, obediently telling stories of the child Geoffrey Steine – 'Well, he was always arresting other children, of course. He would catch them committing minor misdemeanours and march them down to the police station. We took no notice. We put it down to normal boyish exuberance. And then one day we took him to the London Zoological Gardens in Regent's Park, you see, but he disappeared and we were so worried. And do you know where he had gone? To His Majesty's Stationery Office in the City! He wanted to study the latest edition of the Highway Code!'

This crowd was accustomed to a diet of crude dancing, clashing music, sparkly outfits and catchphrase humour. Wouldn't such wholesome and heart-warming stuff be totally lost on them?

'Enjoying it, dear?' Mrs Groynes would ask, from time to time. But she often found him with his eyes closed, controlling his breathing. It was in this state that he managed to miss two singing stars of yesteryear, a magician, a trapeze artist and a comedian who did a comic monologue about West Indian immigrants, which of course broke no laws at the time, but would one day (thankfully) be sufficient cause for prosecution.

It was after half-past nine when the star of the show took to the stage, and Steine reluctantly opened his eyes. Huge applause went up as the band in the pit played the signature music for Professor Mesmer, Last of the Phrenologists ('Nice Work If You Can Get It' by George and Ira Gershwin), and Mrs Groynes nudged him.

'Cheer up,' she said. 'This bloke's very good by all accounts, dear.' Then she nudged him again. 'Oh, look, there's the sergeant over there. Yoo-hoo, Sergeant Brunswick!'

While the curtain parted to reveal Professor Mesmer and a row of dining chairs painted gold, Steine stood up (to the annoyance of the people behind him) and looked to where she had pointed. Brunswick was indeed here, in the far aisle, evidently clinging to a curvaceous young woman in a rather ostentatious show of affection and relief. He appeared to be in tears. Steine could scarcely believe it. 'What on earth?' he said. 'What's he doing?'

'He's with that Maisie.'

'Maisie?'

'I expect she's been messing him about again, leading him a merry dance. Some people never learn, do they? Ooh, but look, dear. Here he is! Professor Mesmer! They say he's at the height of his powers, whatever that means!'

Before he sat down, Steine was briefly conscious again of the flash of uniform in the front row; he also spotted (at the back of the hall) the young reporter from the *Argus* who had been at the Theatre Royal on the night of Crystal's murder. Was the uniform in the front row Constable Twitten's, by any chance?

Looking again, he thought it might well be, which would be quite a coincidence, what with Brunswick being here as well, and Mrs Groynes – and then suddenly all the doubt and fear that Steine had banked up inside himself was released in a glorious dam-burst, because now he *knew*! He knew for sure! If all these people were here, and pretending not to see him, this must all be part of the *This Is Your Life* conspiracy!

Why else would a reporter be present here tonight? Why else would Brunswick be here with his girlfriend, canoodling like the rest of the *hoi polloi* so as not to draw attention to himself? Perhaps Twitten's lengthy disappearance from the station had all been connected to the plans for the show as well! Perhaps he'd been ferrying Mother from Croydon Airport!

Steine stopped worrying about the Hippodrome audience. He thought of his famous childhood misdemeanour at the HMSO shop and glowed with pride. It would make a wonderful story for the television viewers. A little boy running off from the zoo to check the exact wording of the paragraph 'Disregard of Traffic Signals', with reference to Section 49 of the Road Traffic Act, 1930!

'What he said at the time,' continued his mother in this fantasy, 'was that: "An elephant would always look the same,

Mummy! Whereas Section 49 of the Traffic Act was rightly subject to legislative revision!"'

* * *

When the whole affair was over, Steine was forced to concede that he was glad to have seen Professor Mesmer 'at the height of his powers', because right up to the climactic moment when the tragedy occurred, it had been a truly magnificent show.

Initially, Mesmer himself was hard to make out under the beard and hat and bushy eyebrows, but in any case the distinctive thing about him turned out to be his voice. The accent was classless, the tone warm and open, the effect reassuring. In fact, the impact he had on the audience was so profound that it was inexplicable in rational terms: one moment they were a rowdy, overexcited crowd, spitting grape skins on the floor and starting small, localised fights; the next, they were quiet and focused, and not even chewing, with expectant smiles on their faces.

There was nothing solemn or forbidding about Professor Mesmer, however. He merely projected – in a genial, relaxed way – authority. The blazing lights, which had rendered all the other turns garish, conferred on him a godly radiance. Using charts and jokes, Mesmer spoke first about the old art (or science) of phrenology, with all its highfalutin' language of 'organs'. This elicited the expected sniggers. But then he turned serious, insisting that phrenology *did not lie*. Finally, he announced that he would be reading some heads and also doing a couple of safe experiments with 'phreno-magnetism' – and then the show began.

'Who will be first, ladies and gentlemen?' he asked. A drum rolled, and Mesmer put a hand up to shield his eyes from the light as he scanned the audience for likely subjects.

'Me! Me!' came cries from sections of the auditorium, as Mesmer's gaze swept over them. One young woman shouted, 'I love you, Professor Mesmer,' and it made him smile, but he carried on scanning.

Steine had never experienced anything like this. Was it entertainment, really? Should it perhaps be banned? And then Mesmer shouted, 'You, sir! In the uniform!' and the drum roll was rounded off with a cymbal ('Tsh!') and Steine stood up to look round again and see who had been picked out, and realised that, weirdly, everyone was looking at him.

'It's you, dear,' said Mrs Groynes.

'*What?*' Steine sat down. 'Are you sure?'

There was a murmur from the crowd – mostly a groan of disappointment that the chosen person was nobody they knew.

'Would you care to come up, sir?' Mesmer said, extending his hand.

Steine hesitated. Could he plead he was on duty? Could he feign a nosebleed? If he ran for the door, would anyone stop him? While he was quickly considering all these attractive options (he liked the nosebleed best), Mrs Groynes got up and pulled him to his feet.

'He's coming,' she yelled. 'He's coming if I have to drag him up, dear!'

To laughter and applause, she started to march Steine towards the stage.

'Care to come up yourself, madam?' Mesmer asked. 'I've got plenty of room.' He indicated five elegant chairs lined up on the stage.

But Mrs Groynes flapped her hands at him as if to say, 'Come off it', and went back to her seat, to a ripple of laughter.

Meanwhile Steine found himself walking up the steps onto the blindingly bright stage, where Professor Mesmer waited, arms open in a gesture of welcome and reassurance.

Steine noted that the smell on the stage was a powerful mixture of face powder, Brylcreem, lavender, rubber adhesive and explosives, but a quick search of his memory failed to explain why this could possibly be significant.

'Now, I'm known for how perceptive I am, and I'm guessing you're a policeman,' said Mesmer, with a smile.

The audience responded with a mixture of laughs, whoops, jeers and boos.

Steine introduced himself. There was a very small buzz of recognition when he gave his name, which was somewhat disappointing. Just one person shouted, 'Hooray!' and Steine had a horrible suspicion it was Brunswick. He felt sweat trickle down his cheek. It was hot up here. When he turned to look back to Mrs Groynes, he could see nothing beyond the footlights. This was not like talking on the radio.

'Have you ever been phrenologised before?'

'Of course not. I mean, I don't think so. I mean, no.'

'Well, there's no need to worry, it won't hurt.'

'Oh, good.'

Mesmer repeated this for the audience, as if it was exceptionally witty. 'He said, "*Oh, good,*" ladies and gentlemen. Now, I need you to sit on this chair, sir, and I'll stand behind you, and I'll place my hands on your head. I can already see you have some interestingly *enlarged organs.*'

The crowd laughed and whistled.

'I do apologise, sir. But that's Brighton for you.'

Steine sat down, full of dread. His mind was racing: when was *This Is Your Life* going to break this up? Why hadn't this awful crowd ever heard of him? And then Mesmer's hands were on his head, and he felt something he had never felt before: all the apprehensiveness in his mind – indeed, all the tension in his entire body – dissolved and flooded out of him.

'Ladies and gentlemen, what I find here immediately,' pronounced Mesmer, 'is a man who knows the difference between right and wrong. Am I correct?'

Steine nodded, dumbly. It was as much as he could do not to weep. The crowd was agog. Mesmer's hands were lightly pressing all over Steine's cranium, each finger finding a new spot, as if his head were an accordion.

'Now, there are people who are good,' continued Mesmer. 'And there are people who just know the difference between right and wrong. This man, I would say –' here he concentrated on the upper regions of the head '– *is* a good man, and a trusting one. What I'm feeling here is someone who is not afraid to take things at face value. Is that right?'

Again, Steine didn't speak, so Mrs Groynes called out from her seat. 'That's uncanny, dear. He does take things at face value, bless him.'

'He is a leader, by nature. Not a follower. I am seeing a rather serious child, ladies and gentlemen – a child perhaps that parents didn't understand; if they didn't have much imagination, they might even have found him unlovable. But that was their failing, not his. Perhaps he was always playing the policeman? Yes? On the side of law and order? Maybe sometimes his zeal for right and wrong made him a bit unpopular with his little friends?'

Steine sniffed. This was a far cry from what he'd been expecting tonight, but at the same time it was astonishing, and he didn't want it to end.

'He's a lousy rozzer!' shouted someone from the audience. Mesmer held up a hand.

'Now, stop that,' he said. 'Many men in the position of Inspector Steine are cynical and self-seeking. They are, in short, lousy rozzers.'

The audience laughed.

'But, believe me, I find nothing remotely corrupt – or even corruptible – about this man. He is if anything too trusting. But if he sees the goodness in people rather than the badness, I for one celebrate it as a breath of fresh air. Brighton is lucky to have such a man. I salute you, Inspector Steine!'

And with that, Mesmer removed his hands from Steine's head, and the audience applauded with enthusiasm – especially the large criminal element, for whom this information was extremely useful.

When it came to standing up again, Steine found that he couldn't, but Mesmer said – wonderfully –'No, you can remain seated, sir. I've had an idea.' So Steine was able to stay on the stage, which was a great relief. The idea of stumbling back down into the smelly pit, and rejoining the mortals, was horrible to him. He felt he now deserved to be part of this show for ever, and if Eamonn Andrews had walked on at this minute, interrupting everything, the inspector would have leaped up and punched him on the nose.

'Yes, I've had an idea,' Mesmer continued. 'I'd like to ask that lady to come up, after all.' And he called Mrs Groynes up onto the stage, amid cheers. Then Mesmer looked down to the front row, and indicated Twitten.

'There's another policeman down there, ladies and gentlemen,' he explained. 'Let's get him up here too and have some fun.' The men sitting either side of Twitten gave him a push up, and he actually climbed straight onto the stage, without using the steps, which to Steine seemed slightly odd, especially when Twitten, wild-eyed, lunged for him, saying, 'Sir, thank goodness, I must talk to you! It's very important! It's enormous!'

Steine was alarmed: was Twitten threatening to ruin this wonderful show? He was relieved when Mesmer grasped the constable by the shoulders and moved him forcibly to the other end of the row of chairs – where Twitten, still agitated, sat down.

'Now, please tell me your name and why you are here tonight with a senior policeman,' Mesmer asked Mrs Groynes.

'I'm the station charlady, aren't I? My name's Palmeira. Palmeira Groynes.'

The audience applauded. They approved of Palmeira already.

'Palmeira? Like Palmeira Square in Hove?'

'Named after Palmeira Square in Hove, in fact. I was conceived in the gardens there, by all accounts.'

'So you might equally have been called Russell?'

'That's right, dear. A lucky escape.'

'Now, Palmeira. I'd like to use phreno-magnetism on you. It's a kind of hypnosis. Is there any skill that you wish you had? Can you stand on your hands, for example?'

'I don't wish to stand on my hands, thank you.'

'What about singing? Can you sing?'

Mrs Groynes seemed to think about it. 'Not a note, dear. Sadly.'

'Is that true?' Mesmer asked Inspector Steine.

'Well, she does hum a bit while she's mopping.'

The audience laughed, while Mesmer repeated it. 'She hums a bit while she's mopping!'

Under cover of the laughter, Twitten slid along the row of chairs and tugged at Steine's jacket. 'Sir! I don't know what's going on here, sir. But I know everything else and Mrs Groynes is –'

'What's all this?' said Mesmer, smiling.

'I've no idea,' said Steine, pushing Twitten away. 'I can only apologise. He's very keen.' He addressed Twitten. 'This can *wait*, Constable.'

Reluctantly, Twitten returned to the chair at the far end. Steine tried not to look at him.

Then Mesmer turned back to Mrs Groynes, who was now seated in front of him, and began the bump-feeling process again. Once more, there was an intense hush.

'Ladies and gentlemen, I must inform you that this lady is far cleverer than she looks,' said Mesmer.

'Golly, you can say that again,' muttered Twitten.

'But what I find most enlarged on this head is the organ of Loyalty. Palmeira is a very caring person when it comes to people close to her. She also has a massive organ of Precognisance. Are you very good at planning, Palmeira? Am I right?'

'Yes, dear. I am.'

'When you plan ahead, you think of everything?'

'Yes, dear. I think I do.'

'Every last detail?'

'That's right.'

'Because sometimes a lot depends on it.'

'That's right. But never fear, dear. Never fear. We're nearly there.'

There was a moment when Mesmer seemed to be taking stock, and the audience held its collective breath. Sitting beside Mrs Groynes, Steine was as bemused (but enchanted) as everyone else. Then Mesmer broke the spell.

'But it's the singing we were going to talk about! I need you to trust me now, Palmeira, and let yourself lose control. Just for a moment, you see, you must *give* control.'

Mrs Groynes was motionless under his hands.

'So, imagine you are mopping the floor and humming, mopping and humming, and I take the mop from you – gently, gently – and now I've got it, you see, but it goes on smoothly, mopping, mopping, it goes on smoothly, the only difference is that I'm doing it, not you.'

He took his hands away, and the audience gasped. Mrs Groynes was in a trance. 'Can you hear me, Palmeira?'

'Yes, dear.'

'Can you sing?'

'I can, dear. Like a canary, if I say so myself.'

'That's good. Now, I'd like you to sing "The Boy I Love is Up in the Gallery" – can you do that?' He looked down to the orchestra pit. 'Maestro?'

The audience was spellbound. Inspector Steine was spellbound. Brunswick and Maisie, in the third row aisle-seats, were both spellbound. Twitten alone, watched closely by thugs in the front row – and spotting thugs guarding the wings at both sides of the stage – was in turmoil.

And then the orchestra struck up the introduction, and Mrs Groynes rose from her seat, had a little cough, clasped her hands to her chest, and sang.

* * *

After the applause died down, Mesmer turned to Twitten.

'Young man,' he said. 'You don't seem very comfortable up here.'

'I'm not.' There were boos from the audience, and cries of 'Shame!'

Twitten raised his voice. 'I'm not here of my own free will, for a start!'

Steine shot him a very stern look. He found Twitten's unsporting attitude to all this intensely embarrassing. 'Look, if it's good enough for me, young man,' he said – and earned a round of applause.

'I don't wish to do anything you're not happy with, Constable, but I've had an idea,' said Mesmer, moving along the row of chairs to stand behind Twitten. 'It sounds a little dangerous, but I promise there will be no permanent effect.'

He stood behind Twitten and placed his hands in position.

'It's as I thought! Ladies and gentlemen, this young man has an exceptional head, an amazing head. The head, I might say, of a genius.'

Twitten, who had just drawn breath to make another loud protest, stopped and bit his lip. 'Really?' he said. 'You can tell that?'

'Yes, I thought you'd like that,' said Mesmer, to a laugh from the audience. 'But I never flatter. I can honestly say that this is the cleverest person I've ever had under my hands – and I'm afraid that includes you, Inspector. And you, Palmeira. The sharpness of intellect here is phenomenal. What do you say to that, young man?'

'I'm amazed.'

'Amazed that you're a genius?'

'No, of course not! That you can tell I'm a genius from feeling my head, when phrenology has long been discredited as so much unscientific mumbo-jumbo!'

Steine winced with embarrassment.

'And I hope you realise,' Twitten went on, 'that phrenology as a system has always been eagerly adopted by eugenicists and racists?'

Steine adopted a thoughtful, faraway look.

'He forgets, ladies and gentlemen,' laughed Mesmer, 'that I'm quite clever, too. Now, I'm not going to put you into a trance, young man. In your case, I am simply going to use a trigger word while I have your full attention. And given the circumstances, the trigger word for this experiment will be "Einstein". Are you listening?'

'Yes.'

'Is Einstein acceptable to you? Einstein?'

'I'd rather you didn't use a trigger word at all, sir.'

Again the audience started booing.

'As I said before,' Twitten went on, 'I don't like this, and I am here under duress, and I need to speak urgently with the inspector about a very dangerous person who is in our midst *right now*. But thank you very much for calling me a genius.'

'Well, I'm sorry to disappoint you, Constable, but my experiment has already begun.'

'What?'

The audience laughed.

'I have already spoken the trigger word, and believe it or not you are in a state of hypnosis, so it would be highly inadvisable to break off suddenly. When you next hear the word from me, the experiment will be over, and you'll be restored to normal. Do you understand?'

'It doesn't feel like I'm in a state of hypnosis.'

'But you are. Trust me. You are in my power.'

'You won't make me sing?'

The audience laughed.

'No, no. We've done that.'

'I still don't like it.'

'Well, there's nothing you can do. I have said the trigger word. Anything I suggest to you now, you will simply believe until I say the word again.'

'Anything you suggest to me? Like what?'

Twitten's mind raced. *Mrs Groynes must be behind this, but how would she get this phrenologist to go along, and what would she ask him to do anyway, and why choose the bally word 'Einstein', that was a bit insulting –*

'Now, the lady sitting to your right – can you name her?'

'Yes. Mrs Groynes.' *She is behind this,* he thought. *Of course she's behind this. But what is she playing at?*

'She's the station charlady,' Mesmer said.

'Pardon?'

'She's the station charlady? She mops the floors?'

'Yes.' Twitten shrugged. 'And she makes jolly nice cups of tea.' *And she kills people and she's devious and she's up to something, but I can't bally well think what it is!*

Mesmer gave a big smile to the audience. He signalled for a drum roll from the pit. Twitten closed his eyes.

'Ladies and gentlemen, I suggest to this young man that Palmeira here, who makes jolly nice cups of tea is, in cunning disguise, a *master criminal*.'

'Oh, my good gawd,' exclaimed Mrs Groynes, as the audience tittered with laughter.

'Good heavens,' gasped Steine. 'The idea!'

'And that you, with your gigantic intellect, have worked out that this funny cockney charlady is behind all sorts of robberies and murders!'

Time stood still. The drum roll was still going. Steine was agog. Mrs Groynes was agog. The whole place was nothing but agog. All eyes were on Twitten. Had it worked?

'But she is!' cried Twitten, as cymbals clashed, and the audience began to applaud. 'She was behind the Aldersgate Stick-up, sir, that's what I wanted to tell you. And she shot Mr Crystal at the theatre the other night, and she had me coshed in London – coshed, sir – and she's got umpteen henchmen operating in this very theatre *at this minute*. This is maddening, sir!'

'Incredible!' exclaimed Steine, jumping up and clapping. He patted Mesmer's arm in congratulation, while the audience cheered and applauded and drummed their feet. What an amazing display of mind control.

'Stop! Stop applauding!' Twitten begged. 'It's a trick!'

'Of course it's a trick, dear,' said Mrs Groynes, wiping her eyes.

'Of course it's a trick,' agreed Mesmer. 'It's a really good one.'

'Well, I'll tell you something else!' Twitten was shouting to be heard, and had to wait for the laughter and applause to die down. He was stolidly refusing to be a sport about this. 'I'll still believe she's a master criminal even after you've said "Einstein" again.'

'No, you won't,' said Mesmer, smiling.

'But it's true, sir! I'll still say she shot Mr Crystal. So how are you going to explain that? Go on. Say "Einstein" again, Professor Mesmer. Say it now and we'll see whether I'm right or not.'

Mesmer turned to the crowd. 'Shall I say it, ladies and gentlemen?'

There was a roar of mixed 'No!' and 'Yes!' – with the 'No' contingent definitely in the majority.

'I can't quite hear you, ladies and gentlemen,' said Mesmer. 'Shall I say it?'

Which was when the tragic events of the evening suddenly irrupted. While the audience were shouting 'Yes!', and 'No!', and Mesmer was exaggeratedly cupping a hand to his ear, two young women rushed down the aisle of the auditorium from the back; a blonde woman Steine vaguely recognised as an actress from the Theatre Royal, and another – dark and intense-looking – with a telltale bulge in her raincoat pocket.

Brunswick – who had been shouting 'No!' along with most of the excited audience – spotted these two figures coming, and stepped out to block their path.

'Now calm down, ladies,' he said, gripping the arm of the blonde woman. 'Where do you think you're going? There's a show on here.'

'Let me go, Sergeant,' said the blonde, which was when he realised it was Penny Cavendish, and that the other woman was Jo Carver.

'Bobby!' cried Penny, trying to push past him.

'Bobby!' shouted Jo.

'Bobby?' said Brunswick, confused. He looked up at the stage and for the first time (at last!) clocked the identity of Professor Mesmer. '*The Professor is Bobby Melba?*'

But there was no time for the unfortunate sergeant to process such a huge piece of new information, or to start the arrest procedure. While the audience were baying their answers at the stage ('I can't quite hear you, ladies and gentle-men!'), Jo Carver produced a gun from her pocket and shot Sergeant Brunswick in the leg.

* * *

The audience kept on shouting. It was only when Jo (with Penny close behind) climbed onto the stage – and Professor

Mesmer backed away from them with his hands up – that people realised there was something wrong. All the previous calm and control gave way to confusion and alarm.

'What's she doing here?' muttered Mrs Groynes.

'Penny, you shouldn't have come!' said the Professor.

'That woman's got a gun!' said Steine.

The audience began to react – some people got up, but many remained frozen in their seats, watching events unfold. Was this part of the act, or not? On the stage, no one moved, but Bobby Melba's arms dropped to his sides as Jo moved closer to him and held the gun at arm's length, aiming it at his chest.

'Who's this woman?' said Steine.

'Bobby, you framed me,' said Jo.

Bobby swallowed. He breathed heavily. 'I did, Jo. It was unforgivable. But please put down the gun. I'm so sorry.'

'Who's Bobby?' asked Steine. 'Who's Jo?'

'You planted a wig and some jewellery in my dressing room.'

'We can talk about it, Jo. There's no need for the gun. It was a stupid thing to do – an unkind thing to do. I can only say I was desperate. The police were on to me, and they thought I'd committed a *murder*. But you know I'd never kill anyone!'

While he was talking, Bobby was slowly removing his hat, and peeling off his eyebrows and beard. He said, quietly, 'Does anyone know if this gun is loaded?'

To which Brunswick called out from the auditorium, 'Of course it's flaming loaded! She flaming shot me!'

The bemused audience tittered nervously. Whatever else came out of this astonishing scene, poor Sergeant Brunswick's Brighton underworld catchphrase was now destined to change from 'Eating flaming ice cream' to 'Of course it's flaming loaded!'

Bobby stood before her without his Professor Mesmer paraphernalia. His voice was steady and reassuring, but if you looked closely you would see that his hands were shaking. Steine noticed for the first time that the ends of his fingers were odd-looking, somewhat like little hammers. Again, this information rang no bells in particular.

'Look, it's only me, Jo. It's your friend Bobby. Give me the gun, dear. Give me the gun.'

'It's a trick!' said Twitten. 'It's a put-up job! I am virtually certain that this is all a put-up job!'

But even Mrs Groynes was looking very serious. Meanwhile Penny's expression was one of utter terror. Her lips were moving as she said to herself, 'Give him the gun, give him the gun… don't shoot him… please don't shoot him… give him the gun.'

But Jo did not give Bobby the gun.

'How about you give *me* the gun, dear?' said Mrs Groynes, gently. 'There's a good girl.'

But Jo did not look round. Instead, she cocked the hammer.

Steine wondered whether he ought to be joining in with this negotiation himself, and made a decision. 'Twitten,' he ordered, 'instruct this woman to give you her gun.'

But Twitten didn't get the chance.

'I thought you cared about me, Bobby,' Jo Carver said. 'I thought some day –'

Bobby lunged for the gun, catching Jo by the wrist – possibly forgetting that she had the strongest wrists of any woman who ever lived. He screamed when she easily bent back his hands. As the two of them dropped to the stage and began to fight, with the gun out of sight between them, Penny rushed forward but was held back by Mrs Groynes.

'Bobby, no!' Penny cried.

People in the audience were standing on the seats to get a better view of Bobby and Jo, rolling around downstage. They shouted excitedly, 'He's on top now!' and 'She's on top now!' and 'He's back on top!' and (from those who hadn't quite caught up with what was happening), 'This is what I call entertainment!'

And then *Bang!* – the bodies stopped rolling, with Jo on top, crying, 'Oh, Bobby, I'm sorry.' All gasped in horror. And then there was another *Bang!* And Jo went limp, and both of them lay still.

'Bobby!' wailed Penny, still being held back by Mrs Groynes.

'No!' groaned Mrs Groynes.

'Crikey,' said Twitten.

'Oh, good heavens,' said Steine. 'Shouldn't somebody do something?'

There was a momentary silence, and then Brunswick yelled, 'Call for a flaming ambulance! And no one leaves this theatre!'

Twitten was stunned. It was all too much.

'So, do you still think this is a *trick*?' said Steine. 'With two people dead?'

As if on cue, Bobby stirred, groaning. The audience gasped, while Twitten ran to his side. 'Say "Einstein", Professor Mesmer!' he begged. 'Please, say "Einstein"!'

The audience booed. Steine booed as well. What a selfish – and perfectly shocking – reaction to this tragedy.

Twitten knelt beside Bobby, and took his hand. 'Just say "Einstein", sir. Please?'

But Bobby spluttered and mouthed the words, 'I'm sorry' – and that was it. The curtain was lowered, and in the auditorium, Maisie began to scream.

* * *

The rest of the evening was undramatic by comparison. A man with a Greek accent barged onto the stage and took control, directing men from the St John's Ambulance as they lifted the bodies onto stretchers and removed them. Someone identified him as the Punch & Judy man from the beach, but Steine didn't know or care if this was true, as long as someone took those awful bodies away.

Meanwhile Brunswick's leg was attended to – and Brunswick forgave a weeping Maisie when she said she was sorry for making him worried about her all day. She said she'd been perfectly safe, and there had been no man called Twitty responsible for her disappearance. She'd just wanted to give him and Vince a fright, to see how much they both cared about her. (What she neglected to say was that Mrs Groynes had promised her two tickets to Frank Sinatra at the Albert Hall, to get her to do it.)

'Well, you certainly did give me a fright, Maisie,' said Brunswick, wincing and clutching his leg. 'But I wish you'd chosen a better day to do it. I was close to flaming arresting that man for the murder of Jack Braithwaite, and now I never can!'

Twitten sat on his chair, stunned. He still wanted to believe it was all a trick – but how to account for Penny Cavendish, who was genuinely distraught with shock and grief? Throughout all the proceedings, he had watched Mrs Groynes, and she had stopped looking triumphant the moment Jo and Penny had arrived in the theatre. 'What's she doing here?' she had said. Obviously his own hypnotising had been part of a plan – but the shooting, too?

Right now, however, he couldn't ask her. She was busy apologising to Inspector Steine, who was looking dazed and had undone the top button of his tunic.

'I'm so sorry I got you here, dear. It's all my fault you saw this! Look at you now, all undressed.'

'Now, don't be silly, Mrs Groynes. It's not your fault at all.'

'No, dear. I'm afraid I have to tell you something – something I kept from you. The thing is, dear, I got a message today to telephone some people. Some people from the programme *This Is Your Life*, dear.'

'What?' said Steine, affecting disbelief. '*This Is Your Life*? What did they want to talk about?'

'Well, you, dear. They wanted to talk about you.'

'What, to be the subject of a *This Is Your Life* programme? Me? I'm sure I'm not famous enough!'

Mrs Groynes laughed her agreement (a bit tactlessly, in Steine's opinion). 'I know! I was surprised myself. I mean, I know you're famous, but I didn't think you were *that* famous. I mean, no offence, but I wouldn't watch it myself if you were on, and I'm someone who knows you! Anyway, that's why I asked you to come here tonight. It was a ruse, dear. Nothing more than that.'

Steine looked at the floor where the two bodies had been. 'There's not a speck of blood, look,' he said. 'I suppose that's because they were face to face.'

'So I just wanted to say sorry, dear, not to have told you the truth. But they said it had to be a secret. "*Don't let on,*" they kept saying. "*If he knows, it will be ruined!*" And then when they phoned again at six o'clock to say it was all off, I didn't see how I could tell you it was off – not having told you it was on in the first place!'

She laughed, weakly. He tried to laugh too. 'So it was called off, you say?'

'Yes, dear. They were furious. Eamonn Andrews was really looking forward to it, he said. But I thought, well, the inspector doesn't even know about it, so he can't be upset. I mean, what you don't have, you don't miss – that's what they say, isn't it?'

Steine sighed. He looked round, remembering the scene on this stage as he had pictured it earlier: Eamonn Andrews with his big red book, and arrayed on chairs, all smiling at him and singing his praises, former police colleagues, old friends from the Operatic Society, childhood arrestees(!), glamorous royal personages, and his elderly mother in that strange khaki safari outfit that she nowadays always wore, with the long brown knee-socks, and around her neck a big silver locket containing a picture of the dear departed Hugh Lees-Chetwynde.

In place of that vision, what he saw now was a scene including his prone sergeant, bleeding from the thigh; a hysterical actress wrapped in a blanket; and a gibbering constable who had been hypnotised into thinking that all the crime that ever happened in England had been orchestrated by the inoffensive, wittering charlady currently confessing to a highly understandable white lie.

'Any idea why they cancelled it?' he asked.

'Sorry, dear?'

'Why did they cancel it?'

'Oh. Something about Princess Margaret, they said.'

'Princess Margaret!' It came out as a wail so loud and agonised that many people looked round.

'Princess Margaret was going to come?' the inspector whispered.

Mrs Groynes put her hand on his arm. 'She was, dear. She wanted to. But that's why they cancelled, you see. It turns out your mum disapproved!'

A Bit After That

Twelve

The following Monday, at 8 a.m., Constable Twitten reported for duty for the second time at Brighton Police Station. He found it deserted, aside from Mrs Groynes, who welcomed him warmly and made him a cup of tea.

Since the events at the Hippodrome, Twitten had spent time at home in Oxfordshire with his parents, recuperating and considering his future as a policeman. He'd had a lot to think about. For example, was he too young to retire at twenty-two? Should he join the church instead? Or should he turn his talents to anthropology – as his father had always hoped? After all, those kinship systems in the Fens wouldn't untangle themselves, would they? (That was indeed part of the problem.)

But he had to ask himself: was he suffering from real disillusionment with the career he had chosen, or was it simple wounded pride? It was very hard to take, after all: that on the same night as he was proclaimed a genius (by an expert), he had been roundly outwitted by this middle-aged woman in a housecoat and turban, who was currently having difficulty shaking fig rolls from a packet onto a little tin tea-plate.

'You came back, dear,' she said, smiling. 'I wasn't sure you would.'

'I needed to ask you a few things.'

'Fair enough, dear. Fig roll?'

'No, thank you.'

'Oh, go on. You know you want to.'

'Oh, very well, then. Yes, please.'

He looked round for a place to sit down, and she indicated Sergeant Brunswick's desk. This was all very awkward, especially as Mrs Groynes was behaving as though nothing was the matter.

'He's off with his leg for the time being,' she explained. 'But he's loving the glory of it, so don't feel sorry for him.'

'I went to see him in the hospital yesterday, as it happens.'

'That was nice of you.'

'I told him I needed some facts.'

'And I'm sure that cheered him right up, dear.'

Twitten was not amused. 'Well, I did express sympathy too. It was just as well I went to see him, actually, as he'd started to form a theory that I was a psychopath.' He sipped his tea. 'Where's Inspector Steine?'

Mrs Groynes sat down beside him and put her hand on his knee, as if they were the best of friends. 'He's only down at the Palace Pier, being filmed for the newsreels! Always falls on his feet, that one. Actually, you'll be interested in this, dear. It's only being made public today, it was very hush-hush. You know that Deputy Chief Whatsit in London – what was his name, Peplow?'

'DCI Peplow, yes. From the Met. I worked for him for about a week. He really disliked me for some reason.'

'For being too clever?'

'Well, more precisely for saying, "I wonder what's under this rug, sir?" I think.'

'Well, you'll like this, then. He's dead, dear.'

'Crikey. What happened?'

'Fell through the Pier with that Harry Jupiter in bizarre circumstances. And before you go jumping to conclusions, I had nothing to do with it. It was a godsend to the inspector – a bit like a miracle, as it happens – but I had no hand in it no-how.'

Twitten drank his tea, and looked out of the window. It was a beautiful day. On his walk to the police station, he had stopped to look at the sparkling sea, and watch the seagulls swooping. He had also seen a female pickpocket bump into a nicely dressed holidaymaker in broad daylight, giggle an apology and lift a wallet from his stripy blazer. If he went back to studying those fascinating, interbred semi-aquatic people of East Anglia, wouldn't he miss all this?

'Well, since we're alone, Mrs Groynes, I've been doing a lot of thinking.'

'You want to ask me to clear things up for you. It's only natural.'

'I didn't want to ask you. I hoped I wouldn't have to. But after talking to the sergeant, and thinking I'd got nearly everything worked out, I've realised there's one thing I don't understand at all. So you've got to tell me. It's Jo Carver, the strong lady. I just don't see where she fits in.'

Mrs Groynes raised her eyebrows. 'Really? You haven't worked out how Jo Carver *fits in*?'

'So who is she? I mean, who *was* she?'

Mrs Groynes walked to the door and locked it, then came and sat down. She lit a cigarette. 'I'll pour you another cup before I start,' she said. 'We might be here for some time.'

And so Mrs Groynes went back to the very start of the story, to the days when she was the youthful partner (in crime, as well as other things) of the notorious East End mobster Terence Chambers.

'You see, everything changed for Terry and me around the end of the war when he took on these two young people – you could call them *wards*, I suppose. They weren't his flesh and blood; they were the kids of a bloke who'd saved his life (that's what he said) in France in 1918. They stayed friends after. Terry'd gone in for the life of crime, of course, but this other bloke was a musician and as honest as the day is long. And he was widowed, and he had this daughter and this son he was bringing up on his own, and then one day just before VE Day, he was killed in a bus crash, and Terry brought the kids home and that was that.

'Joan was the girl, and Robert was her elder brother. I remember I wasn't keen on the idea… I wasn't ready for kids. I said they'd get in the way unless we had them climbing through windows for us like in *Oliver Twist* – and Terry, he said, all serious, he'd kill anyone who corrupted them kids! It really took me aback how fierce he was about it. He'd never turned on me like that before, and I was quite upset. He said he wanted Jo and Bobby to have a normal life, and God help anyone who led them astray.

'I'll skip the bits where we bonded at teatimes and visited the Tower of London and went hopping down in Kent and what have you, but we did have some happy times as a little family. Are you comfortable there?'

'Yes, thank you.'

'So, as you rightly guessed, I hit that bank the day before Terry was planning to – but not because I wanted to annoy him, dear – or "earn his everlasting enmity", as you put it.

Oh, no. I wanted to save his bacon – not that he ever thanked me, but there you are. The thing is, dear, I was sure he was being led into a trap. He was working with this new partner at the time – and there was something dodgy about this cove; I could smell he was a copper. "You're being set up, darling," I said. "Think again, sweetheart," I said. "The job's too good to be true, love." But would he listen? So I came up with this plan as the only way to stop him: rob the bank myself the day before.'

'That was very clever.'

'Thank you, dear. But I made a big error of judgement. I needed help, and I told young Jo and Bobby what was going on, and they offered to be my gang for the day, so that no one else was in on it. I should have said no. But at the time, I couldn't see the harm. I didn't see how it would "corrupt" them. Jo could drive the getaway car, so she didn't even need to be inside the bank. But Bobby – well, he might have been older, but he was inexperienced, and he made a mistake.'

'What sort of mistake?'

'Well, although we had the masks and all that, he let that Crystal man see his hands.'

Twitten had already discussed this with Sergeant Brunswick – how easy it was not to spot the giveaway fingers; how clever Bobby Melba was in keeping them moving, so that you didn't notice.

'I'd told him to keep them covered, but he sneezed. He put his hand up automatically, you see. And there was just a split second, in the middle of everything, when Crystal saw them. And then Bobby said – oh, my good gawd – he said, "Sorry, Auntie Palmeira!"'

'Lumme.'

'Yes, dear. *Lumme* indeed. That's why I put the bag over Crystal's head, dear. It's why I fired the shots. I wanted to scare him into forgetting what he'd seen.'

'Because if Mr Crystal had remembered the funny fingers, Terence Chambers might find out you had corrupted his wards?'

'That's right. And then he would have killed me. Simple as that. For leading them into violent crime.'

'I see.' Twitten was thoughtful. 'Wasn't the word *sneeze* already on Crystal's list?'

'Not *already*, no. He'd only just written it when I shot him, dear. Before that, the list only had the bags, and *Palmeira*, and the run-over policeman – which I notice is a detail you never even got started on, dear.'

'The problem I'm having with all this, Mrs Groynes, is that the Aldersgate Stick-up wasn't a violent crime, was it? It was pretty peaceful. No one was hurt.'

'Ah. I'm afraid that's just the myth, dear. No one inside the bank was hurt, that's true. But while Jo was waiting in the car in a quiet side-street near to Smithfield, she spotted Terry's new partner –'

'The one who was dodgy?'

'Exactly. And he saw her too. And when she realised he knew who she was, and what she was doing there, she panicked and she ran him over.'

'What?'

'I know.'

'She killed him?'

'That's right. He was the *run-over policeman*. Crystal hadn't remembered that incident, of course. Miss Sibert must have led him to it.'

'Did she do it accidentally? Jo, I mean.'

'No, I don't think so. She reversed over him to be on the safe side.'

'That's awful. How old was she?'

'Eighteen, dear.'

'Just out of the blue, she did that?'

'That's how it seemed, yes. Of course afterwards I asked myself whether there had ever been any warning signs, and I'm afraid there had. She was what they nowadays call a *bad seed*, dear. Looking back, it's quite possible she shoved her own father under that bus! But she had Bobby, didn't she? Young Bobby to protect her and cover up for her – that's often what happens with orphans, isn't it? He looked out for her all their lives.

'Anyway, when we came out of the bank, Bobby and I had no idea what she'd done – and when she told us, we all swore then and there that Terry must never know any of it.

'That's how I came down here to Brighton. When I started here at the station, it wasn't because it was a brilliant place to operate from – although it *is* – it was because it was a good place to hide. But then, when I looked about me, I started to realise how easy it would be to divide and rule in this town. And of course you know the rest.'

'So what did Bobby and Jo do then?'

'They both went to drama school, which Terry paid for, none the wiser. He's still very proud of them. He wanted them both to be actors on the legitimate stage, but he's happy with the careers they've got. I'd already got Bobby interested in phrenology, and he took to it so well that it was quite a natural thing for him to make it his livelihood.'

'And Jo became a strong lady. Was she always strong, then?'

'No. While she was at drama school, she had a silly run-in with another student. I think she just laughed at him when he was doing a love scene, something like that. She was never very tactful; it's like she's got a bit missing, you see. A bit missing.

'But this other student was a vengeful sort of person, it turned out. She thought he'd forgiven her, but he was just biding his time – and one day they had fencing practice and he deliberately wounded her, and she ended up in a wheel-chair for a while. And that's when she started strengthening her wrists and arms – and discovered, in the end, she could tear up telephone books and whatnot.

'I have to say I was a bit worried about her combining phe-nomenal strength with that bad-seededness of hers, and so was Bobby – but he was always there to look after her, you see. They were so close, Bobby and Jo. They toured everywhere together. They just kept it a secret that they were related.'

Twitten remembered with some embarrassment that he had asked how Jo Carver 'fitted in'. It was too late now to re-phrase the question. And Mrs Groynes had evidently not finished yet. She got up and poured them two more cups of tea.

'And then Bobby turned to crime anyway?' he prompted, as he took the cup and saucer from her. 'He dressed up as a woman from the Opinion Poll. Does Terry know about that?'

'Oh, no, dear. Definitely not. The thing is, after the Stick-up there was a piece in the paper about this undercover police-man who'd been run over near Smithfield. I'd been right, you see: he *was* a lousy rozzer all the time. And guess what? He'd been a war hero, just like Jo and Bobby's dad. Bobby couldn't live with the guilt of it, and he persuaded Jo that they should send money anonymously to the policeman's widow. The way they funded it was with the proceeds of the Opinion Poll scam, which they did together. Sometimes the lady was Jo, but more often it was Bobby dressed up. They never kept a penny for themselves.'

Twitten wasn't quite convinced by this justification for a crime that robbed innocent people of their prized possessions, but he let it pass. In the relativist world-view of Groynes, the Opinion Poll scam had been in such a good cause that it was practically a charitable enterprise.

'Why red hair?' Twitten asked.

'Well, when Bobby dressed up as a woman, he always took me as his model, for some reason. His auntie Palmeira. I was very touched by that. I've got red hair, you see. It doesn't really go with being a charlady, so I keep it covered. Sometimes he even used some of my expressions and whatnot. For his own amusement. I didn't mind. I liked it.'

'Didn't Bobby put the sergeant onto Jo as a suspect? That wasn't very brotherly.'

'Yes, but that was just a way of buying time. She had a solid alibi, didn't she? She'd have been out next day without charges if she hadn't panicked and escaped. But that's Jo and Bobby for you. Bobby always thoughtful and protective, and following the plan to the letter; Jo always unpredictable and prone to outbursts of sickening violence. It takes all sorts, dear. It takes all sorts.'

* * *

At the Palace Pier, Inspector Steine was thanked for his time as the newsreel men packed up their equipment. It was such a nice day, he thought he would pop to Luigi's before returning to the station and facing the Twitten Problem that he knew awaited him. Having a permanently hypnotised constable on his team was not a happy prospect.

On that fateful night at the Hippodrome, people had taken it in turns to say 'Einstein' to Twitten, but to no avail. The boy continued to maintain that Mrs Groynes was a criminal Mrs Big, and to dismiss every piece of common-sense reasoning from the same insane perspective.

'Where is your evidence against Mrs Groynes?'

'She destroyed it, sir!'

'We have a typed confession from Jack Braithwaite to the murder of A. S. Crystal.'

'But Mrs Groynes wrote it!'

The inspector pictured the scene in the future: the telephone rings with news of a post-office robbery in the Fiveways district of the town. First of all, Sergeant Brunswick pipes up, 'Permission to pose as a postman, sir,' and then Twitten chips in, 'I think we need look no further than Mrs Groynes!'

As he walked, he realised there was someone following a pace or two behind. He stopped to see who it was.

It was the young reporter from the *Argus*, who seemed to pop up everywhere. He had been present at the Hippodrome on Steine's big night; his excellent report – using vivid, verbless sentences in homage to Harry Jupiter – had been a great hit with the editor, who not only re-hired but promoted him.

'They've made me Crime Correspondent,' said Oliver. 'So I thought I should let you know we'll be working together in the future, sir.'

'Excellent,' said Steine, pleasantly. 'Congratulations.'

'Thank you, sir.'

'Assuming there's any crime for you to write about.'

'Oh, I think there will be, sir.'

They walked together.

'Off the record, sir –'

'Yes?'

'I talked with DCI Peplow at length on the morning that he died, sir, and I got the impression there was no love lost between you.'

'Between me and Peplow? That's odd. I hardly knew the man.'

'Well, he very much disliked you, sir.'

'Really?'

'Yes. He considered you overrated. I told him my theory that you had knocked Mr Jupiter into the sea – but that Mr Jupiter's memory loss saved you from facing charges – and he burst out laughing and stated that your entire career was built on flukes.'

'Flukes?'

'Lucky accidents, sir.'

'I know what flukes are, thank you.'

'I just wondered whether you saw things in the same light yourself, sir. Off the record.'

Steine scowled. This was outrageous.

'I mean, he did have a point, sir. For instance, it was very lucky for you that the Middle Street Massacre came out as a triumph for you personally,' Oliver persisted, 'and it was lucky for you that just as I was about to establish the truth about your knocking Mr Jupiter into the sea, he went in the sea *again*, together with a rival policeman who was delighted at the prospect of your being exposed.

'Also, you have a very high reputation as a policeman, but it's not based on any actual success in fighting crime: it's based on telling people the history of lighting-up time, and whether they can carry a tray of potted geraniums on differ-ent sections of the London Underground. And now, in the case of the deaths of Crystal and Braithwaite, a confession just turns up out of the blue that absolves you of any need to detect other culprits.'

The reporter laughed, but Steine did not. He didn't like the sound of any of this.

'What are you implying?' he demanded.

'Nothing at all, sir.'

'Oliver, that confession of Braithwaite's is patently genuine.'

'If you say so, sir.'

'The murderer is the only person who could have written it. No one apart from the police knew the detail of the regimental sword. In fact, outside the police station, even the method of killing was unknown. *Ergo*, the guilty man wrote it.'

'Absolutely, sir. I appreciate that. But the fact remains: it's still lucky for you that he did, isn't it? There was no earthly need to leave an explanatory note! That's why I just wanted to ask you, off the record, whether you've ever acknowledged the fact that you are a freakishly fortunate policeman?'

* * *

Back at the station, Mrs Groynes stood up, and was about to grab the mop, when Twitten remembered something.

'So who did kill Jack Braithwaite?'

'Ha!' laughed Mrs Groynes, sitting down again. 'I'm really enjoying talking to you like this. This is better than a weekend in Bognor.'

'I'm assuming he didn't *kill himself*?'

'No, no. Jo again.'

'*What?*'

'I'm afraid so.'

'I don't believe it. Why?'

'Because Jack Braithwaite was the student who had wounded her at drama school, and it was the first time she'd seen him since then – and according to Bobby, she went berserk.

'Bobby had no idea Jack was staying at that house, of course. He'd seen Jack a few times in the intervening years, but had always shielded Jo from knowing about it, because the mere mention of Braithwaite made her so angry. So they went in together to rob the house, and split up – Jo went upstairs, Bobby started in the front living room. And suddenly there was Jack, waiting for him. Jack jumped on him, but when he saw it was Bobby, he was so dumbfounded that he stopped. He poured himself a drink – Bobby had one too, to steady his nerves.

'Naturally he was quite anxious about Jack unveiling him as a criminal; but he was much more anxious about what would happen if Jo came in and found Jack Braithwaite there.

'And then, while he was still trying to think, she came in, saw Braithwaite and attacked him with this sword she pulled off the wall.'

'Oh, crikey! How awful!'

'Bobby tried to stop her. All the disarray in the room was because he was struggling with her. Apparently Braithwaite just cowered on the settee, pleading for his life.'

'No!'

'But Jo was stronger than Bobby. It's the story of their lives. The next thing he knew, the room was a bloodbath.'

Once again, Twitten reflected with embarrassment that he had only wanted to know how Jo Carver 'fitted in'. He felt a bit sick.

'You all right, dear?' Mrs Groynes asked, kindly. 'Are you feeling a bit like a soppy ha'p'orth?'

'Well, yes, quite frankly, I am. But I was also thinking that Sergeant Brunswick *had* already identified Bobby as the

Opinion Poll lady. He'd done some very good detective work. He was getting close. I wonder why he didn't search the dressing rooms for bloodstained clothes and so on? Why didn't he do that?'

'I think he did his best, dear. And with no help from me, as you can imagine! Sending him on a wild goose chase looking for Maisie was the best I could come up with to buy Bobby a bit of breathing space. Yes, you're right. He did very well, Sergeant Brunswick, this time.'

* * *

Lying in his hospital bed, Sergeant Brunswick idly perused *Behind the Eyes of a Killer* (by the world-famous criminal psychologist J. R. R. Twitten), and waited for his auntie Violet. He was utterly fed up. If only her flat wasn't on the second floor, he'd be allowed to go home, but it would be a week or more before he'd be safe to tackle stairs. The only advantage to being cooped up in hospital like this was that he knew now what a narcissist was (and it was a bit disappointing).

The events at the Hippodrome still buzzed in his head: first, arriving there with Vince, and the gale of relief when he found Maisie safe and well; then a long and agonising period while all his colleagues from the police station were called up on the stage – which was all very unfair, what with Brunswick being the one who loved the Hippodrome, and who idolised Professor Mesmer.

But instead of being called up to take part in the act himself, he'd had to watch while Inspector flaming Steine's great qualities as a policeman were announced to the world – and then, to top things off perfectly, Brunswick had been shot.

Lurking behind his sense of outrage were, however, deeper stirrings of doubt and self-blame. It was hard for him to visit one particular suspicion – but it wouldn't go away. Had Melba/Mesmer played him for a fool?

He kept remembering with anguish his visit to Mesmer's dressing room, just minutes after he'd seen the Opinion Poll lady enter through the stage door. Mesmer had been so calm, so helpful, showing such kindness to a fan, offering to *feel his head*. And then – well, twenty minutes had mysteriously disappeared.

'You were gone half an hour!' Maisie had insisted, repeatedly, the next day. And he'd accused her of exaggerating. But what if he *had* been gone half an hour? Could it explain why he never put two and two together, that Bobby was the professor?

'He hypnotised you, Jim, that's what,' said Maisie, when he talked to her about it at morning visiting time. 'What a bastard.' She was chewing gum, and it made beautiful dimples dance in her cheeks. She also bumped up and down on her chair, so that her bust jiggled.

'But possibly I just missed everything,' he said, gloomily. 'I can be a bit star-struck, Maisie. For one thing, I took him to be a much older man. I didn't even look at his fingers. I missed the biggest giveaway of them all: the fact that the Opinion Poll lady's hands smelled of Brylcreem.'

'You were looking for a woman, Jim.'

'Good point, Maisie, thank you.'

She laughed. 'And now they've got that suicide note it turns out you were barking up the wrong tree anyway.'

Brunswick rolled his eyes in misery, and Maisie gave him a mock-stern look. 'Listen. You're a very good policeman, Jim. Blimey, you keep getting shot, for one thing!'

He attempted a smile.

'Here,' she said, pulling out her gum until it formed a thin string, and then gobbling it back again. 'Now don't get jealous, darling –'

Brunswick glowed when she called him 'darling'.

'– but Vince wanted to take me up London, and I said yes. I mean, what with you laid up here for months, I need a bit of fun. And it's Frank Sinatra. At the Albert Hall. I couldn't say no, now could I?'

Brunswick felt helpless. How could he compete with Frank Sinatra? He'd looked into it once, and the tickets cost more than his auntie's monthly rent.

'Well, I wish you wouldn't, Maisie.'

'I know you do!' she laughed. 'I told him you'd be jealous. But you know what? It made him all the more determined. Here, I should play you two off against each other a bit more, shouldn't I? I wouldn't mind seeing that Mario Lanza some time, would you? What d'you say to that, Jim? You can take me to see Mario Lanza!'

* * *

Back at the station, Twitten realised – somewhat belatedly – that there was something wrong in the way Mrs Groynes had told him all these stories.

'Mrs Groynes, I might be missing something, but didn't you indicate that you *loved* Bobby and Jo?'

'I did love Bobby very much, dear, yes. Jo slightly less, on account of all the random violence, and also on account of being terrified of her personally.'

'So why aren't you weeping or upset?'

'No need, dear. We made a plan and it went like a dream. Apart from a certain Clever Dick Constable shouting, "*It's a trick! It's a trick!*" that is. But luckily you're so discredited, dear, that no one took any notice, did they?'

'So the shooting *was* a trick!'

'Course it was.'

Twitten groaned. This day was getting worse and worse. 'You mean even Penny Cavendish was in on it? It was her reaction that convinced me it was all real.'

'No. I'll admit she was the icing on the cake, dear. She wasn't supposed to be there. But everything else was planned: the gun having one live shot in the barrel – for wounding the sergeant. As for the rolling and wrestling and the double-dying, dear – Jo and Bobby have practised that little charade for years, and they've never done it better. There was only one thing I wasn't happy with: the St John's Ambulance men got there suspiciously quickly, didn't you think? Almost as if they were waiting in the wings. I had to have a little word with Vince about that.'

She rummaged in the pocket of her housecoat and produced a postcard. It had been sent from Dover.

'Bobby says he and Jo are on their way to France. He wants to tell Penny the truth but he can't, can he? He'll always have to look after his sister. But he says he's very glad never to have to ask anyone again to list the different ways they cook potatoes, so there you are, something good's come out of it.

'He's a good boy, you see. A very good brother. As for Penny, it's best for her to move on. But I tell you what, dear, she'll make a fantastic Gertrude one day, you mark my words.'

Mrs Groynes folded the card and put it back in her pocket.

'Poor Miss Cavendish,' said Twitten, solemnly.

'You're right. They really fell for each other, those two. But when you think about it, they only knew each other for less than three days, so I expect she'll recover in time.'

* * *

And so we will leave them, with Constable Twitten still officially undecided about his future. What he has to ask himself is whether catching criminals is for him a purely moral issue, or whether he's actually much more interested in establishing facts to his own satisfaction.

Sergeant Brunswick, on the other hand, feels more strongly than ever that bad people should be caught and punished. Lying in his hospital bed, he is thinking of new ways to convince Inspector Steine that undercover work is the way forward – even for a man with a giveaway limp. He sees himself posing as a limping fisherman, or a limping seaside photographer, or perhaps a limping gardener tending a Hove Lawns floral clock.

The fact that every criminal in Brighton knows what he looks like – and can quote back to him the hilarious 'Of course it's flaming loaded!' – never occurs to Sergeant Brunswick. It thrills him to imagine the moment of truth when he throws off his disguise and says, 'All right, Chalkie. The game's up. I'm a policeman and you're nicked.'

And Inspector Steine? Nothing has changed. He still wishes, more than anything, for Brighton to be a quiet and well-ordered society; for criminals to take their business elsewhere. As he eats his Knickerbocker Glory in Luigi's, he is glad that last week is over. First there was the critic killed, then the playwright, then Jupiter and Peplow, then Professor Mesmer and the strong lady – the final body count doesn't bear thinking about. Two, four – no, he can't go on.

On whom should this horrible sequence of events ultimately be blamed? he wonders. There must be someone who can be held responsible. Braithwaite must take his share of culpability, having two of the deaths firmly attributed to him. But as he spoons the glacé cherry from the glass (he's kept it specially for the final mouthful), Inspector Steine decides that the person he blames most for all this is actually Graham Greene.

Meanwhile, in the world of the theatre, the myth of the tragic-heroic Jack Braithwaite is already beginning to bubble into life, conferring on *A Shilling in the Meter* something of the literary status of the odes of John Keats. That a young and magnetic writer should feel so strongly about the death of his friend that he would commit murder and suicide stirs the imagination of disaffected youth. When an important playwriting prize is later established in Braithwaite's memory, there is no hesitation in naming it the Bang Bang Ta Ta Prize. There is good reason for thinking that Braithwaite, had he lived, would never have achieved comparable status, although that doesn't really justify his murderer getting away with it.

Back at the station, Mrs Groynes makes another cup of tea for the constable, and finds a nice piece of left-over coconut ice in a tin with a picture of the Coronation on it. The coconut ice is a bit brown and crusty round the edges, but still sweet and sticky within. Twitten takes it from her, uncertainly.

'Go on, dear. You need your strength if you're staying. Or if you're buggering off elsewhere, for that matter.'

He finds that tears have come to his eyes.

'What's the matter, dear?' she asks. 'Need a huggie?'

'I don't know what to do, Mrs Groynes.' It comes out as a wail.

'About what?'

'About being a policeman, now that I know what I know.'

She sits beside him again, and says, gently, 'Then I'll tell you. It's quite simple. Don't cry, dear. You have to accept defeat graciously, that's what.'

'But you're a criminal. A major criminal. And people here tell you anything, *all the time*! You were able to write that confession – and have everyone believe it – because you knew things *no one outside the police station knew*. I have to do something about you.'

286

'But you don't, because you can't. Think of it as a kind of freedom. Look at it that way. You did your best and you lost, dear; there's no shame. And now you're off the hook. So when the inspector comes in today, you just say that you'll never accuse me again because you understand it's a totally mad idea that was planted in your brain by a naughty hypnotist in front of a thousand witnesses.'

'I don't think I can do that,' he snivels.

'Yes, you can. The alternative would be to have Inspector Steine saying "Einstein" at you all the time, which would actually be worse.'

Twitten half-smiles, but he isn't ready to agree with her. Not yet.

'Come on. That would be maddening, wouldn't it, dear? Him jumping out of cupboards saying "Einstein"?'

He hangs his head, while she waits.

She looks at the ceiling. He continues to look at the floor.

Finally, he takes a deep breath. 'So, say I do all that,' he says. 'Say I promise Inspector Steine I'll never accuse you again of being a master criminal, or say you shot Mr Crystal. Where will we stand, then, you and me?'

'You and me? Blimey, haven't you guessed? You and me will be ever the best of friends!'

She moves closer, so that their knees are touching.

'So what I have to ask you is this, and don't look so scared, dear. You've got to answer me this one thing honestly or not at all.'

'What is it?'

'What's your favourite cake, dear? And don't say cherry Genoa because that's gone.'

Acknowledgements

Since the characters in this novel have a pre-history on radio, I have a large cast of people to thank for helping me form them, not least my producer Karen Rose, who managed to persuade the commissioners at Radio 4 to give me not only four series of *Inspector Steine*, but also a final Christmas special. Our wonderful cast of regulars comprised Michael Fenton Stevens, John Ramm, Matt Green and Samantha Spiro (replacing Jan Ravens after the first series). Writing scripts for such talented comic actors was throughout a real privilege.

But that was radio, and it was *not the same*. When it came to adapting and expanding (while at the same time firmly reining in) the scripted material in order to create *A Shot in the Dark*, I have fewer people to thank, but I thank them wholeheartedly: Alexandra Pringle and Alison Hennessey at Bloomsbury, and Anthony Goff at David Higham Associates. First Alexandra backed me to write a bona fide crime novel, and then Alison patiently showed me how. Meanwhile my wonderful agent Anthony loyally cheered the book along, which meant a lot to me.

I've never written acknowledgements for a novel before, but now that I've got the hang of it I am going to carry on, and thank my gorgeous doggy companions, Hoagy and Django, for all their support while I was writing (cleverly disguised as either begging noisily for treats or pawing at doors to be let out). Finally, I would also like to take this opportunity to say that, obviously, if anyone should shoulder the blame for all this, it's not me, it's Graham Greene.

READ ON FOR THE NEW
INSTALMENT OF LYNNE
TRUSS'S JOYFULLY QUIRKY
CRIME SERIES . . .

THE MAN THAT
GOT AWAY

One

It was a blazing day in July. The threepenny deck-chairs on Brighton seafront were in high demand; ice cream was melting fast; the aroma of cockles in vinegar wafted on the breeze, mixed with the distinctive smell of unprotected human flesh being slowly and painfully cooked on the bone. What a day to be at the seaside! If you closed your eyes, you could faintly hear – beyond the fluttering of the overhead bunting – a romantic medley from *The King and I* played by the brass band of the Grenadier Guards. Holiday-making parents watched proudly from their deck-chairs on the shingle as their pasty, knobbly offspring cavorted in ill-fitting swimsuits under the scorching sun. If they considered the issue of infant catastrophic sunburn at all, it was only to make a (small) mental note to buy calamine lotion before the end of the day.

'You look like a ruddy lobster, Charlie!' mothers called, cheerfully. 'I shall have to pop into Timothy White's, the way you're going!'

Or, 'You mark my words, Dawn! You'll bleeding well suffer tonight!'

This being 1957, of course, attitudes to tanning were not sophisticated. You exposed pale city skin to solar rays for the first time in twelve months; some of it went a nice colour while some of it burned; the burned stuff could ultimately be peeled off by a skilled relative, with the larger sheets preserved for a while as souvenir curiosities. As for sun*stroke*, the same blithe unconcern applied. A child screaming and delirious in the night was just the price you paid for a day at the seaside, like Nan breaking her last molar on a stick of rock, or having to beat your carpets outdoors for the next fortnight to get rid of all the sand.

Along the Prom, two young women immaculately dressed like flying-boat hostesses – in white high heels, buttoned blue jackets, mid-calf skirts and smart little brimless hats – smiled regally at the tourists as they walked.

'Good morning,' they said, in a general kind of greeting. 'What a lovely morning! Welcome to Brighton. Good morning. Good morning. What a charming day!'

'Cor!' was the main response, and rightly so. These two elegant figures represented a body known as the Brighton Belles, attractive women hired by the council to make themselves useful to tourists during the summer.

'Enquire of a Brighton Belle!' ran the slogan on the posters on the wall outside the station, on hoardings and even on the sides of the buses. No one arriving in Brighton could miss the advertising, which depicted nicely dressed holiday-makers (small children holding multi-coloured beachballs aloft, mothers in headscarves and fathers in hats), all with happy cartoon question marks over their heads as they approached the blue-suited beauties.

Whatever you want to know,
Wherever you want to go,
Enquire of a Brighton Belle!

Incidentally, it had taken a small committee of men in suits around two hours to come up with that slogan. It was the grammar that worried them. Did you enquire *of*? Or enquire *from*? Opinion was divided equally, and there was an awkward *impasse* until the young clerk employed to take the minutes piped up unexpectedly that he couldn't listen to this any longer, and that 'enquire from' was technically illiterate, so at last they had their answer.

But the members of the committee were not embarrassed. They were pleased to have undertaken such a lengthy deliberation in the public interest. At this time in Brighton's iffy town-planning history, when great swathes of venerable Regency architecture were being demolished on a say-so to oblige the interests of dodgy developers, it was important that other matters municipal should appear to be above board.

Anyway, the slogan worked. Whatever they wanted to know and wherever they wanted to go, holiday-makers did enquire of a Brighton Belle. The whole scheme was a massive success. People asked the Belles everything they could think of: the quickest way to the station, how many pebbles were on the beach, which horse to back in the three-forty-five at Doncaster, where was the nearest place to spend a penny, how to tell the difference between heat rash and smallpox, and (most frequently) what time they got off work, and did they favour a Babycham, 'the genuine champagne perry'?

It wasn't easy to become a Brighton Belle: the prerequisites eliminated 99 per cent of the female population at a stroke. You had to be tall, shapely and fair of face, with excellent posture; also well-spoken, courteous, blind to class difference and fluent in at least three foreign languages. You must be helpful and kind – and a total pro at brushing off sexual advances without causing offence. Basically, you had to be Grace Kelly, only without the recent romantic attachment to a member of the House of Grimaldi (because you also had to be single).

And sometimes you didn't even wait to be enquired of.

'Good morning, madam, I see you've written some post-cards!' said one of the Brighton Belles now, stopping to speak to a slightly startled pensioner, seated in a blue-and-white-striped deck-chair. 'I can post those for you if you like.'

The pensioner – a Mrs Tucker from Bow in East London, wearing a warm coat with a fur collar despite the tempera-ture – instinctively gripped her postcards tightly. She couldn't imagine why this uniformed glamour-puss with the cut-glass accent was bending over her with white-gloved hand outstretched.

'Mavis?' she said, uncertainly. 'Woss appnin? Woss she want?'

'She's offering to post them, Mum,' explained the buxom red-haired woman in yellow gingham, sitting beside her. In this woman's hand was an open paperback book with a draw-ing of a Regency buck on the cover; she'd chosen it randomly from the stall beside the Palace Pier, and the edges of its pages were browned and crisp from being displayed for weeks in the sun.

'I expect posting other people's cards is her job, poor thing,' she said, looking up at the two Belles. '*Is* it your job, dearie?' she asked, sympathetically.

'Well, yes,' said the Belle, whose name on a little gold lapel-badge was given as Phyllis. 'It's *part* of my job, anyway. I could also direct you to the Pavilion in Italian, if you wished. My colleague Adelaide here could point you to the public library in Serbo-Croat!'

Phyllis smiled and continued to hold out her hand, but the old cockney woman refused to surrender her postcards. This was the trouble with dealing with the public, Phyllis was beginning to realise: they never quite followed the script. You

298

imagined they would be thrilled when someone who sounded like a lady-in-waiting offered them menial services; instead, you got awkward scenes like this.

'Let the poor girl do her job, then, Mum,' sighed the gingham woman, wresting the postcards from her mother, and checking they had stamps on. She handed them over quite grandly.

'There you are, dear. With our compliments. And I hope you won't mind my saying it, but I do hope you get a proper job soon.'

Luckily for Phyllis, the woman's attention was then caught elsewhere.

'Charlie!' she shrieked (with laughter) at a passing child. 'Bloody hell, you're so red now, you're blue!'

———

On such a bright day, it was a shame to find yourself inside a gloomy, airless wax museum, but such was young Constable Twitten's fate this morning. The great Inspector Steine, famous as a wireless personality and star of the Brighton Constabulary, had last week received an invitation from the historic 'Maison du Wax' in Russell Place, begging in very flowery language that he agree to the creation of an Inspector Steine mannequin. Hence the unusual visit.

All that was required of him (the letter had said) was his gracious consent, plus a short hour of his time sitting for the Maison du Wax's legendary blind model-maker Pierre Tussard (never for legal reasons to be confused with Tuss*aud*, the similarity of the name being a mere unfortunate coincidence); it would also be appreciated if Inspector Steine would provide without charge a spare uniform and a pair of shoes, and the standard donation of thirty-five pounds ten shillings for unavoidable expenses such as wax, human hair, rent of building, fire insurance and so on.

The generosity of this 'invitation' had of course caused general hilarity at the station.

Sergeant Brunswick, a down-to-earth man, chuckled, 'Thirty-five pounds ten! That's more than most people earn in a month! And I bet the inspector still falls for it!'

Mrs Groynes (the amusing charlady) had wholeheartedly agreed, saying that she would bet her entire – and famously comprehensive – collection of scouring powders on a positive outcome.

Only young Constable Twitten had loyally chosen to believe that vanity would not always prevail with Inspector Steine in the face of an obvious scam. Which was why, when Steine of course accepted the invitation without a second thought, Twitten had felt morally obliged to go with him to his first sitting, on this bright July day when the world outside was sizzling with life and ozone, and the world inside was airless and quiet, creepy and murky, and full of weakly spot-lit livid-coloured effigies helpfully labelled 'Winston Churchill' or 'Shirley Temple'.

Directed up the echoing stairs, Steine and Twitten passed through a room of such exhibits – the constable horrified by the general tawdriness, the inspector making enthusiastic remarks such as, 'Over here, Twitten! I had no idea Queen Mary looked like this! It turns out she's got a face like a bun!'

This particular wax museum had been part of the Brighton entertainment landscape for many years, and for this reason alone it demanded to be admired: for the way it had managed to survive despite its sheer and utter terrible-ness. To be fair, it owed its continued existence mainly to factors beyond its control, such as the regularity of sudden coastal squalls driving holiday-makers indoors, the system of landladies strictly locking out their guests until half-past four, and above all, the British seaside visitor's heroic determination to enjoy him- or herself, even when nothing remotely enjoyable was on offer.

Based loosely on the lines of the famous Madame Tussaud's, Brighton's Maison du Wax featured grisly execution tableaux (Mary Queen of Scots, complete with little dog under her skirts), effigies of notorious murderers (Dr Crippen, Neville Heath) and figures from modern-day entertainment (Gloria Swanson, Mr Pastry) – all bearing scant resemblance to the people concerned, although Robert Newton's peg-leg and threadbare parrot gave the onlooker a sporting chance of identifying him as Long John Silver. When you looked round in the gloom, you saw everywhere the same illuminated staring eyes and preoccupied (somehow constipated) expressions, the same wiry hair springing at unnatural intervals out of visible pocks in the scalp.

On the plus side, however, the museum charged only tuppence for admission, which made it the cheapest attraction on the entire South Coast.

Inspector Steine and Constable Twitten were greeted at the top of the stairs by Angélique, the middle-aged daughter of Pierre Tussard – and there was no mistaking her for someone unconnected to this dusty, moribund, phoney business. She was dressed in a high wig of ribboned brown curls and a full-length, short-sleeved frilly frock of acid green, like a revolutionary Parisian at the time of the Terror.

'Ah, *Inspecteur*!' she trilled, in a laboured French accent. 'We are *honaired* by your *press-ance*. Did you *remembair* ze thirty-five-pounds-ten?'

'I did, yes.'

'Excellent! *Zut alors*. Step zis way.'

Upstairs, in the special 'measuring room', Twitten sat in a corner, taking the whole thing in. For a keen amateur social anthropologist (and incorrigible know-all) such as he, it was all bally fascinating.

'You will meet *mon père* very soon, *monsieur*,' this bizarre figure twittered, encircling Steine's cranium with her tape measure.

'I see,' said Steine, keeping still.

'You have a fine as-we-say-in-*ze*-world-of-waxworks *bonce*, *monsieur*.'

'Well, thank you very much.'

'The making of the *statue de cire* is a combination of science and art, as you will *discovair*. Of measurement most precise, and of art most *accompli*.' She giggled in a theatrical manner and then added, 'It does not 'urt one *beet*.'

The inspector, who had seemed a little tense until now, was visibly relieved.

'It doesn't hurt, you say?'

'*Non, non, non.*'

'So you won't be turning me upside down and dipping me in hot wax like a toffee apple?'

Twitten started.

The woman shrieked with laughter. '*Non, non, non!*' she said.

This was good news for Steine. He'd been seriously wondering where they would put the stick.

'I think someone has been to see *Monsieur* Vincent Price in *ze* film *House of Wax, peut-être*?' trilled the woman.

'Well, yes,' Steine admitted. 'But not me, I assure you. I rarely visit the cinema. No, it was my sergeant. He went to see *House of Wax* several times, and said it was terrifying. He also said that if I spotted a boiling vat in here, I should exit the premises at once, the extorted thirty-five-pounds-ten notwithstanding.'

Twitten, from his corner, watched Angélique's reaction. Had she noticed the word 'extorted'? Apparently not. She worked on with her pretty tape measure, unperturbed. But she did explain that whereas the Vincent Price film *House of Wax* had been quite a shot in the arm to the entire wax-model business (admissions had more than doubled the year of its release), it had also engendered some very misleading and unhelpful ideas about how the models were made. In the film, Vincent Price basically killed people and then coated them in wax (like, indeed, a toffee apple). Here at the Maison du Wax, by contrast, sitters could remain alive throughout. They merely had to submit to an examination by touch – a touch so light and gentle! – from Angélique's dear blind papa.

At this point Angélique was called away to the telephone, leaving Steine and Twitten alone with a wall of hand-tinted photographs of famous people gamely posing alongside their Maison du Wax figures and looking understandably uncomfortable. Some of the figures weren't even the right height, and the celebrities were obliged to crouch slightly, or raise themselves on the balls of their feet. If you hadn't known the old model-maker was blind to begin with, you would certainly be able to deduce it from the results.

'Sir,' said Twitten, carefully. Should he mention how dreadful the wax models were here? Should he point out that '*remembair*' and '*discovair*' were not proper French words, and that 'bonce' was not a specialist term?

'What now?' snapped Steine.

Twitten decided against it. 'Nothing, sir,' he said. And, on balance, he was probably wise to do so.

Things were still uneasy between Inspector Steine and his clever new recruit. In general terms, the twenty-two-year-old Twitten's quickness of mind combined with his inability to shut up about anything – *ever* – was simply irksome to the inspector, who valued a sense of ordered calm. Moreover, Twitten's zeal for raking up old cases that had been – quite satisfactorily, in Steine's view – filed away under 'unsolved' was both unnecessary and intolerable.

However, something in particular had caused a greater strain between them. Within days of joining the Brighton Constabulary, young Constable Twitten had publicly denounced Mrs Groynes the station charlady – and this bears repetition: he had denounced *Mrs Groynes the charlady* – as a criminal mastermind responsible for a massive network of underworld operators in Brighton as well as for cold-blooded murder!

Under pressure from all directions, Twitten had now formally retracted his absurd allegations, and pledged never to repeat them, on pain of being dismissed from the force. But seeing as Mrs Groynes had happily admitted to him in private that she *was* a criminal mastermind responsible for a massive network *et cetera* (and had been getting away with it for years), this wasn't easy. In fact, it had brought him close to tears of frustration.

'Don't cry, Constable dear,' Mrs Groynes had told him, quite kindly, when they had discussed his unusual predicament. 'You have to accept defeat graciously, that's what. Everyone believes your insane idea about me was planted in your brain in front of hundreds of witnesses by a hypnotist, who was then unfortunately shot dead in a bloody fracas before he could de-hypnotise you. I beat you, dear; just admit it. I'm a genius who destroyed your credibility in a single stroke.'

'You *are* a bally genius, Mrs Groynes,' he had conceded, 'and I take my hat off to you. The hypnotism ruse was brilliant.

No one will ever believe me now when I point the finger at you. They'll say it's all in my mind.'

'That's right, dear.'

'But you forget that you're still an enormous criminal, with a vast underworld network of ruffians, and as an officer of the law, I have to do something about you.'

'But you *don't* have to, dear!' she had expostulated. 'Because you've been stitched up like a kipper, dear! So now, in a way, you're off the bleeding hook, do you see?'

And after a day or two to think about it, Twitten had reluctantly (and miserably) accepted her argument, because remaining a police officer was more important to him than anything else, and because plotting the eventual downfall of Mrs Groynes could be better done from inside than outside the force. And so here he was, accompanying the famous Inspector Steine in his public duties, and being careful not to say anything contentious. He was determined to fit in. Just two days ago, he had been issued with a brand-new white helmet, the traditional, exotic headgear of the Brighton policeman. Putting it on for the first time had been quite an emotional moment – until Mrs G privately pointed out that the introduction of white helmets had actually been her own idea. ('It means we can spot a bleeding rozzer a mile off, dear!')

'I've never spent much time in a wax museum before, sir, have you?' he said now.

'No, none,' said Steine.

'Actually, my parents did take me to Madame Tussaud's once, when I was nine, but we didn't stay long because I started pointing out what was wrong with the exhibits.'

'Why does that not surprise me, Twitten?'

'Well, I believe you'll sympathise, sir. I don't know if you've heard of the famous model of a policeman on the stairs that's supposed to be so lifelike people ask him what time it is?'

'Yes, thank you. I *have* heard of that wax policeman. Everyone has.'

'Well, sir, naturally I rushed to see him, and people were crowding round, saying, "Ooh, isn't he lifelike?" and "I keep expecting him to speak!" and also, of course, "Up yours, you filth! Your lot stitched up our Jimmy!" And what do you think, sir? *The buttons on his tunic didn't match with the style of his helmet!*'

'What?'

'That's how bally un-lifelike he was, sir.'

Steine was shocked. 'Are you sure?' he said. 'In Madame Tussaud's?'

'Yes, sir. The buttons were Metropolitan; the helmet was City of London! What a blunder! Any schoolboy knows the difference! You would think they'd be interested, but when I pointed it out, they asked Father to take me away at once!'

At Luigi's, the inspector's favourite ice-cream parlour, where the jukebox was playing Perry Como's 'Papa Loves Mambo', and all the top windows were open, a distinguished-looking middle-aged man in a homburg hat and light raincoat plonked a holdall on to one of the shiny brown tables, with his frothy coffee beside it.

It was a glorious day to be at the seaside, and Luigi's was buzzing with youthful customers (quiffs, bobby socks, ponytails) ordering banana splits and Knickerbocker glories, and also respectable couples in their twenties drinking coffee from stylish Pyrex cups and saucers.

One such young couple smiled across to the man, who introduced himself with the single word 'Melamine', and warmly shook their hands. Fifteen minutes later, the couple left, hysterical with laughter. As they told their friends back in Palmers Green afterwards, 'Lord Melamine' had really taken them in to begin with. He sounded so very posh!

At the police station, they were having a quiet day. Mrs Groynes poured Sergeant Brunswick a cup of tea and offered him a slice of gala pie, complete with a segment of hard-boiled egg. He sat down to receive both at his desk.

'Lovely, Mrs G,' he said, appreciatively. 'That's lovely, that is.'

Mrs Groynes smiled. She knew how to keep her boys happy. As it happened, their needs were absurdly simple, but she had genuine affection for them anyway, especially Sergeant Brunswick. She liked to think of herself as a sort of substitute mother to the well-meaning sergeant – a substitute mother with just a bit of a dark side. On the one hand, she brought in tasty things for him to eat because she knew he liked them; on the other, she might arrange for him to be shot in the leg if it served a wider purpose.

It was a beautiful relationship, and the sergeant certainly cherished it, and never got impatient with Mrs Groynes when (say) important bits of criminal evidence, left in his desk drawer for safe-keeping, were accidentally thrown away with the tea leaves.

'I've got some of those so-called London cheesecakes for later, dear,' she said now, her eyes twinkling. 'With that nasty shredded coconut on the top.'

'I'd be as fat as butter if you had your way, Mrs G.'

'You deserve it, dear,' she said. 'Now … how's the leg?'

Sergeant Brunswick winced at the reminder. He had indeed recently been shot in the leg at close range, as part of a classic criminal master-plan that climaxed at the Hippodrome in Middle Street. This master-plan had, of course, been entirely conceived by the dowdy woman in a paisley overall now swabbing the lino with a mop.

'The funny thing is, it's quite itchy,' he said.

'You're right, dear,' said Mrs Groynes, thoughtfully. 'That *is* funny.'

Brunswick sighed, and sat munching his pie and sipping his tea in contented silence for a little while, while Mrs Groynes mopped. He was such a nice-looking man, she thought, it was a shame he never had a girlfriend. The trouble was, women seemed to sense his desperation.

'Did young Clever Clogs Twitten show you that book he's reading, Mrs G?' the sergeant asked at last, the gala pie now reduced to a few pastry crumbs.

Mrs Groynes stopped mopping. 'What book's that, then?'

'Blimey, you're lucky!' said Brunswick. 'He's flaming obsessed with it. It's called *Noblesse Oblige*, if you please.'

'Never heard of it, dear.'

'Well, it's written by this la-di-da woman, and it's about how the so-called "upper class" have got different names for things from the rest of us.'

'Have they?'

'Well, so this book says. So if you say a word like *radio* or *serviette*, people can tell, just like that – ' Brunswick clicked his fingers ' – you're not upper class.'

'But everyone says *radio* and *serviette*, dear.'

'I know!'

'And who wants to sound upper class, anyway? That's daft.'

'I know. Young Twitten asked me what I'd call *that*, for instance.' He indicated a mirror on the wall.

Mrs Groynes was confused. 'What you'd call what, dear? The mirror?'

'Exactly. I said, "What would I call that mirror? What would I call it? I'd call it a mirror, son, because it *is* a flaming mirror!"'

'No flies on you, dear.'

'But he said an *upper-class* person would say "looking-glass".'

Mrs Groynes shrugged and gave an exaggerated sing-song, 'Ooh.'

'I know,' agreed Brunswick. 'Talk about pointless. But apparently everyone's buying this book and talking about it.'

Mrs Groynes sighed heavily as if to ask what the world was coming to, lit a full-strength Capstan from a lady-like pack of ten, took a thoughtful drag and then handed the sergeant the latest *Police Gazette*.

'Hot off the press, dear,' she said, expertly exhaling at the same time.

'Oh, good.' He loved perusing the *Police Gazette*, which was just as well because it was part of his job to read it every day. It was Mrs Groynes's usual practice to read and digest it first, of course. The information in it was invaluable if you were a vigilant master-criminal with a network of around two hundred villains. But today it had arrived later than usual and she hadn't had the chance.

'Here,' Brunswick said, 'imagine when a toff goes to buy the *Daily Mirror* and he can't say it! He keeps asking for the *Daily Looking-Glass*!'

Mrs Groynes laughed. 'They wouldn't know what he meant! Poor bleeder would be there all day!'

Back at the Maison du Wax, things were less harmonious. In fact, they were quite sticky. Constable Twitten was pointing at a full-length mirror propped against the wall in the measuring-room, to the confusion of his senior officer. And he was beginning to wish he had never started it.

'That mirror, you mean, Twitten?'

'Yes, sir. But please let's drop the subject, sir. I'm sorry. It's just a book. By Nancy Mitford. *Noblesse Oblige*, sir. It's been quite controversial. It's basically about the differences between what she calls "U" and "Non-U", and truly, sir, it's bally fascinating, and I'm sure the whole field of socio-linguistics has practical applications for police work, you see, but people keep getting annoyed when I talk about it, so I should probably bally well belt up about it, sir.'

'No, look, hang on. You started this, Twitten. You're asking me what I would call that mirror?'

'Well, yes.'

'I'd call it a mirror, Twitten. Good grief.'

'So, not a looking-glass, sir?'

Steine swallowed hard. 'I don't understand what you're getting at, Twitten.'

'There's no need to be irritated, sir.'

'But it *is* a mirror, Twitten. Of course I'm irritated.'

'Even if I tell you that "mirror" is a "Non-U" indicator, sir?'

'Especially if you tell me that.'

At that moment, luckily for Twitten, the great blind model-maker Pierre Tussard made his entrance, wearing a crimson velvet cap-and-robe ensemble and shuffling behind his daughter, his hand dramatically on her shoulder, his head strangely angled, his eyes closed. Despite the ridiculous picture they made, Twitten couldn't have been more pleased to see them. Would he be allowed to leave, now? To go outside in the sun and read the rest of his book?

The answer was yes and no. 'You make yourself scarce, Constable,' said Steine, still sounding agitated. 'But don't leave the building. We haven't finished discussing this mirror business.'

'Yes, sir. I mean, no, sir. I'll wait on the landing, sir.'

Meekly, Twitten donned his shiny white helmet and left the room.

Outside, at the top of the stairs, he stood for a while, just thinking. How defensive everyone got on this issue of U and Non-U words! It made no sense to him. Why weren't they fascinated by the revelation that upper-class people said 'preserve' instead of 'jam', or 'wireless' instead of 'radio', or 'mad' instead of 'mental'? Wasn't it worth knowing that an upper-class person would despise you for referring to your fish-knives or your cruet set, or (worst of all) your toilet? Snobbery was a living thing in modern British society! Surely it was important to know how it operated?

He was so deep in thought that at first he didn't notice the small crowd of visitors gathering on the staircase below him, looking up with interest. And then he realised what was happening, and froze. A policeman at the top of a flight of stairs in a wax museum! Did they think he was a model? Crikey. Thank goodness his tunic buttons and helmet were stylistically complementary.

The small crowd approached, to look more closely.

'That *is* bleeding lifelike,' said a young man with a Brylcreemed quiff and prematurely blackened teeth. ''Ere, what's the time, mate?'

Twitten stopped breathing. Understandably, he was tempted to reply 'Half-past nine, sir', but worried about the accident it might cause. What if alarmed holiday-makers stepped backwards into space and then tumbled in a heap down the stairs?

The teenaged girl on the Brylcreem-boy's arm laughed and gazed up. 'Shall I pinch him, Roy?' she said. 'Shall I knock his helmet off?'

'Go on, Em. I dare you,' said an older woman.

Twitten mentally braced himself, but luckily the girl decided she didn't have the nerve and the group passed on to the upper floor, giving him an opportunity to exhale. But at what point could he move? It was while he was pondering his predicament – and continuing to stand completely still with a fixed expression – that he happened to overhear a conversation between a pair of star-crossed young lovers that would – given what happened later – haunt him for the rest of his life.

———————

Back on the seafront, Brighton Belles Phyllis and Adelaide decided to stop at Luigi's for a refreshing glass of hot milk before continuing with their duties, and found themselves sitting beside a man in a felt hat with a heavy bag in front of him on the table.

'May I introduce myself to you lovely ladies?' he said. One of his eyes pointed in slightly the wrong direction, which was unsettling, but he had a beautiful voice.

'I'm the Fifth Marquess of Colchester,' he said, in a confiding tone. 'But you can call me Melamine.'

They smiled at him and shook his proffered hand. He registered the names on their little lapel badges. The brunette was Phyllis; the girl with the rich brown hair was Adelaide. As it happened, Adelaide's hair was technically chestnut, while her eyes were almond-shaped, and hazel-coloured. As her mother used to say (presumably as a compliment), Adelaide had been born with all the nuts.

'Now,' Melamine said, shifting the bag a little closer to them, 'I'm wondering if you've ever heard the story of the gold from the battleship *Potemkin*?'

The two women exchanged glances. They'd been warned about con men, but they'd somehow imagined that a con man would be a little bit harder to spot.

'I don't think so,' said Adelaide, amused. 'Have *you* heard of the gold from the battleship *Potemkin*, Phyllis?'

'Not me,' said Phyllis.

'Russian gold! Imperial gold!' enthused Melamine. 'It was thought to be lost during the uprising of 1905, sunk in the depths of the Black Sea. But in the 1920s it turned up in the possession of none other than Rudolph Valentino!'

The Belles raised their eyebrows at each other. This man was possibly the least convincing liar the world had ever seen. They now understood the comments they had overheard from a young couple they had bumped into outside Luigi's. 'He was hopeless, Alfie!' the woman had said, and the man had replied, 'Yes, but you can't fault him for trying! Rudolph Valentino!'

'Gosh,' said Phyllis, now, trying to keep a straight face. 'Rudolph Valentino. That's very romantic.'

'Yes, it *is* romantic,' said Melamine, clearly making a note of a useful word that had previously not occurred to him. His faraway look was weirdly enhanced by the fact that his eyes pointed in different directions.

'But the Nazis sadly got hold of it, and then – ' He leaned closer, surreptitiously pushing the bag towards them, and quickly opening it to reveal the presence inside of several large gold-coloured bricks ' – General Eisenhower liberated it from

Berlin. And he placed it in the safe-keeping of my father, the Fourth Marquess, not realising that the poor, sad man was seriously mental and would forget where he had left it.'

'What a truly incredible story,' said Adelaide, between lady-like sips of warm milk. She turned to her friend, eyes twinkling. 'That is literally incredible, isn't it, Phyllis?'

'It is, yes. Literally.'

Melamine seemed pleased. 'Thank you very much,' he said.

'May I ask why you're carrying it around, sir?' said Adelaide. 'The gold? It's rather careless of you. Someone might steal it.'

'But I have to get rid of it, that's the point! I don't usually go around talking about my family's Russian gold to total strangers in coffee bars. No, I'm in a fix, my dears, and I need help.'

'Here it comes,' murmured Adelaide.

'Ladies,' Melamine announced, solemnly. 'For complicated reasons too shaming to relate, I'm willing to sell this gold of mine to you for as little as twenty-five pounds a brick! What you see before you is a desperate, desperate aristocrat.'

A less convincing story would be hard to imagine, and the kind thing would have been to stand up, plead an appointment elsewhere and go. But Adelaide had indeed been born with all the nuts, and was enjoying herself.

'Oh, I'm so sorry to hear that,' she said, reaching over to pat his hand. 'But I don't understand completely. What sort of complicated reasons? And why are they shaming?'

'Can't you guess?' he said.

'Well, no.'

'Tax!' he said, with what sounded like genuine frustration. 'It's all about tax and those dreaded new-fangled death duties. "You've never had it so good," the man says on the radio, but not if you inherit a country house and estate in 1957!'

'I see.'

'You can't imagine how hard things are for the landed gentry. My father dealt with nothing, being too mental. He didn't declare this hidden Russian gold, which is worth – each brick! – just under five hundred pounds! The ancestral home is on the verge of collapse. All over the country, families like mine are selling their silver cruets and serviette rings! Yes, it's a topsy-turvy world we live in, ladies, but the long and short of it is this: if I'm still in possession of Father's confounded gold at the end of the month, I'll be ruined!'

So what was the momentous conversation Twitten overheard at the wax museum? It was only because he had spent five minutes standing immobile on the landing that he noticed something that would never otherwise have caught his eye: at the top of the stairs, in the wall that (he calculated) ought to comprise the back of the building, was the well-disguised outline of a jib door.

'A secret door?' he said aloud. He wondered what to do. Should he stop pretending to be a waxwork and investigate? There was someone approaching the stairs below – he could hear footsteps echoing through the entrance hall – so he would have to make up his mind quickly. But too late! A scratching sound came from behind the secret door, then it opened and a young woman stepped out nervously.

'Peter?' she whispered.

It took Twitten all his presence of mind not to look round to see who Peter was.

'I'm here,' said a voice, and a thin young man came running up the stairs and put his arms round her. 'Deirdre! You came! Does this mean … ?'

'Yes, Peter,' she said, quietly. 'It does. I want to go with you. I want to run away. But we have to be so careful!'

'Oh, my love!' he said.

Twitten was extremely uncomfortable about overhearing all this private lovey-dovey stuff, especially when it emanated from people who might be minors. But again, he was also aware that if he exhibited the slightest sign of life, he might scare them out of their wits.

'Peter, stop. Stop!' said young Deirdre. 'This is serious. You know what my brothers would do if they found out. Or Mum! She calls you Weedy Pete! Weedy Pete Dupont! And the boys join in and laugh. They're all beasts!'

Twitten was just making a mental note about the reprehensible solipsism of the young when the girl said something that truly surprised him.

'And don't forget what they did to Uncle Ken! The police only found one bit of him in that suitcase at the station. No one's ever found his head!'

Staying completely immobile while this conversation was playing out was possibly the hardest thing Twitten had ever done. The urge to take out a notebook and lick the tip of a pencil was overwhelming. *Uncle Ken's head?*

'We'll meet tonight at nine at the coach station in Pool Valley,' said the girl, who seemed to be in charge of arrangements.

Nine, repeated Twitten to himself, silently. *Pool Valley. Peter Dupont. Deirdre who? Secret door to … where?* And again, *Don't forget: Uncle Ken's HEAD??*

'Don't say anything at work,' she reminded her boyfriend. 'Especially to Mr Blackmore.'

'All right, I'm not stupid!' laughed the weedy boy.

Mr Blackmore, Mr Blackmore.

And then the boy took Deirdre's hand and held it tenderly. They both hung their heads. Twitten's eyes moistened. For the first time, he realised that this scene being played out in front of him was jolly lovely, in its way; it was a privilege to witness it. He was reminded of those short-lived hopeful bits in tough modern films like *On the Waterfront*, where wide-eyed young love expresses itself so sweetly and poignantly (usually with a light woodwind accompaniment), against a backdrop of inevitable violence and doom.

Peter squeezed Deirdre's hand. 'I know what to do, don't worry,' he assured her, quietly. 'It's a good plan and you're very brave. But if anything happens to me, remember you can trust Hoagland.'

Hoagland? Who's Hoagland? Oh, bally hell, this is getting harder.

'Don't talk like that, Peter! Nothing will happen to you, so long as we get away now. I'll get the money from the safe. Dickie said he'll help me.'

The boy reacted with alarm. 'You didn't tell Dickie?'

Dickie?

'I had to tell *someone*!'

Yes, but why Dickie?

It was at this point that they both happened to look round, and spotted Twitten for the first time.

'That's new,' said the girl, frowning. 'That policeman. It wasn't there yesterday.'

Twitten felt his new helmet slip slightly on his forehead.

'It looks a bit good for in here,' said the boy, suspiciously.

But just as Twitten's legs began to tremble, the door to the measuring-room burst open, signifying the end of Steine's sitting, and the boy and girl sprang apart and scarpered with all the energy of the young – the weedy Peter boy back down the stairs, the girl with the de-boncified male relative back through her secret door.

'Ah, there you are, Twitten,' said Steine, beaming. He turned and waved goodbye to Angélique.

'*À bientôt*, Inspector,' she called.

'Yes, sir,' said Twitten, almost crying with relief that he could move at last. 'Shall we go, sir?'

They started to walk down the stairs towards the sunshine outside.

'Well, I don't want to rub it in,' said Steine, 'but you won't believe what you missed by being out here.'